THE HIRED MAN'S Clock

THE HIRED MAN'S Clock

BY DALE S. MARSHALL

THE HIRED MAN'S CLOCK

By: Dale S. Marshall

Published by
GOSPEL FOLIO PRESS
304 Killaly St. W.
Port Colborne, ON L3K 6A6
CANADA

ISBN:9781926765952

Cover design by Danielle Elzinga

All Scripture quotations from the King James Version unless otherwise noted.
All Scripture and hymns use single quotation marks.
Italics indicate a character's internal thoughts.

Printed in USA

Introduction

The Hired Man's Clock is a story demonstrating how the life of one simple, but godly man, even after his death, was used by the Lord for His glory.

The Hired Man's Clock is not a true story—but events and circumstances from the author's life have influenced the story.

The Hired Man's Clock is a series of stories. Each chapter is complete in itself yet each has connections with the others. In every chapter, some details which seem insignificant become meaningful in others.

May the Lord be honoured and may He be glorified through the story of *The Hired Man's Clock*.

—Dale S. Marshall

Contents

chapter one

summer, 1915

The Hired Man

Jedidiah Harriston stood at the open door of his modest little dwelling at the north end of the coastal village of Rogers Cove. He pushed his gnarled fingers through his thinning hair as he observed his friends, George and Dorothy, set off over the narrow path across his front yard. The couple turned onto Sawmill Road and walked side by side towards the village where they lived near the wharf.

Before they passed from Jedidiah's view on the far side of the thick trees, they faced him and waved. "The Lord be with you, Jed," he heard George call out to him. He returned the wave and then watched as his friends moved out of his sight.

The elderly man hesitated momentarily on the doorstep before he slowly backed into his kitchen and closed the door behind him. He stood there nearly a minute, took a deep breath and then let it out. He crossed over to the table and sat down on one of the worn kitchen chairs. "Now what?" he said aloud, and he placed his elbows on the table and put his head in his hands.

Suddenly the clock on the shelf over the table gave five strikes. It told Jedidiah in no uncertain tones, "Gone. Gone. Gone. Gone. Gone."

When the offensive chiming ceased, he moaned aloud, "It's so hard! And I'm all alone." He dropped his clenched hands to the table and lowered his forehead to his crossed arms. And then he wept until his shoulders shook.

About nine miles out from Rogers Cove lay Bunchberry Island where the lighthouse keeper and his family resided. Thomas Palmer was a quiet man in his mid-thirties who valued the solitude of his island home. He took his lighthouse duties seriously and enjoyed the challenge of developing and managing part of the island for farm use. Thomas was trying to encourage his sixteen-year-old son to be useful as well as hardworking.

This afternoon, Mr. Palmer and David were working near the woodshed leaning against the lighthouse. They were cutting eight-foot lengths of logs into firewood size to be later split and stacked to dry in the sun and wind of the open air. As they worked either end of the long cross-cut saw, Mr. Palmer could not help noticing that his son was nearly as strong as he was, but that the young man had more endurance. *That's good,* Mr. Palmer reasoned as he and his son pulled alternately on the saw. *David's growing up, he's nearly a man—but needs more experience.* The stove-length piece of wood toppled to the ground. The young man promptly pushed it away with his foot, and at the same time, he repositioned the longer chunk ready for the next cut. *He does a good job. I'd like him to take over my duties here some day. He's getting the training and should be able to step right into it in another four or five years—maybe less. He'll be married by then and can settle down here. Me and Mildred and young Bobby could then go back to the mainland. I'd like to try my hand at fox farming. Bobby by that time could go to the new school that's started in Rogers Cove.*

The piece of wood fell to the ground at their feet, but before David yanked on the remaining long length of tree trunk, he stopped and stood facing his father. Mr. Palmer waited for him to speak. "Pa," the young man said, "I'd like to go to school in Rogers Cove beginning this fall. Two more years should do it. Figure I could board somewhere handy to there. After that, maybe go to college. Or even go out west." David was serious, but not demanding.

Back on the mainland, Jedidiah Harriston remained at the kitchen table with his head resting on his arms. *Why did the Lord allow this to happen? Why did He take away my wife—all I had left? My only son's gone, too—it's been thirty-six years already.* The man sighed deeply. *I'd like to give up on the Lord. I don't feel any of His love for me right now.* He sat up and with a scowl on his weathered face, he stared through the kitchen window and off into the distance. *But the Lord has promised never to leave me, and He has promised to not give me burdens greater than I can bear.*

Jedidiah stroked his chin, and he shifted his gaze back into his kitchen. On the wall between the door and the window hung the framed cross-stitched text his wife had made several winters ago. He knew the verse without looking, but he read it deliberately word by word. *'If we confess our sins, He is faithful and just to forgive us our sins and to cleanse us from all unrighteousness. 1 John 1:9.'* He once more took a deep breath and let it out slowly. *My Heavenly Father, I confess I have sinned in wanting to give up on Thee. I have not trusted Thee completely. I thank Thee Thou art faithful and just to forgive me of my sin of not trusting in Thee. Thou art just in forgiving me because the Lord Jesus paid the penalty for my sin. And I thank Thee for cleansing me from all unrighteousness.*

He was now aware of the summer sun which was beginning to spill into the kitchen from the west window. His eyes were drawn out between the drapes to his well-kept vegetable garden in the side yard. *My Heavenly Father, continue to lead me in my life, and may Thy presence be known to me at this difficult time.* The man's scowl was gone, and he was nearly smiling.

On the island, the lighthouse keeper's wife came around from the main door of the structure. Her long dress brushed the taller grasses and wildflowers as she moved along the footpath to where her husband and older son were working near the woodshed. "Supper's ready," she called to them.

After he and David worked the saw blade through the log, Thomas balanced the cross-cut saw on top of the long lengths of uncut trunks. David walked along the path towards the lighthouse, and as he went he brushed the sawdust from his clothing.

In the main room of the lighthouse, Mr. Palmer picked up his younger son. "Bobby," he told the little fellow who was delighted to see his father and big brother again, "it's supper time." He carried him to the table and lowered him to the booster seat he had designed and made to fit over a kitchen chair. Thomas and David washed their hands in the basin on the side table.

David sat across from Bobby. He removed a butter knife from the cutlery container in the centre of the table, and after sinking the knife into the jar of molasses, he spread the dark fluid over a thick slice of his mother's fresh bread. He then broke off a small hunk and handed it to Bobby, who grinned broadly at him. Bobby watched his big brother shove the molasses-soaked bread into his mouth, and he copied every move. David put his elbows on the table and held the slice of bread in both his hands as he ate. Bobby did the same. When David realized his little brother was copying him, he rocked his head from side to side as he chewed. The young boy did the same. David then stuffed the remaining bread in his mouth and wiped his hands on his shirt. Bobby grinned and did the same.

Their mother turned from the stove with a steaming pot of potatoes. "Bobby," his mother exclaimed, "don't wipe your hands on your clean shirt. I just changed you."

The little fellow looked over at her and grinned. "David," he informed her with satisfaction. She then glared at David but said nothing.

In Jedidiah's house on the mainland, the old gentleman could feel the cat rubbing himself against his legs under the table. "Why, Skipper," he greeted when he leaned over to stroke him. "Have you been neglected these past few days?"

The cat gave a quick, "Meow," as he looked up at him with his big green eyes.

"Well, that'll never do," Jedidiah told him. "What would Myrtle feed you? Let's see what's here." He stood up and removed the feed sack draped over the basket the McNeills had left him. "Have a look-see at all these good things George and Dorothy gave us. A loaf of bread, six eggs, a jar of milk. And here's chicken and a hunk of dried fish. And look, here's some of Dot's dory plugs. I'll give you a lunch, Skipper—but you know, you should be out mousing for your own supper."

The cat began to purr and to rub himself on the chair legs as he looked up expectantly at Jedidiah. *My friends are good to me,* he realized. *They shower me with their love and the love of Christ.*

Jedidiah cut several small pieces of chicken and some dried fish and dropped them onto a saucer. After lowering the saucer to the floor by the wood box, he held back the hungry cat with one hand and poured some milk into the saucer nearly to its brim. "There you go, Skipper. Enjoy!" Next, as Jedidiah began to sing, "To God be the glory, great things He hath done," he sliced a thick piece of bread for himself and placed two chicken drum sticks on a small plate and filled a glass with milk. He sang, "So loved He the world that He gave us His Son, who yielded His life an atonement for sin and opened the life-gate that all may come in."

When David was through eating his evening meal with his parents and little brother in the lighthouse, he rose up from the supper table and returned outside. Soon could be heard the sound of firewood being split. "David," Bobby exclaimed as he grinned at his parents at the table.

Mrs. Palmer smiled and nodded in acknowledgment. "He's a good worker," she commented to her husband who with his elbows on the table was draining the last of his tea.

Mr. Palmer grunted in agreement and then he said, "I was hoping David would take on more responsibilities here and then in a few years he could apply for duties as lighthouse keeper. I know he'd be well-qualified by then."

Bobby began to squirm in his seat and his mother lowered him to the floor before she answered her husband. "I know you'd like David to take over here someday. You've put too much into this place to turn it over to a complete stranger, and we're sure David would do a fine job here. He needs to make up his own mind, and he'll be happier that way and do a better job, too."

Mr. Palmer had to agree and then told his wife, "He says he wants to finish his schooling in Rogers Cove. Board on the mainland this fall and winter—maybe college after that or go out west to work." He placed his empty cup on the table, leaned back in his chair and put his hands behind his head.

"Yes, I know," Mrs. Palmer answered as she lowered another stick of wood into the stove. "He mentioned that to me the other day. I told him he should go talk to his pa."

Mr. Palmer stood up and crossed over to the door. "David's a man now—a young man anyway. He can make up his own mind. We've been preparing him for this and I'll not stop him any."

His wife dipped hot water from the large pot on the stove and poured it into a basin to wash the dishes. She turned to face her husband. "It'll be hard to let him go," she said.

Mr. Palmer nodded before reaching for his hat on the catch-all shelf by the door. "Chores to do," he said, and he went outside.

Jedidiah awoke the next morning on the other side of the bed from where he usually slept. *Yes*, he had to admit, *Dot was right. I won't miss Myrtle so much if I sleep on the other side of our bed.*

Before getting up, he committed himself to the Lord for this day and he thanked Him for His Son the Lord Jesus Christ. "I thank Thee for giving Him to be my Saviour," he told Him. "And because I trust in Thee, I belong to Thee and can truly call Thee my Heavenly Father, and I thank Thee I am Thy child."

As Jedidiah crossed the kitchen floor to the woodstove, he began to sing, "Praise Him, praise Him, Jesus our blessed Redeemer." He set up the fire but before he reached for a match, Skipper appeared on the outside window sill near the wood box, impatiently looking into the kitchen. Without interrupting his singing, Jedidiah opened the window and the cat squeezed in and dropped to the floor with a thud.

After starting the fire, Jedidiah filled the kettle with water from the pail and positioned it on the stove. "Good morning, Skipper," he said when he finished the chorus of the hymn. "Looking for your breakfast are you?" The cat continued to rub himself on his ankles as Jedidiah sliced more meat and dropped the pieces onto the saucer near the wood box. Skipper began to eat and Jedidiah fixed breakfast for himself.

"Well," Thomas Palmer said to his wife after breakfast in the lighthouse, "if I leave now for Rogers Cove, I could be back before dark." He took advantage of the flow and direction of the tides to row both ways on the same day and during daylight hours. He laced up his boots and put the shopping list in his shirt pocket. "David's going to work some in the garden," he told his wife. "And there's more splitting to do."

Mildred crossed the kitchen and stood next to her husband as he buttoned up his coat. Her hair was pinned back behind her head. "Bye," she told him. "Don't forget to check if there's any mail." Thomas nodded in reply.

He never said, "Good bye," but his wife knew that although he was away, she was in his thoughts.

As he left the lighthouse and followed the well-worn path down to the beach about a half mile through the mixed woods, he glanced over at David who was working with the firewood. David paused with the axe in his hands and he exchanged nods with his father.

Late that afternoon, Jedidiah closed the door of his little house and stepped off the stone landing. As he followed George along the path, he quickly glanced over at his cat curled up in the sun on the wooden wheelbarrow under the apple tree. "I'll be back, Skipper." The cat stretched out all four legs and then relaxed and resumed his late afternoon nap.

The two men moved single file along the narrow path through the tall grasses of the front yard. When they reached Sawmill Road, Jedidiah came alongside George. "Nice of you and Dot to invite me to your evening meal," he told George who smiled in reply.

Jedidiah and George approached the brow of the hill and started their descent towards the McNeill house just above the wharf. Several minutes later, he could see beyond the grove of hackmatack trees to the well-kept house and property of his friends the McNeills. *George and Dot are good friends to me,* he reasoned. *I thank the Lord for them and their kindness and encouragement. It's nice of them to offer for me to stay with them for the winter. I have to admit, I can't manage on my own very well.* He stepped across a shallow washout which zig-zagged across the road, the result of a recent rainstorm. *I can't be sponging off my friends. I need to earn my keep, but there's nothing to work at in this area. And I couldn't keep up no more with those young fellows at the sawmill—don't have the strength I once had.*

The thick spruce woods on their right-hand side between the road and the cliff above the beach gave way to a narrow, grassy area. Jedidiah and George now had a clear view over the water beyond the cove, and they automatically looked out to Bunchberry Island nine miles to the west. They could see a small boat moving with the tide, and the two men knew it was carrying the lighthouse keeper back to his home and duties on the island.

Jedidiah cleared his throat. "George, I've been thinking some this afternoon," he told his friend. His eyes dropped to the dirt road at his feet, and then he peered out over the water. "Thomas Palmer was at the general store when I was in there before noon." George glanced sideways at him but said nothing. "Told the men there that his son wanted to come to the mainland and attend school over this winter. Said he'd be looking for someone to do light work while David's boarding here at the village."

The two men walked in silence for nearly a minute. Finally George spoke. "And you've been thinking about applying." It was more of a statement than a question, and Jedidiah slowly nodded once. The men paused on the road and turned to look at the island and the dot which was becoming smaller as it slowly moved closer to its destination.

"I don't feel sure about it yet, one way or the other," Jedidiah admitted. "I need to pray about it more." George nodded in agreement, and the two friends continued their walk together towards the McNeill house where supper was nearly ready.

About two weeks later, the timing of the tide was again suitable for Thomas Palmer, the lighthouse keeper. His son David had his back to the mainland as he rowed his father's dory towards Rogers Cove. Thomas guided the young man past Fearful Rocks and into the calm water of the cove. Thomas looked beyond his son's shoulder towards the wharf. "George and Jed waiting to greet us," he stated.

When Thomas and David were within hearing range, George McNeill called out from the wharf, "Morning, Gentlemen."

"Morning to you, Sirs," Thomas answered. David maneuvered the dory up against the wharf, and his father tossed up the mooring rope to George who grabbed hold of it and tied the rope securely to a post.

Thomas climbed the ladder onto the wharf and shook hands with George and Jedidiah. He then reached down for the basket of eggs David held up to him. "Carrots, too," Thomas told him. "And pass them pears up, Boy."

"Nice looking squash you have there," Jedidiah commented. "I'd like to purchase one of them from you." The produce was spread out on the wharf, and David climbed up from the dory and joined the men.

Thomas picked up the basket of eggs. "Want to get these to the store," he remarked. "Someone might want them for noon meal today."

George looked over at Thomas. "You men stay for noon meal." He glanced from Thomas to his son. "Dot's expecting you since we first seen you out across the water."

"Sure," Thomas replied. "Can't turn that down." David grinned and nodded. He was pleased he was included as one of the men.

"Let me carry these for you," Jedidiah offered as he picked up the pail containing the carrots.

George headed back to his house and the dory he was building in his side yard. As he cradled Jedidiah's squash in his arm, he observed the three men loaded down with produce from the island farm. He could see his friend between Thomas and David as they moved up the steep road towards the village store. George began to smile broadly and when he reached his yard, he balanced the squash on the top of a fence post next to the road for Jedidiah to pick up when he came by later. "Thy will be done, Lord," he said quietly. "Thy will be done."

Later that afternoon, Thomas Palmer and his son David, accompanied by the McNeills and Jedidiah Harriston, went to their dory tied up alongside the Rogers Cove wharf. "I'll row, Pa," the young man offered as he placed their parcels on the edge of the wharf. He climbed down into their boat and waited for his father to hand him the packages.

But first Thomas turned to George and Dorothy. "Thanks for having us to noon meal and afternoon lunch," he told them.

George nodded, and his wife smiled. "Oh, you're welcome, Thomas, I'm sure," Dorothy told them. She held out a cherry pie to Thomas and quickly glanced down at David sitting in the dory. "Tell your mother we'd like to have a visit with her," she said.

Thomas climbed into the dory, and Jedidiah handed him the remaining things which were to be carried over to the island with them. As Jedidiah stood with his friends, he looked out across the water to the island. "Looks like you'll have a good trip." He shielded his eyes from the late afternoon sun and then added, "See you tomorrow, Thomas."

David gently pushed one of the oars against the wharf. The dory with him and his father seated amongst their parcels glided away from the folks standing on the edge of the wooden structure. Jedidiah stood with George and Dorothy, and he watched as David rowed the loaded boat out of the cove, past Fearful Rocks, and into the open water between the mainland and the island.

George and his wife headed back to their house, and Jedidiah remained alone on the wharf and watched the departing dory growing smaller as it moved towards Bunchberry Island. "Jed," he heard George call out, "will we see you at supper, Boy?"

He slowly turned and faced the McNeills who were waiting for his reply. "No," he simply stated. "I want to go back to my place, but thanks, Friends." Jedidiah let his head drop, and he gazed absent-mindedly into the deep water just off the wharf at his feet. For several minutes he let his eyes follow a jellyfish which slowly and gracefully propelled itself past him, and then the creature dropped out of sight beneath the dark water.

"Mr. Harriston."

Jedidiah lurched and looked over his shoulder to a young woman a dozen feet away. "Why, it's Miss MacDonald," he greeted pleasantly. "You startled me, Lorna."

The young lady smiled shyly. "Mr. Harriston, this is the Bible your wife lent to me. When I seen you here I figured it was a good time to return it to you."

Jedidiah took several steps towards her. "Have you been reading it?" he asked her.

"Oh, yes, every day. I now believe the Bible is God's Word. I know it's the Truth." Lorna paused and because Jedidiah could see she had more to say, he waited. "The Bible has things written in it I've never heard tell of before," she told him. She frowned slightly as she added, "Some things in the Bible are different to what I've growed up with."

Jedidiah smiled and nodded. "Well, in that case, you keep the Bible—I want you to have it. And keep reading God's Word—the Truth. Read it for yourself every day, and ask Him to help you to understand His Word. And I know Myrtle would want you to have her Bible."

Lorna held the Bible close to herself, and a look of gratitude spread across her face. She turned and started back to her parents' house on the wooded slope overlooking the cove.

"You want a lunch, David?" Thomas asked from the stern of the dory.

David let the oars drop and he moved to change places with his father. After he sat down, he tore off a hunk of bread from the loaf they had brought with them that morning. "This here cheese for me, too?" he asked.

Thomas nodded. "You going to mind boarding at the McNeills', Boy?" he questioned as he began his turn at rowing.

David bit into the bread and chewed it slowly. "No, I don't mind," he answered before he swallowed. "Why'd you ask?"

"The McNeills are some religious," his father told him, and he watched for his son's reaction.

David shoved more bread into his mouth. "Don't bother me none." He gave his shoulders one quick shrug.

"Jed Harriston's religious, too," Thomas commented between pulls on the oars. "Nice folks, George and Dot—and Jed as well. Myrtle was, too." He pulled on the oars several times before continuing. "Religion's alright, I guess, but best not overdo it. The McNeills and the Harristons make religion a big part of their lives. Religion isn't necessary everyday - once a week's enough. My father and his father got along alright without much religion. Reckon I'll just stay that way, too."

David brought out a large apple from the feed sack, snapped it in half in his two hands and bit into one of the pieces. When he finished his lunch, he asked, "Want me to row now, Pa?"

After Jedidiah climbed down off the Rogers Cove wharf onto the stony beach, he followed the row of debris a recent high-tide had deposited there. The dark line of knotted-wrack at his feet made a large sweeping curve a short distance from the base of the bluff and it stretched all along the shore next to the rock cliffs on the far side of the cove. *I hope Myrtle's Bible will bring Lorna to the truth of Christ, her Saviour,* he contemplated as he observed the tide which was slowly retreating. *I'll pray she'll be saved, and she'll grow to know the Lord and know Him well.* As Jedidiah tramped along, he could see here and there amongst the seaweed, bright orange, empty crab shells. *This is a big step for me—and at my age,* he recognized. *I thank the Lord for His guidance and for peace from Him. I want to follow in the way He has prepared for me to go at this time in my life, and I want to have the assurance I'm in His will.*

Farther along the beach, Jedidiah spied a white buoy, and when he came to the carved wooden piece, he noticed the narrow, red-painted band which circled one end. "Why, this buoy belongs to Elijah Bean," he realized as he continued on by it. "I'll pick it up on my way back and leave it on the wharf for him."

About ten minutes passed, and Jedidiah came to Indian Head jutting out into the cove. "Can't go no farther," he said aloud as he put his hands against the face of the dark, damp, cold rock. "Time to go home. Anyway, must be nearly supper time by now." He turned to look back towards the wharf. In the distance he could see the McNeill house, and he could make out several other village houses and fishing shacks. *I don't think I've ever seen the lower part of the village of Rogers Cove from this here viewpoint before.* He began his hike back along the high-tide line. *Better get going. Skipper will be wondering where I'm at.* As Jedidiah moved along he remembered, *I need to fix a box tonight to carry him in.*

❧

As the dory transporting the Palmer men neared Bunchberry Island, the lighthouse and its tower became lost from view on the far side of the woods above the high cliffs. David continued to pull on the oars past Porcupine Point and headed for their small wharf.

Thomas and David placed the things which they had carried over with them onto the wharf and then dragged the boat up above the high-tide line. Since they would be making another trip to the mainland the next day, they did not return the dory to the boathouse. Thomas brought the wheelbarrow down onto the wharf, and David and he loaded it for their trek up to the lighthouse.

"I'll carry that there pie," Thomas said as David grabbed the handles of the wheelbarrow and pushed it along the wharf to the flat area just above the stony shore.

The half-mile path to the lighthouse was mostly uphill. Thomas and David did not converse as they laboured up the road through the woods of maple and birch and a few spruce and pine trees. About halfway along, Thomas took the wheelbarrow, and David carried the pie.

Several minutes later when the roadway was nearly leveled out, David announced, "Ma and Bobby." They were waiting for them at the sheep fence which crossed their path. Mildred slid back the fence rails when the men approached, and young Bobby eagerly staggered towards them.

"Whoa, Boy!" David blurted out as his little brother grabbed his leg and held tightly. "Cherry pie here, My Son." David continued to walk with the laughing youngster hugging his leg and the pie held high above his head. Mrs. Palmer promptly seized the pie, and David lifted Bobby up onto his shoulders.

"Good trip," Thomas told his wife. He moved the wheelbarrow to the pasture side of the fence and repositioned the rails across the roadway. "I got me a hired man, and David has a place to board."

The next morning after his breakfast, Jedidiah Harriston returned to his bedroom off the kitchen and dropped to his hands and knees. From beneath the bed he dragged out a wooden trunk and opened it, leaning its lid back against the bed. *Lots of room in here for my things,* he determined.

Jedidiah reached into the trunk, took hold of a pair of boots and lifted them out. *Don't know why I hang onto Dwight's boots—wishful thinking, I reckon. They're all I have left of him. Likely don't fit him no more.* The man placed them under the bed out of his sight and continued with his packing. *Even when I put my clothes in here, there'll be lots of room left over. I need to take my bedding and I want my Bible. I should take that text over our bed.* He looked up at it and read it once more. *It's in confidence or faith in the Lord and not having anxiousness that in quietness and in confidence will be my strength. Yes,* he agreed, *I have strength to go on. The Palmers shouldn't mind that in my room.*

From the kitchen came the sound of the clock striking the half hour. "I'll take my clock, too," Jedidiah said aloud as he grinned and looked towards the open door. The man returned to his kitchen, and after picking up the timepiece, he carried it into the bedroom and carefully placed it on the bed. As he hesitated, he reflected, *I wonder what Myrtle would think of me doing all this?* He then gathered the blankets around the clock and lowered the bundle into the trunk. *And now for the rest of my things.*

"We need to get a move-along," Thomas said later that day to the small group gathered on the Rogers Cove wharf. "Tide's been going out for a while now." He glanced over at David who was standing with the McNeills. Thomas moved over to his son, and without any expression on his face, he shook the young man's hand. He said nothing to him and then turned to George and Dorothy. "Thanks for supper." George nodded, and Dorothy grinned.

Jedidiah shook hands with George and Dorothy. "Bye, Friends," he said to them as he tried to smile.

George replied, "The Lord bless thee and keep thee, the Lord make His face shine upon thee and be gracious unto thee, the Lord lift up His countenance upon thee and give thee peace." Jedidiah nodded in acknowledgment, and then he crossed over to the edge of the wharf. He climbed down the ladder and took his place on the seat beside the box which contained his cat. And then he glanced over to his trunk with his belongings which David had earlier placed in the bow of the dory.

David knelt on the wharf, and after he untied the mooring rope, he let it drop into his father's dory. "See you in a couple weeks, Pa." With his hand, Thomas pushed against the wharf, and when they were clear, he lowered the oars into the water.

When the dory carrying the two men left the cove and was beyond Fearful Rocks, Jedidiah rotated in his seat and waved to the three people who were still standing on the wharf and looking towards him. After they returned the wave, he faced the bow of the dory and stared out over Thomas's shoulder to Bunchberry Island - his new home and a new chapter in his life.

What would Myrtle think of me doing this? he wondered again. *It sure is strange doing things without her!*

Later that night, Jedidiah Harriston stretched and rolled over. He was finding it difficult to sleep in a strange bed and in the darkness of an unfamiliar room. *My frame don't suit the humps and hollows of this here straw-tick mattress,* he concluded. *Have to do something about this tomorrow.* He sighed and frowned slightly. *Perhaps it wasn't a good idea I brought our mantel clock to here.* He could tell just where it was in the blackness and he turned his head to face its familiar rhythmic ticking. *It reminds me of Myrtle and our life together. How I miss her!* He listened as his clock seemed to say, "Myr-tle, Myr-tle, Myr-tle," over and over again. He slid his hand sideways between the bed sheets, and when he did not feel the warm body of his wife, he left his hand there limp and empty and cold. "I miss you, Myrtle," he said in a subdued tone.

Suddenly his timepiece struck the hour. The loud clanging seemed to shout out at him repeatedly, "Gone! Gone! Gone!" Jedidiah jerked back his hand to himself. He suddenly threw back the bed covers, dropped his feet to the floor, stood up and crossed the floor through the blackness. The sound of the mocking chimes came to an end just as he touched the offending clock, but he still heard, "Myr-tle, Myr-tle, Myr-tle." He placed his hands on the timepiece for several seconds and then abruptly tipped it away from him. The ticking stopped immediately but as he returned the clock to its upright position, the pendulum swung back and bounced against the chiming rods, taunting him one more time.

Jedidiah slowly made his way back to his bed in the dark, now-silent room. After feeling his way in between the sheets, he curled up and brought the covers up over his head. *It's all so difficult,* he lamented to himself. *I feel miserable. Was it the right thing for me to come away over here? I already miss my friends, the McNeills. George and Dot are people I can have fellowship with. Is it the Lord's will I not have that Christian fellowship I long for and need so badly?* He took a deep breath under the covers. *But I felt it was the Lord's will I come here, and so did George and Dot as we prayed together. And somehow I still feel I'm in the Lord's will. So why am I fretting?* He pushed the covers away and breathed deeply the air of the bedroom. *Lord, forgive me for doubting Thy will for me. Keep me in the knowledge of Thy will, and give me peace.*

He was now aware of a rhythmical sound he had never heard before in his life. The noise was muffled and barely audible, and although it reminded him of a moan, the ongoing sound was somehow peaceful and comforting. *And when I lie still,* he realized, *I can feel it through the bed. Thank You, Heavenly Father for this small comfort.*

Jedidiah noticed the odors in this room were not the same as he was used to at his home on the mainland. The smell of fuel oil was stronger here than he was accustomed to and through the open window drifted in a variety of farm fragrances. *And I think I can smell that pear tree just outside my window,* he figured, and he smiled. *It will be nice to have some pears for a change.*

When Jedidiah turned to look behind him and above his head, he could see flashes of light every few seconds coming from outside the window. He had seen this light many times before, but he had never been this close to its source. He studied the flashes for several minutes and then he recalled, *Each beacon has its distinct characteristic. This one is: one flash, and then dark, four flashes, dark, and then three flashes, dark. That spells, "I love you,"* he suddenly realized. *Yes, that's what it says.* He watched it go through its sequence several times. *And the Lord loves me,* he reminded himself.

As he observed the flashes, he said aloud the words the beacon spelled out to him. "I—love—you. I—love—you." *Thank You, Heavenly Father, for showing Thy love for me by giving Thy Son who bore my sin in His body when He shed His blood and died in my place. Thank You, Lord, for sending the Holy Spirit, the Comforter, who gives me peace and strength through my difficult times. Thank You, for Thy love for me, and thank You for this flashing beacon to remind me of Thy great love.*

Jedidiah took a deep breath. He let it out and relaxed. *Lord, may Thy will be done for me. Work in me and work through me. May I be the person You want me to be, and may I be used by Thee to reach others. May I be a good influence on Thomas and Mildred Palmer and their family.* Jedidiah Harriston rolled over and then promptly fell asleep.

chapter two

about a year and a half later—late winter 1917

"Just As I Am"

Thomas pulled on his boots and lifted his heavy coat from the hook by the door. He moved across the large main room in the lighthouse towards his wife. Mildred's hair was pinned to the back of her head, and her full-length apron, powdered with flour dust, covered the front of her dress. The kitchen table creaked rhythmically as she kneaded another batch of bread, the second this week. "Well, it's early afternoon," Thomas remarked to his wife. "I better get a move-along."

Without pausing in her task, Mildred looked up at him and then glanced quickly out the window and across the snow-covered yard to the stand of spruce trees along the edge of the cliff. "It's breezing up somewhat," she remarked. "Thomas, I left the letters there." She nodded in the direction of the catch-all shelf by the door. "And please find out how David's doing at school." The hired man's clock on the shelf between the woodshed door and the window struck the half hour.

Thomas put his big but gentle hand on her large abdomen and said, "You two take care." He buttoned up his coat, slipped the letters into his pocket and stepped out into the cold winter air without saying, "Good bye."

Mildred felt she should continue to pray for her husband. She had been committing him to the Lord everyday for a long time.

Thomas began the half-mile hike to the beach where his boathouse and wharf were. As he walked briskly along the path through the exposed clearing, he could feel the winter wind gently tugging at his beard. He concluded, *It seems it's always windy up here on top of Bunchberry Island, but it's the best place for the lighthouse. We enjoy it here even if it's a bit lonely by times. We have the island all to ourselves.*

The road soon dipped into the shelter of the cat spruce and the taller maple and birch trees. The snow was deeper here in the woods than it was in the small, open fields at the top of the island. *But it isn't all that lonely,* Thomas decided. *There's often folks here in the summer—even groups of people—nearly every week. It's nice to see them come, but sometimes it's even nicer to see them go. Right now Lorna's staying a few months and helping out. She's good company for Mildred.*

Thomas arrived at the boathouse and wharf. Soon he had his dory ready and was on his way across the now-choppy water to Rogers Cove on the mainland about nine miles away. "My, it's right cold," he told his boat as he rowed with the tide, "and this stiff breeze don't help none even when it's pushing me along."

Because of the sea conditions and the cold, it seemed to Thomas to be a long trip over to the mainland. He had a good while to think. *Jed sure knows the Bible, and he lives it too. Says God loves me so much that He gave His Son to take the penalty of my sin, and if I trust in Him, I'll be saved from God's judgment. Jed says I'll have a new life—whatever that means. I can see Mildred's different since she believes in the Lord.*

"Come on, Jed, you! I think you've carried enough firewood for now," Mildred half scolded, half teased. "You'll have the wood piled up to the kitchen ceiling before we know it, Jed Harriston! Here, I've made you a tea to go with your lunch."

Most of the maple and birch were split and Jedidiah stacked them neatly against the wall. As he stopped to catch his breath, he reached up and ran his bony fingers through his thin hair. He found it hard to hum when he was out of breath. *I wish these young people wouldn't tell me what to do,* he reflected, *but Thomas and Mildred treat me good, and it was kind of them to take me in after Myrtle passed away. The Lord has been good to me—I have a nice place here to stay, and I'm earning my keep, too. But I can't help wondering about Dwight. It's been thirty-eight years since he left me and Myrtle.* Then he said aloud, "One more load, and that's it for now, I reckon. I'm beginning to feel a mite faint, so I'm looking forward to that lunch, Mildred. Thanks."

The woodshed was attached to the house, and Jedidiah was grateful he did not need to go outside today in the wind and cold. He gathered an armload of firewood and headed back to the kitchen. Part way across the room, the old gentleman suddenly stopped, and the wood he was carrying slipped from his arms and tumbled to the kitchen floor.

"Jed! Are you all right!" Mildred quickly lowered the pan of freshly baked bread to the kitchen table. Jedidiah stood there with both hands to his chest and there was a distressed look on his face. Lorna moved quickly to him and tried to catch him as he began to sink to the floor. The kitchen cot was handy and she managed to lower him onto it.

Just then young Bobby appeared from the backroom. "What was that noise, Ma? Ma, why's there firewood on the floor?"

"Bobby, hurry, go fetch your pa," Mildred ordered him.

The boy replied, "But Pa's gone to the mainland."

Jedidiah's body was now limp and his face was relaxed. Mildred slowly took off her oven mitts as she stared wide-eyed at his lifeless form on the cot and then she clasped her hands together.

"Ma, why is Jed lying on the cot?" the youngster questioned.

"Because he's, he's—" She paused and then realized what had to be done. "Come on, Lorna, help me here." Lorna moved towards the kitchen cot. The younger woman pulled on the lounge while Mildred pushed. The two ladies maneuvered the lounge fairly easily for it was on roller casters.

"Look, Ma, there's the truck I lost! It was under the cot. Look, I found it!" Bobby made engine sounds as he pushed his red, toy truck through the pieces of firewood scattered over the floor.

When Lorna came to the doorway, she hesitated. "What if it don't go through?" she wondered.

"You'll have to lift the cot a smidgen to get it over the threshold," Mildred told her. The kitchen cot fit through, but Lorna raised Jed's leg up onto the cot to clear the door frame. Mildred and Lorna rolled the lounge to a clear spot next to the window near the stairs to the tower. The two ladies gazed down at the lifeless face of the old gentleman, and Lorna reached out and brushed back a long, stray wisp of Jed's hair which lay across his forehead. They hurried back to the kitchen and closed the door behind them.

This door was usually kept open in the colder months to allow the heat from the kitchen to go up into the tower where the light mechanism was situated.

"Ma, why did you put Jed out there?" Bobby wondered as he glanced at the closed door. "Why did you and Lorna take out the kitchen cot with Jed on it?"

His mother replied, "Bobby, help us pick up this firewood." They had the wood picked up in short order, and Lorna fetched the broom and swept the kitchen floor.

Bobby held his toy vehicle and added cheerfully, "Well, I'm glad I found my truck."

The empty place where the lounge had been made the ladies feel uncomfortable. Mildred looked over at Jedidiah's untouched lunch on the side table. "It's getting dark - almost time for me to go up and light the beacon," she spoke as calmly as she could.

The daylight was slowly departing from the sky when Thomas rowed his little boat past Fearful Rocks and into the sheltered water of Rogers Cove. At the wharf, he climbed out of his dory and up the wharf ladder, and then he secured the rope to a post. It had been a rough crossing, and he was chilled through. He wiped the frost from his mustache as he turned to look back through the twilight to his island home. Even though he was anxious for some warmth, he stood there and watched as the beacon went through its sequence. *Mildred is looking after the light while I'm away,* he contemplated. *Not only the light, but she has her usual everyday duties as well: preparing meals, looking after Bobby, and must be a dozen other things.*

One flash, dark, four flashes, dark, three flashes, dark, then the beacon repeated its characteristic over and over again, and it would continue all night until daybreak. Thomas remembered Jed had pointed out to them that the light flashed, "I love you, I love you."

Thomas replied as he observed the flashing light over the dark water, "I love you, Mildred, and you too, Bobby." And then he turned and made his way up to the warm house with the comforting light in the window where David was boarding.

Thomas knocked and promptly walked in. "Thomas! Welcome!" Mr. McNeill said in surprise. "Come on in," he greeted as he stood and extended his well-worn hand. And then called out, "David, your pa's here." He added more wood to the kitchen stove. "We wasn't expecting you today, Thomas, with this wind and all."

"Wind's some sharp," Thomas replied, removing his boots. "Cut the whiskers right off your face." After he removed his coat and hung it by the door, he deposited his boots behind the woodstove. David could be heard coming down the narrow stairs from the attic-room over the kitchen. He shook hands with his father, and then he moved to stand near the stove. The stubble on his face made him appear more mature than his father had seen him three weeks previously.

"You must be hungry," Mrs. McNeill said to Thomas, and she wiped her hands on her apron. "I'll get you something for nourishment."

"Thanks." He nodded. "How's you folks, anyway?"

"We're not getting any younger." Mr. McNeill grinned. "How's Mildred doing?"

Thomas sat down at their kitchen table. "Well, we figure she's got about a week to go yet. Lorna's with her." Thomas appreciated his friends and felt at home at their place, even when they did talk about the Lord.

"How's Jed Harriston?" asked Mrs. McNeill. "We haven't heard from him for a while, and we don't get over much to visit you folks at your place in winter."

"Oh, he's doing fine—just fine. Keeping busy. Good worker for an old fellow."

"The last time we seen Jed," Mr. McNeill remembered, "he said he felt the Lord could come at any time. He reminded us, as I recall, that in the last-times people would be boasters and proud and unthankful."

Thomas nodded and said, "I can see people's like that now more than they was when I was a lad."

Mrs. McNeill smiled. "Jed would say he thought he wouldn't die," she remarked, "but that the Lord would come first."

There was a long thoughtful pause, and then David spoke. "Pa, I've landed a job at the sawmill."

His dad nodded. "Good, My Son. Good."

David added, "It's after school and all day Saturdays."

Thomas was proud of his older son, but he was not in the habit of showing it. "Your ma wants to know how you're doing at school, Boy."

* * *

Neither Mildred nor Lorna had eaten much for their evening meal. Both were silent, deep in thought as they washed the dishes and put things away. Finally Mildred spoke as she hung the dishcloth on the line over the stove. "Well, I guess I'll have to signal for Thomas to come home."

Lorna looked over at Mildred. "You'll have to use the fire signals, won't you?"

"Yes," she replied. "We need four fires. Two fires on the beach means someone's ill. Three fires—a doctor's needed. And four fires mean a death. I'll have to go down to the beach and away over to Porcupine Point and build four fires and hope Thomas sees them."

Bobby was listening in. "Build a fire!" he piped up. "Can I help? I know how. Pa showed me."

"Mildred," Lorna told her, "you shouldn't be tramping out and away down to Porcupine Point in your condition." And then it dawned on Lorna that she ought to go. "I'll go," she said with apprehension.

Mildred lifted down the hurricane lantern from the shelf and told Lorna how to get a bit of oil in a pail. Bobby was directed to get birchbark from the woodshed and stuff it into Lorna's coat pockets. "Take a generous handful of matches," Mildred advised her. "You'll have to build the four fires along the beach so they can be seen from Rogers Cove."

"Ma, can I go and help Lorna?" Bobby pleaded. "I know how to build a fire. Pa showed me how."

"No, Bobby, it's too dark and cold and windy for you." She figured she had better not discourage him any more than that, or it would make it even harder for Lorna. "Come on, you get ready for bed, and then we can watch Lorna go across the yard from the window in Jed's room. We'll read a story after you get into bed."

"A Bible story," Bobby told his mother.

Going down to the beach to light the fires, thought Lorna as she buttoned up her coat, *is a good excuse to get away from the lighthouse with a corpse in the tower.*

Lorna opened the lighthouse door and stepped out into the yard and the dark of the night, but she was soon aware of the bright flash of the light beacon radiating high overhead. She turned towards the path which led down to the beach. *It's some cold—and windy, too!* she realized as she moved along the path. *It nearly takes my breath away. I wish I had a third hand to hold my scarf over my face. I hope this lantern don't go out. But Mildred said it wouldn't—they don't call them hurricane lamps for nothing.* Then she whispered aloud, "My Heavenly Father, I thank Thee for Your promise to be with me. Help me to be brave and to do good at making the four fires."

The front pockets of her long coat were bulging with birch-bark which she could feel with every step. *I'm walking in a sphere of light, but the wind and cold blows clean through. Jed said our light—our lives—should shine for the Lord and we should let the attitudes and things of the world blow clean through.* Lorna turned to face the lighthouse. *Bobby is watching from Jed's window right now,* she remembered. She swung the lantern back and forth several times and laughed when she imagined Bobby being amused at her waving the lantern to him and his mother. Before Lorna turned towards the dark woods, she looked up at the light beacon over the lighthouse. One flash, dark, four flashes, dark, three flashes, dark. "Thank You, Lord, for Your love to me," she expressed to Him.

When Lorna moved down into the woods, she realized the wind was not as forceful here. She was out of sight of the warm lighthouse, and Mildred and Bobby could no longer see her nor the light she was carrying. She knew she was now on her own except for the Lord, and she walked boldly along the path, deeper into the woods. She had no reason to be afraid for she knew no one could be here and there were only domesticated farm animals which were sheltered in the barns.

Lorna soon came to the pasture gate which was left open for the winter. *Jed Harriston really wasn't so bad,* she began to reminisce as she stepped by the railings poking through the snow. *He was never in the way. He was always helpful, and he never imposed himself on others. He never went to school, but he learned to read so he could read his Bible. He said he used to read the Bible to his wife who was finding it harder to see the past few years. Jed was good to have around. He was never owly or ugly, and he seemed to be always humming or singing a hymn or chorus, (I think he made up a few of them), or quoting a passage of Scripture. I wish I had shown him more appreciation. It's sad to think that his only child, when he was in his late teens, up and left home for the big city and never kept in touch all these years, not even once. Jed probably now has several grandchildren he could only imagine about.*

Lorna was conscious of the sound of the continual thunder of the crashing waves since she left the shelter of the lighthouse. *Jed helped me to realize the importance of a daily, private, quiet time with the Lord,* Lorna remembered.

The booming of the waves was becoming more distinct as she descended the steep hill towards the beach. *Is the tide in or out?* she wondered uneasily. *It sure sounds like there's a real sea on—and right handy, too. Sometimes when there's a high tide and the wind is right, the waves will wash right over onto the storm beach and push the driftwood back.* Every step brought Lorna closer down to the turbulent shore. *The tide must be in!* But then she remembered what Thomas had told her recently: *"At the quarter moon, the tide's in at six o'clock, morning and evening."* Lorna recalled when looking at the calendar with Bobby that the quarter moon had been today, therefore the tide had been in a couple of hours ago about supper time and was now on the way out.

A cold gust of wind in her face told her she was nearly at the beach. She stopped and lowered the pail of oil to her feet, and she shielded the light of the hurricane lantern from her eyes. *Yes, there's the boathouse - I can barely make it out. I'll have to go away along the beach to the right, towards Porcupine Point over that way somewheres.*

Lorna grabbed hold of the handle of the pail of oil and headed into the penetrating wind. To her left, the heavy doors of the boathouse thumped irregularly in the gusty breezes. The stony shore here was sometimes strewn with large pieces of driftwood, tree branches and roots pointing in all directions. The sound of the tumbling, crashing waves, just beyond her lantern was loudly threatening, always rushing towards her but never coming too close. It reminded her of an angry, barking dog at the end of its chain. She reasoned, *That's like the Lord not permitting danger to harm us, but of course it's important we not purposely step out of His will.*

As Lorna proceeded along the beach, she pondered, *The tide's always moving—it never stops. There's no normal water level, it's either coming in or going out over all these smooth stones all along the beach and right around the island.* As the water receded after each wave, she could hear the smaller beach stones knocking together. Lorna remembered Thomas saying, *"The height of the tide in this area's about thirty feet, and that's about one vertical inch each minute. High-tide's about every twelve hours and twenty-six minutes. That's an enormous volume of water that moves in a little over six hours."*

She passed through the driftwood and other debris the recent tides had tossed up. Her swaying lantern caused shadows to quickly dart from side to side. Beyond her immediate circle of light, she could see nothing but blackness. *In one year,* she concluded, *there are over seven hundred high-tides on this beach. There have been tides here for thousands of years—winter, spring, summer and fall.*

Here in the open, the wind was much stronger. Lorna's hands were cold because of the pressure of the handles of the pail and the lantern as she carried them along the beach. Her nose and cheeks were nearly numb.

Lorna stopped and held the lantern behind her and she peered off into the distance to see if she could detect any lights of Rogers Cove. She was disappointed that she could not. She then struggled farther along the dark and blustery shore and once more searched through the darkness across the rough water. "Oh good!" she said aloud when she discovered a few faint lights in the direction of Rogers Cove. She went forwards a short distance and then hung the hurricane lantern low on a hooked branch of driftwood and she carefully put the pail of oil nearby. The lantern swung slightly in the wind causing shadows to gently shift left and right, left and right. *Mildred said the fires should be no closer than fifty feet apart—that's about twice the width of the lighthouse,* she visualized.

Lorna gathered some dry sticks and deposited them next to a thick log nearby. She positioned the wood over some of the birchbark she had pulled from her coat pocket and had placed in the shelter of the log and then she splashed about a quarter of the oil over the pile. To give even more shelter, she knelt close to the heap she had made. Her fingers were stiff with cold but she managed to remove a match from her inside pocket. As she dragged the head of the match across a stone, it flared up but the wind promptly extinguished the little flame.

Lorna tried again with more determination. The second burning match, she carefully but quickly placed on the oil-soaked birchbark. The fire shot up rapidly, causing her, from her squatted position, to spring back and lose her balance. As she was sprawled out over the smooth stones, she watched the fire grow until she could feel its warmth. She was much relieved and encouraged, but she stood up and hurried farther along to make the second signal fire.

After the fourth fire was burning well, Lorna glanced around at the now-visible beach and the cliffs. She saw that the trees nearby were illuminated with warm light. The hurricane lantern which had given her much comfort was pale in comparison to the four fires. She stared into the fires one by one and considered, *The lantern I'm holding here must be like us knowing the Lord while still here on earth. Jed would now know Him so much more, like these large fires, than anyone could know the Lord here.* She felt drawn to the warmth of the fires which she could feel on her exposed face, and she was pleased she had accomplished her task, but she was longing for the refuge of the lighthouse where Mildred was awaiting her return. "No doubt anxiously," she giggled as she glanced up into the dark sky. She could make out the flashing of the beacon through the swaying tops of the spruce trees near the edge of the high cliff.

Lorna headed back along the beach with the lantern, stepping over and around the driftwood. When she came to the boathouse, she lingered several minutes, leaning against the side which was sheltered from the wind. *Thank You, Lord, for being with me and helping me,* she prayed as she watched the tall flames of the four signal fires dancing wildly in the gusts of wind.

When she got up this morning—it now seemed a long time ago—Lorna had no idea she would be away down here on the beach this cold, dark, and windy evening. *Jed would have been embarrassed to know I was here on account of him. And thank You, Lord, for sending him to encourage us.* After she had rested, Lorna left the empty pail by the boathouse with a heavy stone in it, preventing the wind from blowing it away. She started back up the long, steep hill to the lighthouse carrying only the lantern. Her free hand she put in her now empty pocket and succeeded in warming it somewhat.

"I've made up the bed for you, Thomas," Mrs. McNeill told him. "Same as before. Would you like some more tea? Help yourself to the dory plugs, You."

He replied, "I've had enough, Dot, thanks. And thanks for the supper."

Suddenly there was a knock on the kitchen door, and when it was not opened immediately, the knock came once more, but louder. "Who could that be, George?"

Before Mr. McNeill could reach the door, one of the neighbour boys burst in. "Is Thomas Palmer here? Ma seen him come in here earlier." Then the young fellow saw Thomas. "Mr. Palmer, there's four fires on your beach, Sir!" he exclaimed with excitement. "Pa seen them just a few minutes ago. I scurried over to here right away to where you're at to tell you. Someone died, didn't they!" He was all out of breath.

Thomas stared blankly at him, then promptly crossed over to the kitchen window facing the Rogers Cove wharf and Bunchberry Island away off to the west. David followed and looked over his father's shoulder. Several long seconds later, Thomas turned to face the others. "Four fires," he said with concern.

David wondered, "Who could it be, Pa?"

Thomas once more peered across to his island home. He cleared his throat. "Well, your ma's there, and Bobby and Jed," he said thoughtfully.

"And Lorna," David added. Thomas could not possibly make the return trip tonight and probably not tomorrow either. He was storm-stayed on the mainland for now.

The next morning Mildred climbed the stairs to the second floor of the lighthouse. She entered Jed's room and crossed over the braided rug to the window and after parting the drapes, she looked through one of its frosty panes. Whiffs of smoke were still rising from the beach where Lorna had been the evening before, and thin lines of gray could be seen stretched out across the sky by the stiff wind over Porcupine Point. Far across the restless water, she could make out the houses and fishing shacks of Rogers Cove. Beyond the village could be seen the gently curved summit of Bennys Bump silhouetted against the pale sky. She knew her husband could not return home today for the seas were far too high, besides, there were many heavy chunks of ice in the waves. The winter ice had broken up in the river on the mainland to the north and was now in the open water between the mainland and the island.

Poor girl! Mildred shook her head. *Lorna was gone almost two hours, and about half frozen when she got back. I know Thomas would've seen the fires, and he'll come as soon as he can. I've looked after the beacon—had to pass Jed lying there. She glanced around Jed's room absent-mindedly. My, I wish Thomas was here—he'd know what to do. He's good at knowing what to do at times like this. Like the time the Parker boy fell from the cliff on the other side of the island. It was Roy's twentieth birthday; a couple years older than David is now. Been hunting for gull's eggs, slipped and fell to the rocks on the beach below. Just like that! Alive one moment, dead the next.* Mildred shuddered, and she again pushed aside the curtain and peered out the window.

"Ma, I'm hungry," she suddenly heard coming from downstairs. "Can I have something to eat?" Mildred was abruptly brought back to the present time and the difficult circumstances they were now experiencing.

"I'll be down in a minute, Bobby," Mildred called to him, and she quickly glanced around the room again. *There's Jed's Bible, opened to where he had been reading from. My, I'm thankful he told me about Jesus, the Son of God taking my sins and dying on the cross for me. The Lord Jesus took the penalty for my sin, and I accepted God's gift of salvation, and now I'm saved—saved from the wrath of God and from the penalty of my sin. But I wish Thomas would trust in Jesus Christ, too.* Mildred returned downstairs, hurrying past Jed's body on her way. She entered the kitchen just as the hired man's clock struck twelve. And then she remembered, *Jed gave us his mantel clock—said it was too loud for him in his little room, besides the ticking at night reminded him of his wife and their home together.*

The gale continued to blow all that day, and the tower creaked during the occasional heavier gusts. Any loose snow around the lighthouse had blown across the field and into the woods, or over the cliffs to the rocky shore far below. On the paths in the clearing, the hard-packed snow remained and looked like dirty, white ribbons laid across last summer's lifeless vegetation.

The next day, Mildred and Lorna brought in firewood with Bobby's help. Mildred attended to her duties in the lighthouse. The lamps had to be filled with oil each day, the chimneys cleaned, and the reflectors polished, and the weights cranked up from the cellar far below. Each day Mildred looked out the window in Jed's room towards Rogers Cove. It was hard to tell the difference between the white caps and the ice chunks, but she could tell the ice was being blown away as well as breaking up and melting in the salt water. *Thomas won't be coming today, either,* Mildred realized as she placed Jed's Bible in the top drawer and straightened the dresser scarf.

That afternoon, Lorna suggested to Mildred that they move Jedidiah's body to the woodshed where it was colder than it was in the tower and to allow more heat up into the tall structure where it was needed. As the ladies pushed and pulled on the kitchen cot, Mildred said, "I think we should sing something."

Lorna looked at her in surprise. "Sing! What would we sing?"

"How about, 'Just As I Am'. That was one of Jed's favourite hymns."

"Yes, it was," Lorna agreed. "And come to think of it—wasn't that what he was humming just before he died? He didn't finish singing it." When Mildred and Lorna had moved the kitchen cot with its load into the woodshed, they stood at either end and sang, "'Just as I am, without one plea, but that Thy blood was shed for me, and that Thou bidd'st me come to Thee, O Lamb of God, I come.'"

By the fourth day the wind had died down somewhat, but the seas were not calm enough for anyone to venture out in a small dory. Thomas had spent much of his time staring out the window in the McNeill's kitchen and standing on the wharf looking beyond Fearful Rocks towards Bunchberry Island. *Mildred and Bobby, Jed and Lorna,* he kept thinking.

Mildred's contractions were coming more frequently, and they were harder now. She prayed that the delivery would be in the night and Bobby would sleep through the birthing process. *If Thomas was here,* she knew, *and if the delivery was during the daytime, he could entertain Bobby outside, and Jed had been good with him, too.* Everything was ready, and Lorna would be a great help. She had recently assisted in several births in her home community and beyond.

I didn't realize how much Jed really was a big part of our lives, Mildred reminisced as she sat in the stuffed chair in the main room of the lighthouse. *I noticed a week or so ago when I was reading Second Peter that the epistle starts and ends with the knowledge of our Lord Jesus Christ. I mentioned that to Jed. He said that the Lord's people get to know Him in three ways: by reading His Word, by talking to Him in prayer and by meditating on Him. These three ways have one thing in common—the Holy Spirit. The Holy Spirit guides us and gives us understanding when we read His Word. The Holy Spirit guides us and helps us when we pray. And the Holy Spirit guides us and gives us understanding when we meditate on the Lord. The Epistle of Peter ends with glory to the Lord both now and forever, and that glory comes from our knowledge of Him or how much we know Him.*

Captain Rafuse had a large boat with an engine, and he offered to take Thomas back to his island home when the seas were somewhat calmer. In the evening of the fifth day, Thomas and Captain Rafuse decided to attempt the crossing the next morning if the wind did not pick up again in the night. David would also travel with them.

The seas had lowered considerably overnight allowing the men to set out at daybreak towards Bunchberry Island. During the crossing they ploughed through a few clinkers, and even with the powerful boat, it took longer than usual to cross to the island. None of the men spoke as Captain Rafuse's boat carried the men past Porcupine Point where the four fires had been.

Lorna and Bobby were in the kitchen preparing their noon meal when Bobby happened to look out the window and across the wind-swept clearing. "Look! Pa's coming! Come have a look-see, Lorna! There's Pa and David and someone else."

Lorna left the knife in the loaf of bread as she rushed over to the window. She and Bobby watched as the men moved along the path towards those in the lighthouse. "Mildred," Lorna called to her as she held her long braid, "Thomas is coming."

Bobby opened the door, and the men promptly entered. "Hi, Pa! Hi, David!"

"Where's Mildred?" Thomas immediately demanded as he scanned the room.

"Over here, Thomas," she answered from the stuffed chair behind the door. Her husband quickly turned to face in her direction. "This is Joshua Palmer," she announced proudly to him. "He arrived early yesterday morning." And then she said softly, "Joshua, this is your pa."

Thomas stood there a few seconds and then moved over to his wife and newborn son. "Well, hello there, Joshua," he answered, gently stroking the baby's soft cheek with his large, rough hand. And then he bent over and kissed his wife. David grinned as he stared at his youngest brother.

Mildred explained to her husband, "Jed died the day you left. We moved his body out to the woodshed where it's cooler."

Her husband replied, "I was anxious to tell him I have put my trust in Christ."

Mildred looked up at him and grinned. "Thomas, I'm so glad you're saved! I've been praying for you."

Thomas answered her, "The way Jed lived convinced me that what he said about the Lord was true. And now I believe the Bible where it says Jesus the Son of God took the penalty for my sin, and I accept His gift of salvation."

"Jed was faithful," Lorna put in, "and he sure was a good influence on all of us."

Yes," Mildred added as the hired man's clock began to strike, "each of us could tell by Jed's life that he belonged to the Lord."

chapter three

about ten years later—summer 1927

Spruce Gum

"But I did see it," insisted ten-year-old Joshua as he and his brother hiked up the steep roadway through the woods towards the lighthouse. The young fellow was wearing baggy, hand-me-down pants held up by faded yellow suspenders.

Bobby, who was several steps ahead, grinned back at him. "Aw, go away with you, Boy," he retorted. "You were seeing things."

"No, I wasn't. I saw it with my own two eyes in that spruce thicket back of Porcupine Point. You know that big old spruce tree we can see from the beach? I was checking it for gum." Joshua quickly glanced back in that direction.

"Spruce gum. Get any for me?" fifteen-year-old Bobby asked. He was wearing overalls with patches on both knees, and then he reminded Joshua, "We've been all over this here island, and we've never seen nothing like that before." The older boy grinned at his brother, not believing him.

Joshua took several quick steps and came alongside Bobby. "Maybe so, but we've never been in that thicket before," he persisted. "When you were on the other side of the point at that recent rock-fall, I went into the woods there for gum. Pushed my way through those thick spruce trees up on that flat area, and back in there I saw an old dory. I did too, Mister, I tell you."

Bobby shrugged his shoulders. "Well, I reckon you did," he finally admitted. "Let's check it out later, Joshie. Hey, where's my gum?"

"I didn't get none. I came looking for you to tell you about the dory." And then Joshua put his hand over his abdomen.

"I'm hungry something fierce!"

His brother told him, "Well, you ought to be, My Son. It's high-nigh dinner time. We better get a move-along." With his arm stretched out, he gently pushed him into the ferns along the side of the roadway. "Race you to the lighthouse," he called back, and he laughed and scurried ahead.

As Joshua walked along the road, he kept an eye on Bobby running towards the rail fence stretched across their path. He grinned as Bobby vaulted over the fence without slowing down and continued his run as the sheep in the clearing scattered.

The two boys had lived all their lives here on Bunchberry Island with their parents. Their father had been the lighthouse keeper for about thirteen years. Because mainland folks sometimes came to visit them, the Palmer family did not mind the isolation. There was plenty to do looking after the sheep, their two cows, several pigs, and a dozen hens. The boys had chores with the animals as well as work in the vegetable garden. They also enjoyed and made use of the woods and the beach surrounding their island home, and they had great times together.

When Joshua came to the fence across his path, he took his time and climbed over it. Then, because he could see Bobby was nearly halfway to the lighthouse and just poking along, he broke out into a fast but noiseless jog along the roadway towards him.

Joshua caught up to his brother when he was several yards from the lighthouse door. He quickly brushed by Bobby, knocking him off balance. The family cat which had been napping in the sun on the stone step scampered away in alarm. Joshua came to an abrupt stop at the wooden door with his arms spread out and the side of his face pressed against the door. He slowly turned to see Bobby's reaction. "Beat you!" he told him with glee. Bobby grinned, and he opened the door and entered the main room of the lighthouse. Joshua glanced over at the cat now crouched behind the tall grass next to the woodshed and studying the situation nervously. "Sorry about that, Uncle Hairy," he informed him.

Spruce Gum

When the noon meal in the lighthouse was nearly finished, Mr. Palmer gave instructions to his sons regarding that afternoon. "Mr. Thompson will be working at the boathouse later today. I want you boys to carry things down for him before then. He'll tell you what to take." Mr. Palmer glanced over at Mr. Thompson with his elbows on the table sipping his tea.

"Yes, Sir," Bobby replied for both of them. Joshua looked at Mr. Thompson who was in his mid-twenties. The man nodded at him, lowered his tea to the table, and grinned at the boys. The clock which Jedidiah Harriston gave the Palmers struck one o'clock.

"And when you're through there and before supper," their father continued, "bring in firewood for your ma. Bobby, be sure you split enough kindling for several days while you're out there in the woodshed."

Bobby nodded and replied, "Yes, Sir."

"Joshua," his father reminded him, "when you take out the garbage, please chuck it farther into the woods towards the cliff, will you."

"Yes, Sir."

Uncle Hairy appeared from outside the open window. He squeezed under it, dropped to the floor with a thud, and crossed the room to where Mrs. Palmer was standing by the woodstove. After rubbing himself against her ankles, he inspected the saucer under the stove and began to lap up the milk.

"Okay," Mr. Palmer announced, "let's read a bit of Scripture before we leave the table." He reached over for his Bible on the side table, and Mrs. Palmer returned and sat down. Mr. Thompson looked disinterested and glanced out the window, but he remained where he was seated during the reading of God's Word.

When the noon meal was over, Mr. Thompson and the boys gathered the tools and supplies which were needed down at the boathouse. They loaded the wheelbarrow, and the two boys left with Bobby pushing it along the path. When they reached the fence at the far side of the sheep pasture, Joshua lifted and slid back the rails wide enough to allow the wheelbarrow through.

The two men remained near the woodshed attached to the lighthouse to cut firewood into stove-length chunks. The boys would later separate the wood to be split from the remaining smaller pieces which were stacked to air-dry in the sun and wind.

Bobby and Joshua left the wheelbarrow and its load near the boathouse and took off along the beach towards Porcupine Point. As they moved along, they hopped or jumped from rock to rock, they tramped over the unstable, smooth stones, and they walked along the occasional logs thrown up by the waves. When they were about one hundred yards from the thicket, Joshua could sense Bobby was anxious to see the old boat he had found that morning. Joshua tried to lead him along, but Bobby kept one step ahead of him. Joshua ran past him, and then they raced side by side. When the boys reached the narrow grassy area up from the beach, Bobby rushed ahead of Joshua to the thick spruce trees.

Joshua told his older brother, "Wait, I'll show you where I went into the woods." He came up behind Bobby.

"I can see where you've been at," he answered with a grin. "The grass is tramped down here, and these spruce boughs have been turned back. You went in here." He pushed into the thicket with Joshua close behind him. The trees were tight together here, and the boys carefully maneuvered their way between the dry, bare, lower branches. The heavy green boughs overhead kept out the direct sunlight, and there was no movement of air as the boys tread over the pale, reddish-brown carpet of spruce needles at their feet.

"See the dory, Bobby?" Joshua questioned, pointing through the trees. "Over there, see?" He and Bobby made their way over to it. They stood a couple yards away, staring at it.

"Well, I never!" Bobby exclaimed, and Joshua grinned at him. "You sure found something of interest, Joshie." Joshua's grin grew larger.

The old dory was about twelve feet long. It was partly upside down, leaning against the largest spruce tree in the area. The boys studied it in silence. The wind could be heard in the branches high overhead, and off in the distance was the familiar sound of the waves unceasingly washing over the stones along the shore. Bobby moved around to the other side of the old boat. "This is some pretty little dory," he exclaimed. Most of the paint had worn off, but there were still traces revealing its former colours of blue and white. The side of the boat which was resting on the ground was partly buried in the spruce needles and was beginning to separate from its nearly flat bottom.

Bobby expressed amazement. "I didn't know this old dory was back in here."

"How'd it get back here anyhow?" Joshua wondered aloud.

Bobby answered, "It was dragged up to here before all those trees growed up around here." He swept his hand in the direction they had come in. Bobby then circled the dory, touching and tapping the hull where he could reach it through the skinny trees.

"This dory's been here some long time," Joshua figured. "Probably before I was born. I wonder if Pa knows about this."

Five minutes later, the boys pushed their way out of the spruce thicket and stepped into the bright sunlight and onto the grassy area above the stony beach. They took the easier route along the high-tide line, back towards the wharf where the boathouse was and the roadway to the top of the island.

Mr. Thompson, the assistant lighthouse keeper, had started his job of removing the old, weather-worn shingles from the west wall of the boathouse. "Hey, boys, I have a riddle for you," he said when they stopped to watch him work. "What is as light as air yet a strong man can't hold it for more than a few minutes?"

The two brothers stared at him blankly. "I don't know," Bobby had to admit. "How can something be as light as air, but a strong man can't hold it for very long?"

"Give up?" Mr. Thompson asked. He paused his work to grin at the boys, and they looked at him expectantly. The man then pushed the pile of old shingles with his foot before answering. "His breath," he told them.

Bobby and Joshua grinned at Mr. Thompson, and a minute later Bobby told him excitedly, "Josh here—he found an old dory in the woods—over there up from Porcupine Point."

The man grunted in acknowledgment as he held his pipe between his teeth. "Lots of old dories around," he informed them after he removed his pipe. "When them old dories break their backs or spring a leak that can't be fixed, they're hauled up on shore. And there they stay until they rot through." He placed his pipe back in his mouth, yanked the nail out of the wall and let the damaged shingle drop to the ground at his feet.

A look of disappointment came across Joshua's face as he momentarily stared at Mr. Thompson. He pushed his hands into the pockets of his loose-fitting pants and then looked over at Bobby who spoke up. "No, Sir, this dory isn't an old dory—I mean it wasn't an old dory. It got old back there in the spruces." He gestured along the shoreline towards Porcupine Point. Mr. Thompson glanced over to where Bobby had pointed, but he said nothing as he sucked on his pipe.

Joshua stepped a little closer. "It looks like it's been there a long time, Mr. Thompson," he declared with enthusiasm.

The boys turned to leave for the roadway up to the lighthouse. Mr. Thompson repeated, "An old dory in the woods."

The boys stopped and faced him. "Yes, Sir," they both replied.

The man said, "And she was in good shape when she was hauled up to there where she's at now."

Joshua answered, "Yes, Sir. Appears so, anyhow."

"Help me here, Boys, and shortly we'll go take a gander." Joshua and Bobby gathered up the old shingles and set aside suitable ones to be taken up to the lighthouse for kindling. The remaining pieces were left in a safe place to burn on the beach at a later date. When the work was completed, Mr. Thompson said, "Let's go, Boys." He turned his pipe over and gently tapped it against a rock, and then he lowered the empty pipe into his shirt pocket.

The brothers walked side by side as they moved along the beach and a step or two behind Mr. Thompson. When they reached the narrow grassy area, the man hesitated allowing the boys to lead. Bobby gave Joshua the honour of directing them into the spruce thicket. Bobby followed Mr. Thompson, who had to turn sideways several times to allow his tall frame and broad shoulders to pass between the tightly packed trees.

"Well, blow me down!" Mr. Thompson blurted out when he saw in the dim light the overturned boat surrounded by the bare lower trunks of the spruce trees. "Never in all my life!" The man then stood motionless, and he leaned forward slightly with a frown of concentration on his face. As Joshua grinned at him, he noticed a twig caught in the hair of the surprised man.

Mr. Thompson studied the dory for nearly a minute. "This dory was dragged into here—and a long time ago," he figured. "These spruce trees are stunted—they're older than they would look back on the mainland. Growed up after the dory was left here." He glanced from the dory to the direction they had entered the thicket and then back to the dory. "Some strange," he concluded as he scratched through his two-week-old beard. He moved forward and squeezed between the trees to have a closer look and then he made his way around to the elevated side of the little boat. When he lowered himself to kneel on the brown thicket floor, a dry, bare branch snagged his shirt, pulling it out from his trousers. He carefully leaned forward and turned his head to look inside the overturned dory. "Oars still into her," he announced, "the other side of the thwart there." He retrieved his pipe which had fallen from his pocket and onto the old spruce needles.

Both Joshua and Bobby looked at each other and joined Mr. Thompson still crouched over on his hands and knees. They peered into the dark overturned boat. "Yeah, there they are," Bobby agreed. "Caught under the thwart like Pa does it."

Joshua added, "A porcupine's lived under here, too."

"And look," Bobby said when he pointed to the ground under the dory, "that looks like an old coat or something there."

Mr. Thompson stared at it with a frown of wonderment, and then he carefully stood up. "Pretty dory—at one time." And then he remembered, "More work to do before supper. Got to get a move-along, Boys." He and the two brothers left the dory in the shady spruce thicket and stepped out into the bright light of the open shoreline.

As Mr. Thompson quickly returned to the boathouse, the boys wandered back at a leisurely pace following the high-tide line. Along the way, Bobby discovered a wooden buoy half buried in the line of seaweed cast up onto shore by the last tide. As he knelt in the pea-size stones, he pulled on the knotted-wrack twisted around the long shaft and rope of the buoy. "Some snarled up," he exclaimed as he yanked off a bunch of seaweed and chucked it aside. "Pa will know whose buoy this is."

Joshua sat on a large rock nearby to watch his brother work. About half a minute later he said, "Bobby, do you know what Mr. McNeill means about getting saved? He says something about believing in God and in Jesus dying on the cross. I believe all that—doesn't everybody?"

Bobby sunk his fingers into a mass of brownish-green seaweed and struggled with it until he broke off a large handful. "He doesn't mean just believing or knowing about God," he answered, "he means trusting in Him."

"Trusting in Him?" Joshua repeated with a frown. "I trust in God. But Mr. McNeill says I need to be saved." He put his elbows on his knees and his chin in his hands. "Pa and Ma say they're saved," he continued, "but I don't think I am. Are you saved, Bobby?"

Bobby looked over at his brother sitting on the rock. "Yeah, I got saved a couple weeks ago."

"You did? How'd it happen? What does it mean to get saved, anyway?"

"Well, Jesus died on the cross for us. That's how He paid the penalty for our sin. He was punished for us—in our place."

Joshua shrugged his shoulders. "Yeah, but I'm not a sinner like Mr. Thompson," he insisted. "I don't smoke a pipe. I don't swear. Hey, Mister, I'm not a bad person—I never killed nobody." He scowled at Bobby. "Why do I need to be saved?"

Bobby worked off more seaweed and tossed it down. "The Bible says, 'All have sinned and come short of the glory of God.' Remember that verse, Joshie? It's in the Bible somewhere—Romans, I think. Mr. McNeill made us say it until we could say it without looking." He glanced towards Rogers Cove, the closest village on the mainland where the McNeills lived.

Joshua answered without hesitation, "'For all have sinned and come short of the glory of God.' Romans chapter three, verse twenty-three."

"The Bible says we've all sinned," Bobby explained to Joshua. "Even Mr. McNeill says he has sinned. To sin means that we have broken one of the ten commandments—like stealing or lying or something else like that. Even if we broke only one of the commandments only once, we would be guilty of sin." The buoy and its rope were now clear of seaweed, and Bobby stood up.

Joshua looked thoughtful. "So Jesus died on the cross to pay the penalty for our sin—He was punished for us. I get it now. To be saved means to be saved from the penalty for our sin."

"Yeah, that's right," Bobby replied. He cradled the wooden buoy in both his arms as he stood among clumps of seaweed scattered about him. "Those who aren't saved are already heading for hell until they are saved."

Joshua looked off into the distance over the water. "But how does a person get saved?" he asked. "How did you get saved?" Joshua turned and looked into his brother's face and waited for him to reply.

Bobby did not answer immediately. He looked thoughtful as well as pleased. Finally he spoke. "Well, Joshie, I told the Lord I knew I was a sinner. I told Him I was sorry I had sinned against Him and I thanked Him for giving His Son the Lord Jesus Christ to take the penalty for my sin. I told Him I was now trusting Him to save me. And then I thanked Him for saving me."

Joshua looked at Bobby in surprise. "And that's all there is to it!" he spoke up in amazement. "It's so simple. There must be more to it than that. Aren't there other things I have to do?" Bobby grinned and started back along the beach with the wooden buoy over his shoulder. Joshua followed at a distance.

At the boathouse, Bobby left the buoy resting against a large rock where his father could see it. The boys gathered up the old shingles and dumped them into the wheelbarrow. Bobby grabbed hold of the handles and started up the steep roadway through the mixed woods.

"Mr. Thompson's nice, I guess," Joshua said as he took his turn with the wheelbarrow which bounced over a tree root snaking across their path.

Bobby answered, "Pa says he'll make a good lighthouse keeper. He's catching on real quick what needs to be done around here. I guess Pa's a good teacher. I hope Mrs. Thompson likes it here." Joshua struggled with the heavy wheelbarrow and after a while he stopped momentarily.

"Here, My Son, let me take that," Bobby told him, and Joshua stepped back. Bobby took hold of the handles and rushed up the roadway pushing the loaded wheelbarrow.

Joshua laughed as he scampered after him. "Go, Bobby, go!" Without stopping, Joshua scooped up a shingle which had come free from the load and tumbled onto the roadway.

Bobby soon slowed down but did not come to a stop until they were halted by the rail fence across their path. Joshua dropped the shingle into the wheelbarrow and then slid back the rails. Bobby, breathing hard, stood waiting next to the wheelbarrow. When the wheelbarrow was on the pasture side and the rails were repositioned, Bobby climbed into the wheelbarrow and lay back on the shingles. "Okay, Josh, give me a ride home, Boy."

Joshua pushed the wheelbarrow with his brother in it over the level ground, past the lighthouse and through the scattering chickens near the barn. They entered the barn by the open door and Joshua parked the wheelbarrow in one of the empty cow stalls. He giggled as he tried to sit down beside Bobby on the shingles in the wheelbarrow. "Move over, Mister," Joshua ordered. "I'm bushed." Bobby refused to move as Joshua crowded against him. In the struggle which followed, the wheelbarrow tipped over and the boys giggled as they sprawled in the old shingles and fresh straw bedding.

Bobby suddenly jumped to his feet. "We've got chores to do before supper," he remembered. "Come on, Josh, let's go."

At the supper table that evening in the lighthouse, the boys reported to their parents regarding the dory in the spruce thicket. "It's about as long as from here to that window over there," Bobby informed his father.

Mr. Palmer showed only polite interest in what they had discovered. "You never know what you might find in them trees next to the beach," he told them as he leaned back in his chair. "A storm can toss things up into the woods if there's an extra high-tide and the wind's fierce enough. Bobby, you split kindling before supper?" he asked.

Bobby nodded. "Yes, Sir. And we brought up some of the old shingles for kindling, too." The hired man's clock gave six strikes.

"But, Pa," Joshua insisted, "that piece of ground is up high, and the dory is back quite aways."

Mr. Palmer took a deep breath and let it out slowly before he responded. "Someone—probably one of the former lighthouse keepers must have dragged the dory back in there years ago because it had finished its duty."

Mr. Thompson spoke up. "It looks like it was in good shape, nearly new when it was left there. Oars still into her, too. Badly cracked now and separated on her starboard side."

Mr. Palmer looked over at him. "You saw it too, Ian?"

Mr. Thompson nodded. "I reckon it was a right pretty dory when someone left it there," he replied. "Some curious, I'd say."

Mrs. Palmer checked the water on the stove. "We've been here thirteen years this past May," she said when she replaced the cover over the large pot. "And we didn't know there was a dory in the woods down there."

"Pa, will you come and see it this evening before dark?" Joshua wanted to know. "Me and Bobby can show you right where it's at."

Mr. Palmer looked at Joshua and then Bobby who were seated at the long side of the table. A slight smile of pleasure swept across his face as he observed his eager sons. He said, "How about tomorrow morning?" It was more of a promise than a question. The boys were obviously pleased and they grinned at each other.

"Bobby, Joshua," their mother said to them when they stood up to leave, "this is bath night for you two. And by the looks of your clothes and the bits of straw in your hair, you've been on the barn floor again." Her sons stood still and faced her as she spoke. "And don't forget, Boys, Mr. and Mrs. McNeill are planning to come tomorrow morning if the seas are fairly calm. We don't want them to think you two are just growing wild out here."

Bobby and Joshua left the lighthouse for their evening responsibilities with the animals. Uncle Hairy ignored the boys as they passed by him near the woodshed. He jumped up onto the log on the sawhorse and began to sharpen his claws.

A couple hours later before the boys climbed into their beds, Bobby slid the oil lamp on the dresser closer to his bed. He opened his Bible and began to read. Joshua watched him but said nothing until he closed the book several minutes later. "Why'd you read the Bible now, Bobby?" he asked as he partly sat up, leaning on one elbow. "Pa's read it to us. Isn't that enough?"

Bobby looked over at his brother. "Because I like to read it. I decided I'm going to read the Bible for myself everyday," he informed him with determination. "The Bible is the Word of God, and it tells us about Him and about the Lord Jesus Christ. And it tells us how to live the way He wants us to live."

Joshua looked at him blankly but said nothing. He laid back down in his bed and brought the covers up to his chin. Just as he was going to close his eyes, he asked in surprise, "What are you doing now?"

"I'm praying before getting into bed," Bobby answered as he knelt on the braided rug between the beds.

Joshua did not respond; he rolled over and said no more.

Bobby and Joshua did not need to be called for breakfast the next morning. They were down and at the breakfast table in good time. When they checked out the window, they could see the top of the island was in full sunlight with clear, blue sky overhead, but there was thick fog over the water all around the island, and it was up about level with the top of the island.

To the boys, breakfast seemed to take more time than usual. Even the Bible reading was longer. Joshua thought the seven strikes of the hired man's clock were slower than they had ever been before. Mr. Palmer had several small, daily jobs which he needed to do, and it seemed to Joshua that his father took his time. Finally Mr. Palmer grinned and said, "Okay, Boys, let's go."

As Bobby and Joshua followed their father from the lighthouse, their mother stood at the door. "Boys," she called after them. "We have company coming this morning. Please don't get your clean clothes mussed up."

After waving in reply, Bobby caught up to his father, and he tried to match his long strides. Joshua traveled on one side of the roadway for a while and then skipped across to the other to examine something in the vegetation close by or off in the woods.

"Pa," Bobby began when he tried to make conversation, "Mr. Thompson's working out real good, isn't he?" His father smiled in agreement as he glanced over at him.

Bobby continued. "Hope his wife likes it here." Mr. Palmer nodded. Bobby kept alongside his father and said, "Living on the mainland will be different for us. Joshua will miss it here."

His father looked thoughtful and nodded. "Your ma's finding it hard here. Needs female company," he said to his son. "And the work here is getting to be too much for me."

Bobby added, "Living in Rogers Cove will be good for all of us, won't it, Pa?"

Mr. Palmer knew that what his fifteen-year-old son had said was meant to be a reassuring statement rather than a question. *Bobby's maturing*, his father realized, and he grinned but said nothing.

When they reached the boathouse, Mr. Palmer had a quick look at the west wall. "Nice work," he commented, and then he surveyed over the water and the thinning fog in the direction of Rogers Cove on the mainland.

Bobby followed his gaze. "Fog will be about gone soon enough," he reported to his father.

Joshua threw several stones into the water. "Come on, let's go," he urged, and he led the way along the beach towards Porcupine Point. When the three of them reached the narrow grassy area, Joshua bounded ahead and pushed into the spruce thicket. Mr. Palmer signalled for Bobby to enter before him. Joshua called back, "Over this way, Pa."

Their father squeezed his way between the close, stunted trees until he was standing near Bobby within several yards of the boat. Joshua grinned broadly. "How do you like it, Pa?" His father stood without expression, staring at the dory. Joshua was beginning to think he and Bobby had dragged him away down here for nothing. Mr. Palmer moved to another position which brought him closer to the old dory. Without saying anything, he studied the rotting hull, barely moving his head as his eyes swept from bow to stern and back.

Joshua stood looking disappointed, and he lowered his hands into the front pockets of his baggy pants. There was silence in the damp and shady thicket, and because there was no wind, the spruce trees gave no sound, but off in the distance he could hear the outgoing tide as it made its way around the rocks on the beach. The boy studied the faces of his father and his brother, and for the first time he thought he could see what his mother meant when she said Bobby looks just the way his father did when she first saw him many years ago. *Ma says,* Joshua recalled, *that several years after meeting Pa, she fell in love with him. But I can't imagine anyone falling in love with my brother Bobby or wanting to marry him, and I can't imagine him wanting to get hitched to a girl.*

After what seemed like a long time, Mr. Palmer spoke. "This is some peculiar!" he told them. "Whose dory was this? Why's she away back at this place? And how long has she been here?" He then looked over at Joshua. "You found this here dory, Boy?"

Joshua grinned. "Yes, Sir." And Joshua could see his brother was grinning at him, too.

Bobby reminded him, "Oars still into her."

Mr. Palmer squeezed between the skinny spruce trunks and knelt on the ground where he could see under the up-tipped boat. "Yup," he agreed, "the other side of the thwart. Old coat here, too." He then leaned back against a spruce tree and remained in that crouched position for several minutes looking thoughtful. After a while he said, "Better go." And from his cramped quarters, he stood up gingerly.

They emerged from the spruce thicket and stepped into the clear sunlight on the beach. Mr. Palmer immediately squinted across the water towards Rogers Cove. "Fog is mostly gone," he observed.

Bobby nodded in response. "McNeills are probably well on their way by now," he decided.

When Mr. Palmer with his sons reached the boathouse, the lighthouse keeper climbed the ladder leaning against the side of the building, crawled up to the peak of the roof and examined the water off towards Rogers Cove. After he returned to the boys he told them, "Stay here and carry things for the McNeills. They'll be here in about three quarters of an hour."

"Yes, Sir," Bobby answered him as he nodded, and Mr. Palmer headed for the roadway to the top of the island.

An hour later, Bobby and Joshua led Mr. and Mrs. McNeill up the steep path in the shade of the mixed woods. "It sure was nice of you boys to meet us at your wharf and help carry these parcels," Mrs. McNeill told them. The boys grinned in reply.

Mr. McNeill added, "Must be gentlemen, I'd say."

Between the four of them, they carried several boxes of groceries, the latest weekly newspaper and Bibles belonging to the McNeills. "I have a letter here for you folks from your brother David out west," Mrs. McNeill said. "I picked it up at the post office the day before yesterday."

A minute later, Joshua looked over at Mr. McNeill. "I've memorized Psalm One," he told him shyly.

"You did!" Mr. McNeill exclaimed with pleasure. "Good for you, My Son. Can you say it now, Joshua?"

When the young fellow completed the psalm, Mrs. McNeill remarked, "That was well done."

Mr. McNeill said, "You sure earned that dime I promised you." And Joshua grinned.

After greetings were exchanged at the lighthouse with Mr. and Mrs. Palmer, Mrs. McNeill remained to help Mrs. Palmer with the noon meal and Mr. McNeill returned outside to inspect the garden with Mr. Palmer and the boys.

On their way back to the lighthouse, Mr. McNeill reached into his pocket and pulled out a dime. "Here, Joshua," he told him, "and remember, for a person to be strong and stable in his life, he needs to value the Word of God and enjoy it." Joshua took the dime and grinned, and then he carefully examined one side of the coin and then the other.

Mr. Palmer did not read the Bible after noon meal. It was planned that Mr. McNeill would read a passage of Scripture and comment on it after the ladies tidied up from their meal. Mr. Thompson hastily finished his tea, and he left the table and went outside. Bobby brought his Bible down from his room, and he sat beside Joshua on the kitchen cot and waited. The ladies quietly conversed as they worked, and the two men discussed something political and of no interest to the boys.

Joshua stood up and reached deep into his front pocket and when he sat down, he again studied the dime which Mr. McNeill had given him. His brother tried to see the coin, and when he leaned closer, it was yanked away from his view. "Hey, Boy," Bobby protested, "I only want to have a look-see."

Joshua giggled as he held the dime at arm's length from Bobby. "It's mine, Mister," the younger boy stated as he moved away from Bobby to the far end of the lounge.

Bobby grinned at him. "I know it's yours. I just want to see it." He leaned away over, supporting himself on one elbow and extending his arm towards Joshua.

Joshua liked to challenge his brother. He then held the coin high over his head as he sat on the cot. "No, you don't," he said to Bobby as he continued to giggle.

Bobby accepted the challenge, and he enjoyed showing his superiority over his young brother. "You think so, Boy?" he questioned defiantly. Bobby stood up, faced Joshua and grabbed his wrist extended high over his head. Joshua laughed as he made a tight fist around the dime. He leaned back against the wall and holding his closed fist up, he raised his foot and put it against Bobby's chest. Bobby gave Joshua an exaggerated grin knowing that laughter temporarily weakens a fellow. As he continued to grin in his silly fashion, he ignored the foot on his chest and reached for his brother's closed fist. The younger boy continued to laugh which drained his strength to push Bobby away.

Mr. Palmer glanced over at his noisy sons. "Boys," he addressed them quietly, but firmly. And then he gave them a short, "Shh." Bobby immediately released his grip on Joshua's wrist, and he sat down at the far end of the kitchen cot and picked up his Bible. Joshua promptly stood up, slid the dime into his pocket and sat down. He took a deep breath and let it out slowly as he grinned sideways at his brother.

The two ladies came to the kitchen table with their Bibles and sat down. Mr. McNeill opened his Bible, and Mr. Palmer reached over to the side table for his. Bobby moved closer to share his Bible with Joshua even though the younger boy could not read well. Mr. McNeill gave a message from God's Word and then closed in prayer after the little group sang a hymn.

The two couples remained in the lighthouse to visit. Bobby listened in on the adult conversation between his father and Mr. McNeill. About twenty minutes later, the man turned to Bobby. "And what have you been up to, Boy?" he asked as the hired man's clock struck two.

Bobby grinned politely. He quickly glanced at Joshua beside him on the kitchen lounge. "Me and Joshua's been looking at an old dory he found in the woods," he revealed to Mr. McNeill. "In that spruce thicket back of Porcupine Point."

Joshua added excitedly, "The dory's been there a long time. It wasn't old when it was put there."

Bobby quickly put in, "Oars up inside her, and an old coat under it, too."

Mr. McNeill stared at Bobby and Joshua. His wife abruptly stopped her talk and turned towards the boys. The cheerful faces of their visitors suddenly became somber. Mr. McNeill looked over at the boys' father who informed him, "Looks like she was left there many years ago. Spruce trees in front of her growed up since."

Mrs. McNeill moved closer to the men. She looked troubled as she stood near her husband. There was silence in the main room of the lighthouse, and Mr. and Mrs. Palmer and their sons were puzzled as they studied their friends, the McNeills.

Uncle Hairy, the cat suddenly appeared at the open window having jumped up from the ground outside. Mrs. McNeill lurched and gasped, but was relieved when she saw it was only the family cat.

Mr. McNeill spoke. "Thomas, could you tell if the dory had been painted blue and white?" he asked anxiously. The two boys were wide-eyed, and they could tell the McNeills knew something they did not.

Mr. Palmer looked at Mr. McNeill with a puzzled expression. "Yes," he told him solemnly, "at one time it was painted blue and white." Mrs. McNeill took a sharp breath and placed her hand over her mouth. Mrs. Palmer stared at her not knowing what to think. Mr. Palmer then suggested, "George, would you like to see the dory?"

Mr. McNeill did not reply. He stood up, glanced at his wife, and then reached for his coat hanging on the hook by the door.

About a half hour later, Bobby and Joshua led the two couples to the edge of the spruce thicket back of Porcupine Point. The boys entered in first followed by Mr. McNeill and their father. On account of their long dresses, the two ladies remained on the narrow grassy area. Bobby and Joshua pushed their way through the spruce trees and quietly waited beside the dory for the two men. Mr. McNeill made his way over to them, and Mr. Palmer stayed nearby. At first, no one said anything as they stood there solemnly gazing at this mysterious, abandoned boat.

Nearly a minute later, Mr. McNeill took several steps closer towards the dory. He rested his hand on the rotting hull and then he crouched down. Without facing the others, he said simply, "This is my dory. I built her many years ago—thought I'd never see her again." The boys looked at each other in amazement but said nothing. Mr. McNeill slowly moved around to the side of the dory which was leaning against the large spruce tree. He knelt down on the pale brown, spruce needles and gazed into its dark interior. "My oars," he stated thoughtfully.

Bobby spoke up. "Would you like me and Joshua to get them out for you, Mr. McNeill?" he volunteered.

"No!" the man quickly charged him. "Leave them be—don't touch them." Bobby frowned in bewilderment and looked to his father. And then they watched as the older man examined the ground under the old dory. "There's his coat," they heard him say. "I remember him having that coat."

Several minutes later, the men and the boys joined the two women waiting at the narrow part of the grassy area. Mrs. McNeill studied her husband's face. "It's my dory," he reported to her with a slight grin.

Mrs. McNeill gasped. "We've found it after all these years!" She smiled at her husband, and then Mrs. Palmer who still had a puzzled expression on her face.

On their way back up to the lighthouse, the McNeills explained to the Palmer family the story behind the old dory now resting in the spruce thicket. "Back when Martin was in his late teens," Mr. McNeill began, "he was spending time with Jedidiah Harriston, and I didn't like him filling my son's mind with any of his senseless and useless religion. You see, I wasn't saved back then, and I didn't know the Lord." Mrs. McNeill smiled and nodded.

"Me and Dot would give Martin a hard time. Well, it was mostly me coming down hard on him," Mr. McNeill admitted. "I didn't trust Mr. Harriston—he quoted the Bible a lot. Why anyone would take the trouble to memorize any of it was far beyond me. And he was always happy and at peace, no matter what happened. I couldn't stand it—and I couldn't stand him." He paused as he looked over at Mr. Palmer.

"I realized later that I couldn't stand him because he had something I didn't have—something I needed, but at that time, I didn't know I needed anything," Mr. McNeill revealed to the boys as the group moved along the beach. "One day Martin told me he had gotten saved. Well, I lit into him something fierce right there and then. I hit him so hard he fell over backwards onto the firewood we had been stacking by the side of the house." Joshua gasped as he and Bobby stared at Mr. McNeill with widen eyes, and their mouths dropped open.

"Mr. McNeill had a terrible temper back then," Mrs. McNeill explained, "but the Lord helped him with that after he confessed it as sin."

Mr. McNeill went on with his story. "Martin picked himself up out of the sticks of firewood and walked away. I hollered at him to come back, but he ignored me and kept going." Mr. McNeill stopped talking, he sighed deeply and then bowed his head. They were now in the area of the boathouse.

"Martin didn't come back that night," Mrs. McNeill explained to the others, "nor the next day. Nor the day after that." The two couples and the boys started up the roadway.

Mr. McNeill continued. "My dory was missing—so I figured Martin took it. A week went by, and my son never came back. We were really concerned now and I could have killed that Mr. Harriston. And then about a week and a half after Martin went missing, he showed up. Me and Dot were eating our noon meal. He just walked in, or staggered in, was more like it. He didn't say nothing. He collapsed onto a kitchen chair, and I thought he was going to fall to the floor." Bobby and Joshua listened attentively as they climbed the steep hill.

Mrs. McNeill spoke up. "Martin was in pretty poor shape. He was sick and in no condition to talk to us. He slept most of the remainder of that day and then all night. It wasn't until the next morning that he could tell us what happened." Her voice began to break, and she looked over at her husband. "All Martin could remember was that he took his father's dory and started to row away over to here, to Bunchberry Island. On the way across it started to rain, and then the wind picked up. It was the month of May—not warm weather by any means. He remembered he was soaking wet and shivering badly as he was rowing, and that it was getting dark. But the Lord's hand was upon him." The little group steadily moved up the roadway to the top of the island.

Mr. McNeill said, "The next thing my son remembered is waking up in the lighthouse, and the keeper's wife eyeing him. Mr. Griffin told us later he found Martin in his boathouse. He said he was wet and shaking and couldn't talk any sense. Mr. Griffin could see that the young man wasn't at all well, and he managed to get him up to the lighthouse where he got him dry and warm. He said that because of the dampness and thick fog, the signal fires would not have worked. Martin slept off and on the next several days while Mrs. Griffin nursed him back to a resemblance of health. And then when he was well enough to travel, Mr. Griffin brought him back to Rogers Cove, and that's when he came home to us." The four Palmers were listening with rapped attention. "He probably stayed the night under the overturned dory, but because of the wet and the cold he nearly died. We know the Lord had His hand on him."

Mrs. McNeill smiled as she looked at the boys. "It was soon after that that both Mr. McNeill and I found the Lord. It wasn't Martin's experience that made us want to be saved, but it did convince us that God was real and in control. And we had to admit - we were sinners." Mr. Palmer slid the fence rails back, and the little group passed into the field where the sheep were grazing. Mr. McNeill grinned and added, "The Lord has been real to us ever since as we've grown to know Him more and more. And our son Martin has been labouring for the Lord in Kenya—eighteen years now."

Mrs. Palmer slipped her arm under Mrs. McNeill's. "Thank you, Dot, for telling us about your son Martin, and about you and George."

***

When the McNeills arrived back at the lighthouse and had had an afternoon lunch, they took advantage of the incoming tide and left for their home in Rogers Cove. Bobby and Joshua were pleased to be asked to accompany them to their boat. After the McNeills were on their way across the water, Bobby hurried back to the lighthouse to help his father and Mr. Thompson with several jobs, but Joshua remained alone in the area of the boathouse.

Just before supper, Bobby wondered where Joshua was. "I don't know where he's at," his mother said to him. "I thought he was with you menfolk. Go fetch him will you, Bobby. He probably doesn't realize how late it is. Supper's in half an hour."

"Last I seen Josh," his brother admitted, "was down at the boathouse when we saw the McNeills off. I know he's not around these here parts."

***

Bobby began a slow steady run along the path across the clearing. He vaulted over the rail fence at the far side of the sheep pasture and continued his brisk pace through the woods and down towards the beach. When the boathouse and shoreline came into his view, he halted and called out, "Josh! Supper time." No response. *Probably on the beach somewhere wondering why he's so hungry,* he figured and he moved down the path and stopped next to the boathouse. He faced towards Porcupine Point and cupped his hands to his mouth. "Josh! Time to eat." The younger boy soon appeared on the narrow grassy area in front of the spruce thicket. Bobby waved, and the younger boy returned the wave as he started back along the beach.

When Joshua came up to Bobby, he told him, "I'm some famished!"

"Well, you ought to be, My Son," his brother scolded him. "It's nearly supper time. We better get a move-along." The two boys headed up the roadway through the woods. "What were you doing in that spruce thicket, Josh? Haven't you seen enough of that old dory?"

Joshua removed a couple of lumps of spruce gum from his pocket and handed one to Bobby. "I was talking to God," he said. "I told Him I knew I was a sinner and that I wanted to be saved from punishment because of my sin—like the Bible says. I thanked Him for giving His Son the Lord Jesus to be my Saviour. And I told the Lord I am now trusting in Him." Joshua grinned at Bobby.

Bobby dropped the lump into his pocket, and he smiled as he placed his hand on his brother's shoulder. "I'm glad," he said to Joshua. He then pushed him into the ferns along the side of the roadway. "Race you to the lighthouse, Joshie," he challenged as he rushed ahead up the path.

chapter four

eight years later—late summer 1935

The Letter

Joshua sat on the edge of his bed in the front, upstairs room he shared with his brother. He ran his fingers across his bristly chin and crossed his sock-feet on the braided rug between the two beds. On the dresser was the letter he had received the day before yesterday. He reached for the envelope, drew out the single sheet of paper, and laid it down beside him on the patchwork quilt covering his bed.

Eighteen-year-old Joshua did not need to read the letter again. He had read it six or seven times since his mother had picked it up from the post office at the back of the village general store. Instead, he stood up and crossed over to the chair next to the open door, sat down, and leaned back with his hands behind his head. I don't know what I should do, the young man pondered. Pa passed away nearly a year ago, and now this offer has come from David.

About half a minute later he heard his mother downstairs exclaim, "Oh, no! It can't be!" Joshua leaned forward and turned his ear towards the door.

"You can see the smoke from the brow of Wharf Road," his brother related excitedly, somewhat out of breath.

"Oh, no!" Joshua heard again. He rose to his feet and leaned through the open door.

"Where's Josh?" he heard his brother ask.

"Upstairs."

"Josh!" Bobby called up to him from the bottom of the stairs as Joshua came along the second floor hallway. "The lighthouse is on fire!" Joshua came down the stairs in his sock-feet two steps at a time. His brother was now waiting for him at the porch door.

Their mother stood at the counter by the window preparing chicken to fry with potatoes for their evening meal. "Oh, no!" she exclaimed once more. Joshua pulled on his work-boots by the woodstove. Bobby remained with one hand on the knob of the door and with the other he stroked his bearded chin.

The two young men hurried along the dirt road towards the wharf at the lower end of the village of Rogers Cove. Several other people were moving quickly in the same direction. "You know, Pa always said, that there chimney needed to be replaced," Joshua reminded his brother.

Bobby nodded and added, "He reported it several times."

Four minutes later when they arrived at the brow of the hill, they had an unobstructed view of Bunchberry Island, nine miles away. At first, neither young man spoke as they looked across the water. Thick black smoke billowed upwards, forming a tall column which drifted slightly to the left. Soaring flames could be seen dancing wildly at the base of the dark smoke. "Must be those drums of fuel," Bobby figured. "They were stored in the tall grass on the far side of the tower."

Joshua and Bobby were joined by other onlookers, some concerned, others only curious. "Look!" Joshua pointed out. "There's a boat headed over—and there's another one."

"There's nothing nobody can do," Bobby put in. "I feel so useless."

"All they can do," Joshua replied, "is bring back the Thompsons and the little bit they might have managed to save." He shifted his weight from one foot to the other and shoved his hands deep into his pockets. Bobby waved to their older friends, the McNeills, who were standing in the doorway of their house a stone's throw from the wharf.

Joshua said, "Never seen so many people at one time since Pa's funeral."

Bobby nodded in agreement. "Let's go, Josh." He turned in the direction of their house. "Ma's probably waiting. We better get a move-along."

Supper was ready by the time the Palmer brothers had returned home. Sometimes their mother prepared enough for four people rather than the three of them as it was now.

"There's more chicken there, Boys, if you'd like," Mrs. Palmer said when they were nearly through their meal.

"Pa improved that place quite a bit," Joshua commented. "I'll have another piece, Ma." He half stood as he leaned over the table to reach the platter.

"Yeah, he did," replied Bobby. "He even built one of them there barns."

"Remember that rope swing we rigged up in the hayloft, Bobby?"

"Yeah, that was some fun."

Mrs. Palmer got up to fix the tea. "I was glad for the work your pa did on the cupboards in the kitchen," she said with appreciation.

"And he built closets in the bedrooms, too," added Bobby. "What's for dessert, Ma?"

"I made apple pie this morning."

About six hours later in the dark and quiet house, Joshua awoke, rolled over and fluffed up his feather pillow. He could hear his brother quietly breathing, and somewhere in the distance, a dog barked several times. *I'll miss Bobby when he leaves next month,* he knew. *I'm not ready to get hitched yet. But he's five years older than me, and he's working full-time. He knows what he's doing—he's got it all together. Says he feels the Lord is directing him to the Blake Eberness place. Mr. Eberness is asking eight and a half hundred for his property which is more than Bobby has right now. Bobby offered him five hundred, but he said he wouldn't take less than eight. Bobby's just waiting on the Lord to see what happens.*

I'm pleased he asked me to stand up with him. What will I get him for a wedding gift? I mean them—I must not forget Eva!

The mantel clock downstairs gave one strike. The timepiece at one time belonged to Jedidiah Harriston, his father's hired man on the island. *It's either one o'clock,* Joshua figured, *or it's half past something.*

A fire sure can be so destructive! It can come suddenly and cause a lot of permanent damage. We seldom think that things won't remain the same. That lighthouse on Bunchberry Island is now gone forever. I was born there eighteen years ago this past spring. Several days before I was born, (Joshua had heard this story many times), *Pa came here to the mainland for supplies, and while he was here, the hired man died right there in Ma's kitchen. Pa couldn't get home because of the weather, but finally showed up the day after I was born.*

I grew up on the island. It was my home until we moved here to the mainland when I was ten. Me and Bobby had some great times there on the island. We played in the fields and the woods and down on the beach, too. I remember I played with the truck Mr. McNeill made for Bobby. It was painted red. One day Bobby said I could have it for keeps. I was some pleased! I think I had it with me all the time—the first few days, anyway. Joshua grinned and sighed.

One day in winter, me and Bobby coaxed one of the pigs out of the barn. We got her to come onto the ice where we was sliding next to the shed. She promptly slipped on the ice. Did a double split! After several minutes we could see she couldn't get up on her own—no way! It took the two of us quite a while to push her along the ice on her belly, squealing all the time until she could get a foothold on the tufts of grass at the edge of the ice. Joshua nearly chuckled aloud. *We were some glad we were on the other side of the barn and out of sight from the kitchen window.*

Once we played church in the loft of the barn—just the two of us. We sang a hymn. I didn't know the words, so just followed along with Bobby. Now that I think of it—he probably made up most of the words. Then I took up the collection. We had a tin can and I passed it between the two of us. We each dropped in a stone or two, making sure they made a clatter. And then Bobby preached. I sat there spellbound - my brother could preach! I thought he done as good as any preacher I'd heard in my young life up until then.

I liked it when Bobby called me, "Joshie". It made me feel I was important to him. But I hated it when anyone else called me "Joshie"—that was Bobby's name for me.

I hardly knew David. When I was born, he was the same age as I am now. He was boarding with the McNeills and going to school and working at the lumber mill here in the village. When he did come home, I shied away from him. "David's your big brother," they'd say, but I knew Bobby was my big brother, not this guy with the whiskers.

Things change. I used to live on an island, and now I'm living in a village on the mainland. Dave has moved out west and has set down roots out there. Pa has died—his life here on earth is over. I'm about a quarter way through my life—if I don't die prematurely, or the Lord doesn't return before then. What did Pa say? "Only one life, 'twill soon be past; only what's done for Christ will last."

The hired man's clock again sounded once. *It's either one o'clock or half past one,* Joshua knew. *Half an hour from now it'll strike again. If it strikes once, it'll be one-thirty. If it strikes twice, it'll be two o'clock.*

Then Joshua remembered, *I've got to answer David's letter soon, and I don't know how.*

The next time Joshua awoke, he could see the pale gray sky through the narrow slit between the curtains. The smell of fried mackerel drifted up and into the bedroom, and he could hear Bobby with their mother downstairs in the kitchen. Joshua thought of his day ahead. *I plan to work in the garden—need to bring in the squash and fix the chicken coop roof. And I want to make inquires at the lumber mill. Bobby says they might need help there come this winter.*

Joshua dressed and went downstairs. As he entered the kitchen, Bobby left for his job at the lumber mill. "See ya later, Ma, Josh," he called out.

Joshua sat down to breakfast of fried fish and potatoes left over from supper. "Ma?" he asked when he reached for the butter which he had churned the day before. "What do you think I should do? I'm at a loss."

Mrs. Palmer hesitated and then replied thoughtfully, "You mean regarding the letter from David?"

"Yeah."

She did not reply immediately, but she crossed the kitchen to check the water on the stove. "You have to decide, Son," she finally answered as she returned the cover to the large pot. "Your pa would want you to do what you think is best for you."

"Yeah, but Ma—you need me here."

"I'll manage. Besides Bobby and Eva will be handy to me. Will you be wanting more of anything to eat?"

"No thanks - this is fine. There's a lot more work out west, and there's not much doing around this neck of the woods."

"David's done good out west. You will too. He'll keep an eye on you 'til you get settled in."

"Yeah, I'm sure he will." Joshua stood up and carried his plate over to the stove. After he opened the damper, he lifted the lid and dumped the fish bones into the smoldering fire.

"Son, you need to let the Lord guide you."

Joshua was taken back somewhat, and he thought, *Let the Lord guide me! Here, I'm a Bible-believing Christian, I belong to the Lord, I should have thought of that.*

He heard his mother say, "I found a good Bible verse for you." She brought a small piece of paper from her apron pocket and handed it to him. He took it and quickly read it over before he folded it and pushed it into his back pocket. "I'll keep praying for you, Joshua. This is a big step for you."

Before Joshua left for the outdoors, he went back to his bedroom for his private time with the Lord. He reminded himself that the Holy Spirit is the Author of God's Word and He speaks to us when we read His Word, but we hear Him only when we are willing to listen to Him.

Joshua gathered up the squash and pumpkins, and put them on shelves in the porch. In the fall when it was cool out there, he would bring them in and store them under a couple of the beds in the house. Next he picked up a few cedar shingles from the woodshed to repair the chicken coop roof.

That evening after supper, Bobby and Joshua went along the road towards the Rogers Cove wharf. When they came to the brow of the hill, they looked out over the water to Bunchberry Island where they could see smoke hovering in the motionless air, and they detected a whiff of smoke ascending from the foundation of the lighthouse.

The young men climbed down to the stony beach where about two dozen seagulls were congregating, and when they came near, the birds scattered. Bobby and Joshua followed the line of seaweed the last in-coming tide had deposited along the high waterline. Joshua kicked an empty sea urchin shell and exclaimed, "I wish I knew how a fellow's to know the Lord's will."

Bobby leaned over and picked up a stone and tossed it into the rolling waves a dozen yards away. "Well, the first thing he ought to do is pray about it and then he should wait for the Lord to show him." He again grabbed up another pebble and continued, "The Holy Spirit won't speak to us when we don't have ears to hear, and He won't lead us when we're not willing to follow Him." He chucked the stone towards the water and with his eyes, he followed it as it dropped into a crashing wave which then broke on the rocks of the beach.

"I have prayed about it," Joshua insisted with a scowl, and he picked up a stone and flung it out over the water, "and I am willing to follow."

"Sometimes the hardest part is to wait on the Lord," Bobby told him. "We want Him to act now, and we don't understand what's taking Him so long." Joshua stomped on a hollow crab shell in his path.

The brothers walked on towards the cliffs without speaking and farther along the shore, the gray, massive form of Indian Head slowly grew larger as they approached it. Several times Bobby stooped to pick up stones which he threw into the advancing breakers. Joshua stepped on the empty, pale green shells of sea urchins and any orange crab shells he could see along the way. Another group of gulls split up as the young men drew near.

"Let's pray about it now, Joshie."

The two fellows made their way over to a log on the bank above the high waterline and sat down on its silvery-gray surface. Bobby prayed, "Our Heavenly Father, we pray Joshua would be guided by You so he would do Your will, Your way and in Your perfect timing. Give him peace in this matter, we ask."

For several minutes, Joshua and Bobby remained on the log at the edge of the cove. Joshua parted his lips slightly, and he gently whistled a nonsense tune. Bobby dug his heels into the coarse sand, making two parallel trenches. The stony beach several yards away, sloped down to the ever-tumbling waves at the water's edge. The brothers scanned the cove and Fearful Rocks and beyond to Bunchberry Island, their childhood home and once-familiar terrain. *Some pretty!* Joshua reflected as they gazed out over the water. *Hey, I could paint a picture of this—for a wedding gift!*

The evening sun abruptly broke through the clouds, and the glare off the water momentarily caused the fellows to squint and divert their eyes in another direction.

Bobby stood up and looked back towards the wharf. "Well, let's get a move-along, Boy."

"Tide's coming in," Joshua replied, and they retraced their steps along the beach, climbed onto the wharf and started up the road for home.

"Bobby! Joshua!" a voice called out to them. "Lovely evening, I'd say." It came from Mr. McNeill who sat on a wooden, kitchen chair on the front veranda of his house.

"Hello, Mr. McNeill," Joshua answered, and Bobby nodded. As Bobby crossed the road, Joshua followed, and they stepped up onto the veranda.

The old gentleman glanced over at Bobby. "Thought you'd be up country a bit, on a nice evening like this," he commented.

Bobby grinned and replied, "I can't be wearing out my welcome by showing up every evening."

The old gentleman nodded in agreement. "Right sorry to know the lighthouse is gone." The young men turned to follow his gaze across the water to the island. "Don't know when it'll be rebuilt or even if it will be."

The men saw the blue paneled door of the house open. "George, I thought I heard you talking with someone out here." Mrs. McNeill stepped out onto the veranda. "Why, it's the Palmer boys!"

"Good evening, Mrs. McNeill," Bobby replied as he and Joshua stood up.

"Good evening to you, Gentlemen," she answered as she glanced from one to the other. "And while you're on your feet, won't you come right in and have some pie? I made three cherry pies this afternoon, and me and George can't make more than a dent in them." Without waiting for a reply, she turned towards the door. "We can't have the cherries going to waste, you know," she continued. "I made some of them into pies and some into preserves for winter." Before they could respond she returned to her kitchen. Mr. McNeill stood up, and Bobby and Joshua followed him into their house.

The three men sat at the kitchen table while Mrs. McNeill went to the cellar door between the kitchen and the sitting room. She returned smiling and carrying a golden crusted pie which she carefully lowered to the table. The hostess beamed as she placed a generous slice of cherry pie before each of them.

The older man gave thanks, and they began to eat. "Pie's some delicious, Mrs. McNeill," Bobby told her after several bites.

"The last summer we were on the island," Joshua said, "the Barns girl stayed with us for a while. What was her name?"

"Katie," Bobby answered with a mouthful of pie.

"Yeah, that's right. Katie Barns. Well, she made a plate of sandwiches and proudly carried it outside so we could have a picnic out there handy on the grass—you know, on the east side of the lighthouse there under that pear tree. She had been talking about a picnic for days but because of the weather, we couldn't. Well, finally the weather was just perfect. The sun was shining, but there was some wind—there's always some wind up there on top of the island."

He took a bite of pie while the others waited for him to continue his story. "Katie spread a quilt out on the grass and put the plate of sandwiches down in the middle of it. I was in a good mood, so I took off my shoes and then my socks. It was a beautiful day in summer, and I got a mite carried away. I threw my socks up into the air and the wind caught them. I realized too late my mistake!" Joshua paused for effect and looked over at Bobby and then Mr. McNeill. "They came down and landed, wouldn't you know, right smack draped over the sandwiches Katie had made. She was some horrified! Owly! She came after me something fierce, let me tell you, thundering at me for all she was worth. I took off running down that rough path in my bare feet. I could hear Bobby laughing as I tried to make my escape." He chuckled as he glanced over at Bobby who had nearly finished his piece of pie. The older man grinned at Bobby and then Joshua. Mrs. McNeill set a cup of tea before each of the men and one at the end of the table for herself.

Mr. McNeill lifted his fork loaded with pie. "Joshua, can you still repeat Psalm One?" he asked him.

"Yeah, I sure can, Sir! I remember we were visiting here at your place, and you said you'd give me a dime if I memorized Psalm One." He placed his fork on the empty plate and picked up a pie crumb from the table.

Mrs. McNeill wiped her hands on her apron and asked, "Would you like another piece, Joshua?"

"No thanks, this is just fine." He raised his cup of tea and rested both elbows on the table.

The older man continued, "Back then you didn't know what a dime was—never seen one before in your young life."

"Yeah, that's right, but I memorized it, and when you crossed over to our place two weeks later, I said it for you."

"Yes." Mr. McNeill grinned. "And I was so pleased, and so were you."

"I've memorized other passages of Scripture since then. I think it's more useful to memorize passages than to memorize only individual verses."

"Yes, that's right. And in that way we're more likely to get a more complete handle on the mind of God."

Mrs. McNeill spoke up. "I was thinking the other day. Before we can know what the Word of God means, we need to know what it rightly says. It's very important we first get rid of any wrong ideas we might have by taking note of what it does not say. Only then will we see clearly to know what it really means."

"Yeah, that makes sense," Bobby agreed as he leaned back in his chair with his hands behind his head.

A little later, Mrs. McNeill said, "Joshua, remember the time you locked Elsie in the outhouse?"

"I didn't know she was in there. Honest!" he quickly protested. "We was in the house, and suddenly she gets up and says she needs some fresh air. A few minutes later I leave for chores in the barn. I find the outhouse door unlocked, so I locks it. How was I, as a seven or eight-year-old shaver to know that when a girl says she needs some fresh air, what she really means is she needs to make a visit to the outhouse!" Mr. and Mrs. McNeill grinned broadly, and Bobby tipped back his head and laughed.

When there was a lull in the conversation, Mrs. McNeill told Joshua, "One time when the Snows and us were visiting with your folks, you Joshua, took a real fancy to their young daughter Alice. You told us you were going to marry her when you grew up."

"Alice?" Joshua replied, somewhat surprised. "Alice Snow, who lives a couple miles over from here? I said that? In front of everyone!" He grinned and made out he was embarrassed.

"Yeah, that's the one," answered Mrs. McNeill, and she lifted the kettle of boiling water from the woodstove. "Alice is a lovely girl—and she knows the Lord," she stated as the young man looked over at her.

Several minutes later Mr. McNeill said, "Joshua, we know what Bobby's plans be, but what about you, My Son?"

Joshua stared at the pitcher of knives, forks, and spoons in the centre of the table and then dropped his eyes. "David wants me to come out west to him, where he's at," he responded as he fingered the edge of the worn oil cloth. "There's work out west, but there's nothing in these parts round here. I've been praying about it but don't feel much settled about nothing yet."

Mrs. McNeill spoke up. "Going out west might be attractive to us, but it's so important to do what the Lord wants us to do. The past few days I've felt I should be praying for you, Joshua, and now I know why, and I'm right glad you dropped in this evening and told us what's going on in your life."

Mrs. McNeill returned to her tea as her husband nodded in agreement. The older man said, "There's a verse in Isaiah somewhere that tells us the Lord is gracious and merciful as well as being a God of judgment, and we're to exalt Him. It says He's waiting for us to wait for Him, and we'll be blessed as a result of waiting for Him."

Mr. McNeill paused as he studied the young man's troubled face. "Joshua, I'm glad you understand we don't ask the Lord to bless the plans we've made for ourselves. We ought to ask Him what His plans be for us." Joshua gave a quick nod of acknowledgment.

"Let's pray about it right now," Mr. McNeill said as he placed his empty teacup on the table. He stood up and knelt at his chair. Mrs. McNeill and the two brothers did likewise.

"Our Heavenly Father," the older man began, "we thank Thee that in the Name of the Lord Jesus Christ we come boldly and unafraid into Thy presence. We come before the throne of grace because the righteousness of Your Son has been given to us, and now You see us as righteous even as He is righteous." Joshua listened as Mr. McNeill prayed with confidence and conviction, and he leaned forward and pressed the top of his head against the back spindles of the chair.

"Heavenly Father, we pray You would show Joshua what he should do and give him peace in this matter. Make it clear to him whether he should stay here in these parts or go out west to his brother. And we pray that David would see his need of the Saviour, Jesus Christ the Lord. May Joshua's life be such that David will recognize in him Thy greatness and goodness. We pray these things in the Name of the Lord Jesus Christ our Saviour."

The others in that modest kitchen gathered together in His Name added their, "Amens," and they remained in their kneeling positions for several seconds.

"Thank you, Mr. McNeill," Joshua told him as the little group stood up. "It's good to have friends who care and will pray for us."

"Yes," he replied, "we need to pray often for one another. And it's nice to pray with each other, too." He reached over and touched Joshua's shoulder. "And remember, fellows," he added, "prayer is not telling God what to do. We don't insist on anything as though our demanding of Him is proof of our faith in Him. We are the Lord's servants to do His bidding. Prayer is acknowledging our dependency on Him, and it is seeking His will for us."

Mrs. McNeill gathered up the plates and cups, and she put the remainder of the cherry pie onto a dinner plate.

"I think we best get a move-along, Josh," Bobby suggested. "It's getting late." The young men moved towards the door, and Mrs. McNeill crossed the kitchen to the cellar door. She returned with a full pie.

Mr. McNeill leaned back against the counter and said, "I heard just before supper that Blake Eberness passed away this morning. Bobby, you heard tell of him, haven't you?" Bobby turned around and looked at the older man and then at Joshua who was leaning with one out-stretched arm against the door-jamb. Mr. McNeill added, "It was unexpected and without warning."

The four of them stood there, and then Mrs. McNeill held out the pie to Joshua. "Would you boys like to take this pie home with you?"

"Sure would!" Joshua grinned. He reached for the pie and carefully held it with both hands.

"Thanks, Mrs. McNeill," Bobby replied for both of them. "We'll take good care of it."

A couple days later, in the early afternoon, Joshua gathered up his painting supplies and then hiked along the narrow road which passed through the woods along the brow of the hill overlooking the wharf. He leaned his stretched canvas against a pile of freshly-cut logs and studied the scene before him. On the white surface, he quickly drew a loose composition using a narrow, bristle brush. He sketched in Bunchberry Island and then beyond that, the far-distant mainland, miles away to the west. He would paint bright, billowy clouds to break up the deep blue sky. To give a sense of depth to his painting, he planned to include foreground rocks and shrubbery in the lower third. The middle distance would include the McNeill house and woodshed, the fishing dories hauled up on shore, and the Rogers Cove wharf.

As Joshua worked, there came from between his lips, a low, soft whistle like the sound of the wind through a knot hole. To hold the composition together, he included the trunks of the tall pine trees in the foreground on the left hand third of the canvas. On the right-hand third, Joshua drew in the cliffs along the shore including Indian Head and then the hills rising up farther to the right. Several old, moss covered tree trunks lying on the forest floor would guide the eyes of the viewer towards the main subject, Bunchberry Island. Joshua knew Bobby would value this painting because the island meant so much to him.

Suddenly Joshua heard, "What are you doing, Joshua Palmer?" It was the neighbour boy who lived several houses over from his place.

"I'm setting up to paint a picture. What are you doing, Lawrence?"

The nine-year-old fellow came closer to have a look. "Hey, that's Bunchberry Island and the McNeill's place!" he piped up as he ran his fingers along the red suspenders holding up his baggy pants. "You're a good artist."

"I like to paint," Joshua told him.

The boy pushed back his straw hat and asked, "Are you going to show the lighthouse even when it's not there no more?" Joshua gave him a quick nod.

Lawrence studied the painting for nearly a minute and then said, "I have a question for you, Joshua. What are blue but are pink when they're green?"

Joshua abruptly stopped, looked at him in surprise and repeated, "They're blue but they're pink when they're green! How can that be, Boy?" He frowned and then grinned at the youngster. "I don't know what are blue but are pink when they're green. You'll have to tell me."

Lawrence giggled and replied, "Blueberries are pink when they're green!"

"Blueberries!" Joshua exclaimed with a chuckle. "Why of course. Blueberries are pink when they're green." He resumed his work, and Lawrence stood there quietly watching him.

Next Joshua covered the whole canvas using a wide brush and a wash of the basic colours of the objects to be painted, making sure the white canvas was completely covered.

Lawrence resumed his boyish chit-chat. "Bunchberry Island is farther away than it looks, isn't it? I wouldn't want to row over there by myself! Nine miles is some far to row anyway, especially against the tide. It would take me all day and probably all night. Pa says the tide's some strong and I shouldn't take the dory out farther than I could talk to someone on shore, but Ma says I can holler pretty loud by times. Pa says I'm not to go near Fearful Rocks. Did you know Elijah Bean nearly bashed up his dory there the other day? Albert says he was probably sloshed."

"Yeah, he probably was," Joshua agreed.

Lawrence chattered on. "The McNeills have a good view from their place, don't they? I'd like to live there. I could look away out across the water to Bunchberry Island except when it's foggy, but it's not foggy all that often—mainly the mornings this time of year." He stopped to scratch his arm. "Albert says you used to live over there—I mean on Bunchberry Island. I bet that was fun! You could do so many exciting things over there."

Lawrence turned to leave. "I better get a move-along. I'm supposed to stack some firewood before supper."

"Okay, see you later." Joshua glanced over at the boy as he scurried along the woods road. He then called out to him, "Lawrence! Don't eat the pink blueberries because they're still green." The boy stopped, turned, and waved.

Joshua began to apply heavier layers of paint on his canvas without concentrating on any particular area. And then he went over the painting again, putting in details using a narrow brush. In order to avoid giving a stiff appearance to the painting, he was not overly careful nor fussy but he laid fresh paint onto the wet paint already applied to his canvas. Joshua enjoyed painting in this thick, 'juicy style', as he referred to it.

Several hours after he began, Joshua decided there was nothing more that needed to be done to his painting. The brushes he washed out in turpentine and then he packed up his things to leave. He carefully took the painting by its wooden stretcher and headed for home where he hid the painting in the woodshed. He positioned it vertically preventing mice from traipsing across the wet paint.

Just before supper, Bobby returned home from the lumber mill. "Ma! Joshua!" he called out as he entered the kitchen. Several small wood-shavings were still caught in his hair. "Mrs. Eberness came looking for me at the mill this afternoon. She wants to sell the property to me for five hundred dollars."

Mrs. Palmer paused at the side of the kitchen table with three dinner plates in her hands. Joshua lowered the load of firewood into the box behind the stove before he turned to face his brother. Mrs. Palmer and Joshua stared at Bobby, neither one saying anything.

"And that includes the furniture," Bobby added, grinning at both of them. "She says she's going out west to live with her son where he's at."

Mrs. Palmer set the dinner plates on the table, and Joshua leaned over the firewood as he brushed off his sleeves. He crossed the kitchen to his brother. "Hey, Bobby, that's great!"

Mrs. Palmer said, "You prayed, and you waited patiently on the Lord. He answered your prayers in a greater way than you could have imagined. I've been praying for you too, Son."

"Yes, the Lord does care about us," Bobby replied. "I'm realizing that real prayer is not only trusting but it's expecting Him to guide us and to provide for us and sometimes in unexpected ways." He dipped water from the covered pot on the stove and poured it into the basin to wash up before supper.

The Palmers sat at the supper table, and Bobby gave thanks for the food. He also thanked the Lord for causing His will to be done for him regarding the property, and he prayed again for Joshua and for their mother. "Amen," both Mrs. Palmer and Joshua said when Bobby had finished praying.

After supper, Joshua climbed the stairs and went along the hall to the room he shared with his brother. He closed the door behind him and picked up his Bible from the dresser. After he sat on his bed, he opened his Bible and laid it across his knees.

Since it was the third of the month, Joshua read Proverbs chapter three. When he had read the first twelve verses, he noticed there were six commands here, each followed by a promise. He came to the promise in verse six which says, 'and He shall direct thy paths,' and he recognized this was from the Lord for him at this time. He backed up to the commands which accompanied this promise in verses five and six. *The first command,* Joshua noticed, *says to me, 'Trust in the Lord with all thine heart.' I'm to trust in the Lord and rely on Him fully. The second command tells me to 'lean not unto thine own understanding.' I'm not to do anything the way I think is best or what I want, for His ways are best and for my good and for His glory. And the third command says, 'In all thy ways acknowledge Him.' I'm to give Him the credit for all things in my life—the little things as well as the big things. And here's the promise: 'and He shall direct thy paths.' That's what I need. He directs, not forces.*

Joshua leaned over and pulled from his back pocket the piece of paper his mother had given him with the Bible verse she had printed out on it. He slowly read it again, *'Be careful for nothing but in everything by prayer and supplication with thanksgiving let your requests be made known unto God. And the peace of God which passeth all understanding shall keep your hearts and minds through Christ Jesus.' Philippians 4:6 and 7.* He took a deep breath and considered: *I'm not to be anxious, but I'm to pray about things which concern me, and I can be thankful for this privilege of prayer. And it says in His Word that I can have peace beyond understanding.*

Joshua now knew for sure what he should do regarding the letter from his brother David. *I will not be impatient, but I will pray and wait for the Lord and have complete confidence in Him and expect His will to be done. Neither will I do what I think is best without first praying about it. I now recognize Him in all areas of my life—in small things as well as big. And with thanks I look forward to the Lord leading me in every way.* He stood up, reached over to the dresser, picked up the envelope, and drew out the single sheet of paper. After unfolding it, he laid it down on the bed next to his open Bible.

Joshua stood with his knees resting against his bed. He clasped his hands behind his back and bowed his head. "I have spread it out before the Lord," he said quietly, and then he dropped to his knees on the braided rug. "My Heavenly Father," he prayed aloud, looking over at his Bible opened to the Proverbs, "Thy Word says, 'Trust in the Lord with all thine heart… In all thy ways acknowledge Him.'" (Prov. 3:5-6). Joshua closed his eyes, bowed his head into his hands with his elbows on the bed, and continued aloud, "And then comes Thy promise for me, Lord, 'and He shall direct thy paths.' I am patiently waiting and trusting Thee to direct my path. Thank You, Heavenly Father. So let it be."

Joshua did not know how long he had remained in this kneeling position with his head in his hands. *This great peace I have must have caused me to fall asleep,* he reasoned as he ran his fingers across his bristly chin. He stood up and moved over to the chair next to the door, and then he sat down and leaned back with his hands behind his head. *You know, I think I'd rather be poor and have only the basic necessities but have peace than to be rich and have whatever I wanted to buy but not have peace. And I'd rather be sickly and be in poor health but have peace than to be well and have lots of energy but be without peace. And I can also say I'd rather be unknown and have few friends but have peace than to be known for my successes and have influence on others but not have peace. I value peace or contentment above everything else - above wealth, above health, and above position.*

He crossed his socked feet on the braided rug and glanced out the window. *The Lord is in control of my life and the things which happen to me. His will for me is for my good. This gives me peace. And when I have to make a decision in my life, I can ask the Lord to give me wisdom to make that decision, and if I still don't know what is best, I know He will cause me to do the right thing. This gives me peace. Even when I make the wrong choice or do the wrong thing, if I've first committed myself to Him, He will overrule or He will cause good to come out of my mistakes. This also gives me peace.*

Jedidiah Harriston's clock in the living room struck the hour, but Joshua did not count the chimes. Instead he crossed to his bed where he picked up the letter from his brother David, refolded it and returned it to its envelope. As he opened his dresser drawer and dropped the letter into it, he said, "Thank You, Lord for directing my paths and for giving me peace in my life."

chapter five

five years later—1940-1941

Whiskers and Company

"Joshua, they're here," his wife called out to him. She turned from the kitchen window and placed the dishtowel over the line behind the woodstove. Her long, thick braid hung loosely down her back.

Joshua opened the kitchen door to the woodshed and storage entrance as the approaching truck came along the dirt driveway. He crossed to the outside door and passed the mother cat perched on the stack of firewood and batting at a fly in the window. "Catching a little snack, are you, Pussycat?"

Joshua opened the outside door, smoothed back his mustache, and shielded his eyes from the bright morning sun. It promised to be a beautiful autumn day. He stepped to one side to allow Alice to join him on the stone landing, and they watched the truck stop next to the lilac bushes.

"Morning, Joshua, Alice," greeted Joshua's brother Bobby as he and his wife came through the grass towards them. With his foot, Joshua gently pushed the corrugated cardboard box to the edge of the landing.

"Hello," Joshua replied. "Come on in, you two."

"Joshua," Alice said to him with a giggle, "we ought to greet our guests at the kitchen door."

"Oh, that's all right," Eva replied. "We're family." And then she grinned shyly.

"Well, if I'm not mistaken," Alice put in after she gave her sister-in-law a hug, "you two are adding to the family. That's great!"

Bobby and Joshua exchanged glances, and Bobby shrugged his right shoulder. He asked, "Can you use these here eggs?"

Bobby handed Joshua a basket of brown eggs. The two couples entered the woodshed, and Bobby said, "Catching a little snack, are you, Pussycat?"

Alice giggled and told Eva, "That's exactly what Joshua said." He looked back at his brother who shrugged his shoulder again, and then Bobby bent down to untie his boots.

"Oh, Bobby, don't take your boots off," Alice told him. "Joshua never does."

"Don't worry," he assured her. "I changed my socks just this morning."

Joshua put the basket of eggs on the kitchen table and lifted his canvas hunting bag from the rocking chair near the stove.

Alice asked, "How's it going with you people? We're really pleased you're expecting." She grinned again at Eva. "Any other news?"

Eva glanced over at her husband. "We got another letter from Betty," she told them as she turned to face Alice and Joshua.

"Still no sign of David," Bobby added, and he scratched through his new beard. "Been gone over a year now. Maybe he's had an accident somewhere and hasn't been found."

"Yeah, where's he at?" Joshua asked as he had many times before. "Sometimes I think I should go out there myself and have a look around." No one responded, and he moved towards the door with his bag in his hand.

Eva broke the silence. "Me and Bobby's been praying every day for David and his wife."

Alice nodded, and then Joshua looked over at his brother. "I'm ready, Bobby. Let's get a move-along." He glanced at the hired man's clock his mother had given to him and Alice when they married, and then he reached for his red and black checkered hunting jacket and cap on the hook on the door. Bobby got up from the kitchen chair, stretched, and moved towards Joshua.

"You men be careful," Eva told them and she kissed her husband. "Bye," she added.

Alice remarked, "We expect you fellows back here for supper." She squeezed her husband's hand and he leaned over to kiss her.

As the brothers passed through the woodshed they could not help noticing the cat in the window. "You haven't caught your snack yet, Pussycat!" Joshua chided her. He stepped onto the stone landing outside the door and picked up the corrugated cardboard box by the cord encircling it. Before he climbed into Bobby's truck, Joshua carefully put the box in the open back and leaned his bag against it.

"Let's pray before we leave," Bobby suggested after he slammed the door closed.

"Good idea," Joshua agreed, and he removed his cap and planted it over his knee.

Several minutes later they were on the Hannah Road, the dirt road which headed towards Rogers Cove, near their destination. "Tell me about it again, Josh," his brother said.

"Well," he began, "I was bush-whacking it through that neck of the woods back of Rogers Cove. You know, to the north there this side of Bennys Bump. It was spring before leaves were out on the trees, so I could see into the woods real good. I was looking for a picture to paint."

When Bobby saw a vehicle coming towards them on the narrow road, he eased up on the gas pedal, rolled up his window and geared down to a crawl. The approaching vehicle also decreased speed which cut down on the dust billowing up behind the vehicles, and it made it safer to meet on the narrow dirt road. Bobby nodded to the other driver before he stepped on the accelerator again.

Joshua continued, "There's an area there back a ways of thick spruce trees which I had to skirt around. I followed along the brook best I could and just as I came over the brow of a little hill, I suddenly came upon an old cabin there up against the spruce trees on a small flat area. It was the old camp which some folks call the Brown Beans Camp. The brook's handy to the cabin there. I could see an area of ground that looked like someone was working it up for a garden. It was partly dug up, freshly turned over—in fact, a shovel was planted there in the soil. It looked like someone had just left several minutes ago. This was all news to me, so I just stood there. Didn't know nobody lived back here at this camp."

The brothers gave each other a quick glance. "I could see a bit of smoke coming from the chimney. Didn't want to startle anyone who was there so I hung back some—about a hundred feet. I hollered out, 'Hello,' several times, then slowly walked towards the cabin. The cabin door opened about six inches, and I stopped. I said, 'Hello,' once more, and someone behind the door said, 'Go away.' He sounded a bit hoarse, and I could hardly hear him. I stood there and tried to see who was in the cabin. I could make out someone standing just inside the door, so I said, 'I didn't know anyone lived back here.' And he again said, 'Go away.' So I backed up, and then I slowly turned around to leave. It was strange—I didn't know what to think."

Joshua paused as he and Bobby glanced over at the field to their right. "Nice flock of sheep," Bobby commented.

"Yeah, sure is," Joshua agreed. He continued to relate his experience. "I had gone, oh, maybe twenty—thirty feet when I heard, 'No, wait.' I stopped and turned and I could see a man standing in the doorway. I could hardly believe my eyes—yes Sir, I tell you!" The brothers exchanged glances again. "It was one of them hermits. I heard there's a few of them around, but never laid eyes on one before. They like to be left alone."

"I'm sure my mouth must have dropped open." Joshua grinned at his brother. "He had a long stringy beard. Must've been halfway to his waist. And his hair was past his shoulders. We stood there staring at each other for the longest time. Didn't know if I should turn and leave or what I should do. I didn't feel he was harmful, but I thought he was hiding from something. I stood there not knowing what to do or say. The guy took a couple of steps away from his cabin, and I could see he wasn't armed or nothing. He was uncomfortable, maybe as much as I was. He seemed to want me to stay, but he didn't say nothing. He went over to a rock nearby and sat down. I took this as a signal for me to come closer, so I slowly came a little nearer to him. He watched me intently. Seemed to be studying me, and I was getting more uncomfortable. I tried to look friendly. The guy didn't seem to be afraid of me - only looked kind of nervous. And I got the feeling he hadn't seen nobody for a long time."

Bobby drove through the village of Hannah, and a minute later he decreased his speed for another truck, and he raised his hand in acknowledgment when they met on the narrow road.

"I came up to about twenty-five feet of him, and there I stopped," Joshua informed his brother. "He looked harmless enough. He still didn't say nothing, and I couldn't think of nothing to say, but I had a lot of questions I wished I could ask. Finally I said, 'I didn't know anyone stayed back here.' The guy didn't answer. We stared at each other. He made no attempt to speak or to hide from me. In fact, it seemed he wanted me to stay."

Bobby brought the truck to a stop at the intersection and made a right-hand turn onto the Rogers Cove Road.

"I thought I had to say something, so I asked him if he had lived here very long, but he didn't answer me. So I said, 'Is there anything I can get you?' He seemed to be a bit uncomfortable. I asked him if he had any family or friends. Again he looked uneasy and stared at the ground at his feet."

Bobby slowed down for a truck loaded with lobster traps, and Joshua said, "Soon he took to looking at me, almost as though he was pleading with me. I just stood there, and he just sat there, and neither one of us said nothing. Five minutes or so passed and I said that I better be going. It looked like he wanted to say something so I stood there another minute or so and waited, but he didn't say nothing again. So I slowly turned to leave. I walked away several yards and thought I just had to say something, so I stopped and said, 'Would you like me to check on you again?' He lurched back a bit, but then he gave me a little nod. I turned again and left in the direction I came in. But then I stopped where I first seen his cabin, and I turned to face him again. He was still looking my way. I called back to him, 'See you later,' and I walked away."

The two brothers could see Bennys Bump as it came into view up ahead. Its gently curved summit was crowned with green pine and spruce in contrast to the reds and yellows of the mixed, surrounding lower forest. Joshua thought, *That there might make a good painting for me to do sometime.* Bobby geared down and came to a stop on the shoulder of the road near the Elijah Bean property. The dust slowly drifted by as they cranked up the truck windows.

The brothers retrieved their hunting bags, and Joshua lifted out his cardboard box by the twine. "Come on, Whiskers, let's go," he said, and they crossed the ditch and entered the woods.

The colourful, leafy canopy overhead was becoming thinner, and it allowed the sun to penetrate deep into the woods. Underfoot, the dry leaves provided rhythmic swishing as the men walked along. "Some pretty in the woods this time of year," Bobby exclaimed.

Joshua grinned and nodded. "Love this. Hear some folks say they feel closer to God when they're out in nature like this. They call it 'God's country'. But I don't feel any closer to the Lord when I'm here in the woods."

Bobby did not respond immediately. He carefully released a spruce bough preventing it from swinging back against his brother. "Neither do I," he had to admit.

"The first chapter of the first epistle of John talks about being close to God. It says our fellowship is with the Father. And it says that our sins get in the way of that fellowship or closeness that we should have with our Heavenly Father."

Joshua added, "And when we confess our sins, we are cleansed by the Lord, and only then can we feel close to Him."

The brothers stepped over the rotting trunk of a fallen tree, and Bobby reasoned, "Some people may feel closer to God when in nature, and it's probably because they are less distracted by the ordinary things of life. They can think about God because they have less on their minds, but it's the confession of our sins and the cleansing of it that makes us closer to the Lord."

The men hiked on in silence for several minutes. A deer darted for the cover of a spruce thicket off to their left. "Look at that!" Bobby exclaimed. They watched as it bounded out of sight.

Joshua grinned. "Some pretty!" He switched his heavy bag to his left hand and the cardboard box to his right.

"Yeah," his brother agreed. "Most people think of the beauty of nature as an act of God's creation, but really, much of what we call beauty is a result of God's condemnation. The cliffs we see at Rogers Cove and the large mountain ranges out west came into being because of His judgment on the sin of mankind. He caused a worldwide flood which not only destroyed all flesh as the book of Genesis tells us, except for Noah and his family, but it altered the face of the earth."

Joshua agreed. "Yeah, and more than half of the earth is still flooded today, and that means that twice as much of the surface of the earth is covered with water than there is dry land."

They sprinted across a narrow brook and then scampered up the face of the bedrock protruding through the forest floor. "This bag's some heavy, I tell you!" Joshua grumbled as the rock leveled out. "Alice really stuffed it jam full."

"Don't complain, My Son," his brother grinned at him. "Your wife thinks of you as being a strong man."

Joshua stopped and lowered his bag and box to the ground. "Well, that's a nice way to look at it, but it's still heavy, and I'm near famished. Let's stop for a lunch."

Joshua and Bobby dropped to the base of two maple trees. "Have a look-see at the stuff in here!" Joshua exclaimed when he opened his canvas bag. "She sure is generous!" He lifted out a package of toilet paper and a large box of matches and laid them on the ground. He then opened the bag farther. "Ahh, this must be for me—has my name on it anyway." He looked over at Bobby. "What did you bring for the guy?"

"Well, let's see." He folded back the flap of his bag and enlarged the opening. "Package of raisins, bar of soap."

Joshua frowned and grinned at the same time. "Bar of soap!"

"Yeah. For creature comfort." He shrugged his right shoulder. "And a bag of something. Must be oatmeal flakes."

Joshua peered into his bag again. "Here's a Bible and a handful of tracts and several weekly newspapers. Hey, no wonder it's so heavy - must be a dozen tins of milk in here! And look, here's a pair of scissors."

Bobby glanced over at him and grinned. "Probably for creature comfort." He shrugged his shoulder again and then he opened his lunch bag. "Eva packed me a half dozen hard-boiled eggs. Want one, Boy? How about two?" Bobby tossed him two eggs before his brother could answer.

Joshua threw him a hunk of pork wrapped in waxed paper and then picked up one of the eggs. "Hey, this one was intended for you, Bobby. It has a very personal message on it." He winked at him and tossed it back. Bobby read the printing penciled on the shell and grinned. He picked up another egg and after examining it, he chucked it to his brother.

When Joshua opened his jar of milk, he took several gulps and then handed it over to Bobby.

Ten minutes later Joshua stood up, removed his cap, ran his fingers through his hair and pressed his cap back on his head. Bobby stretched his arms up and over his head and then dropped them down. "Let's go, Whiskers," Joshua said. He picked up the box and his bag, and then he pushed through a couple of young pine trees.

"Wait for me," Bobby called to him. "Hey, I'd like to see the guy's face when he opens your box."

"Yeah," Joshua replied, "and I'd like to see the kitten's face when she sees him! Probably arch her back and hiss at him!" The brothers laughed, and then Joshua added, "Maybe she'll be good at swatting flies like her ma." Bobby grinned and shrugged his shoulder.

Neither fellow spoke as they followed along the edge of the brook. Ten or fifteen minutes later, Joshua who was in the lead suddenly stopped. "Listen!"

Bobby took a couple steps and stopped at his brother's side. "Sounds like someone's splitting firewood."

"Must be him," Joshua concluded looking pleased.

The brothers quietly moved through the trees in the direction of the sound of the chopping. Joshua turned to Bobby. "I think you should stay back out of sight until the guy gets used to me. Don't want him to think he's being ambushed," he said in a hushed voice. "He should recognize me. I'm wearing the same jacket and cap I had on when I was here last spring. Give me five minutes or so." Bobby nodded in agreement.

When they came to the brow of the little hill, the Brown Beans Camp came into view about a hundred feet ahead of them. The sound of the man splitting wood was much clearer here at this closer distance. Bobby crouched down behind several thick spruce trees, and Joshua nodded at him before he walked forward a dozen paces and stopped.

Joshua could see the hermit was between his cabin and the garden with his back to them. His hair appeared to be longer and more stringy, and as he worked, it flew about his shoulders. Joshua waited for the man to complete his swing and after the pieces separated and fell to the ground, he called out, "Hello." The man abruptly spun around, eyed him briefly, then looked towards his cabin door in a panic. He then stared back at this unexpected intruder and waited. A few seconds passed and then Joshua slowly came closer to the man who was visibly uncomfortable.

"You remember me," Joshua called out to him as he halted next to a stand of wire birches. He stood holding the bag and the box, and he reminded the hermit, "I was here last spring. I told you I'd be back, Boy." Joshua smiled pleasantly and took two steps forward.

The man studied him for several seconds, took a deep breath, moved and stood near the rock he had sat on last spring.

Joshua came forward and stopped at about the same place he did before. "How are you doing?" The man continued to keep his eyes on Joshua but he did not reply. Joshua lowered himself to the ground and tried to look relaxed. He lay back and supported himself on one elbow. Joshua could see the hermit's hair sway in the breeze as the fellow continued to stare at him. He shifted his gaze to the man's pile of firewood. "Splitting wood's a chore." The man said nothing.

He sat on the rock and nervously stroked his beard. Joshua tried again. "Has anyone else come to visit you?"

The man hesitated and then shook his head once. Joshua pulled on a long piece of grass growing up through a fern plant. He did not know what more to say. From his reclined position, he glanced from the cabin to the woodpile and then to the man's garden. "How was your garden this past summer?" The hermit surveyed his garden, and Joshua told him cheerfully, "My wife and I had a good crop of squash."

The man's mouth suddenly dropped open, and he stared intently at Joshua. He looked like he wanted to say something, but then changed his mind and showed disinterest. From this distance of twenty-five feet, Joshua thought he could see tears in the man's eyes. *Probably doesn't have a family that cares for him, let alone a wife. I didn't realize I have so much.* The strange man lowered his head and stared at the vegetation near by.

Several minutes later, Joshua heard a twig snap behind him. Without looking, he knew it was Bobby approaching. Joshua saw the man jump up and glare at this new intruder coming in their direction. "No!" the hermit protested hoarsely, scowling at Joshua.

"This is my brother," Joshua quickly got across to him as he glanced back at Bobby.

"No!" the man insisted once more. As he took a step towards his cabin, he quickly surveyed the woods beyond Joshua and Bobby.

"But this is my brother—he's okay," Joshua tried to assured him. "We're your friends." Joshua knelt on the ground and held his open hands toward the frightened man. "We won't harm you, Boy."

The hermit slowly sat down again and stared at Bobby who was cautiously coming through the trees. Bobby stopped several yards behind Joshua, lowered his bag and squatted down. Joshua could see over his shoulder that his brother was trying to look pleasant. The man had tears in his eyes, and Joshua thought he could see him trembling. *This man's a nervous wreck,* he realized. "I think we better go, Bobby," Joshua said quietly. "We've stressed him enough." The man promptly jumped up and hurried into his cabin and closed the door behind him.

"Yeah, let's go," Bobby agreed and the brothers quickly unloaded their hunting bags onto the ground. Bobby dug out the remaining hard-boiled egg from his lunch and positioned it next to the bar of soap. The pile of supplies looked strangely out of place under the trees and amongst the decaying ferns and other wild plants of the woods. A leaf fluttered down and settled on the package of toilet paper. Joshua could hear a muffled 'meow' coming from the box which was tipped sharply and was threatening to roll over.

The brothers moved several yards away, and Joshua turned and informed the nervous man who had retreated to his cabin, "We're leaving now." The little dwelling was silent, but he thought he could see the hermit through the darkened window. "Bye," Joshua called out. "I'll check on you in the spring."

When the brothers were back over the brow of the hill, Joshua questioned his brother. "So, what do you think?"

"The fellow values his privacy. And, like you say, he's hiding something or from something, but he's not a bad guy. I think he's harmless."

"I wish there was more we could do for the hermit," Joshua said.

"I think we're doing the best we can," Bobby quickly responded. "We're praying for him. We're helping him in his needs—some of them anyway. And we're showing him friendship. If there's anything else we should do, I'm sure the Lord will show us because He knows we've made ourselves available, and we're willing."

Joshua nodded. "Yeah, you're right."

Everyday that winter, Joshua prayed for the hermit who was living at the Brown Beans Camp deep in the woods. He asked that the Lord's will would be done for him. He prayed that the fellow would read the Bible they had left him, realize he was a sinner, and then put his faith in the Lord, and that he would have real peace in his life.

Over the next several months, Joshua figured that this winter had been colder than normal and that they had had more snow. Alice thought they might have had a bit more snow, but she didn't think it was any colder than other winters. She told him he probably felt that way because of his concern for the man he had befriended who was alone in the backwoods and had had no contact with anyone but him. She reminded him that the kitten would be good company for the hermit.

He grinned when he remembered the playfulness of the kittens they had had when he was a youngster. "Yeah, they sure can be entertaining," he told her.

Joshua could now see that spring was definitely coming. The daylight hours were increasing and the sun was higher in the sky. For over a week now, the daytime temperatures were well above freezing, while the night-time temperatures were just below freezing. The open fields which lay in the full sun were void of snow and were a dull, washed-out yellow, but the snow still lingered in the shadows of the buildings and the thick trees. As well, it carpeted the north facing slopes. Another sure sign of spring was the appearance of flies emerging from the cracks of the woodwork of the house both inside and out.

Finally Joshua felt he just had to go and check on the hermit in the woods. He retrieved his canvas bag from the attic above the attached woodshed, and Alice packed him a lunch and put together some supplies to leave with the fellow.

Joshua lifted his coat from the hook. "I wonder if I'll get invited in this time." He glanced over at his wife and grinned, and then he added, "Probably not, and I'll not push it any."

Alice returned the grin. "Do you mind carrying these five small cans of beans?" she asked him as she brought them from the pantry. "I don't want to overload you like I did last time."

"What do you mean, overload me!" he remarked in mock surprise. "I can carry them."

"I didn't mean you couldn't carry them," his wife quickly answered. "I just didn't want to give you so much to carry."

Bobby would not be accompanying Joshua this trip as his wife was expecting any time now. Besides the hermit was more stressed with both men there. It was normal for the roads to be muddy in spring and deeply rutted in places, and this year the Hannah Road was no different. Joshua traveled to the Rogers Cove Road and parked his car on the side of the road close to Bennys Bump. *Not only does the drive take longer when the road's muddy,* he reasoned when he removed the ignition key, *but it seems longer when a fellow's anxious, and it seems longer when he's by himself.*

Joshua lifted his bag from the seat beside him and after stepping onto the muddy road, he reached back and closed the door. He jumped the water in the ditch and pushed his way through the alders and spruce trees and entered the woods. He could clearly see the green top of Bennys Bump off to the west through the leafless branches of the maple and birch trees he was walking beneath. There was plenty of snow on the floor of the woods, especially on the shady side of the thick spruce trees and where the terrain sloped down to the north. Those areas which received the most sunlight and were well protected from the harsh winds showed signs of new growth.

Joshua made a short detour to avoid the deep snow close to a dense thicket of spruce trees, and soon he came to the brook which was now spring-swollen. He walked along it to where it was narrow enough to jump across.

After what seemed like a long time, Joshua finally came over the brow of the little hill, and he looked towards the Brown Beans Camp.

He halted abruptly in his tracks, his mouth dropped open, and he stared wide-eyed at the cabin in the little clearing. Joshua held this pose for about ten seconds, and then he ran towards the little dwelling tightly clutching his bag. At the spot where he had sat other times, he stopped and hugged his bag as he stared at the cabin.

"Oh no!" he moaned aloud. "No! It can't be!" One side of the roof was collapsed into the cabin with nearly two feet of snow still covering the roof. A side wall had fallen out and the top of a young spruce tree was poking out from beneath it. One of the other walls was away from the roof and was leaning heavily against a nearby maple tree. The other half of the roof was dislodged and at a precarious slope, causing the remaining wall to be badly twisted.

A minute or two later, Joshua slowly lowered his bag and left it resting on the damp ground. He moved hesitantly towards the collapsed cabin and stopped about a yard from the wall which was lying back in the snow inside up. As he stood there, he peered into what was left of the structure.

Joshua supposed that the collapse of the little building had caught the hermit unawares for there was evidence his activities had been suddenly interrupted. He could see, still on the woodstove, a saucepan with its lid in place. Joshua imagined, *The guy wouldn't leave the pot on the hot stove if he wasn't cooking or heating up something.* The metal chimney had separated from the cast-iron stove and was leaning back against the wall. He could tell that although the fire had continued to burn in the stove, it had not spread to the now ruined cabin.

Joshua figured the weight of the roof had broken the chair's back, but the little table knocked over onto its side was unharmed. *There's his dinner plate on the floor,* Joshua noticed. *It smashed when it fell from the table. And there's his knife and fork on the floor near the woodstove.*

Several metal canisters and some cans of food were lined up in a row on a shelf which was now tipped at a sharp angle but still fastened to one of the walls. Joshua recognized the scissors which were dangling from a nail. The wall at his feet was partly covered with several inches of snow and had what looked like items of clothing on it buried under the recent snowfall. "What happened to the guy! Where is he?" he demanded aloud as he stared into the mess.

Joshua moved around to where the cabin walls had split apart. The sun was melting the snow on the roof and he could hear water dripping to the ground in an irregular but somehow peaceful fashion. As he cautiously leaned forward into the cabin, he could see the kitten's cardboard box with a five inch hole cut through one side and some bedding inside. As he studied what he could see of the interior of the cabin, he pondered, *I hope Whiskers was good company for the man, and I hope the man was good company for Whiskers. But I don't see either of them. Where are they?*

The collapsed roof laden with snow appeared to be resting on the bed. On the floor nearby lay the Bible Joshua and Alice had given the man and under the bed were five or six squash. Close to Joshua on the wall was printed in pencil, 'Therefore being justified by faith, we have peace with God through our Lord Jesus Christ: By Whom also we have access by faith into this grace wherein we stand, and rejoice in hope of the glory of God' Romans 5:1-2.

"He underlined 'peace' and 'rejoice'," Joshua stated thankfully. "He found the Lord! The hermit read the Bible and found the Lord!"

Joshua glanced down and saw within his reach a book which was swollen by having been exposed to the dampness. He bent over, picked it up and read the title, 'Homesteading in the Northern Regions'.

"I've got to know if the guy's here," Joshua said as he held the damp book in his hand. He slowly lowered himself to a crouched position and looked between the roof and the man's bed.

Joshua gasped, jerked back, and nearly lost his balance. He looked once more just to be sure. In the dim light under the caved-in roof he could see the hand of a man hanging limply from the bed. It was angled down in the direction of the Bible on the floor.

"Oh, no! It's him," Joshua moaned. "The hermit's dead." He hung his head, closed his eyes, and squeezed the book he was clutching. His mind was blank, yet at the same time it was full. He was then once more aware of the sound of the peaceful dripping of the melting snow as it dropped from the dislodged roof. Behind him and several yards away, he could hear the water of the brook gurgling unconcerned as it passed unceasingly under the winter ice. After several minutes, he stood up and cautiously backed away from the demolished cabin.

Joshua glanced down at the book he was tightly clutching, and with trembling hands he opened the front cover. He read the name penciled near the top edge, and he gasped again even louder, and then he respectfully closed the book. He stared at the collapsed cabin for about a minute before slowly walking backwards to his hunting bag under the wire birches. After placing the book in his bag, he turned to leave. He took a dozen or so steps towards the brow of the little hill and then glanced back at the cabin. *I want to go—I want to get out of here,* he determined as he hugged his bag, *but I also want to stay.*

Before reaching the top of the little rise, he stopped to survey the scene once more. About a minute later he slowly turned and moved out of sight of what was left of the Brown Beans Camp.

At first Joshua's walk was brisk, but then he increased his pace, and finally he broke out into a run as he crashed through the undergrowth. Five minutes later he stopped and leaned back against a maple tree. His breathing was fast and hard, and he slid down the trunk of the tree to sit at its base in the sun with his bag at his side, and there he remained for about ten minutes. Finally, he began to talk to his Heavenly Father in prayer, and then he had a bite to eat and a drink of milk before proceeding through the woods again. After walking the remaining distance, which to Joshua seemed to take a long time, he finally reached the road; and he started his car, turned it around, and headed for home.

As Joshua approached the house he and Alice were living in, he could see Bobby's truck in the yard. Joshua parked close to the door of the attached woodshed and shut off the engine, and then he took hold of his bag and stepped out into the yard.

Without taking off his boots, he entered the woodshed and moved past the cat which was swatting flies in the window. He stood just inside the kitchen door and stared at his wife and brother who were seated at the kitchen table having coffee and freshly baked bannock bread.

"Joshua!" his wife greeted him as she stood up. "Eva had her baby this morning. Joshua, you're an uncle." Without expression, he looked from Alice to Bobby but did not reply. He lowered his bag to the floor, still bulging and heavy with supplies meant for the hermit.

Bobby grinned at Joshua and shrugged his right shoulder. He let the hired man's clock complete its hourly chime, and then the new father proudly announced, "It's a boy." Joshua continued to stare blankly at his brother who added, "We've named him 'David'." Bobby shrugged his shoulder once more, and then as he studied his brother's somber face, he became puzzled.

Alice added, "After your brother David." And she now looked with concern at her husband as she stood before him.

Joshua reached down and removed the damaged book from his bag, and as he pressed it to himself, he repeated solemnly, "David." He looked at his wife and then passed the book to his brother. As Bobby held it, Alice reached out to grasp her husband's hand.

Joshua took a deep breath and then let it out slowly. "The guy at the Brown Beans Camp is dead," he reported to them as he bowed his head. "The hermit was David."

chapter six

about nine years later—summer 1950

The Mouse Nest

Joshua Palmer leaned over and placed his hands on his knees as he scanned the bottom shelf on which the bags of flour were located. "Now, which one did she want me to get?" he asked himself as he paused in the narrow aisle of the general store in the village of Hannah. "There it is—that one." He picked up one of the bags of flour and turned to leave.

"Well, hello, Cecil," Joshua greeted the man nearby who was waiting for him to move aside. "Nice day." His neighbour who lived a bit to the east of his place, nodded politely as Joshua held the bag of flour close to his chest and leaned towards the shelves to let him pass by. Joshua saw Cecil retreat to the back of the store and fasten a piece of paper to the notice board near the post office.

Joshua cradled his load in one arm, and when he approached the front counter he announced, "Bag of flour here, Mr. Bent."

The middle-aged man looked up from his papers where he was doing some figuring. "Yes, Sir, Joshua," he replied as he balanced his pencil over his ear. "Nice weather we've been having lately, don't you think?"

"Sure is." Joshua set down his purchase on the long wooden counter. "But I reckon we could do with some rain."

"Rain," Mr. Bent stated as he stroked the top of his nearly bald head. "It hasn't rained in these parts for well over two weeks now."

"That's right," Joshua agreed. He removed his wallet from his back pocket. "Ground's getting some dry, I'd say."

Mr. Bent nodded, and he brushed back his mustache.

Joshua glanced at Cecil who was now arriving with several tins of brown beans. "Beans," Joshua suddenly remembered.

"I'm supposed to get some beans." He pushed his wallet back into his pocket and told the man, "Go ahead, Cecil." And he proceeded to the area of the store where the tinned foods were kept.

After picking up two large cans, Joshua looked over at the notice board. He could see the small piece of paper which Cecil had left secured by a thumb tack. *What's it say?* he wondered, and he moved over to the board which hung between the window and the post office. Joshua leaned forward and read the note which was scrawled out on the partly wrinkled, lined paper. *FOR SALE, PUMP ORGAN. CECIL HILL.* That was all it said. *Well, what do you know!* he exclaimed to himself. *A pump organ for sale.* And then his eye caught a larger piece of paper. *And here's a notice that says something about a divine healing teaching meeting. What next! Don't need that, I'm sure.*

Joshua grinned and then turned back to the front of the store to pay for his purchases. As he returned his wallet to his pocket, he could see through the large front window of the store that Cecil was now driving away in his car towards home.

"I'll get the door for you," Mr. Bent offered as Joshua started to leave with the bag of flour and the tins of brown beans cradled in his arms.

"Okay, thanks."

The storekeeper came around from behind the counter. "Joshua, there's a meeting this Saturday evening you might be interested in," he said to him as he crossed to the door. "A gentleman from away is going to tell us what the Bible says about divine healing." He pulled open the door, causing the bell suspended over it to tinkle, and Joshua carried his things outside.

"Yeah, I saw the notice back there."

Mr. Bent stepped out and stood on the concrete landing and continued. "People say he knows the Bible real good. Knows a lot of verses, I hear." Joshua nodded politely, and Mr. Bent added, "Just thought you'd be interested in something like that."

Joshua said, "Thanks, and have a good evening." Mr. Bent raised his hand in reply, and he turned and re-entered the store.

Joshua went to his truck nearby and laid his purchases on the floor on the passengers' side. He started the engine and pulled onto the road which passed through the village. At the outskirts of Hannah, just before the pavement ended and the road became gravel, Joshua drove by the old schoolhouse which was now used as a community hall. The sign in the front yard read, 'DIVINE HEALING TEACHING MEETINGS'. *I like to learn things from God's Word,* he mused over as he shifted up to a higher gear, *but divine healing? I don't feel right about this.*

The dust billowed up behind his truck as Joshua traveled along the road towards home. A half hour later, he slowed down and turned in at the old Myles Dorey place where Cecil Hill lived near his own house and property. After turning his vehicle around in the yard and parking next to the lilac bushes, he opened the door and stepped out onto the grass.

Joshua paused and listened. *I hear music. Somebody's playing the organ.* He walked up to the side door to the kitchen and leaned forward to listen as the organ music continued. *Some nice,* he decided. *And pretty, too. Didn't know a pump organ could sound so good.* He stood at the door as three verses of the hymn were played. He noticed each verse was played in a different manner or style. *Cecil don't have no company—who's that on the organ?* A final verse was played, and when the music stopped, Joshua rapped on the door.

The door opened shortly, and Cecil stood there. He smiled at Joshua but looked a little uncomfortable. He shifted his weight from one foot to the other but did not say anything.

"About the organ," Joshua began as he looked beyond his neighbour and into the kitchen. "It's for sale?"

Cecil stared at him momentarily and then nodded. "Come on in, Joshua," he invited. He led him through his large kitchen and into the living room of the farmhouse. Joshua considered, *I haven't been in this house since Cecil took over this here place.*

The two men stood before the organ without saying anything. Joshua could tell the instrument was not a real fancy one like the one he had seen some time ago at a funeral in a large church in a distant town. This one was a domestic model similar to ones he had seen in the homes of several of his neighbours. Joshua knew how the pump organ sounded from a distance, but he wanted to hear it again now that he was in the same room. He asked, "How's it sound? Play it again will you, Cecil." He tipped back his hat and then slid it forward again. Cecil shifted his feet but did not answer. "Heard you play," Joshua told him as he glanced over at the organ. "Didn't know you could play, Sir. Sounded real good, I'd say."

Cecil smiled slightly and looked away. "No," he said simply but politely. "I don't play for other people."

Joshua grinned and shrugged one shoulder. He moved closer to the organ and rested his hand on one of the round light-holders as he quickly scanned the instrument. *Don't know much about organs,* he reflected, as he pushed in one of the stops and then pulled it out again, and then he tried another stop. Next he ran his fingers across one of the carvings on the side of the organ, and then he dropped his gaze to the stool. He could see the stool height could be adjusted by rotating its upholstered top. *Alice would love this pump organ,* Joshua knew, and he smiled as he pictured her with this piece of furniture in their living room. He stepped back a couple feet and studied it in silence. After a minute he asked, "How much?"

Cecil paused, shrugged his shoulder, and then told Joshua, "Twenty-five dollars."

Joshua rubbed his chin and then slowly nodded. "Okay," he answered, and then he inquired, "Can I take it now?"

Cecil removed his hymn book from the ledge over the keys of the organ and placed it on the arm of the chesterfield nearby and then he drew out the cover towards him and closed the instrument. He moved to the side of the organ and grasped the handle. Joshua took hold of the other handle and the two men rolled the instrument across the floor to the front door. After Cecil unlocked the door with the skeleton key hanging nearby, they lifted the organ over the threshold and lowered it to the grass in the front door yard.

Cecil paused as he glanced over at Joshua's truck. Joshua questioned, "You think we can carry it from here?" Cecil grinned and nodded in reply.

After the organ was laid down in the back of the truck and Cecil had retrieved the stool from his living room, Joshua slammed closed the tailgate. He then paid Cecil the full amount and slid behind the wheel of his truck. He drove cautiously along the driveway and headed for home where his young family lived and were awaiting his return.

Joshua moved slowly along the dirt road to keep the billowing dust from settling on the prized possession on back of his truck. *How will I get this thing off the truck and into the house?* He parked his truck with the back facing the door to the attached woodshed, and he circled around to the passengers' side where he picked up the bag of flour in one arm and the tins of beans in the other. With his foot, he shoved the truck door closed.

Joshua entered the house through the woodshed and greeted his wife and young daughter at the kitchen table and his two young sons who came into the kitchen from the living room. He lowered the flour and tins to the counter as the two boys scampered off and returned to their play at the back of the house.

"That's right, Martha," Joshua's wife informed their five-year-old girl. "It's a B flat note." She pointed to the page in the hymn book. The book was propped up against a pile of books on the kitchen table and the pages were held back by two clothes pegs.

"Keep going. Next is, 'of Glory died.'" Joshua smiled as he watched his daughter move her small fingers along the wide piece of shelf-paper which was against the edge of the table. It was marked to represent the keys of an organ. His wife slowly counted out the notes. "A, G, F, E, F, G. Can you hear the hymn tune in your head? That's great—you're doing real good, Girl."

Joshua crossed to the woodstove. "Alice, you want me to tickle this fire for you for supper?"

"Yes, Joshua, thanks," she quickly replied. "Martha, that line there ends on a G note."

Joshua opened the chimney flue and then swung back the front door of the stove. He lowered a stick of wood onto the hot coals in the firebox and after closing the door and latching it, he checked that the front air intake was wide open.

"Thanks, Joshua," his wife said to him from the table. "I'll get supper started soon."

The hired man's clock in the living room gave one strike.

Martha was concentrating deeply. "Mom, this is getting too hard. Can I stop now?" She frowned. "My fingers are getting kind of tired, and so is my head."

"Okay," her mother told her. "That's all for now." Alice picked up the paper with the organ keys drawn on it. As she moved across the room, she glanced out the kitchen window. "Why did you park so close to the house, Joshua?" his wife questioned him. "And what's that you have on back of the truck?"

Joshua grinned broadly. "Something for you," he informed her as he took her hand. "Come on, I'll show you." She dropped her paper organ keys on the counter as he led her to the door and through the woodshed to outside.

"What is it, Joshua?" Alice asked as they crossed the grass to the pickup. "A pump organ!" she exclaimed with delight as she gazed at it lying on its back. "Where did you get it? I can't believe it! Joshua, you found an organ!"

"Merry Christmas, Alice," he announced and he grinned broadly at her. "And Happy Birthday, too. And Happy Mother's Day, as well."

"Oh, Joshua, you found me an organ! Thank you, Joshua, thank you."

"Here," he said as he grinned over at her and opened the tailgate. "Let's slide it off and stand it upright." He pulled on the base of the organ until it was balanced on the edge of the tailgate. "Okay, grab that handle on the side there but don't pull on that lamp holder." They carefully lowered the base of the organ to the grass, and Joshua made sure it was steady.

"Oh, it's beautiful!" Alice squealed as she stepped back to examine her organ. "Look at the lovely carvings on the front there, and those cutouts are elegant. Oh, I really like it!" Alice came closer and ran her fingers across the hymn book ledge.

Joshua grinned again. "Cecil Hill wanted to get rid of it so I bought it from him," he told his wife.

Alice watched as he slid back the lid above the keys. She counted, "Eight, nine, ten. There are ten stops." And then she leaned over to examine beneath the key housing. "And there are two knee stops."

Joshua reached back into the box of the truck and lifted out the stool. He set it on the ground in front of the organ. Alice rotated its padded seat back and forth.

"Mommy?" seven-year-old Brent called from the door of the woodshed with his younger brother Drew just behind him. "I'm hungry." He then stared at the fancy piece of furniture on the grass. "What's that, Mommy? Did Daddy bring it home for us?"

"Joshua, I should get supper started." She looked from the organ to her boys standing on the landing. "And you must be needing your supper, too."

Alice returned to the kitchen with Drew, and Joshua and his young son Brent left for the barn to do chores. As Joshua worked he wondered, *How will I get the organ into the house? It's too heavy for me and Alice to lift it up the steps. I'll need some help.*

Immediately after supper, Alice selected one of her hymn books, and without saying anything she hurried out to the front yard where her organ was situated. Her husband watched from the kitchen window as she set her opened book on the ledge. She lowered herself to the stool and placed her hands over the organ keys and began to play. He smiled as he observed her hands moving along the keys and her feet working the two pedals for the bellows. At first Alice played cautiously—the music was slow and deliberate, but as she gained feeling for the instrument her playing became more spontaneous and natural sounding.

The three children soon joined their dad at the window. "What's that noise?" asked Brent as he pushed his nose against the window pane.

Martha remarked, "Mommy makes nice music." She remained motionless to listen.

"What's Mommy doing that for?" Drew asked, and then he returned his thumb to his mouth.

Their dad grinned. "Your mommy can make the organ sing—just listen, Children. Some pretty!"

Mrs. Palmer's hands traveled back and forth along the keys as her feet pushed against the two foot pedals. She leaned forward to concentrate on the written music and at the same time she balanced herself on the stool which was beginning to wobble on the unstable ground.

It was not long before the two boys lost interest and withdrew to play at the back of the house. Martha came out from the kitchen and stood beside her mother at the organ. Joshua came through the woodshed to the landing. He lowered himself to sit on the stone landing and smiled as he watched his wife.

Alice continued to play, oblivious to her surroundings. She tried each of the stops and then combinations of stops. Her husband listened and reminisced, *I haven't heard Alice play the pump organ since we wed. She must miss her parents' organ. She used to tickle that thing softly and smoothly, and then play loud and like thunder—and all the while teetering on that narrow stool. I'm glad I found this organ, but we need to get it into the house tonight.* He studied the sky over the woods nearby. *Might rain. Maybe I can find some boards to rig up a ramp for over the front steps and we can lug it up and into the house.* He came off the landing and headed for the barn.

Suddenly Joshua stopped and stared down his driveway. *What's he doing here?* he wondered. *He's never dropped in to our place before.* The visitor approached Joshua, smiled and nodded. "Hello, Cecil," Joshua greeted as he glanced from his neighbour to his wife who was still playing the organ. "Nice evening."

His neighbour nodded and looked towards Alice. "Thought you might need some help. You know—to get the pump organ into the house." Joshua grinned and moved towards his wife and little girl.

Alice abruptly stopped her music in the middle of a verse. "Oh, I didn't know we had a visitor." She giggled, stood up, and smoothed down her skirt.

Cecil nodded politely at Alice. "Evening, Mrs. Palmer."

"The organ is magnificent, Mr. Hill," Alice told him. "I'm really enjoying it. And it works beautifully, too." She and their little girl stood with her husband near the organ.

They all gazed at the pump organ set up in the grass, and finally Joshua spoke. "About the organ," he said to his neighbour. "Sure could use your help, Sir."

The two men took hold of the handles, lifted the organ five or six inches from the ground and struggled with it to the kitchen door landing. Alice picked up the stool and hurried to open the door for the men. "Thanks for coming," she said to Cecil as she held back the door. "We couldn't have done it on our own."

After several minutes, the pump organ was in the place in the living room which Joshua and Alice had prepared as supper was cooking. Martha watched from the chesterfield and her two brothers peered into the living room from the doorway. This piece of furniture looked large in this room, but Alice was clearly pleased, and Joshua grinned at her as she set the stool in position. Their neighbour Cecil moved across the room to leave. He paused to quickly study several of Joshua's paintings hanging on the walls.

"Thanks, Cecil," Joshua told him sincerely. Cecil nodded and turned to leave.

"Yes, thank you," Alice agreed as she positioned the hymn book on its ledge. "Won't you stay a few minutes? We'd like to hear you play. Joshua says you play real good."

Cecil grinned. "No," he said as he retreated. "Need to get a move-along." Joshua followed him to the door. Before Cecil stepped off the landing, he turned to Joshua and said, "I'm glad my pump organ has gone to a good home. I can see you'll take good care of it." Joshua grinned and nodded, and Cecil walked along the driveway to return to his house a short distance down the road.

Even before Joshua came back to the living room, he could hear the music of the organ. *Sure sounds grand,* he contemplated. *I'm glad we finally have an organ, and I'm glad my wife can play. 'What can wash away my sins? Nothing but the blood of Jesus.' Perhaps someday Martha will make nice music, too.*

For the next few days Alice was at the pump organ every spare minute she had. Her playing technique steadily improved each day.

Saturday night, Joshua attended the divine healing teaching meeting in the village of Hannah. He listened as the man from away in the smart suit explained. "The gospel of Mark chapter sixteen says that Jesus commanded His disciples to go into all the world and preach the gospel, and that signs would follow—including laying hands on the sick, and they would recover." He went on and commented that we, His disciples, can do healing today; in fact, we are commanded to heal.

Is that really so? Joshua wondered as he balanced his unopened Bible on his thigh. *We haven't been taught that, and I've never seen it that way.*

He heard the man relate, "Believers all through the centuries since Pentecost have been healing the sick for the glory of God."

Joshua groaned within himself. *Well, I don't know about that. I've never heard such a thing before.*

The man continued. "This teaching isn't something new, but it's gaining greater acceptance as Christians are getting back to the Word of God in these last days as never before."

Are we really away from His Word? Joshua questioned in his mind.

The man said, "The Spirit of God is moving in these end times in marvellous ways all around the world. Multitudes in many countries all over are experiencing miracles of healing."

As soon as the meeting was over, Joshua quickly left the community hall without speaking to anyone. The sun was low in the western sky as he returned home along the familiar dusty road.

"How was the meeting, Joshua?" his wife asked after he entered the kitchen and hung his hat on the peg next to the door.

He looked over at her sitting in the rocking chair near the now-cold stove and shook his head. "It was different alright," he expressed in disappointment. "Never heard nothing like it before. Claims we should be healing today just like the early disciples did—you know, in the book of Acts there." He sat on a kitchen chair and leaned back.

Alice lowered her mending to her lap. "Well, doesn't it say they went everywhere preaching and healing?"

"I'm confused," he admitted, somewhat agitated. "The guy quoted Scripture all over the place. Have we missed out on teaching about healing? The guy waved his Bible at us and said, 'Welcome to the Word of God, Friends.'" Joshua frowned and shook his head again. "We hardly opened our Bibles at all."

Alice looked concerned. "We'll have to look into it, won't we, Joshua?"

He nodded in agreement. "What's for a bite?"

After a lunch and before retiring for the day, Joshua went to the hired man's clock in the living room. He picked up the key and wound the timepiece in preparation for the coming week.

Late that night, Joshua had trouble sleeping. *I just don't know,* he contemplated. *I don't want to miss out on any Scriptural truth or anything the Lord has for us—and I'm willing to learn. He rolled over again. If we're supposed to perform miracles of healing, then why aren't we doing it? I want to be obedient to the Lord and be a faithful witness for Him.* He could hear his wife breathing peacefully, and he, being wide awake, gently fluffed up his feather pillow.

Sunday afternoon, Joshua's brother Bob and his wife and young family came to visit. Joshua and Alice met them in the front yard. "I hear you have a pump organ, Alice," Eva informed her. "Oh, I'd love to see it, and I want to hear you play, too." They passed through the attached woodshed. "I can't believe you finally have one—just what you always wanted! You must really enjoy it."

"Some eggs here for you folks, Josh," Bob reported, and he left the container on the counter just inside the door.

The two ladies moved to the living room, and the children followed. The men remained in the kitchen to visit. "Heard you went to the divine healing teaching meeting, Josh," Bob said as he sat at the kitchen table. "How was it?" The organ began to sound in the living room.

Joshua slumped forward on the wooden chair and put both elbows on the table. "Didn't think much of it. The guy quoted the Bible a lot, but we didn't open our Bibles much." His brother leaned back and put his hands behind his head and let Joshua speak. "Bob, I don't know what to think," he continued with a frown. "I want the truth, and nothing but the truth."

The two brothers sat in silence as the organ music wafted in from the other room. Nearly a minute later, Bob spoke. "In order for the Holy Spirit to show us the truth, we must be willing to learn things in God's Word. We must be open-minded, but not so open-minded that our brains fall out. And don't just tell us what the Bible says—show us in the Bible what it says.

We'll even find it ourselves in His Word if we put out the effort to study it out." He paused and rested one elbow on the table. "The Holy Spirit will show us where we're wrong and will correct us, but only if we're willing to be corrected," he continued.

Joshua looked over at Bob and nodded in agreement but said nothing. As they sat in the kitchen, the men could hear one of the familiar hymns being played on the organ. The children passed through the kitchen and went outside to play in the orchard behind the house. Both men said at the same time, "Don't get your Sunday-go-to-meeting clothes dirty."

"Do you realize, Josh," his brother began, "that every single miracle of healing that Jesus did was for illnesses and diseases that were hopeless? There was no known cure." Joshua nodded from across the table. "And," Bob continued, "for each and every disease there was instant healing or nearly so within a few minutes—no one had to wait any period of time."

"Yeah, that's right," Joshua agreed as he sat up straight.

Bob went on. "And the healing was complete—there was no partial healing where the one who had been sick had to come back later for more healing." His brother grinned and nodded. "And the healing held. The disease didn't come back the next day or even the next week or month."

Joshua quickly added, "Jesus was one hundred percent successful each and every time." He grinned broadly at Bob.

The organ music from the living room suddenly sounded a little strange and Eva stopped playing. The men in the kitchen heard, "Oh, no. Something's gone wrong here."

Martha pumped the bellows with her feet as she rested her hands on her hips. One note continued to sound without it being held down. "A key is stuck," she said with concern and when she stopped pumping, the room was silent.

Alice then sat at the organ, and as she pumped the bellows causing the stuck note to sound, she quickly fingered each of the keys down to her left until the constant sounding note was reached. "There it is—it's that low E flat note here," Alice determined.

"I wonder if Joshua can fix it." She depressed the key several times, but it persisted in sounding even when the key was released.

Joshua and Bob, who were still sitting quietly listening from the kitchen now looked over at each other. Joshua stood up, and he and his brother joined their wives in the living room.

"Oh, Joshua," his wife reported to him with disappointment when he appeared, "this note is stuck." She demonstrated by tapping it several times as she worked the bellows.

"Yeah, so I hear," Joshua agreed as he stepped up to the organ. "The back panel can be opened." He took hold of the side handle, and Alice picked up the stool and moved it aside. When the organ was angled into the room, the two men examined the back side of the instrument.

"Some screws along there," Bob remarked as he pointed them out.

Joshua nodded as he knelt next to the organ. "And hinges here. This top half folds down. I can get into it from here and take apart the inner workings. Probably a bit of dirt fell inside and messed up something. I can get at it tomorrow evening, I reckon." And he returned the organ against the wall.

Bob and Eva and their young children left to travel home and prepare supper for themselves. Before they set off, Alice handed Eva a large jar of milk and two loaves of bread. "It was nice to see you two and your family again," called out Eva as she herded her children into their car. The brothers nodded to each other across the front yard.

Later that evening after their children were in bed, Joshua and Alice sat in their living room on the chesterfield which was facing the now-muted pump organ. Joshua related to his wife what Bob and he had discussed that afternoon. "So if miracles of healing are to be done today," Joshua said to her, "it must happen in the same way as when Jesus did it. If not, we must have detailed instructions from God's Word how it is to be carried out. And we don't."

Alice considered it and had to agree. "That's right. And when we read the book of Acts, we see that the healing miracles the apostles did were just the same as Christ did. No known cure for the disease, instant healing, complete healing, and the healing lasted." She grinned at Joshua.

Joshua added, "And it says somewhere in Acts that many signs and wonders were done by the apostles—the sent ones—not the believers in general. The apostles were to be identified as being with Jesus by the miracles they did, and it says the priests took note that these men—the apostles, had been with Jesus. Paul said he did the signs of an apostle. What signs? It doesn't mention anyone else who did miracles except for Stephen who was very closely associated with the apostles."

Alice realized and spoke for both of them, "So often we miss the straight forward, simple things in God's Word. How do people get off into wrong teachings?"

"Well," Joshua speculated, "they don't carefully look into things, and they rely heavily on what others say. Also, their interest is often in emotional experiences—ours is simply believing what God has said."

The next evening after the children were in bed, Joshua picked up his screwdriver from his toolbox. After he pulled the pump organ out from the wall, he began to remove the screws from the upper back panel. It was not long before the panel was loosened and folded down, resting on the lower half of the organ back. Joshua stared into the interior of the organ, and then he leaned forward for a better look. "Hey, Alice," he called to her in the kitchen. "Come have a look-see."

Alice left her baking and came into the living room to where Joshua was kneeling on the floor. She leaned over holding her long hair back and peered into the mechanisms of the organ.

Joshua pointed to something inside on their right, and Alice studied it for several seconds. "It's a mouse nest," she decided in surprise. "A mouse nest inside the organ. Imagine! At one time a mouse lived right here inside this pump organ."

Joshua reached in and began to carefully remove the nest. "Wait," Alice said. "I'll get some newspaper to put it on." She withdrew to the kitchen to the wood box beside the stove.

When she returned, Joshua resumed his removal of the mouse nest. He placed it on the paper Alice held out for him, and then she started for the stove in the kitchen.

"No, Alice, wait," he informed her. "I'd like to paw through it tomorrow and see what's there, if anything. Might be a part of the organ workings." She handed him the newspaper with the nest, and he carefully positioned it on the top ledge of the organ.

"Well, it's getting late," Joshua realized as the hired man's clock behind him began to strike. "I'll work on this thing again tomorrow night."

Alice returned to the kitchen as he swung the back panel up in place and put in one screw to hold it there. After he slid the instrument back against the wall, he joined his wife in the kitchen for a lunch.

"Fresh biscuits," Joshua stated with pleasure, and Alice smiled at him. He settled himself on a chair at the table and watched as his wife carried over the plate of biscuits.

She placed the lunch down in front of her husband, and then she reached for the pot of tea and filled two cups.

Joshua took a biscuit, broke it in two and spread currant jelly on both halves. "I don't think Cecil knew the mouse nest was there," he remarked to Alice as she sat opposite him. "He would've cleaned it out."

"Yes," Alice agreed, "I'm sure he would've gotten rid of it."

Joshua took another bite of biscuit and added, "Carting the organ over here on its back shook it up a bit and something fell into the plunger contraption and messed it up."

"I'm glad you're going to fix it, Joshua—I really miss it."

Joshua picked up another biscuit and glanced out the window. "Look," he stated. "It's starting to rain. I better close the truck window."

"Well, that's an answer to our prayers," Alice replied as her husband left his lunch and hurried outside.

The next day after work, Joshua dropped by the general store in the village of Hannah. There was no mail for the Palmer family, and as he passed by the counter to leave for home, Mr. Bent remarked, "Good rain in the night."

"Yes," Joshua responded as he grasped the doorknob. "We needed it for sure."

"Saw you at the divine healing teaching meeting the other night, Joshua."

Joshua released his grip on the doorknob. "Yeah, I was there." He turned to face the storekeeper behind the counter.

Mr. Bent remarked, "Good meeting—interesting. That guy from away knows what he's talking about—seems to anyway."

Joshua had a doubtful expression on his face, and he moved closer to Mr. Bent. "God doesn't specialize in the miracle of healing more than any other miracle," he stated with certainty. "Why healing? "Why not make it rain since we needed it?"

"Yeah, but sick people—they're made well," Mr. Bent replied hesitatingly. "And rain? Well - that might not work."

"Might not work?" Joshua questioned him. "Can't the Lord do anything?"

Mr. Bent began to look uncomfortable, and he stroked his balding head. "Well sure," he admitted. "God can do anything. But make it rain? How would we know God was doing it? And healing is a lot more dramatic—and this healing seems to work."

Joshua challenged him. "And what about the other miracles the Bible says the apostles were to do? Like speaking with new tongues, taking up serpents, and drinking deadly things. It mentions those in the same passage."

The storekeeper looked surprised. "It says that? I didn't know that was in there, too. They're sensational, I'd say—taking up serpents and drinking deadly stuff."

Joshua leaned forward with his hands on the counter and grinned. "Did you read your Bible for yourself, Mr. Bent—to see what it says?"

"Well, the guy from away was here to teach us," he defended himself. "I reckon he knows what the Bible says—he can tell us. Why should I take the time to study it out when he can tell us what it says? That's his job."

"Did you believe that guy several years ago who tried to sell you some kind of miracle potion to make your hair grow?" Joshua reminded him, and then he answered for him. "No, you looked into it for yourself and studied up on the subject."

Mr. Bent snickered and stroked the top of his head again. "Yeah, you're right. And, well, I have to admit that I wondered last week if a miracle of healing would give me back my hair. Why not? But I don't have the faith for that, I'm afraid."

"You don't have to have faith," Joshua informed him. "The man who was healed at the gate of the temple by Peter the apostle had no faith. No one is healed because they have faith in their faith. It says Peter lifted him up, and only then did his feet and ankle bones receive strength. His faith, or lack of it, had nothing to do with it. That's what the Bible says." Joshua grinned and then added, "Welcome to the Word of God, Friends."

Joshua heard the door behind him open, and the bell gave a jingle, and then several people filed into the store. He and Mr. Bent exchanged pleasantries with them, and Joshua started for home.

Later as Joshua left the barn for the house and supper with his family, an unfamiliar car pulled into his yard. He watched as the vehicle came to a stop, and the driver bounded out. The well-dressed man grinned pleasantly as he approached Joshua. "Good day, Sir," he greeted with enthusiasm and an out-stretched hand.

Joshua nodded politely and shook hands with him. The man told him, "I've seen you at the divine healing meetings."

Joshua replied cautiously, "I was there the first night."

"Well, we'd like you to come back again," the man said, still smiling. "We're preaching the Word of God. I trust you know the Lord?"

"Yes, I know the Lord," Joshua assured him. "And I have the Holy Spirit who directs me in my life as I study His Word and allow Him to teach me."

"Praise the Lord, Brother!" the divine healing preacher beamed, looking pleased.

Joshua then reported to him, "I believe the Bible is the Word of God. It was authored by the Holy Spirit, and it's without error." As Joshua spoke, the man nodded in agreement.

"Praise the Lord, Brother!" the man exclaimed. "Praise the Lord!"

"I believe," Joshua stated, "that the Word of God can be understood by any believer who truly wants to know what the Lord wants them to know. Real believers want to learn what the Word of God teaches, and they are open to be corrected of any error they might have."

The man grinned as he stared at Joshua, who continued. "If you were wrong in your understanding of something in Scripture—in this case healing—would you want to be corrected? Or do you wish to hang onto what you prefer to believe even if it's actually wrong?"

The well-dressed man looked surprised and a bit hurt. "I've studied the Bible for many years," he quickly protested, "and I know what it says about biblical healing." The friendly grin slowly faded from his face and was replaced by a forced smile as he tried to explain. "I don't need to be corrected of anything—I know I'm right in what I believe. I've experienced biblical healing in myself and countless others, and I'm convinced without a doubt that what I believe and teach is right; I've experienced it."

Joshua answered, "But surely you don't think we learn spiritual truths through our experiences! Believers don't learn by what we experience. We learn by faith—that is, believing in what Scripture actually teaches."

The man's stiff smile was wearing thin. "Here's an illustration for you," he offered Joshua. "If your wife was to serve some cookies, and to me they looked like chocolate cookies, they smelled like chocolate cookies, and they tasted like chocolate cookies, I would know by my experience that they were indeed chocolate cookies. Don't tell me what I experience doesn't mean anything or prove anything." The well-dressed man looked agitated, and he shifted his feet.

"Hold it!" Joshua exclaimed. "I know what my wife puts in her cookies. She puts in carob—not chocolate—and that's a fact. Her cookies don't have any chocolate in them. You thought they were chocolate cookies, but they were actually carob. Your experience deceived you. I ask you—could that also apply to your understanding of healing?"

The well-dressed man looked disturbed as he fidgeted with the knot of his tie. Joshua continued. "I believe anyone who alters the Bible to suit themselves and what they fancy have corrupted the Word of God." The man frowned, and he began to look away. Joshua told him, "And anyone who uses the Word of God to uphold his personal beliefs could be in danger of deceiving the people. Surely you know that one of the major subjects of the New Testament is a warning to believers about false teachers," he stated as he looked directly at him. "False teaching is heresy."

The divine healing preacher was speechless, and he continued to scowl as he rubbed his chin. He suddenly turned and marched to his car nearby. Joshua watched the vehicle as it left the yard and moved along his driveway towards Hannah Road.

Joshua returned to the house where his wife was waiting. "Joshua—who was that gentleman?" Alice asked when he entered the kitchen. She was holding an extra dinner plate.

"Oh, just the divine healing preacher from away," he told her. "He seems a nice enough fellow. He asked us to attend his meetings. 'Welcome to the Word of God, Friends.'" Joshua glanced out the kitchen window and noted, "He suddenly left in a hurry." Alice returned the plate to the cupboard.

After supper and as Alice was getting the children ready for bed, Joshua went to the organ in the living room. He slid the instrument out from the wall, and as he did so he looked at the sheets of newspaper on the top shelf of the organ which had held the mouse nest. *That's strange,* he thought, *I told Alice I wanted to check through the nest to see if there were any parts of the organ in it, but the nest is gone.* He returned to the kitchen where she was getting a lunch for the children.

"Did you see anything in the mouse nest before you threw it out, Alice?" he asked as he stood in the doorway.

She stopped slicing the bread and looked up in surprise. "I didn't throw out the mouse nest, Joshua. I haven't even been in the living room since we were there last night." He looked over at their three children, and his wife told him, "I don't think they've been near the living room today either."

Joshua shrugged his shoulder and went back to the organ and removed the single screw holding the top panel in place. After he folded the panel down he glanced into the inside of the instrument. He stared for several long seconds, and then called to his wife. Alice came into the living room trailed by their three children. Joshua said nothing as he pointed into the organ, and Alice followed his direction. Her mouth dropped open as she leaned over. "The mouse nest! Oh, there's the mouse nest again! Joshua, how did it get back in there?"

Joshua laughed. "The mouse carried it back inside to where it used to be—piece by piece." And then he pointed out, "Probably through the bottom there and up the side of the bellows."

"The mouse!" Alice exclaimed and then giggled. "Joshua, you mean we now have a mouse loose in the house?"

Martha looked pleased. "A mouse in the house!" she exclaimed as she glanced at her parents and brothers. "I'd like to see a mouse."

"Sure looks like we have a loose mouse in the house," he informed his little girl as he knelt on the floor. "Get out the mousetrap." And he grinned at his wife and children.

Alice giggled again. "I thought I saw evidence of a mouse in the pantry this morning."

Joshua grinned as he looked up at her. "The mouse traveled to here from Cecil Hill's place inside the organ. That must have been some trip for the little critter!"

"Yes, it sure would," Alice agreed, and she giggled again. "Just imagine!"

Joshua's face became solemn. "Oh, Alice," he remembered, "I heard in town today that Cecil has left the area for out west somewhere. Left yesterday in fact."

His wife stared at him and then remarked, "That's why he got rid of the pump organ. We should've been more friendly with him—shown an interest in him."

Joshua looked disturbed, and he nodded. "Yeah, you're right of course."

"Come, Children," their mother said to them, "let's finish your lunch and leave your father here to work."

Joshua cleaned out the nest for the second time. He gently pulled it apart to inspect it and finding nothing of consequence, he wrapped it in the sheet of newspaper and carried it to the kitchen stove. After he removed the organ stop mechanism, he was able to clean out any residue of the mouse nest. Joshua circled around to the front and without opening the lid, he worked one of the foot pedals a few times. The offending note did not sound. "Good!" he said with satisfaction, and then he called out, "Alice. Organ's working again." He slid open the lid for her, and when she arrived, he said, "Want to check it out before I close up the back?"

* * *

Later that week as Joshua drove through Hannah on his way home from work, he again glanced over to the community hall. "Well, look at that!" he expressed aloud as he stared out the side window of his truck. "There was supposed to be a meeting there tonight—but the sign is gone. That's an answer to prayer." He grinned as he shifted up and continued along the Hannah Road. And then he considered, *It's so important to understand God's Word properly. We don't interpret the Bible according to what we want it to say, but according to what the Holy Spirit shows us it says.* As he drove towards home, he thought it through and grinned. *And we don't interpret the Bible according to our experiences but according to what it actually tells us.*

* * *

When Joshua arrived home, he parked his truck at the usual place in the front yard. He passed through the attached woodshed and into the kitchen. The sound of the pump organ drew him along and towards the back of the house. At the doorway of the living room, he stood and watched as his young daughter sat on the edge of the stool at the organ. He could see that, with determination, she fingered the keys and at the same time she worked the foot pedals for the bellows.

Martha glanced up at her mother at her side. "How does this sound, Mom?" she asked with delight.

"That's just great," she answered as she smiled down at her daughter. "Your father will be so pleased."

Joshua was pleased. He grinned as he continued to observe his wife and daughter at the organ. He stood there several minutes, and when there was a lull in the music, he gently cleared his throat.

"Oh, Joshua, you're home!" his wife remarked as she and Martha turned to face him.

His little girl beamed up at him. "Listen, Daddy," she told him as she rotated on the stool. Alice moved to stand with her husband. The young girl played one note at a time, and when she was finished the verse of the hymn, she turned and grinned as she faced her parents.

Martha's father said nothing; he smiled, and the little girl could tell her father had enjoyed her playing.

Martha suddenly jumped up off the organ stool. "Dad!" she reported excitedly. "We caught the mouse." And she giggled.

chapter seven

eight years later—summer 1958

Brooster Rhymes with Rooster

"And something else I heard in Hannah today," Mr. Palmer began as he leaned back against the counter where his wife was preparing supper. He smoothed back his mustache with his thumb and forefinger.

She quickly glanced at the woodstove. "Oh, Joshua, would you mind moving the vegetables away from the direct heat. I'm trying to get these old potatoes peeled in time for supper. It'll be nice when these are gone and we can have new potatoes."

Fifteen-year-old Brent entered the kitchen from the dining room. He stood in the doorway, and after removing his comb from his back pocket, he quickly gave his hair a once-over, and then he leaned back against the door frame. "When are we going to eat, Mom?"

His dad moved the pot of vegetables to the far right side of the stove. "We're going to eat when supper's ready, Boy," he informed him. "And not a minute sooner."

Mrs. Palmer continued her work. "Brent, call Martha and Drew, will you? What did you hear in town today, Joshua? I'm trying to listen to you."

"I saw Elijah Bean at the post office. He says someone's taking over the old Myles Dorey place. Wanted to know if I knew anything about it seeing we live handy to there. Told him I don't know nothing about any new neighbour folks." His son moved to the stove and lifted the lid of the pot. "Brent," his dad asked him, "you seen anything of new neighbours?"

Brent answered, "When I biked by there this afternoon, I seen this red Studebaker with black fenders backed up to the house. Nice truck."

Mrs. Palmer placed the bowl of hot, peeled potatoes on the kitchen table. "It'll be nice to have another family nearby," she said. She untied her apron and dropped it onto the counter-top. "I wonder what they have for children."

"I'm glad someone's taking over that place," Mr. Palmer said. "Been empty since Cecil Hill left—must be eight years ago now. Be a shame if it deteriorated any farther. Nice house—and barn, too."

"Brent," his mother reminded him, "call Martha and Drew for supper."

"Where are they at?"

"Martha is at the pump organ, and Drew is outside somewheres."

Brent took a deep breath and raised his cupped hands to his mouth. "Martha! Drew!" he shouted loudly in the kitchen. "Supper!" The cat on the window sill near the table opened her eyes wide and stared uneasily at Brent with her ears laid back.

His mother stopped part way from the stove to the counter with the pot of vegetables and momentarily closed her eyes, "Brent, I wish you wouldn't holler in the house."

Martha, who was thirteen, came into the kitchen. "Thanks for letting me know it was supper you were calling us for," she informed Brent dryly. "I could have thought the house was on fire." Her long braid rested on one shoulder.

The kitchen door slammed, and eleven-year-old Drew stood near the stove and he glanced around at his family. "What's up, Bubs?" he asked cheerfully with his big, fake smile. And then he asked, "What's for supper, Mom?"

His dad answered, "It's a surprise."

Brent quickly added, "Because, Boy, you don't know yet what's for supper."

Drew looked over at Martha. "Did you hear about the two old guys who had just met each other?" His sister looked at him blankly. "The one guy asked the other if he was retired. The second old man said, 'No, I'm not retarded, only a little hard of hearing.'" And Drew laughed at his own joke. "Hey, here's another one," he told his family. "Three old ladies were out somewheres. The first old lady said, 'It's windy.' The second one said, 'No, it's not Wednesday, it's Thursday.' The third said, 'I'm thirsty too. Let's go get something to drink.'" Drew threw back his head and laughed again.

The hired man's clock on the shelf in the kitchen struck once. "Drew, wash your hands here at the sink," his mother told him. "It's time to eat."

Brent said, "Yeah, it would be nice if we had new neighbours. Someone I could spend time with. Go hunting—and stuff like that."

"New neighbours?" Martha asked as she flipped her braid off her shoulder.

Her dad answered her, "Family's moving into the old Myles Dorey place."

"There is? That's great! I hope there's a girl I can be friends with."

Drew looked disgusted. "A girl! I'd like to have a guy to hang out and fool around with." The water dripped from his hands to the floor at his feet. "Mom, where's the towel at?"

"Right there where it usually is." She placed sliced bread on the table and said, "It would be nice if the family were Christians."

"Yeah, that's right," Mr. Palmer agreed. He stood next to his chair at the kitchen table. "Okay, come and sit down, and we'll ask the blessing."

Sometime later, Drew asked, "Do you know what really good soup is called?" His family ignored him. "Super soup," he told them. "Super soup for supper."

"Will we be having dessert, Mom?" Brent wanted to know. He stuffed the remainder of his bread into his mouth.

"I made store-bought, instant pudding," she answered Brent. "You can get it from the cellar for me. Be careful how you carry it, will you."

When they had finished eating, Mr. Palmer remarked, "Good supper, Alice. Even the old potatoes are good the way you fix them up." He stood to leave the table, and as he turned, he glanced out the window.

"Can you help with the dishes, Martha?" Mrs. Palmer asked as she collected her apron and checked the water on the stove.

"A truck's coming along the driveway," Mr. Palmer announced as he studied the approaching vehicle.

"Oh, no!" his wife responded in alarm, "And I don't have time to get the underwear off the clothesline."

"Don't worry about it," her husband told her. "It's on the line at the back of the house."

Brent came over behind his dad and looked over his shoulder. "That's the Studebaker I seen at the old Myles Dorey place," he informed his dad, and then he used his comb to straighten up his hair. "Nice looking truck—red with black fenders." Mr. Palmer grabbed his hat and went outside closely followed by Brent.

The truck came towards the house and stopped under the maple tree. A man emerged from the cab and then leaned against the far side of the truck-box as he faced Mr. Palmer and Brent. "Hello there. Lovely evening," the man greeted pleasantly. "We've taken over the old Myles Dorey place. You know, just down the road a piece." He pointed in that direction with a tilt of his head.

"Hi. My name's Palmer—Joshua Palmer. I'm pleased to meet you." Mrs. Palmer was now at his side, and Martha and Drew were close by. "This is my wife, Alice, and these are our three children."

The man nodded at Mrs. Palmer but ignored the children. He came around the truck to where Mr. Palmer was standing. He wore gray overalls and a red plaid shirt.

"We have a bit of a problem," he revealed to Mr. Palmer as he put his hands in his overall pockets. "Our dog has run off. Jumped from the truck as soon as we got here. Not used to traveling, I guess. Just a medium-sized mutt. Black with a white tip on the end of his tail. We named him 'Tippy'. Kind of a silly name for a dog, but that's what we call him. If you see him, latch onto him. He's friendly." He removed his hat and ran his fingers through his hair.

"We haven't seen your dog around," Mrs. Palmer said as she glanced at her children, "but if we do, we'll let you know."

"Well, thanks," he replied as he put his hat on. "We don't want to cause any trouble." The man turned to get back into the cab and saw Brent studying his truck.

"Like my truck, Boy?"

The teen nodded.

"Fifty-one Studebaker. Had her since new. Change the oil regularly. Keep proper air pressure in the tires. Don't let nobody else work on her. And don't let nobody else drive her." Brent nodded once more and shoved his hands deep into his pockets. He took two steps back from the truck.

Mrs. Palmer spoke up, "Our children are anxious to know if you have any children. We don't have any close neighbours with children."

The man stared at her for several seconds. He began to smile, and then threw back his head and laughed. "Children! Nope! What would we do with children? More mouths to feed. They need clothes. They don't earn their keep. Hardly do what they're told." He laughed uneasily.

Mr. Palmer felt he had to say something positive. "Well, we're proud of our children."

"Well, sure," the man told him sincerely. "Some folks can handle it, others can't."

Mr. Palmer shrugged his shoulders. "Well, I best get a move-along," the man said, and he opened the truck door. "Nice to meet you folks." He paused with one foot on the running-board. "Name's 'Brooster'. Rhymes with 'rooster'. B. r. o. o. s. t. e. r."

"Nice to meet you, Mr. Brooster," Mr. Palmer said and nodded.

His wife added, "We'll be on the lookout for your dog, Tippy."

Mr. Brooster gave a quick nod, and climbed into his truck, started the engine and backed away from under the tree.

"He's a nice neighbour—I think," Mrs. Palmer remarked to her family. They watched the truck as it went along the driveway and turned onto Hannah Road. "I wonder what his wife is like."

Mr. Palmer and the two boys had chores in the barn, and Mrs. Palmer and Martha returned to the house. When the work in the kitchen was completed, Mrs. Palmer and Martha sat on the swings hanging from the large spruce tree between the house and the barn. After about a minute, Martha was swinging at maximum height, causing the tree above them to rotate back and forth. Mrs. Palmer was content to swing at a much slower pace. "This could be dangerous," Martha piped up.

"Well," her mother replied, "you sure are going high."

"No. My braid keeps slapping me." Martha let the swing slow down, and several minutes later Mr. Palmer and the boys came from the barn over to where Mrs. Palmer and Martha were.

"Hey, Martha," Drew called out to her, "come take a gander at what me and Brent do in the stable." The two boys left for the barn, and Martha jumped from the swing and followed them.

Mr. Palmer sat on the swing Martha had vacated. "Mind if I join you, Alice?"

"I was hoping you would," she replied and smiled at him. They swung back and forth slowly, out of sync, with the thick spruce trunk between them.

A minute or two later, Mrs. Palmer stopped swinging and brought her heels up against an exposed, crooked root. "I'm very concerned about Brent," she said. "He's stubborn about admitting he's a sinner, and I'm afraid he's going to discourage Drew from becoming a believer. Sometimes he gives Martha a hard time about her faith."

Mr. Palmer nodded in agreement. "But what more can we do?" he wondered aloud.

Suddenly Martha emerged from the barn and hurried along the path towards her parents. "Mom, do you know what the boys do in the stable? They catch flies in their bare hands," she said in disgust. "When they see a fly on the wall or the window sill, they give one quick clap just over the fly, and it goes right into their hands." She had her fists on her hips as she looked over at her brothers who were approaching.

"Yeah, I caught nine flies," Brent said proudly.

"I got only six," Drew admitted.

"Look at your hands, Brent!" his mother blurted out. "No, Drew! Don't wipe your hands on your pants!"

"Must be a boy," his father remarked as he shook his head.

Mrs. Palmer stood up. "Come, Martha, help me get the clothes in before they get damp from the evening air."

Later, just before dark, Brent, who had been outside, opened the kitchen door and shouted into the house where his parents and sister were. "Mr. Brooster is coming along the driveway. 'Brooster' rhymes with 'rooster'. B. r. o. o. s. t. e. r."

"Why would he be here again so soon?" Mrs. Palmer wondered aloud.

"Maybe he found his dog," Martha replied, "and he wants to let us know. It'll be nice when we have telephones in this area."

Brent added, "Yeah, and then we'll be able to listen in and find out what's going on—who did what and stuff like that." He removed his comb from his back pocket and dragged it through his hair several times.

Mr. Palmer got up from his chair and went outside. Mrs. Palmer and Martha followed. "Maybe his wife came this time," Mrs. Palmer remarked to Martha.

The Studebaker came to a stop under the maple tree, and Mr. Brooster climbed out and leaned against the truck-box facing the Palmer family. Drew came from behind the house and lowered himself into the tall grasses nearby.

"Hello there. Nice evening," Mr. Brooster greeted before Mr. Palmer could say anything. "We've taken over the old Myles Dorey place. You know, just over a bit." He pointed with his head in that direction.

Mr. Palmer said nothing but stared at him. Mrs. Palmer's mouth dropped open. *He must have forgotten he was here earlier,* she decided.

Mr. Brooster came around the truck to where the Palmers were standing. Martha held her long braid in one hand. She could see he was wearing a blue plaid shirt under his navy blue overalls. Her eyes widened.

"We have a bit of a problem," the man began. He lowered his hands into his overall pockets. "Our dog has taken off. Bolted from the truck as soon as we got here. Doesn't like traveling in the truck. He's just a mutt—medium size. Mostly black but with a white tip on his tail. We call him, 'Tippy'. Kind of a funny name for a dog, but 'Tippy' it is. If you see him, grab onto him; friendly dog, he is." After removing his hat, he ran his fingers through his hair.

Mrs. Palmer stared at him and blinked several times. *I must be dreaming,* she tried to reason. *We've already experienced this a couple hours ago.* She stepped closer to her husband. Drew pulled on a long piece of timothy grass, held it between his lips, and looked thoughtful.

"We haven't seen your dog," Mrs. Palmer heard herself say. "But when we do, we'll be sure to let you know." She tried to smile.

"Well, thanks," Mr. Brooster answered, and he returned his hat to his head. "We don't want to inconvenience anyone."

Brent moved over to the truck and made out he was studying it.

"Like my truck, Boy?"

"Yeah," Brent answered with a sly grin.

"Fifty-one Studebaker," Mr. Brooster told him. "Had her since new. Change the oil regularly. Keep the tires properly inflated. Don't let nobody else work on her. Don't let nobody else drive her." Brent nodded and tried not to laugh.

Drew bit off a piece of grass stem and spit it out over his shoulder, and Martha continued to grasp her braid. Neither Mr. nor Mrs. Palmer knew what to say. Brent seemed to be enjoying this peculiar occasion. He turned to Mr. Brooster. "Do you have any children?" he asked, looking innocent and trying to keep a straight face.

Mrs. Palmer gasped. She stared at Brent and then Mr. Brooster. *No! This can't be happening! I must be dreaming!*

Mr. Brooster stared at Brent for several long seconds. He began to smile and then he threw back his head and laughed. "Children! What would we do with children?" he asked in amazement as he glanced at Brent's parents. "More mouths to feed. Clothes to buy. They never earn their keep. Don't do what they're told." He laughed again.

Mr. Palmer did not know what to think. *We've already had this conversation. I'll keep it going and see what happens.* "Well," Mr. Palmer told him, "we're proud of our children."

"Well, that's good," Mr. Brooster said genuinely. "Some folks can handle it; others can't." Brent began to giggle, and his dad found himself shrugging his shoulder just as he had done earlier that evening.

"Well, I better get a move-along," Mr. Brooster said as he opened his truck door. "Nice to meet you folks," he said pleasantly. Before getting into the truck, he paused with one foot on the running-board. "Name's 'Brooster'. Rhymes with 'rooster'. B. r. o. o. s. t. e. r."

Mrs. Palmer heard Brent stifle a laugh. The young man turned to face the other direction with his back to Mr. Brooster, and when he could not hold his laughter any longer, he moved quickly around to the backside of the house. Drew looked thoughtful as he continued to chew off pieces of stem and spit them out to the side. Martha stared at Mr. Brooster, and Mr. and Mrs. Palmer stood there saying nothing but looking stunned. Brent's muffled laughter could be heard faintly in the distance.

Martha spoke up, "If we see Tippy, we'll let you know." Mr. Brooster nodded, acknowledging Martha for the first time. After climbing into his truck and starting the engine, he backed away from the tree, turned around, and drove along the driveway.

Mr. and Mrs. Palmer stared at the truck as it left. Brent came around from the other side of the house laughing so hard he could not speak. He kept slapping his thigh and turning in circles. Mr. Palmer had a frown on his face. "I don't know what to think," he said to his family.

Mrs. Palmer looked bewildered and concerned. "Maybe he's a little senile," she answered.

"Well, I don't know," her husband replied as he glanced in the direction the truck had gone, but it was now out of sight. Brent was still laughing, and his parents could not help but snicker, too.

"What's senile?" Martha wanted to know, looking to her mom as Brent took a deep breath and collapsed exhausted and quiet on the grass a few feet away.

"It's when an older person's mind doesn't work properly," Mrs. Palmer informed Martha.

Martha turned to her mom. "Mr. Brooster's an identical twin," she stated. "I hope they find their dog."

Brent ignored her. He propped himself up on one elbow and faced his family. "I think he's one brick short of a load," he said seriously but then broke into laughter again at his latest pronouncement.

"Brent," his dad said sternly, "don't talk like that."

Drew bit off the last of the timothy stem and placed the long cylindrical green flower over his ear. "I'm going to find Mr. Brooster's dog, Tippy," he announced with determination and with his fake smile.

"Yeah, sure you are," Brent said sarcastically, "and I'm going to adjust the carburetor of the Studebaker."

Drew's family looked over at him reclining in the tall grass and appearing confident. Martha demanded, "And how are you going to do that?"

Drew's fake smile grew larger, and the timothy flower slipped from his ear. "I have my ways," he said assuredly, surveying his family members. He stood up. "See you later, Bubs." And he politely nodded to his two siblings and then headed for the hayloft in the barn.

Brent started for the house. "What's to eat, Mom?" he asked over his shoulder.

Mr. and Mrs. Palmer and Martha followed, and when they had entered the kitchen, Brent got out his comb and smoothed back his hair. He asked again, "What's to eat, Mom?"

Mrs. Palmer removed the knife from the drawer and cut a slice of bread from one of the loaves she had baked that afternoon. "Martha, would you butter these pieces as I slice them? Where's Drew? Brent, call Drew, will you—I think he's in the barn. And Brent, don't forget to wash your hands."

Mr. Palmer came into the kitchen with a jar of milk as Brent took a deep breath.

"Brent," his dad promptly told him with a scowl, "don't holler in the house. Holler outside if you have to."

Brent opened the kitchen door, and although his younger brother was just outside the door, he leaned out and bellowed loudly, "Drew!" Drew immediately snuck into the house and quietly positioned himself several feet inside the door. When his mother saw him standing there casually, she gasped in surprise.

Brent turned back into the kitchen. "Dad," he began, "I'd like to make a go-cart using the wheels from my old wagon. I figured out how to rig up a steering wheel. Mind if I use the steering wheel from the junked car the other side of the stone wall?"

His dad nodded. "There's boards in the shed you can use, too. Help yourself. I'll give you a hand tomorrow evening if you like." And he could tell his son was pleased with his offer.

"Mom," Martha asked, "is raisin bread just ordinary bread with raisins mixed in?"

"Oh, no, it isn't. It's the basic recipe but with raisins, cinnamon, and a bit more sugar."

"Can I help you next time you make raisin bread?"

"Alright," she answered and grinned at her.

Drew reached over and picked up a slice of bread which Martha had just buttered, and he bit off a chunk. "Drew," his mother asked in alarm, "are your hands clean?"

"Clean as a sturgeon's," he calmly replied, and then he laughed in a silly fashion.

"Your hands are clean as a surgeon's," Martha corrected him.

"Are you sure your hands are clean, Drew?" his mother quizzed him.

"Sure I'm sure," he replied. "And Martha just said so, and she's always right; well she thinks she's always right." He laughed again and then said, "Hey, did you know," he questioned no one in particular, "that some animals have much better hearing than people do? Some sounds are a lot louder to them than to us. In fact dogs can hear sounds we can't hear."

After the three Palmer children had finished their lunch and gone up to bed, Mr. Palmer sat at the kitchen table with his papers. He was drawing plans for the barn lean-to and determining what materials he needed. Mrs. Palmer was at the kitchen cot nearby sewing patches on the knees of Drew's overalls.

About a quarter of an hour later, the hired man's clock struck ten times. Since Mr. Palmer had completed his sketch and list of materials required for the barn lean-to and Mrs. Palmer had finished her sewing job, he switched off the light, and they retired to their room next to the kitchen.

Mr. Palmer had left for work when his three children came down for breakfast the next morning. Brent and Martha were already eating when Drew came into the kitchen and sat at the table. "What's for breakfast, Mom?" he asked, and before she could answer, he gave his brother and sister a big fake smile. "Morning, Bub and Bub," he greeted pleasantly, but they ignored him as he continued his silly grin in their direction. "I have a question," he announced after he had assumed a serious expression. "What is black when it's clean and white when it's dirty?" No one responded. "A black-board," he exclaimed with another fake grin.

After breakfast, Brent went outside. He crossed through the orchard and climbed over the stone wall to where the old car was rusting away in the weeds and tall grasses. Martha returned to her room where the morning sunlight coming in was diffused by the large maple tree outside her window. She sat on her bed for her daily, private time with the Lord. Drew obtained several small pieces of meat from his mom, and after cutting them into half-inch segments with the butcher knife, he put his cap on and started along the driveway to the gravel road.

After Brent worked several minutes at removing the steering wheel, he selected suitable boards from the shed and gathered up a saw and hammer along with a variety of nails. He spread these out on a flat area of ground near the shed along with the wheels and axles from his old wagon. "Now, I want it to be as simple as possible," he said aloud. "Don't want it to be too heavy."

Martha opened her Bible and turned to the passage she had been reading the past few days. Before she began reading, she asked the Lord to help her understand and learn, or be reminded of things she needed from His Word at this time in her life. As she read the verses she considered what they meant to the original readers and how they could apply to her today. Finally, she prayed that she would be able to put into practice what the Holy Spirit had shown her.

* * *

Drew turned at the end of their driveway and walked along Hannah Road in the opposite direction from the old Myles Dorey place. He carried the meat pieces in a tin can and casually whistled a nonsense tune as he trekked by the mixed woods on both sides of the road. He was not in a hurry, and he purposely made his presence known.

Just before the bridge spanning the Crazy Man River, he could see off to his right, a black dog crouched under a spruce tree studying him as he noisily passed by.

* * *

Brent cut a thick, wide board to the length he needed for the base of the go-cart, and he secured the two metal wagon axles along the length of two shorter, narrow boards. Over the rear axle he built a seat with a high back-rest. The seat was tipped slightly allowing the driver to lean back. Behind the front axle, he nailed a cross-piece to brace the driver's feet against, allowing plenty of room for the axle to swivel. Next he located a piece of round firewood, three or four inches in diameter, and he screwed the steering wheel to one end. He then tied one end of the rope close to one of the front wheels and coiled it around the steering wheel shaft several times before he fastened the other end of the rope next to the other front wheel. Finally he hammered a couple nails through the rope to the steering wheel shaft. He turned the steering wheel in one direction and then the other and grinned in satisfaction. After giving the wheels a good oiling, he stood back from his go-cart and viewed it from one side and then the front.

Brent quickly glanced up at the house, took a deep breath, and bellowed, "Drew!" There was no response. He pushed his comb through his hair and then returned it to his back pocket. "Drew," he called again, but louder. "Come!"

Martha, who was sifting flour at the kitchen table, looked up from her work and out the window. "Mom, come have a look at what Brent has built." She crossed over to the window carrying the sifter. "It's a go-cart. And it even has a real steering wheel."

"Be careful not to get any flour on the floor, Martha," her mother instructed her. "Why, yes, it's a go-cart," she said when she had joined Martha at the window. "Brent knows how to build working things. He's mechanically inclined."

Brent could again be heard calling his brother. "Drew went looking for Tippy," Mrs. Palmer said to Martha who returned to the table with the sifter.

Martha replied, "I'd like to give Brent's go-cart a try."

Drew stopped, faced right-angle to Tippy, and reached into the can containing the meat pieces. He drew out a small chunk of meat, and without facing the dog he made smacking noises with his mouth. He then turned and took several steps towards home, stopped once more, and ignored the dog as he lifted out the same piece of meat. Again he made noisy eating sounds in full view of Tippy. He did this several times, moving farther away from the dog.

Drew snuck a quick look. He could see the runaway mutt was watching him intently from his crouched position under the tree. He drew out the piece of meat once more and made an exaggerated show of placing it carefully on the road. He then briskly walked off along the road towards home. He stopped and looked quickly behind him.

Tippy was cautiously stepping onto the road from the shallow ditch at the spot where Drew had placed the small chunk of meat. When he looked again, he could see Tippy sniffing at the piece of meat.

Drew figured without looking that Tippy would be watching him. He put another piece of meat on the road and again walked away, but this time even faster. As he quickly came to a halt, he glanced back and saw Tippy snatch up the second piece of meat.

Drew dropped a third piece and started running towards home. About ten or fifteen yards along, he skidded to a stop, and with his back to the dog, he stood in the road with his hands to his side. He held the can with the meat against his thigh and waited.

As Drew stood motionless, he heard nothing, but about a minute later, with his hand over the open mouth of the tin can, he felt the warm breath of the dog on his fingers followed by its cold nose. Drew suddenly took off running, and as he ran he held a piece of meat in his hand stretched back with the can up at his chest. Tippy ran along behind him, and when the dog touched his hand, he released the meat. Drew did this several times as he came closer to his driveway.

"Hey, Brent," Martha called out when she closed the door and crossed through the grass towards him. "Can I try your go-cart?"

"Yeah, sure." He grinned at her as he climbed into the seat. "But first, you push me. I need to test my go-cart."

Martha positioned herself behind the go-cart, leaned over, and shoved against the seat. As she pushed the go-cart along, her braid rested on her brother's shoulder. Brent steered towards the driveway, and when they reached its smooth surface, he shouted out, "Faster, faster!" Martha pushed Brent down the driveway, and as they sped along he steered from one side to the other.

Suddenly Brent stared down the driveway and lifted one hand from the wheel and pointed to the road ahead. Martha looked up from her bent-over posture. She let go of the seat and stood on the hard-packed dirt as the go-cart coasted to a stop. "That's Drew," Brent said in hushed amazement as he leaned forward over the steering wheel.

"And look—there's a dog with him," Martha added excitedly as she watched her younger brother casually but confidently walk along the road.

"Drew found Tippy!" Brent blurted out. "I don't believe it. And Tippy's following Drew without a leash or nothing."

Drew turned his head and looked over at his stunned brother and sister. "Morning, Bub and Bub," he acknowledged courteously with his big fake smile and without slackening his pace.

"He's heading over to where Mr. Brooster lives," Brent said to Martha, and he signalled for her to come. "Come on, let's go. Quick, push me."

"No, wait, we better not," Martha insisted as she stepped closer. "We might spook Tippy and scare him off."

"I have an idea," Brent said. "Let them get ahead, and then we'll go down to the road and wait. When we see them go onto Mr. Brooster's driveway, we'll go along the road to there."

Brent and Martha did not have to wait long before their younger brother and the dog were out of sight at the far side of the alders in the ditch at the end of their driveway. Martha leaned over again and began to push Brent in his go-cart to the end of their driveway. They stopped and watched Drew and Tippy go along the road, and about a minute later they could see them turn off onto Mr. Brooster's driveway.

"Okay, now," Brent ordered from the seat of the go-cart. "Let's go. Push, Martha." He grasped the wheel tightly and leaned forward.

"No, it's my turn to drive."

"Come on. Don't waste time. I want to see what happens. Don't you?"

His sister turned to go back to the house. "Yeah, that would be nice, but I have other things to do," she informed him. Brent rotated in his seat and faced her. "You know how to steer?"

Martha shrugged her shoulders. Brent got up out of the seat and positioned himself behind it. He asked again, "Do you know how to steer? I don't want my go-cart to get smashed."

She lowered herself onto the seat and then threw back her braid behind her, hitting her brother in the face. After she placed her hands on the steering wheel, Brent began to push. Martha called out, "Faster, faster!"

"Are you sure you know how to steer?" he asked again as he ran behind the go-cart.

Martha turned from their driveway onto the Hannah Road and told him, "Faster, Brent! Faster!"

When they approached Mr. Brooster's driveway, Martha turned in, and Brent ceased pushing. When the go-cart came to a stop on the dirt, Martha climbed out and stood beside her panting brother. "There's Drew," Brent said to Martha between his heavy breathing.

"And there's Mr. Brooster coming from the barn," Martha added as Brent reached into his pocket for his comb and tidied up his hair.

Tippy left Drew, ran towards Mr. Brooster, and placed his front paws on his master's chest. Drew stood motionless beside the lilac bushes with his hands in his pockets. Tippy barked constantly and ran in wide circles around Mr. Brooster as the man walked towards the waiting boy.

Brent and Martha could see Mr. Brooster was now talking with Drew. "What's Mr. Brooster saying?" Brent wondered.

"I don't know. Tippy's so hyper I can't hear what's going on."

Drew looked towards his brother and sister, and Mr. Brooster followed his gaze. Brent waved, and Mr. Brooster signalled them to come. Brent climbed into the go-cart. "Come on, Martha, push."

Martha pushed her brother in his go-cart along Mr. Brooster's driveway. Tippy was running excitedly in circles and barking, and Mr. Brooster and Drew were watching the dog until Brent and Martha rolled up to them. Mr. Brooster commanded his dog, "Make yourself scarce." Tippy trotted over to the door of the house and crouched down facing his master and the three Palmer children.

"Nice to have a visit from the neighbours," Mr. Brooster said, and then he spoke to Drew. "Thanks again for finding Tippy and bringing him to us. Thanks very much." Mr. Brooster smiled and nodded at him and then asked, "What's your name, Boy?"

"Drew," he answered, and he glanced over at Tippy still crouched by the door and studying the three children.

"Drew," Mr. Brooster repeated. Brent climbed from the go-cart and glanced around looking for the Studebaker which was nowhere in sight, and Martha stood holding her braid in one hand.

Tippy's ears suddenly perked up, and he rose to his feet. The Studebaker was coming along the Hannah Road. It slowed and turned onto the driveway and moved towards them as they waited. The truck stopped under the oak tree, and after the engine was shut off, the driver got out and stepped around in view of Mr. Brooster and the three children. Tippy wagged his tail and then ran towards the man and placed his front paws on his chest.

Brent's eyes opened wide, and his mouth dropped open. He looked from this man and then to Mr. Brooster and then back to the man who just drove in. Tippy ran in wide circles and barked excitedly.

"Make yourself scarce," the man ordered, and the dog again moved to the door of the house and crouched down facing the small group of people in the yard. The man then addressed the children. "Nice to have a visit from the neighbours. How are you doing?" The children stood there saying nothing.

Mr. Brooster informed the man, "This here young fellow brought Tippy home to us." He pointed to Drew.

The man looked at Drew. "Thanks for finding Tippy and bringing him home to us. Thanks very much." He smiled and nodded at him. "What's your name, Boy?"

"Drew."

"Drew," the man repeated and nodded. Mr. Brooster then turned and asked Brent, "You built this here go-cart, Young Man?"

"Yes, Sir."

The other Mr. Brooster commented, "Did a fine job, I'd say." Both men stood side by side with their hands in their pockets as they examined the go-cart from one end to the other. "Good idea for the steering wheel," one of the men remarked. "From a Model A Ford."

The other man asked, "Rig it up yourself, Boy?"

Brent answered, "Yeah."

One Mr. Brooster scratched his chin and said, "Rope's going to get a bit slack after a while." The Brooster brothers moved around the go-cart as they were speaking.

The other Mr. Brooster added, "What you need is a couple of springs—you know, those coil bed-springs."

The other man continued, "One spring on the end of each rope near the axle there. That should do the trick."

The other added, "The spring would take care of the slack." Brent was finding it confusing keeping straight which Mr. Brooster said what.

"But I don't got no springs," Brent answered.

"Think I saw some of them springs in the shed," Mr. Brooster remembered.

The other man informed him, "You can have a couple of them, Boy."

The other one said, "We'll help you put them on."

"Thanks," Brent managed to say, looking from one to the other.

"Come." The Brooster brothers turned and walked side by side through the long grass towards the shed. Brent followed, and his sister and brother walked behind and were joined by Tippy.

⁂

When Mr. Palmer arrived home before supper, the children related to their parents what had taken place that morning. Martha told her dad, "When Drew found Tippy, he took him to the Brooster's. He knew how to catch him, and he led him without a rope."

Drew sat at his place at the table with his fake grin. "When we get a dog," he announced, "I'm going to call him 'Mister'."

"Mister!" Martha quickly piped up in surprise. "What if it's a girl?"

"Dogs should be boys," Drew answered firmly. "Cats are girls." Martha rolled her eyes to express her disapproval, and her dad snickered.

Brent interjected, "Mr. Brooster gave me some springs for the steering ropes, and then they put them on for me. Works real good."

Drew changed the subject. "They said they were going to bake a strawberry-rhubarb-raisin pie this afternoon. Our whole family is to come over after supper and help them eat it up. Can we go, Mom? Can we go?"

Mrs. Palmer grinned, and looked to her husband.

"Sure," Mr. Palmer decided. "Why not! Right after supper. I'd like to visit with Mr. Brooster and Mr. Brooster."

Martha spoke up, "Didn't I tell you they were identical twins?"

After supper without dessert, the Palmer family trooped over to the old Myles Dorey place where their new neighbours the Brooster brothers were living. Mr. and Mrs. Palmer and Martha walked, and Brent and Drew took turns riding in the go-cart. When the Palmers neared the house with the Studebaker truck parked under the oak tree, Tippy jumped up from his crouched position at the kitchen door. The dog ran in circles around them, barking excitedly as they came along the driveway.

Mr. Brooster opened the kitchen door. "Lovely evening, isn't it?" he greeted, holding a dishcloth. "Nice to see you all again."

The other Mr. Brooster, out of sight inside, called out, "Come on in, folks. Good to see you again."

When the Palmer family entered the large farm kitchen, the other Mr. Brooster dropped the dishcloth in the sink and dried his hands. Both Brooster brothers stood leaning back against the counter with their arms folded across their chests. "Have a seat," one of them offered.

"We have enough chairs for everyone," the other added, and then he grinned and asked, "Who wants a piece of rhubarb-strawberry-raisin pie?"

"I do!" Brent told them. He sat with his elbows on the table.

The other twin said, "Baked it just this afternoon. Still warm."

"Some good!" his brother contributed as he positioned the pie in the centre of the table. The other brother carried over seven small plates.

Drew asked, "Did you hear about the guy in the restaurant who complained there was a little bug in his soup?" His mother was beginning to appear uneasy.

The Brooster brothers looked at Drew and grinned. Drew continued, "The waiter said, 'I can get you a bigger bug if you like.'"

Both Brooster brothers laughed in unison. "That's a good one," they both replied.

One Mr. Brooster looked at Drew. "Knock, knock," he said.

"Who's there?" Drew quickly asked him with a grin.

"Boo."

The boy responded, "Boo who?"

Mr. Brooster replied, "Don't cry, it's only a game."

While everyone was eating, Mrs. Palmer noticed a Scripture text on the wall behind the woodstove. "You must be Christians," she remarked. "So are we."

"No, we're not," one of the brothers informed her.

The other brother said, "We were brought up in a typical Christian home—our parents were believers. I'm sure they had the truth."

The other brother continued, "We've heard the gospel preached many times. Been to lots of gospel meetings in fact. But we haven't seen the gospel lived out. Know what I mean? Haven't seen lives changed except acted out in a religious, non-practical way."

Mr. Palmer spoke up, "Scripture does say that those who put their faith in Him are new creatures; old things are passed away; behold all things are new. And we are told to work out our salvation. Much in the epistles tell us how to live in a practical way. And our lives shouldn't be, like you say, acted out in a religious way by observing things which really do not matter in our everyday lives."

The Broosters listened respectfully, and Mrs. Palmer continued. "Don't let anyone, even believers, rob you of the salvation that God has provided, and don't let anyone discourage you from having the joy He intends for you to have." The two men looked thoughtful, and there was a long pause.

Brent broke the silence. "Can I have another piece of pie?"

Later that evening, the Palmer family was conversing in their kitchen. "Didn't I tell you they were identical twins?" Martha reminded her family once more. "They were pleased with the loaf of raisin bread we left them. They said they had never baked raisin bread before."

"Mr. Brooster, which ever," Brent informed his family, "says I can come over, and he'll show me how to adjust the carburetor of the Studebaker." He grinned broadly. "Maybe I'll even get to help change the oil and do stuff like that." He pulled his comb from his pocket and began to comb his hair.

Drew spoke up, "Mr. Brooster and Mr. Brooster like my jokes," he said to his family. He gave them his big fake smile as he glanced around at them.

"Drew," his dad addressed him, "I have a riddle for you." The boy looked pleased and waited. "I heard this one a long time ago—I was about your age. What is as light as air but a strong man can't hold it for more than a few minutes?"

Brent paused his combing. "How can that be!"

Their dad hesitated and then told them, "A strong man's breath is as light as air, and he can't hold it for more than a few minutes."

"Good one, Dad," Drew informed him. "I like it. I'll have to remember that one."

"Well, Alice," Mr. Palmer said after the children had left for the night, "we never know what or who the Lord will send our way for our good as well as theirs." He leaned back against the counter and smoothed his mustache with his thumb and forefinger.

Mrs. Palmer concluded, "Maybe the Lord will use us to encourage the Brooster brothers in the Lord."

chapter eight

four years later—summer 1962

Making Tracks

Fifteen-year-old Drew bounded up onto the wooden landing, but before he opened the door, he looked back over his shoulder to the path he had just run along through the woods behind the house. "Just checking," he stated to himself. After entering the little building, he left the door ajar and dropped his package on the table. He lowered himself to his hands and knees beside the bunk bed, and once more he glanced through the door he had left open. When he was satisfied no one had followed him, he dragged out from under the far side of the lower bed, an old metal toolbox. He opened it, leaning its scuffed-up lid back against the bedpost. He lifted out the canvas bag, loosened the draw strings and dumped the contents on the floor at his knees. Grinning broadly, he picked up the things and placed them on the table with the package he had brought with him this afternoon.

Drew positioned his chair at the table allowing him to see through the open door and along the path, and then he began to work on his project. He thought, *I'm glad I can come back here and work in private.* He surveyed the walls of his cabin and the bunk bed behind him. *I love this place I built here. Well, Dad showed me how to do it—how to think it through, each step of the way and then left me to work on it during the day when he couldn't be here. I like to hammer, especially those big nails—spikes, that's what they're called. And I like to saw, too. I think Dad enjoyed working here as much as I did. I didn't mind the help from Brent or even Martha, but I prefer to do the work myself. Gives me satisfaction and pride in what I do.*

Drew again quickly looked around his personal retreat. *Uncle Bob gave me most of the lumber here. Said every man needs to build a house some time in his life, but I hardly feel I'm a man—only fifteen and a half. Martha tells me to grow up, don't act so childish. Brent says, 'Act your age, not your shoe size.' That's no fun. I don't see Brent and Martha having much fun.* He picked up a small nail and then his hammer. *Mom says I look like Uncle Bob. Don't know how that can be—he has a mustache.* Drew instinctively reached up and touched his face above his upper lip. *Saw a few hairs there the other day,* he remembered. *Mom says she's glad Dad has a mustache. Yeah, I guess a mustache is alright, but could get in the way when a guy blows his nose. Mustaches are something men have. Aunt Eva says men should look like men, and women should look like women. Makes sense.* He turned his project over to inspect the other side. *Women and girls are alright, I guess, but I'm glad I'm a guy.*

Drew leaned over and grabbed the piece of rubber innertube which had tumbled to the floor. *Dad has given me more jobs to do around the place. At first I didn't like the extra work, but when I realized the jobs were grown-up jobs Dad couldn't get to, I didn't mind doing them. And I like to do things when I need to use my strength. They're man-jobs, that's what they are. And I have a lot more strength now than I did a few years ago, I tell you.* He measured the rubber and cut it to size. *I can see now that the jobs I do are important, and our family is better off because the jobs are done and done right. I have to admit, I like working; in fact I like working hard.*

Nearly two hours after arriving at his cabin, Drew was startled to see Brent coming towards him on his bicycle. He quickly shoved his project into the canvas bag along with the loose pieces on the table. He set his hammer on the floor and planted his foot over it.

His older brother came to a stop just short of the cabin landing. "Drew," he scolded as he stood there straddling his bicycle, "don't you know it's supper time?" Drew looked at him with a blank expression, and Brent added with a scowl, "Can't you tell time, Boy?"

Drew stood up and removed his watch from the front pocket of his denim overalls. "Oh, yeah, it's after five. Time to eat," he admitted. "Maybe that's why I'm so hungry." He gave Brent a big fake grin. "And my stomach's been growling, too." Brent looked at him with exaggerated amazement and then rolled his eyes. He turned his bicycle around and headed back to the house without waiting for his brother. Drew watched him go out of sight. "I try to not worry about things I don't have to worry about." And he snickered.

Drew lowered the bag into his metal box. "Sure hope Brent didn't notice this here stuff," he said aloud, and he dropped his tools onto the metal tray and returned the tray to its box. After he pushed the box back under the bunk and stepped out onto the landing, he closed the door and started his several-hundred-yard jog to the house for his supper.

After the evening meal, Mr. Palmer and his two sons left the house. "Mister, you stay," Drew ordered his puppy who was tied up outside the porch. The fellows crossed the yard to the barn lean-to leaving the disappointed young dog behind.

Drew entered the building and took hold of the shovel leaning against the wall. "Might need that there bush-saw, too," his dad advised them. Brent picked up the saw, and Drew raised the shovel to his shoulder. The three fellows left the area, ignoring the whining of Drew's puppy.

As they passed through the apple trees, Mr. Palmer reached up and twisted off an apple. He cupped it in both hands, and as he walked along, he snapped it in two and bit into one of the halves.

"Where do you have in mind, Drew?" his dad asked when they reached the area of the cabin, and as he munched on his apple.

"I figure over there this side of that oak tree and just beyond them young spruces." Mr. Palmer nodded, and Brent grabbed the shovel from Drew and tossed the saw onto a tiny spruce tree. Brent began to dig a hole into the floor of the woods, and Drew used the saw to remove several of the nearby spruce saplings. Their dad bit into the second half of his apple and pulled the spruce trees out of the way with one hand and dragged them back into the woods. When Brent hit a rock with the shovel, he dug around it. Drew quickly discarded the saw and leaned into the hole. After he lifted the rock out, he dropped it into a nearby hollow.

Neither Mr. Palmer nor his two sons spoke as they worked at the hole. Their dad leaned against a birch tree with one outstretched arm. There was a slight smile on his face as he watched his sons. Brent used his shovel to lift dirt out of the hole and Drew knelt on the ground and spread the earth out with his hands. Several minutes later Brent stopped digging and leaned on the top of the shovel. "Deep enough?"

Their dad and Drew peered down into the hole. "Looks good to me," Mr. Palmer informed them. "Let's build a skid, and then with the truck, we'll drag that outhouse back to here before dark."

Over the next few days, Drew worked on his project in the cabin when he had the opportunity between chores around the house. *I'm glad Brent's away working for Uncle Bob,* he considered, *and Martha doesn't come here often.* He cut several pieces of tube and said aloud with his overdone grin, "I need the privacy." He looked over at his puppy stretched out in the sun in the doorway. "And look, Mister, I'm just about finished," he added with satisfaction. The young dog looked up at him, thumped his tail a couple times, and went back to his nap. "Practicing your snooze, are you, Mister?"

During supper meal the next day, Mr. Palmer commented, "Saw strange tracks in the garden before I left for work this morning."

Drew helped himself to another cob of corn. "Strange tracks," he repeated as the hired man's clock struck the hour. "What kind of strange tracks?" He looked over at his dad with an innocent face.

"Drew," his mom interrupted, "Mister is under the table again. Will you please make sure that dog stays over by the door when we eat. We want him to be properly trained."

Drew dragged his dog over to the door between the kitchen and the porch. "Stay, Boy," he ordered as he shook his finger at him, and then he added, "It hardly seems fair, does it, Mister? You have to stay back but the cat - she has the run of the place—and all the time, too. I sure can see why we call her 'Princess'."

"What's for dessert, Mom?" Brent wanted to know as he mopped a piece of bread across his plate.

Martha threw back her long braid and replied, "We could have that raspberry pie I made this morning, Mom."

"Raspberry pie sounds good," her dad told her as he looked to his wife. "Any ice cream, Alice?"

After supper, Martha, who was playing the pump organ in the living room, called to Drew as he was about to leave the house. She entered the kitchen and held out to him a paper bag with something in it. "This is a house-warming, I mean, cabin-warming, gift for you."

He took the bag and peeked into it. "What!" he blurted out and then abruptly closed the bag. "Why would I want this?" He then slowly opened it again, and as he drew out the contents part way, he looked appalled. "It's pink and has pretty little flowers all over it."

"Yeah, I know." Martha grinned at her brother. "It's to dress up your outhouse a bit. So maybe it's an outhouse-warming gift."

"Well, thanks—I think," Drew replied. "An outhouse-warming gift." He pushed the roll down into the bag, tightly folded the opening several times and awkwardly held it. "Why would I want to dress up the outhouse?"

Martha muttered, "You must be a guy."

"Thanks for the compliment, Girl," Drew replied.

A day or two later, Drew retrieved his bicycle from the barn lean-to. He called out to his mom working in the garden, "Bye. Be back." She waved in acknowledgment, and he hopped on his bike and pedaled down the driveway. After he turned onto the Hannah Road, he quickly glanced back to the rat-trap gripping his bulging canvas bag over the rear wheel. He sped up and grinned as he envisioned once more what he planned to do this afternoon.

About a quarter of an hour later, Drew could see up ahead in a dip in the dirt road, the wooden bridge which spanned the Crazy Man River. *I hope no one's there,* he anticipated, *or stops when I'm there.* He crossed the one-lane bridge, and after quickly surveying the road in both directions, he turned off and rode his bike along a narrow trail above the river's edge. Behind a clump of spruce trees nearby, he dismounted his bicycle, but before removing his bag, he scanned the surrounding area. When he was satisfied no one was in the area, he released the bag from the rat-trap and lowered his bicycle into the tall grasses and the Queen Anne's lace. Drew sat on a rock and dumped out from the canvas bag the two parts of his project. He pushed his running shoes into the footwear he had made, and as he stood up, he grinned and then carefully walked along the path carrying his empty bag.

A vehicle could be heard coming along the dirt road. Drew turned and anxiously watched the truck approach the bridge. "It's Mr. Brooster, whichever," he muttered under his breath, and he squatted down in the tall grass. The Studebaker slowed as it crossed the bridge and then accelerated up the slight grade on the other side. "Good—he went right by," Drew pronounced with relief, and he continued on his way along the trail bordering the narrow river.

Drew moved off the path and took several steps onto the dark, soft ground at the river's edge. A frog jumped from the swamp grass nearby and landed with a plop into the safety of the still water. After taking a dozen steps, Drew looked back at his tracks and laughed. "This is great," he exclaimed aloud. "I sure know how to have a fun time!"

Several minutes later Drew was startled when he heard and then saw a man coming through the bushes towards him. He knew he did not have time to remove the footwear he had made and stash them out of sight in his bag. He stepped a little closer to the tall grass lining the water's edge, hoping it would hide his feet. And there he waited.

"Good day, Young Man," the fellow greeted when he approached with his rod and wicker basket. "Catch any fish yet?" He halted on the trail above the river's bank.

"Ahh—no," Drew replied as he waited with one hand in the pocket of his denim overalls. "Ahh—not today."

The man started to leave. "Ought to try a little farther up, Boy, at that big rock, you know, where the river makes a turn there. I got a few nibbles, but no luck this time." The man grinned, and he took a few steps. "Got to go home now. The wife will be wondering what's keeping me."

Drew politely returned the grin and nodded. "Okay, thanks."

When the man left the immediate area, Drew sighed in relief. "That was close," he said as he shifted his sinking feet. "He didn't even notice I don't have no fishing gear. I guess some men think rivers are only for fishing. But I have another use for this here river, and I don't want nobody around when I'm here. They can come later—and I sure hope they do!" He grinned again and nearly laughed aloud as he joined the path to move farther along the river's edge.

Drew made more tracks in several locations, and then he decided to clean his footwear off in the water. He shook the wet from them and shoved them back into his canvas bag.

On his way back along the trail to his bicycle, Drew looked down to the stretches of dark, damp mud at the edge of the river and grinned. "I sure know how to have a really good time!" he said aloud and laughed. "I really do!"

After supper that day, Mrs. Palmer and Martha started the dishes, and Mr. Palmer and the two boys went outside to work on the winter's supply of firewood at the cellar entrance on the far side of the house. Several minutes later, Mr. Palmer returned to the kitchen. "Alice," he said, "we haven't gone for a walk yet this week. It's a nice evening."

Mrs. Palmer wiped the serving spoon with the cloth in the dishpan and placed it in the rinse water. "Oh, that would be nice. I haven't been outside today except to hang out the clothes and to dump the dishwater on the tomatoes."

Martha spoke up, "You go, Mom. I'll finish up here."

Mrs. Palmer dried her hands and draped her apron over the back of a chair as her husband waited at the door with his hat in his hand.

As Mr. and Mrs. Palmer left the house, they could hear Brent and Drew working at the woodpile. "Drew's handling that splitting axe real good," Mr. Palmer noted.

Mrs. Palmer added, "I'm glad you showed him how to use it safely."

They paused in the yard by the well. "Where'd you like to go, Alice?" Mr. Palmer asked. "You want to go along the path beyond Drew's cabin?"

They passed by the swings hanging from the spruce tree between the house and the barn and walked through the orchard and along the woods road. As they approached the cabin, they glanced over at their old outhouse now in this new location and then stepped up onto the landing of the cabin. Mr. Palmer opened the door and walked in, followed by his wife.

"My!" she exclaimed, "Drew keeps this place some neat and tidy. Even better than his room in the house." She picked up a small nail from off the floor and placed it on the table.

"Yeah, he does," her husband agreed as he stood at the woodstove. "Probably because this cabin is his place, and he has pride in looking after his own place—his domain." He glanced over at the neatly stacked firewood and the box of kindling and birchbark. "This place is satisfying to Drew. He's developing his God-given nature as a male to provide shelter and other basic needs."

His wife smiled and added, "Since Drew's worked on this cabin, he's been less rebellious—I've been really concerned about him. But now he's easier to get along with, and I can see he's relaxed and at peace, too."

Mr. Palmer grinned. "Yeah, I've noticed that as well." He removed his hat, sat on a chair, and leaned back. His wife sat at the other side of the table facing him. Mrs. Palmer continued to examine the interior of the cabin as she fingered the small nail.

Five minutes later Mr. Palmer smoothed back his mustache before putting both elbows on the table. "We're not getting much of a walk, are we?"

"No, we're not, but this is nice." She put the nail aside and reached across to touch her husband's hand.

"Want to go farther along the path?" he asked, and he reached for his hat.

She replied, "Whatever you want would be fine."

Mr. and Mrs. Palmer left the cabin and followed along the woods road, deeper into the forest. "It's beautiful back here, Joshua. You could paint a lovely picture of this." He grinned in response as he glanced around at the mixed woods.

"Look!" Mrs. Palmer exclaimed several minutes later. "That big, old pine tree has finally fallen over." It was lying directly across their path.

"Must have blown over that windy night a couple weeks ago," her husband decided. "Some wind we had back then—remember?"

"Look at the size of it!" she said as they came up to it. "It looks much larger laying on the ground than it does up in the air."

Mr. Palmer stood next to it with his hand up to his chin. "I'll have to get it out of here. Need to keep the road clear for hauling logs next spring." They viewed its massive trunk and its many branches. "I hardly have the time to come back here and chunk it up." He and his wife studied the fallen giant and then left for home.

"Hey, look at this!" Martha called out the next day from the living room. Drew picked up a molasses cookie from the cooling rack on the counter and headed for the porch door. "It says here in the newspaper," she reported as she brought it across to the kitchen table, "that some guy saw strange tracks next to the Crazy Man River just off the Hannah Road. That's just down from here handy to us." Drew froze with one hand reaching out for the doorknob and the other hand holding his cookie an inch from his open mouth. He held this pose as she continued. "He says he was fishing along the river when he saw the strange footprints all along there in the mud."

Brent came into the porch from outside. He brushed by Drew as he stood there motionlessly holding his stance. "What's with you?" the older brother asked as he stared at him suspiciously.

Drew bit into his cookie and then told his brother, "I was listening to what Martha had to say." As he spoke, a crumb dropped to the floor. He followed Brent to the table where Martha had spread out the weekly newspaper.

"The guy says he's never seen anything like these tracks before," Martha said to Brent and Drew as they attempted to read the paper over her shoulders.

Drew finished his cookie and reached for another. His mother reminded him, "Supper will be in about half an hour."

She dumped the peelings from the fresh carrots into the compost pail.

Drew bit into the second cookie. "Strange tracks," he repeated innocently. "What do you think, Brent?"

"Says here," Brent pointed to the article, "that he's going to get in touch with scientists from the university."

"Scientists from the university! Ha!" Drew blurted out, and a cookie crumb flew from his mouth and landed on the newspaper. "What would they know?" He again headed for the porch to leave for outside.

Mrs. Palmer called after him, "Drew, supper will be in less than half an hour."

After supper, Drew planted his right elbow in the middle of the table with his arm straight up. "Arm wrestle?" he challenged his brother with a grin.

Brent who was seated on the opposite side of the table snickered. "Arm wrestle? You? Last time I arm wrestled you, I won—no contest."

"That was a long time ago," he reminded him as he gave him a quick silly grin.

Brent positioned himself with his elbow on the table, and the two fellows clasped their hands together and looked each other in the eye. "This shouldn't take long," Brent informed his brother, and the hired man's clock gave one strike. "Go, Boy!" he shouted at him.

Drew pushed his hand against Brent's, and he responded with equal force. Their fists moved a couple inches in Brent's favour, and then Drew forced him back to the vertical position and then succeeded in moving an inch. The fellows held their breaths, grunted, and took more breaths as each strained with all his might.

"Why do guys arm wrestle!" Martha exclaimed to her mom as they began to wash the supper dishes.

"Well," replied her mom, "it's a male thing. The boys are exploring—they're working out and showing off their masculine capabilities. They need to assure themselves that they have physical strength. They want to use it, and they want others to know they have muscle."

"Oh," Martha responded flatly, "is that it?"

Mrs. Palmer and Martha gave several quick glances at the two brothers straining across the kitchen table. "I think Brent's winning," Martha remarked.

Her mother observed, "Drew's holding his own. He might win."

After a couple of minutes, both Brent and Drew showed signs of fatigue on their flushed faces, and their hands were beginning to quiver.

"Well," Martha admitted as she lifted the dried plates onto the shelf, "it is kind of exciting."

Suddenly it was all over. Drew's fist was on top of Brent's, holding it down on the table. "Got you, Boy!" he proclaimed loudly and with satisfaction to his older brother. And then he gave him one of his phony grins as he released his grip. Drew then glanced over at his mother and sister. "Hey! Did you see that, Ladies? I beat him—I beat Brent at arm wrestling. Ladies, were you watching me?"

"We'll try again tomorrow," Brent informed him, and he leaned back in his chair.

Drew looked across the table at Brent. "Want to help me chunk up the rest of the old pine tree this evening?" he asked. Brent grinned in reply.

Several minutes later, Brent picked up the long cross-cut saw, and the two fellows headed to the swings where they turned and made their way through the orchard. They came to Drew's cabin, and as they passed by, his brother glanced over towards it. "How about us camping over here this Friday night?" Brent suggested with a toss of his head in that direction. "I haven't slept there yet."

Drew answered, "Could be fun."

Several minutes later, they saw up ahead, the fallen old pine tree. Most of it had been cut up and Drew had stacked some of the pieces just off the woods road to be hauled off later. As they approached closer to the toppled giant, Drew began to plan how to tackle this evening's job.

Suddenly Brent pointed to the ground at his feet as he walked along. "Look," he observed. "Tracks. All along here on this soft, bare ground. Have a look-see, Drew!"

"Yeah," his brother answered casually. "Wonder what they are! They must be nearly a foot long. Aren't bear tracks and not people tracks either." He tried to hide the grin he was suppressing.

Brent stooped over to examine the strange tracks more closely. "You didn't see no animal here today?"

"No, I didn't see no animal," he replied as he took several steps towards the pine tree. "I was busy, Man—I was working."

"Maybe you just didn't see the tracks," Brent decided as he stood up and followed Drew. "Or after you went home for supper, the animal passed by here."

"Yeah, maybe so—could be," Drew agreed. "Maybe we'll see him this evening, but probably not. He'll be miles away by now, I reckon."

His brother added, "I bet these tracks were made by that same animal that made them tracks along the Crazy Man River we read about in the newspaper." Drew turned the other way and tried not to snicker.

Brent and Drew began their work on the old pine tree. The branches were cut up and stacked to be hauled off later, and the small limbs were spread out in several low spots along the woods road. Drew grinned when he noticed his brother glance along the road and through the trees nearby and into the forest which was slowly becoming deeply shadowed. "Getting late," Brent remarked, "and getting hard to see. Let's chunk up this piece and then head for home."

"But we have another half hour of light," Drew protested as he positioned the saw against the pine trunk. "Come on, grab the other end, Boy. We've got work to do here."

Brent said nothing as he took hold of the saw, but after the log fell away, he pushed it aside with his foot, and then he started back for the house carrying the crosscut saw. "Come on, let's go," he ordered. "We need to get a move-along. And it's time I had a lunch." Drew grinned and followed his brother.

The next day Drew completed his work at the old pine tree, and when he saw his dad before supper, he reported that the job was done. "Good. Thanks," Mr. Palmer told his son. "Appreciate it. No doubt you did a good job."

"Brent helped some, too," Drew informed his dad who grinned and nodded.

When supper was nearly finished, Mr. Palmer reminded Martha and Drew, "it's just about time to leave for Young People's."

"Yeah, I'm coming," Drew said as he downed his second helping of applesauce. He then looked over at Brent. "You're not going to chicken-out on me are you, Boy? You said, me and you should camp over at the cabin Friday night." Brent grinned at him and rolled his eyes.

Later that evening following the young people's meeting and after having an evening lunch, Brent and Drew left for the cabin. Both fellows carried their blankets, their pillows, and their flashlights, and Drew toted a cardboard box. "Come on, Mister," Drew called enthusiastically to his pup, "time to go." He headed into the darkness in the direction of the barn without turning on his flashlight.

"Some dark," Brent stated, and he switched on his light.

"Yeah, sure is," Drew agreed cheerfully. "I like the dark."

"Yeah, right," his brother replied. "I like the dark, too, except I can't see in the dark."

"Can't see what?" Drew asked.

Brent did not reply, and as he walked along he let the beam of the flashlight sway widely back and forth. The two fellows turned at the swings hanging from the spruce tree, and they tramped between the apple trees in the orchard and then along the trail through the dark woods. Several minutes later they reached the cabin and stepped up onto the landing. Brent quickly pushed open the door and walked into the dark cabin followed by Drew.

Brent shone his flashlight around the room and to the upper bunk. "I'll take the top bed," he challenged, and he threw his blankets and pillow up to there.

"Okay, you can have it," Drew agreed as he dropped his things onto the lower bed. "Top bunk or bottom bunk, don't make no difference to me when I'm asleep, and don't make no difference in the dark because I can't see nothing in the dark anyway." He lit the oil lamp on the table, and Brent turned off his flashlight.

Brent demanded, "What did you bring in the cardboard box?"

"Breakfast," his brother answered as he stroked Mister's chest.

Brent folded back the flaps of the box. "Bottle of some kind of juice, eggs, canned meat and bread." He looked over at his brother. "You going to fix us breakfast?" Brent had a questionable expression on his face. "You've never made breakfast before. You don't even know what to fry eggs in or how to turn them over."

"Could be fun," Drew responded with a big phony smile. "You can stay for breakfast if you want, or you can go back to the house for breakfast. I don't mind—don't bother me none. Could be fun, though."

"Could be fun!" Brent blurted out in annoyance. "Does everything have to be fun? I want a decent breakfast in the morning, not fun, fun, fun."

Drew took on a look of exaggerated astonishment. "Brent, don't you ever have fun, Boy? Don't you know how to have a good time? Why do you like being so uptight? Do you actually enjoy being miserable?" His look of amazement was replaced by his silly grin as he stared intently at Brent.

Brent scowled as he replied, "I've had a long, hard day working for Uncle Bob." He lowered himself to the edge of the bottom bed. "I'm turning in." He leaned over to remove his work-boots.

"Okay," Drew agreed as he began to unbutton his shirt. "Sounds good to me. I'm happy—see." He gave Brent another big fake smile, and his brother rolled his eyes and slowly shook his head.

A minute later Brent hinted, "We could leave that oil lamp on all night." He folded the laces of his boots and pushed them down inside, and then he placed his footwear back against the wall.

Drew agreed, "We could leave the oil lamp on all night. I like the light on—I like the dark as well. Don't bother me none—I'll be asleep anyway. Makes no difference to me; you decide, Boy. I'm easy to get along with." Drew kicked off his boots and left them where they settled, sprawled out on the floor.

The oil lamp was left burning, and the two fellows climbed into their beds. "Hope I don't have to get up in the night," Brent mumbled as he fluffed up his pillow.

"Why not?" Drew asked him. "You don't like our old outhouse since we now have indoor plumbing in the house? I kind of miss the outhouse. But I'm glad we moved it to here where it's at now."

"You like outhouses?" Brent asked in surprise from the upper bunk. "So it must be you that doesn't flush the toilet."

"Flush the toilet?" Drew questioned his brother. "What does 'flush the toilet' mean?"

"Drew, when are you going to grow up?" Brent asked in exasperation.

"Don't worry about me," Drew uttered, and he laughed. "I'm not worried any about me. Some people don't grow up until they're in their twenties. And some folks don't grow up until they're way past thirty or even forty." Drew paused, and then he said with satisfaction, "And some people never grow up at all. I heard tell of a fellow who never grew up, and he lived 'till he was ninety-three. He survived alright. So don't worry none about me, Boy."

Brent decided to change the subject. "You think Mom and Dad would mind us being back here overnight with that strange animal in this area?"

"You mean the animal that leaves them tracks handy to us and other places like along the Crazy Man River? I'd like to see the creature. He might be a friendly fellow. You know, if we could catch him, we could keep him in a cage and teach him tricks. Hey, that would be fun now, wouldn't it? What do you think of that, Brent?"

"I think you're crazy," Brent responded, and he rolled over. "Good night."

"Crazy, but having fun," Drew said. "Good night, Boy."

Early the next morning the sun shone through the east window and onto the table with the box containing their breakfast. Drew awoke, and as he lay there he could tell Brent was still asleep. He silently climbed from his bed, and he found it hard to keep from laughing. He grabbed his pants and shirt, and quietly picked up his boots. He crossed to the door, and he and Mister left for outside, where he got dressed. Drew reached under the landing to retrieve his canvas bag. He quickly dumped out the contents and pushed his feet into his project. "I sure know how to have fun, Mister," he said in a hushed voice to his dog. He stifled a laugh as he walked back and forth on the soft, bare ground between the cabin and the outhouse.

Several minutes later Drew sat on the landing and removed his footwear. He quietly entered the cabin carrying the footwear he had made, which he left out of sight at the far side of the wood box. Then he extinguished the oil lamp and lifted the lid of the stove to light the fire in preparation for making breakfast. Brent rolled over. "You up already?" he said in a groggy voice. "It's Saturday. I always sleep in on Saturdays."

Drew kept his back to him as he placed the frying pan on the stove. "I'm fixing us some breakfast," he answered, struggling not to laugh. As his brother climbed down from the upper bunk, Drew continued to hide his face from him. He busied himself at the stove as Brent hurriedly left the cabin without dressing nor putting his boots on.

Drew leaned over to observe his brother through the window as he crossed to the outhouse in his shorts. He said aloud, "There's nothing like a good laugh to start the day, eh, Mister?" And he cracked open four eggs and placed them in the now-hot frying pan on the stove.

Soon the eggs began to crackle, but suddenly Drew heard a loud gasp coming from outside. "Drew!" Brent shouted. Drew giggled as he quickly sat on the floor and again pulled on his homemade footwear. "Drew, come quick," Brent called to him. "Hurry!" Drew clomped his way to the door and stepped onto the landing. "Drew, look!" Brent exclaimed excitedly. "Tracks here of that animal." He pointed to the ground at his feet. "That animal, whatever it is, was right here in the night just outside the cabin when we were sleeping."

Drew laughed in response and Brent looked over at him as he stepped off the landing. Brent's gaze dropped down to his brother's feet and expressions of horror, disbelief and then dismay came over his face. "Drew!" he bellowed at him. "You made those tracks, you scallywag you, and all them other tracks, too, I suppose." Drew grinned broadly at Brent who with his hands on his hips, shook his head in bewilderment.

"When are you going to grow up, Boy? You irresponsible rooster, you! You're something else for sure." And then there came a hint of a grin across Brent's face.

Drew laughed, and he sat down on the landing. "Some people never grow up," he told him as he started to remove his track-making footwear. "But you have to admit, Brent, I sure know how to have a good time—a really good time."

Brent slowly nodded in agreement and grinned at Drew. And from the open door of the cabin came the strong odor of burning eggs. The brothers looked at one another, and both broke into laughter.

chapter nine

five years later—summer 1967

The Half-Ton Pickup

Martha drove the family car along the Hannah Road and past the farms surrounded by a mixture of forests. She enjoyed these warm, mid-summer days, and as she traveled, her long, straight hair blew in the wind turbulence caused by the open window at her elbow. On the backseat behind her was the dog belonging to her brother.

When the gravel road leveled out, Martha could see up ahead on the shoulder, a disabled, half-ton pickup. The hood was up, and a fellow was bent over studying the engine. She did not give the truck and its driver much thought, but as she came closer, he straightened up and turned to face her. When Martha saw this rough-looking man raise his arm to flag her down, she instinctively gripped the wheel more firmly. *Should I stop,* Martha wondered without slowing down, *or should I just ignore him and drive on down the road?* He was now standing nearly in the centre of the road and looking directly at her. She took her foot off the gas, rolled up the window to about four inches open. She geared down, stomped on the brake, and came to a stop next to him as the dust floated by. She saw that his clothing was that of a labourer and he had a scowl on his face and a beard of several days' growth. Martha figured he was in his mid-twenties.

He stared at her without expression. "Give me a ride to my place, will you," he almost demanded. "My truck quit on me." He swore as he turned in the direction of his vehicle. The lettering on the door read, 'All kinds of Masonry Work'. The back of the truck was cluttered with a cement mixer and a wheelbarrow along with an assortment of masonry tools.

"Wait 'till I get my lunch box," he said without giving her the opportunity to answer, and he cursed once more. The young man started for his truck.

Martha eyed him and thought, *He doesn't give me much choice, does he! Now's my chance to step on it, and get out of here.* But then she had the feeling she should help this fellow. She glanced behind her at her brother's dog lying patiently on the backseat. *I'm glad I brought Mister.*

After closing the hood and picking up his lunch box from the cab, the man slammed closed the truck door with his foot, and once more expressed his frustration by using profanity. *He sure has a limited vocabulary!* thought Martha as she kept her hand on the gear stick knob. The man hurried over to the passenger's side of her car and opened the front door.

Suddenly Mister lunged up from the backseat and growled fiercely, showing all his teeth. The man swore in sudden surprise and jerked back, leaving the car door wide open. Before Martha realized what was happening, the dog bounded over the back of the seat into the front of the car and out the open door. The startled fellow jumped back and bolted across the road towards his truck, followed closely by the mutt. The young man quickly looked over his shoulder at Mister, who was now a couple of dog-lengths from him. As he vaulted up onto the hood of his truck, his lunch box sprung open, and the contents spilled out onto the hood. His thermos rolled across the hood, fell to the gravel, and came to rest against the front wheel. A half-eaten sandwich along with a doughnut and several crumpled balls of waxed paper cascaded from the hood and onto the dirt.

Martha lowered her window. "Get down, Mister!" she shouted at her brother's dog. The man looked at her strangely from his crouched position on the hood of his truck. Mister alternated between barking and peeling back his lips, exposing his teeth to the man who was tightly clutching his open lunch box and leaning in the other direction.

Martha tried hard to keep from laughing, and she bravely opened her door. "Mister's the name of my dog," she informed the uneasy guy as she crossed to the mutt. Mister had his front paws up against the side of the truck and was hopping on his hind feet over the remainder of the man's lunch in the gravel. Martha grabbed the mutt by his collar. "Good dog," she said to him. "Good Mister." She chuckled as the dog attempted to pull away to inspect the demolished sandwich on the road.

Well, I'm safe after all, Martha recognized as she dragged the excited dog back to her car and returned him to the backseat. "Good dog," she said once more approvingly. "You stay there and be quiet." The mutt was obedient but whined softly. Martha grinned as she returned to the driver's seat. *You never know when you start your day,* she told herself, *what might take place to give you a good laugh before the end of the day!*

"Okay," she called over to the young man still on the hood of his truck, "you can get down now, Mister. I'll give you a lift to your place if you still want one."

The man briefly stared at her. He leapt off the hood of the truck and retrieved his thermos and gave it a shake. He cursed again and pitched it over the daisies and into the ditch. He then came over to Martha's car and cautiously got in.

"It's okay, Mister," she said firmly to the dog who was growling again, "he needs a ride." The man gently closed the door and nervously held his empty lunch box on his lap. He glanced back at the mutt who was beginning to whine and wanted to finish the job he had started on this ill-mannered stranger.

"It's okay, Mister," she said to the rough fellow on the seat beside her in her clean car. "My dog doesn't like swearing." He looked suspiciously at Martha who was finding it hard not to laugh. Suddenly he grinned at her and then laughed. *Well, he has a nice smile,* she thought as she shoved in the clutch and put the car in gear, and she continued along the road towards his place.

"I won't swear again," he promised, and he stroked his bristled chin.

He's a fool, thought Martha. *He shouldn't promise anything he can't keep.*

"I need to go home and get Dad's tractor," the young man muttered.

As Martha down-shifted to negotiate the curve, she quickly looked over sideways at him. *I don't like or trust a guy with a tattoo.*

"I know the dog's name," he said with a grin, "but I don't know his master's name."

"His master's name is Drew," Martha informed him.

"Your name is Drew?"

Martha paused several seconds and then said, "He belongs to my brother."

"Okay, I get it," he answered and continued to smile. "And what's the dog's master's sister's name?"

"Her name's Martha," she admitted.

He sat up straight. "Hi! My name's Richard."

Martha allowed the car to slow down somewhat as they approached the crest of Thrill Hill thereby minimizing the hill's popular effect as vehicles sped over its brow.

Several minutes later they passed by the community centre with its neatly cut lawns bordered by colourful flower gardens. The unoccupied swings barely moved in the gentle breeze.

"'Gospel Meetings'!" Richard read the sign situated close to the road. "You are all sinners!" he mocked and then added, "And there's a visiting evangelist." He turned his head and shoulders to keep his eye on the sign. "Look, he has more letters after his name than he has in his name. With all that religious training he must be a really good Christian."

My, he's some disrespectful! Martha decided. *I ought to stop the car and tell him to get out. Mister would love to back me up.*

Richard continued, "Did you hear about the little girl who told a horse that he must be a really good Christian because his face was so long? A bunch of religious fanatics!" He shook his head.

Mister growled from the backseat, and Richard turned in his direction. "I suppose you like gospel meetings, Mister!"

"I do," Martha answered boldly. "And I'm not a religious fanatic either. A religious fanatic is someone who is hung up on religious activities to ease his conscience."

"I believe all roads lead to God," he replied. "You don't have to adhere to any particular religion. They're all just as bad as the next," he said as he snickered.

"I agree with you," Martha said to him. "All roads lead to God, and everyone will stand before Him. God will either be their Saviour or their Judge." There was a long awkward pause, and Richard shifted his lunch box and rearranged his feet. Martha continued, "I've gone to the meetings nearly every night. There's special music and—and everything." She decreased her speed for the approaching farm truck.

"Special music—like what?" he asked, looking over at her.

"Choirs, quartets and solos."

"And a collection," Richard put in. "Don't forget the collection."

"And then there's a message at the end," Martha quickly added.

"A message!" he echoed. "A message from who?"

"From the Bible."

"I've never read the Bible," he answered, and then he asked, "Are you going tonight, Martha?"

"Yes."

"Good! I'll pick you up then." He chuckled and glanced over at her again.

"Oh no, you don't!" she quickly protested. "I'm a Bible-believing Christian. I don't go out with guys who aren't born again Christians. Besides, my dad would never allow it."

He chuckled once more. "You could bring your guard dog."

Martha did not bother to answer, and she and the scruffy young man in her car traveled in silence. Several minutes later Richard raised his hand, pointed ahead, and told her, "That's my driveway up ahead there."

Martha brought the car to a stop at his driveway. She could see the name on the mailbox was 'Jack'. Richard opened the car door and put one foot out on the shoulder of the road.

"Well, thanks for the ride, Martha," he said as he smiled over at her. He grasped his lunch box and swung his other leg out. "See you later." He stood up, but before he closed the door, he turned and leaned over into the car. "Bye, Mister. I've had an exciting afternoon—thanks to you!" Mister growled in reply from the backseat.

As Martha pulled away she realized Richard had kept his promise not to swear.

"Well, that's the last of him!" she told Mister as she drove on home along the Hannah Road.

That evening, several hours later, Martha stepped out from the backseat of the family car and followed her parents and brother across the parking area of the community centre. "There aren't many cars here tonight, Joshua," Mrs. Palmer told her husband.

"It's only ten minutes to," Martha's younger brother Drew replied as he squinted and made a fake smile. "People won't be arriving for another nine minutes."

They entered the porch, and a young man dressed in a white shirt with a narrow, purple tie handed hymn books to each of them. The Palmers moved into the main room and sat on wooden folding chairs near the front. There was hushed talking and whispering as others arrived, and several minutes later a lady sat down at the electric organ and began to play.

At two minutes after the hour, the door to the kitchen opened, and members of the choir marched single file onto the stage. They sang a variation of a well-known hymns, and then a musical group from the city performed three numbers using their own sound system.

The evangelist presented the gospel clearly and illustrated it with interesting stories. The theme this evening was that God was not a distant Supreme Being, but He was much involved in the affairs of the world. He made the earth and everything in it, and all things continue to exist and hold together because of Jesus Christ. God expressed Himself to us by giving us His Son who cleanses us of our sin when we trust in Him.

About twenty minutes later, the last hymn was sung, and the meeting was over. People were milling about, but most were leaving. Mr. and Mrs. Palmer were near the door visiting with some friends from their church, and Drew was outside joking with several other young people.

Suddenly in the surrounding din of conversation and laughter in the main room, Martha could hear a quiet, yet distinct, voice behind her that said, "Did you bring your guard dog?"

It was several seconds before Martha realized the familiar voice was meant for her. She wheeled around, nearly causing her hair to fly. She did not recognize anyone in the sea of faces. A nice looking, clean-shaven young man standing about eight feet away, looking directly at her, suddenly broke out into a smile. "Richard!" Martha exclaimed. "Is that you?"

"I told you I'd see you tonight, Martha," he replied as he stepped toward her.

At first she could not think of anything to say, but several seconds later she smiled and inquired, "Did you get your truck started?"

"Oh sure," he replied. "I towed it home and got it fixed. It's outside." And he nodded in that direction.

Martha told him, "I'm glad it's working now."

Then he asked, "Did you hear about the passenger plane that was about to crash? Someone on the plane suggested they do something religious." Richard grinned at her. "So they took up a collection."

Richard laughed, and Martha found herself joining in. She thought, *What a case!*

"Look, Martha, would you mind if I phoned you later tonight?"

"Well, I guess—I guess that would be all right," she stammered as she quickly glanced down at his arm with the tattoo. "Our phone number is in the book. My dad's name is Joshua Palmer."

Drew came in from outside and called over to her, "Martha, Mom and Dad are waiting in the car."

She waved to him and turned to Richard. "Well, if you'll excuse me, Richard, I must go now."

He grinned and told her, "Good night, Martha."

Martha abruptly left Richard and as she approached the family car, she quickly scanned over the other vehicles in the yard. She could see the half-ton pickup belonging to Richard at the far end of the parking area near the swings.

After she closed the car door, and her dad started the engine, Drew looked across at her. "Was that the Jack fellow talking to you?"

"Yes," she replied hesitantly.

Drew demanded, "Why would he bother to talk to you?"

"Maybe he wanted to," Martha answered. "He's going to phone me later this evening."

"You! Why would he phone you!" Drew blurt out as their dad pulled onto the road and headed for home.

Later that evening the phone rang. "I'll get it," Martha called as she left the kitchen for the living room.

"I hope you don't mind me calling you," Richard began. "I'd like to give you my impressions of the meeting tonight."

"Sure, go ahead."

"You said it wasn't religion, but I can see that there are religious ceremonies involved."

"Religious ceremonies!" Martha repeated in surprise. "What kind of religious ceremonies?"

"Choir members coming in, all dressed the same. Soft organ music. They even brought in an organ when there was a piano there already. And then there's all those people wearing their Sunday morning go-to-church clothes."

"Yeah, but all those things are needed to give order and beauty."

"Order and beauty," Richard repeated. "Maybe so, but it seems to be overdone. It's a show, a performance—and the cute decorations are blinding us. Why not get right to the point?"

"Point—what point?" Martha found herself asking.

"Good question! What point? Why are they doing all this? Are they looking for proselytes to join their happy club? A bunch of squeaky-clean, do-gooders with their pasted on syrupy-sweet smiles, or are they warning people that they need to be saved by the love of God, in order to be saved from the wrath of God? All this pussy-footing around! If the building was burning down with all of us in it, they wouldn't play beautiful music on the organ as we tried to escape, would they?"

Martha admitted, "Well, I hope not."

"Do they really believe what they preach?" he lamented, not expecting nor waiting for an answer. "Well, got to go," he informed her abruptly. "Say 'good night' to Mister for me, will you."

There's a hopeless case! Martha thought with disappointment after Richard hung up. *He'll not show up again at the gospel meetings.* She joined her family in the kitchen and related to them what had taken place that afternoon with the disabled truck. "Mister sure showed his teeth!" she told them. "I've never seen him so defensive."

Drew laughed and put his toast down on the kitchen table. "Mister wouldn't bite nobody!" He dropped to his knees, pulled the dog to him, and grabbed him by the ears. "Would you, Mister!" The mutt thumped his tail on the floor, and the young man allowed him to lick his face.

"Drew!" his mom protested. "I wish you wouldn't let that dog lick your face."

"Yeah," Martha quickly added as she crossed the floor to the fridge. "Mister just cleaned his behind, you know."

As Drew stood up, he informed them, "I don't expect to be kissed by anybody in the immediate future."

Martha approached him with pursed lips and scanned his face as he tensed up and looked at her suspiciously. Finally she moved behind him and planted a kiss on the back of his neck. "There," she told him.

Mr. Palmer picked up a piece of cheese. "It was good the fellow came to the gospel meeting tonight."

"We should pray for him," Mrs. Palmer said, and she plugged in the kettle. "What did you say the fellow's name is, Martha?"

"Richard Jack."

The next night at the gospel meeting, Martha sat again with her family. Before the meeting started she studied people as they came into the large room and took their seats. Some were dressed up, some were casually dressed, some were quiet and thoughtful while others were somewhat loud and boisterous.

There were two empty seats between Martha and the outside aisle. "Are these seats taken, Miss?" a man asked her politely.

"No," Martha answered quietly without looking up. The man sat down next to her. She continued to look in the other direction as people were arriving. *Why would a lady wear a hat like that to a gospel meeting!* she wondered as she fiddled with the zipper of her Bible.

Several minutes later Martha realized the man beside her was still alone. Without turning her head she looked sideways at him through her long straight hair. And then she saw his tattoo. "Richard!" she gasped in a loud whisper as she turned to him. "I didn't think you were coming back—I mean, it's good to see you again." He grinned at her and then with a serious face and without saying anything, he bent over and looked under her seat.

"What are you doing!?" she gasped as she stared at him.

He sat up and whispered, "I'm checking to see if you brought your guard dog." She smiled back at him, and she could feel herself blushing.

Martha's parents in the next seats over were now looking her way. "Richard, I'd like you to meet my parents, Mr. and Mrs. Palmer."

"Hello, Richard," Mr. Palmer replied. "We're glad you could come this evening."

"And that's my brother Drew." The two young men exchanged nods, and Drew grinned pleasantly.

I'm surprised he came back again, Martha pondered, *but I shouldn't be surprised. I prayed for him and so did Mom and Dad.*

The program was much like the previous night but with some variation. During the preaching, Martha found herself praying for Richard. Tonight the theme was 'Jesus Christ, the sinless One'. He was the only One good enough to pay the penalty for our sins because He Himself was sinless. The invitation was given as the lady played the organ, and then the service was over.

After the meeting, Martha's parents and brother made their way through the crowd to the exit. As Martha and Richard stood up, Richard turned to Martha and asked seriously, "Did you hear about the fellow who fell asleep during the church service? While he dozed, the lights went out, and the place was pitch black—couldn't see a thing, but the meeting carried on in the dark anyway." Richard tried not to smile. "Well, after a while the guy woke up. He hollered out, 'Pray for me! I've gone blind!'"

"Where'd you hear that!" Martha laughed as she passed by the rows of empty chairs. She wondered, *Why does this guy bother to come to the meetings!*

"You know," Richard said with sarcastic pride, "I could be a Christian like you, just by changing my lifestyle."

Martha answered, "You might be able to act like a Christian, but you wouldn't be a Christ-one—you wouldn't belong to Him."

"There are a lot of non-Christians out there," Richard declared as he and Martha slowly moved towards the door, "who are better-living than some Christians. Those so called Christians make me sick."

"Yes, you're right," she had to admit. "And I've seen a lot of rotten apples over the years, but that doesn't mean all apples are rotten. Usually it's only the rotten apples that get noticed."

"Would a person have to first change his lifestyle in order to become a Christian?"

"Oh, no!" Martha quickly answered. "We can't become Christians by our own efforts, but we must desire to be free from our sin. We must first confess or admit to our sin, and then we need to repent. Repentance is agreeing with God regarding our sin and wanting to be changed."

"Sin," Richard simply pronounced as he held open one of the double doors for Martha. "You mean, he must desire or want to have a changed lifestyle because of his sin?"

"Yeah, that's right," she replied when they had moved onto the outside landing. Richard looked over at Martha. "So, when did you become a Christian? And how do you know you're 'saved' as you call it?"

"When or how I became a Christian or was saved doesn't matter," she explained to him. "My salvation isn't dependant on a story of an experience in the past that I can tell others about. My salvation is based on the fact that I am saved—saved from the wrath and condemnation of God. That only comes about when I am right in God's sight like Jesus the Son of God is. I am righteous before Him because I believe that Jesus took my sin upon Himself and died in my place, and I am trusting in what Christ has done for me. A dramatic story doesn't prove my salvation, but the proof of my salvation is that right now I am simply trusting in Him."

"Yeah, well, that sounds good." He suddenly walked away but then turned to face Martha. "I need to get a move-along. Good night, Martha."

Martha and her family did not attend the next gospel meeting, but later that evening when everyone in the Palmer household was in bed, the telephone rang. Mr. Palmer answered it on the extension in the bedroom off the kitchen. "Who?" Martha heard her dad respond, and there was a slight pause. "And who are you?" he asked. "Richard?" he repeated.

Richard! Martha jumped out of bed as her dad called up to her. She came downstairs and made her way to the phone in the dark living room. Without stopping to switch on the light, she picked up the receiver and said, "Thanks, Dad, I have it."

Martha stood there speechless with the phone to her ear. "Martha," greeted the voice at the other end of the line.

"Richard?" Martha lowered herself to the couch and brought one leg up under her.

"I know I shouldn't call you so late, but I just had to tell you."

She grasped the receiver tightly and leaned forward in the dark. "Tell me what?"

"I'm trusting in the Lord now. So I'm saved from the penalty of my sin."

"You are!" she answered excitedly, nearly shouting into the phone.

"Yes, I started to trust Him on my way home in my truck."

"In your truck!" she exclaimed as she sat up straight. "That's great! We've been praying for you."

Then he questioned, "Why didn't you tell me I was a sinner and on my way to hell! Why didn't you tell me God gave His Son to die for me because of my sin! Why didn't you tell me all I needed to do was to believe on or trust in Jesus Christ!" Martha did not know how to react. She knew he had heard all those facts before.

"Would you like to come here to supper tomorrow?" Martha invited on impulse and nearly gasped at what she had just said to Richard.

"Well sure," he responded, and then Martha did gasp, and she wondered if she had done the right thing. *Maybe I should have talked to Mom and Dad first.*

The next day, Martha thought the time passed slowly. *It's not even mid-afternoon!* she concluded as she glanced at the hired man's clock high on the kitchen shelf. In other ways the time seemed to nearly fly by. "Look what time it is!" she groaned to her mother. "And there's lots to do yet." Martha looked out the kitchen window and down the driveway for the sixth time. A quarter of an hour passed by, and she knew without looking that the vehicle she heard in the yard was her dad's.

Ten minutes later, supper was nearly ready, and Martha moved to the window once more. She could see the pickup truck was finally approaching along the driveway towards the house. She quickly put Mister in her parents' bedroom off the kitchen and closed the door. Then she left for the living room where her dad was reading the weekly newspaper. After straightening the doilies under the table lamps for the second time that afternoon, she rotated the engine piston on the buffet. The piston was from a vehicle her brother Brent had once worked on. Martha then sat down on the couch across from her dad.

Several minutes later she heard her mom go to the door, and then she could hear Richard say, "Good afternoon, Mrs. Palmer."

Martha heard her mom answer, "Come on in, Richard." He was ushered in, and Mister whined from the other side of the bedroom door. Martha remained on the couch in the living room. She was nicely dressed in a rose-coloured skirt and white blouse. Her long straight hair hung over her shoulders.

"Martha," her mother called to her, "Richard is here."

Martha stood up and casually came into the kitchen. Richard was dressed in clean denims and a long-sleeved, light-coloured shirt. "Oh, you're here," she greeted, and he smiled in response. Martha took the pitcher of ice water from the fridge and began to fill the glasses on the table. Mr. Palmer then entered the kitchen. "Hello, Richard."

"Hello, Sir," Richard replied and nodded.

"Come into the living room, Boy," Mr. Palmer invited.

Richard winked at Martha as he passed by her. She watched him and continued to pour from the pitcher until the cold water spilt onto the tablecloth.

Mr. Palmer and Richard shook hands and then moved into the living room, and Martha could hear they were conversing. Several minutes later they were joined by Drew, and the three men talked as though they had known each other for a long time. *That's nice,* decided Martha.

"There, I think everything's ready," Mrs. Palmer stated. "Call the men in, Martha."

After everyone was seated, they bowed their heads, and Mr. Palmer gave thanks for the food, and he thanked God for His Son the Lord Jesus Christ. Mrs. Palmer then instructed, "Just help yourselves to what's in front of you, and then pass it on." She stood up and crossed to the fridge and brought out a jar of green tomato chow.

"Don't bother putting them in a serving bowl, Alice," her husband said. "They'll do just fine the way they are."

"Why's the table wet here?" Drew wanted to know. Martha scowled at him from across the table, but suddenly stopped when she saw Richard, who was seated next to Drew, wink at her again.

Mr. Palmer took a serving of roast beef and passed the platter to Martha. "Richard tells me he became a Christian last night, after the gospel meeting," he said to his family.

"Yeah," Richard spoke up. "Getting saved is so simple once you understand it," he said with pleasure. He quickly glanced around the table at his new friends. Mister whined once more from behind the closed door.

"Yes, I suppose it is," Mrs. Palmer commented as she reached for the bowl of potatoes and took a helping. "To those of us who have been believers for a long time—we could take its simplicity for granted." She passed the potatoes to Drew.

"What caused me to see that I needed to be saved from my sin," Richard continued, "was when I realized that the suffering and the torture Jesus experienced is an indication of the awfulness of sin—my sin. The Bible says that the Lord Jesus took the penalty for my sin and that if I acknowledged my sinfulness and if I believed or trusted in what Christ did for me, I would receive His righteousness. I find that to be amazing!"

Martha thought, *He sure has a good grasp of salvation!* She handed the bowl of peas to her mom.

"It's so simple, yet so profound!" their dinner guest declared. "And I don't need to do anything—besides there's nothing I'm capable of doing." He started to roll up his sleeves but abruptly changed his mind.

Martha put in, "We can't work to get saved, and we don't work to keep saved—lest any man should boast. Besides, we are His workmanship." She left the table to plug in the kettle and asked, "Who wants tea? Maybe I should make a full pot."

After dessert of blueberry pie and cranberry muffins, the three men went into the living room, and Mrs. Palmer and Martha put the food away and tidied up. "Richard seems like a nice young man," Mrs. Palmer whispered to Martha as she carried the dirty dishes to the counter. Martha grinned but said nothing. Several minutes later they joined the men in the living room.

Mister whined again from the room off the kitchen, and Drew left to open the door and let him out. The dog bounded into the living room, gave Richard a quick sniff, and then he moved over to Martha and sat at her feet. Martha observed, "Well, Richard, it looks like Mister has accepted you." Richard grinned, and the mutt lay down with his back to the visitor.

"I think if we took the Bible more seriously," Drew related as he sat on the organ stool facing into the room, "we would see that trusting in Christ in the first place isn't all there is to salvation. When the Lord saves us, He separates us from the world and separates us to Himself."

Richard was listening with interest. "I can see you folks take your beliefs seriously," he told them. "You have Bible verses on the walls here in the living room and in the kitchen as well."

Drew added, "And don't forget the bathroom." He leaned back with one elbow on the organ, and his feet stretched out over the rug.

Mrs. Palmer asked, "Richard, do you have a Bible?"

"No, I don't," he answered.

Mr. Palmer explained, "When we read God's Word, we'll know what it says. When we study God's Word, we'll know what it means. And when we meditate on God's Word, we'll know more of the mind of God."

Nearly a half hour later, Mrs. Palmer decided to start the dishes, but first she crossed over to the buffet, knelt on the floor, and opened the bottom drawer. Martha watched intently as her mother lifted out a parcel. She carefully opened the brown paper bag and drew out the navy blue, cardboard box. Her mother looked over and studied her husband's face, and he responded with a quick nod. For several seconds Mrs. Palmer held the box thoughtfully in her hands, and after removing the lid of the box, she tipped out the Bible. She pressed it to herself and briefly glanced at Brent's piston on the buffet.

"Mom!" Martha exclaimed. "That's the Bible you were planning to give Brent after he got saved."

Mrs. Palmer sighed, and then she replied solemnly, "Yes. That awful car crash took his life. He never accepted the Lord." The room was silent for several seconds, and the hired man's clock in the kitchen gave eight strikes. Mrs. Palmer crossed over to their visitor. "Richard," she smiled and informed him, "I—that is, Joshua and I would like you to have this Bible."

Martha remembered, *Mom and Dad bought that Bible for Brent, and by faith they put his name in it, planning to give it to him when he became a believer. They were sure he would become saved someday.* She watched as Richard accepted the Bible and reverently held it with both hands.

Later, when Martha stood on the porch landing, she watched as Richard stepped up into his pickup truck. Their guest placed the Bible which had been intended for Martha's older brother, on the seat beside him. After he started the engine, he looked over at her and grinned as he put it in gear. She returned the smile and thought, *I'll get him a new thermos and leave it in his mailbox.*

As Richard started down the driveway, he glanced over at Martha again and waved. She waved back and thought, *There goes a new creature.* Mister wandered over to her and sat on her feet looking for attention, and Martha bent over and stroked his back. She said aloud to the dog, "Behold all things are become new." He wagged his tail in response.

The half-ton pickup turned onto the Hannah Road, and Richard lightly tapped on the horn several times. Martha kept her eye on the truck just beyond the tall grasses at the edge of the field. Soon the truck was out of sight, but its driver was still on her mind.

chapter ten

two years later—September 1969

Signs

"Look, Richard, there's another sign," Martha pointed out, and as she turned her head, her ponytail brushed the back of the seat. "'HIGHWAY VIEW CAMPSITE, NEXT EXIT, TURN RIGHT. OPEN MAY TO OCTOBER'."

Richard and his wife, Martha, were on a touring holiday for a week in mid-September, and when it was suitable to do so, they camped along the way. Earlier this afternoon they had stopped to buy a few supplies at a small grocery store in a village off the main highway to prepare for supper at their next campsite.

Ten minutes later Richard said, "Here's the exit now." He took the off-ramp and then turned to the right onto the secondary paved road.

"There it is," Martha told him when they had traveled about an eighth of a mile along the road. He geared down, put on his directional indicator, and turned in at a sign next to the gravel driveway which led up to a remodeled farmhouse. Next to the house was a sign which read, 'OFFICE', and the arrow pointed to an addition on the side of the dwelling.

"There doesn't seem to be anybody around, Richard."

"Well, it is the middle of September."

A battered brown and white truck was situated near the office, and Richard parked next to it and stepped out. Before he walked over and entered the door marked, 'REGISTER HERE', he rolled down the sleeves of his paisley shirt, concealing the tattoo on his arm.

The room was dimly lit, and stretching across its width was a broad counter. A desk covered with odds and ends occupied space against one wall, and a metal filing cabinet with one drawer partly open was near the door to the house. The room was silent except for the buzzing of dozens of flies. Richard could see a sticky fly coil nearly covered in large black dots hanging from the low ceiling. Neither of the two bare ceiling lights were turned on.

Richard stepped over a broom lying on the floor, and he approached the counter. There was a desk bell near a pile of newspapers, and he tapped the plunger twice. The large, multi-coloured cat reclining on the desk opened one green eye, looked at him with disinterest, stretched, and resumed its nap. The large flies kept up their relentless and pointless maneuvers through the stale air.

Richard sharply tapped the desk bell three times. In the distance he could faintly hear what sounded like a news report on the radio. Two or three flies protested loudly on the coil which he thought was vibrating slightly. He waited several seconds and then rapidly tapped the desk bell eight or nine times.

The sound of footsteps came near, and the door was pushed open several more inches. Richard could barely see someone in the near darkness of the house and then the door opened wide, and a man wearing a gray t-shirt and black baggy pants entered. He turned on the light switch and limped over to the counter. "Yes?" he asked solemnly as he sucked on his cigarette.

"My wife and I would like a campsite for the night." Richard tried to sound pleasant. "Do you have any available?"

The man blew out a stream of smoke towards the ceiling. He brushed away a half dozen flies from the counter-top with his hairy, bare arm and picked up a registration form. With one finger, he pushed up his bottle-bottom glasses to the top of his nose.

"Name?" he inquired without looking up.

"Jack, Richard Jack."

"Address?" Richard told him.

"Phone number?" Richard gave him the number. The man picked up the form and dumped off the fly which had just crash-landed there and was now on its back and spinning uncontrollably in circles.

"How many in your party?" he questioned in near monotone.

"Two."

"How long do you intend to stay?" he asked.

"Just one night."

The man raised his eyes and looked at him as he pushed his glasses back up again. "That'll be ten dollars," he said, and Richard thought he detected a smirk come over the man's face. He gave him the money, and the man shoved it deep into his pocket.

"I'll show you." He came out from his side of the counter and hobbled over to the door, stepping over the broom. Richard followed him outside. The man dropped his cigarette on the ground, adding to dozens of others which were crushed into the dirt, and he climbed into his truck and slammed the door. The latch did not catch, and he slammed it once more.

Richard joined Martha in their car. "What took so long?"

"He wasn't in the office at first," her husband explained when he started the engine. "Guess he didn't hear me."

"You sure smell some of tobacco!"

The truck pulled away quickly, and Richard scrambled to catch up. "He wants us to follow him." A homemade sign fastened to a post near the road had the words: 'MAXIMUM SPEED TEN MILES AN HOUR'. Richard and Martha could see no visitors on the grounds here, and no vehicles were in the area. The playground had several swings, two seesaws, and a metal slide.

The gravel road took a turn and went through woods for a short distance, momentarily obscuring the truck they were following after. The road here was dirt rather than gravel and led into a large field. The truck was barely visible through the dust it had stirred up. It increased speed and continued to the centre of the field where it suddenly stopped. Richard pulled up behind the truck as his dust drifted by. The man looked at him in his rear-view mirror and as Richard opened his car door and stepped out, the man pointed to the grassy area on the side of the narrow road. Richard walked up to the occupant in the truck.

"Over there," the man said without expression, and he left before Richard could reply.

Richard returned to Martha's side of the car, and she rolled down the window about halfway. "This is it," he announced as he tried to smile at her. He got in the car and backed it onto the campsite, and he and Martha climbed out and just stood there. "This is some crazy place!" he said as he planted his wide-brimmed hat on his head and rolled up his shirt sleeves.

Their campsite had a fire area made of four concrete blocks topped with a metal grill, and several feet away was a picnic table. The campsite was defined by a low fence on three sides. The fence was more of a barrier than a wall, and it looked like heavy rope hanging loosely on waist-high stakes spaced about eight feet apart.

Martha stared at the fence and then crossed through the tall grasses to examine it. "Look at this, Richard! It's made of pop bottle caps. There must be hundreds of them—no thousands! All strung together."

"Probably beer bottle caps as well," he figured. "Somebody was very busy drinking and threading, and for a long time, too."

Martha returned to the car for her straw hat. Although they were several hundred yards from the busy highway, the couple were well aware of the constant rushing noise coming from the vehicles speeding along the pavement.

"There's no let-up in the traffic!" protested Richard as he glanced across the field. "How are we going to sleep with that racket all night!"

Martha said with a sarcastic giggle, "Highway View Campsite is a good name for this place, don't you think?"

Only three other campsites were occupied with campers. A tent was set up near the fence close to the highway where several people were sitting on a picnic table oblivious to the constant noise so close to them. Richard pointed over a bit to the right. "And look—there's people at that travel-trailer."

"There's a pup tent at the far end of the field," Martha remarked, "but I don't see anyone there."

Richard opened the car trunk and hauled out their tent. "Hey, it's quieter on this side of the car away from the traffic. I'll move the car so it's between us and the highway." After repositioning the car, Richard and Martha pitched their recently purchased blue nylon tent.

"I'll go look for the washrooms before I start the fire," Richard decided as he returned his wooden maul to the trunk. He headed off in the direction of the buildings in the woods next to the field.

Here, all along the edge of the woods were other campsites. Richard figured none of them were occupied at this time. Most of them had elaborate fences made from a variety of materials. Some had borders of tree branches fastened horizontally or vertically.

He followed the road into the woods where there were other campsites. *The sound of the highway is muffled here,* he realized. *These people would have it much quieter.*

Richard could see no one in this area and there were no vehicles here. He saw that these sites had additional personal touches. Most had wooden platforms with picnic tables placed on them. There was an electrical line strung up through the trees providing each campsite with power. Suspended over the platforms were outdoor lights and some sites were decorated with colourful patio lights. Amongst the trees could be seen refrigerators on or near the platforms. A variety of storage buildings of different sizes, materials, and colours were situated at most sites. "These must be the deluxe sites," Richard commented aloud as he fingered the brim of his hat.

Richard crossed to the first public building on his exploratory tour. The weather beaten sign read, 'MENS'. He opened the torn screen door and stepped into the dark room. The air was damp, and he detected a hint of mustiness. A light switch, he noticed, was several feet from the door in the middle of the wall. He discovered it controlled the bare ceiling light. Five homemade shower stalls, side by side were situated along one wall. Richard could see that the used water from the first stall would run along the concrete floor and under the raised wooden partition. The water would continue its course across the floor into the second stall for that fellow to stand in, and so on, down to the fifth shower stall where the only floor drain was situated. Richard thought, *That poor guy wouldn't have clean feet after standing in all that dirty water!*

There were no toilets here. *Strange! I must be dreaming!* Richard imagined as he switched off the light and stepped outside into the fresh air. He carefully closed the door behind him, and after he took a deep breath of clean air, he found himself wiping his boots on a small patch of grass nearby.

There was another building over a few dozen yards, and when he moved closer he could read the 'MENS' sign over the wide sliding door. A large padlock prevented the open door from being closed. From the outside Richard could plainly see four toilet stalls along the back wall. *I'm still dreaming!* Richard concluded as he stared at this strange set-up. Before entering the building, he turned around and quickly surveyed the nearby deserted campsites.

Richard was tempted to rush back to their campsite where his wife was but decided instead to enjoy the peculiar sights as he leisurely walked along.

When he returned to Martha in the large open field, she was organizing supper. "You wouldn't believe this place, Martha!" he exclaimed to her. "See those campsites over there?" He pointed along the edge of the woods and grinned. "Each one is fenced off with boards and other junk, and one has diagonal boards just to be different." She turned and looked where he was indicating. He continued, "Several campsites even have fancy archways made with junk—for entrance ways onto their own personal property."

Martha suggested, "Let's have a walk-about after we eat."

"Those campsites are most likely rented for the season to people from the city," Richard continued, "probably year after year. They sure spent a lot of time and effort personalizing their bit of rented land. Some even have sand-boxes and those metal, backyard swings for children." Martha grinned at Richard.

He glanced over at their fireplace. "I'll get the fire started," he offered. He saw there were several pieces of burnt wood already under the grill. "That's a good start," he commented, and he crumpled up a sheet of newspaper and added the birch-bark he had saved from their last campfire.

Martha opened the package of two steaks, and after she trimmed them, she placed them in the frying pan. Richard dragged a match across the concrete block and put the little flame against the newspaper. The paper, birchbark, and twigs caught fire, and the flames began to lick the old burnt wood. He stood up and adjusted his hat as the smoke slowly rose into the air.

Martha lowered the frying pan to the grill over the fire which now was burning nicely, and then she reached for the saucepan. "I'll get some water to cook the peas in. Richard, will you shell these while I'm gone?" She handed him the medium size paper bag of unshelled peas they had purchased at a road-side fruit and vegetable stand that afternoon.

"Okay," he answered as she handed him the bag. "These look like nice peas. We'll eat them all now, won't we?"

"Yeah, probably," she called back, and she patted down the top of her hat.

When Martha returned with the saucepan of water, the peas were shelled, and Richard was looking over their supply of food. "I'm starved," he said. "Will we have these rolls?"

"Okay, and bring the butter, too. Do you want the pumpkin pie as well?"

Martha poured most of the water into another pan before she added the peas. She put the lid on and placed the saucepan on the grill. She then turned the steaks, and Richard poured water into the tea kettle and set it over the fire.

Suddenly Richard and Martha looked at each other. "Did you notice that?" Richard asked as he faced the highway.

"Yeah," Martha replied, "it was quiet for a second."

Richard looked pleased. "The traffic is getting less." As their supper cooked over the fire, they realized that as the late afternoon merged with the supper hour, the silent times were gradually becoming longer and more frequent.

Richard and Martha were not aware of the slowly approaching station wagon on the roadway until it was nearly next to them. The man in the passenger's seat nodded politely but then suddenly smiled and waved at them. "He must have thought he knew us," Richard figured as he poked at the fire.

The vehicle came to a halt half a dozen campsites away. The car had hardly stopped when one of the back doors flew open, and a boy scampered out and whooped, followed by another boy about the same age, and then a gray dog tumbled from the station wagon. The man, a lady and a little girl emerged from the vehicle, and the man reached back inside and lifted out an even younger girl. One of the boys jumped up onto the picnic table, closely followed by the other boy, and then they both jumped off the other side into the tall grass. The dog was running around in large circles.

"They're having a hyper good time for sure!" Richard muttered. The man lowered the little girl to the grass and hauled out a tent from the back of his station wagon. He called to the boys, and they pitched the large tent. "It looks like they're well organized," Richard observed.

"Richard, you shouldn't be looking!" Martha turned the steaks again. "I think they've been here before," she added. "They don't appear to be surprised at anything like we were."

Richard pushed the burning firewood closer together. "Why would anyone come here more than once!"

"I don't know," Martha replied. "I'm hungry, and it looks like the steaks are done."

Another vehicle came along the road and pulled in at the campsite next to the station wagon and on the side closer to Richard and Martha. Several young people spilled from the car, and the driver shouted a greeting to the family at the station wagon.

"Oh, no!" exclaimed Richard. "They know each other. It could be a noisy evening."

Martha answered, "The traffic noise is becoming less, but the people noise is increasing."

"Well, let's eat," Richard suggested.

"Richard!" She studied his face closely. "Are you growing a mustache?"

He turned to face her squarely and grinned. "Yes, I am."

She giggled. "Well, that's nice."

"I'm glad you think so," he replied as he placed a steak on each of the plastic plates Martha was holding out to him. She put the plates on the table as Richard drained the water from the peas into the tall grass next to their fence of pop bottle caps.

Richard and Martha sat down at their table, and Richard removed his canvas hat, gave thanks, and they began to eat.

Other vehicles arrived, sometimes two or three together. Everyone seemed to know everyone else. Some people were preparing to stay the night by setting up their tents, and it looked like others planned to be there for the evening only. Lawn chairs were positioned at the two joining campsites.

"I hope it isn't a rowdy party," Richard mumbled. "I don't know which is worse, a noisy picnic or the traffic noise."

Some young people were organizing a game of kick-ball on the roadway. Four men carried over two picnic tables and joined them to the table at the site where the lawn chairs were. The ladies began to place dishes of food on the tables. A man and several boys unloaded some firewood from the back of a truck. They carried pieces to the campsite, next to the tables spread with food, where most of the people were now gathered.

"I wouldn't want to be a part of that bunch even if I was invited!" Martha declared.

Richard snickered and put in, "Not much chance of that."

Richard and Martha could hear someone playing an accordion. "That's a Christian chorus, isn't it?" Richard wondered.

Martha replied, "Well, the tune is, anyway. Probably borrowed—or stolen."

"Oh no, look!" Richard observed. "That man who waved to us when they drove by is now on his feet, and he's looking our way."

Martha agreed and then whispered, "Hey, I think he's coming in this direction."

As the man came along the roadway, he led his dog on a leash, and when he approached Richard and Martha, he grinned at them. "Lovely evening isn't it!" he greeted as he stopped in front of their campsite.

"Yes it is," Richard answered politely but did not want to appear too friendly.

"I noticed your bumper sticker when we drove by," the man related. Richard and Martha both turned to glance at the sticker they had purchased last spring. They had nearly forgotten they had it. The sticker showed an outline of a fish and had Greek letters which made an acrostic for 'Jesus Christ, God's Son, Saviour'.

"My name is Tommy Dodge," the man explained as he stepped off the road onto the grass. He glanced back at the crowd of people around the picnic tables and added, "We're a group of Bible-believers who love the Lord."

"You are!" Richard and Martha exclaimed at the same time. Richard added, "We're Bible-believing Christians too!" He stood up to shake Tom's hand. "My name's Richard Jack, and this is my wife, Martha," he replied cordially. "We're pleased to meet you, Tommy."

"Would you folks care to join us?" Tom asked. "If you haven't had dessert yet, you could eat with us. And later, we'll have a singsong and a message from God's Word."

"Yeah, we'd like to come over and meet you folks," Richard answered as he grinned and glanced at his wife.

"Richard, we could take our pumpkin pie."

"Oh, that's all right," Tom quickly put in. "Don't bring

anything. There's plenty of food. Each family brings more than enough, and we share."

Martha returned the pie to the food-box in the car. "We can wash these things later," she told Richard as he rolled down his shirt sleeves. Before they left with Tom, Richard quickly checked their fire.

The three approached the group, and Tom introduced Richard and Martha to several couples. "Hello, how are you?" greetings were exchanged with, "Fine, thanks," in return.

A man in his mid-twenties shook an ox-bell vigorously and motioned for everyone to come near. When they were quietly assembled, he gave thanks for the food and for the Lord Jesus Christ. "Help yourselves to the grub, People," he called out.

The sun had slipped behind the stand of tall trees nearby, and someone added more wood to the fire. There was much less traffic on the highway, and Richard and Martha had forgotten all about the disturbance from that direction.

People were in groups of various sizes, and they were sitting at picnic tables or on lawn chairs. A middle-aged couple invited Richard and Martha to sit with them. After they introduced themselves, Richard asked, "How often do you people meet like this?"

"Every Friday evening in September," he answered, "and the first week or two of October, if the weather is suitable. The insects aren't bad this time of year."

His wife told them, "Theo has a large army tent we can use if it looks like rain. You wouldn't believe the size of it!"

The man added, "There's enough room inside to swing a cat! And the young people have fun helping to set it up." Richard and Martha were also told that this group was made up of believers from several nearby places.

"Getting together like this isn't convenient for some of us, and it can be costly, too," a father of several teens added. "We close up our family businesses Friday evenings to come here—the most profitable evening to do business. We value this experience for our children and young people as well as ourselves more than the money we could've made this evening. And the Lord honours us for this. Our businesses continue to thrive, and we grow spiritually as well."

When most people were through eating, the man with the ox-bell shouted, "Please don't wander off very far. We'll have a singsong in about twenty minutes."

Tom turned to Richard and asked, "What work do you do?"

"I do masonry work," he replied. "All kinds of masonry work. What do you do?"

"Right now I'm working in a hardware store, but my interest is in Christian summer camps."

Richard responded, "I've never been to a Christian summer camp."

Sometime later when there was still some light in the sky, the ox-bell rang again, and the older man with the accordion picked up his instrument and began to play. The young fellow who was leading the singsong motioned for others to come closer.

The group sang some of the standard hymns and choruses. Interspersed with these traditional hymns were other pieces with the regular words sung to nontraditional tunes, which made the words seem fresh. They also sang new words using well-known hymn tunes. The singing was lively, but not overly fast nor hyper, and it was nice to hear the blending of the different singing parts within the group. The accordion player would sometimes stop playing, even in the middle of a verse and join in the singing with his deep melodious voice. It was hard to tell which he enjoyed more—playing his accordion or singing.

"Last week when we were here we said we would memorize First Corinthians Thirteen." The song leader looked around. "Tommy Dodge, where are you, Sir?"

Tom jumped to his feet and asked as he looked around, "Who can repeat the chapter?" More than half a dozen people raised their hands.

"Okay, let's begin. All together now. First Corinthians Thirteen," he quoted slowly, "'Though I speak with the tongues of men and of angels'." Most of the others joined in with him.

When they had completed the chapter, a girl in her mid-teens asked, "What are we going to memorize for next week?"

Tom answered, "How about Psalm One Twenty-One?"

"I already know that one," a boy with red curly hair called out with a grin.

"Good for you, Victor," Tom replied. "Did you get that folks? Psalm One Twenty-One for next week, if it doesn't rain, and if the Lord doesn't come for us before then."

Tom sat down, and the song leader asked, "Who has anything they can share with us that we can praise the Lord for with you?"

A lady shot up her hand. "The Lord led me to a good used car earlier this week." Several people were obviously interested and pleased.

A man with his arm in a cast stated, "I'm thankful to the Lord for the people who helped us get our garden in."

Tom suggested, "Could we pray now that Ian's arm will heal as it should?" He stood up and thanked the Lord for Ian and his family and their testimony. He then prayed that the Lord would continue to meet them in their needs and that His goodness would be evident to them.

A man with a droopy mustache got to his feet. "Well, I'm thankful the company I was working for finally folded," he stated. There was a brief moment of silence, and some people had puzzled looks on their faces. He explained, "The alcoholic owners were managing the business poorly, and it was ruining my reputation. Our competitors have hired me, and there's room for advancement, too."

"Well, that's an answer to prayer, Joe," another man in the crowd pointed out. "I knew you weren't happy there, and I've been praying for you."

The darkness slowly closed in on this crowd of friendly people, and a young man got up and put several pieces of wood on the fire. After they sang another song, a man wearing a jack-shirt stood up to give a message from God's Word. First he turned to Galatians six, nine and ten. Most people had Bibles, and they followed along as he read aloud. "And another passage," he said. "Turn to Colossians three, twelve to seventeen."

After reading these passages, he told his audience, "We have a well-built fire here this evening." He glanced at the orange flames dancing before them and continued. "A good fire is an illustration of our fellowship one with another. A fire is useful for our warmth and comfort—I can feel the heat from here." He held out his hand towards the fire. "And fellowship with the people of the Lord will result in encouragement and support for us." The man glanced around at the people seated before him.

"A fire needs protection from the wind and the rain." The cracking fire could be heard as he spoke. "Our fellowship with the Lord's people needs to be protected from the busyness and commotion of the world and from Satan's discouragements. That's why we appreciate these times here together." Those before him listened attentively, and several nodded in agreement.

"A fire needs the logs close together to burn well. Close fellowship with the people of the Lord causes us to grow spiritually." He could see the others staring into the fire thoughtfully. The man gave this illustration: "When a burning log is pulled away from the other logs of the campfire, it soon cools off and is in danger of dying. When our fellowship is seldom, our love for fellow-believers might weaken and could be in danger of dying." One of the burning logs settled into the fire causing sparks to fly upward into the darkening sky.

"The heat from a well built fire steadily rises upward like this one, and the sweetness of our fellowship with one another ascends to the Lord and is pleasing to Him. Also, a good fire does not produce any irritating smoke, and fellowship with the Lord's people should not produce anything which is annoying to one another nor to the Lord."

"One final point. Let's look at the words of the Lord Jesus in John chapter thirteen, verses thirty-four and five." The man tipped his Bible towards the light of the fire. He read the verses and explained. "The light of a well built fire attracts those who are in the dark, and the harmony of our fellowship will attract unbelievers and should ultimately draw them to the Lord. We sometimes sing, 'They will know we are Christians by our love'."

When the man had finished his message, he concluded by speaking to the Lord in prayer, and then the song leader stood up again. "What can we sing which fits in with what we have been thinking about?" he asked. After singing several more hymns, some people prepared to leave.

"Before we break up for the evening," the song leader spoke up, "we should talk to the Lord again and give ourselves afresh to Him. Let's ask Grandpa Boates to pray for us."

A smiling, elderly gentleman seated on a lawn chair was helped to his feet by a man and a lady. He stood there in the light of the fire, leaning on his cane and swaying slightly as he continued to smile. The patriarch gave thanks for the warmth of Christian fellowship and for God's Word and those who shared it. He then gave thanks for the Lord Jesus Christ and asked that our love for the Lord would be evident like the light of this fire to those around us including those of our family and friends who do not know the Lord.

The man and the lady carefully lowered the still smiling man into his chair. The fire was then built up to give more light for those who were preparing to leave. The two borrowed picnic tables were returned to their original campsites nearby.

Fifteen minutes later and after many 'Good-nights' and 'Good-byes', Richard and Martha returned in the dark to their campsite. Richard dug out the flashlight and retrieved his hat which he had left on their picnic table. He and his wife slipped into their jackets, and they walked hand in hand along the road towards the lights coming from the washrooms in the woods. They passed by the elaborate fences bordering the dark, unoccupied campsites next to the trees. Richard said quietly, "I like the idea of memorizing a different passage of Scripture each week."

"Yes," Martha said thoughtfully, "I wish I had memorized more Scripture when I was younger."

"And did you ever see so many open Bibles as the guy spoke, even when it was almost too dark to read," Richard went on. "Even little kids who can't read had Bibles. These people respect the authority of God's Word, and that's got to make an impression on kids and all those young people who were there tonight."

"Look, Richard," Martha remarked when they could see the buildings in the trees. "Your washroom door isn't wide open now—it's nearly closed." There were several moths circling the outside light over the door, and they could see the interior was lit up.

Richard walked up to the sliding door, turned sideways, and squeezed through the narrow opening. "Well, hello!" greeted a man with a young boy.

"Hello!" Richard replied. He recognized him from earlier at the campfire.

"My name is Vincent. I didn't have the opportunity to speak to you at the get-together."

"I'm Richard. My wife and I enjoyed the fellowship this evening."

Vincent told him, "Yes, our family comes as often as we can."

Richard motioned to the door and asked, "How did the door get closed up like this? It was wide open this afternoon and locked that way."

Vincent smiled broadly and explained. "The padlock was in place, but it wasn't snapped closed. Victor and I just removed the lock and slid the door to partly closed."

The boy spoke up, "Me and Daddy do it every time."

When Richard left the washroom, he waited nearby for Martha. As they walked back towards their campsite, his wife said, "I like the way the young man leading the singing briefly commented on the words. What he said reminded us of what the words are all about."

As Richard and Martha left the woods and crossed the field, they heard only one vehicle traveling along the highway. Richard commented, "Probably people from the group tonight."

The campfire was still burning nicely where the get-together had been, and someone was erecting a tent nearby. There were lights placed on six or seven tables at other campsites or hung in the tents of those who were staying overnight. Their own campsite was in darkness except for several dull red, dying coals between the concrete blocks. Richard and Martha walked in silence and used their flashlight only when they could feel they were on the edge of the roadway. When they arrived at their campsite, they entered the tent and were soon in their double sleeping bag. Richard said quietly, "Nothing was done this evening for the purpose of being emotional."

"Yes, that's right," Martha answered in agreement. "The evening was emotional, but that was the outcome, not the aim or the purpose of the get together."

"It was genuine honour to the Lord," Richard concluded, "and these people enjoy their Christian lives. Let's talk to the Lord right now, and thank Him for this evening." They thanked their Heavenly Father for Christian fellowship and most of all for His Son the Lord Jesus Christ who makes life worth living.

Martha fluffed up her pillow and remarked quietly, "That elderly gentleman must be very close to the Lord. He prays as though he knew Him really well."

"Will I be as sweet as he is when I'm his age?" Richard wondered aloud, and Martha reached over and touched his hand.

"Hey," Richard whispered, "I don't hear any traffic on the highway."

"That's right—and listen to the crickets!" Martha added. "There must be dozens of them!"

"Yeah," Richard answered in a hushed, sleepy voice, "They're the only ones who are having the late night party."

Martha added quietly, "I think they're having a singsong—listen!" Richard did not answer. He was asleep. Martha rolled over and peacefully drifted off with the melody of the crickets' choir encircling their tent.

The next day when Richard and Martha awoke and crawled out of their tent, they could see the sky was heavily overcast. "It looks like rain," Martha noted as she brushed her hair.

"Yeah, let's have breakfast and head for home."

The station wagon slowly passed by, and Richard waved to the occupants. Tom rolled down the window. "Have a good day, Folks," he greeted.

"Yes, we will. You, too." Richard and Martha waved as the vehicle moved away. Richard turned to his wife and remarked, "They have a good start."

"You said they were well organized," she replied as she opened the food-box. "Do you want the rolls or the pumpkin pie?"

"Pumpkin pie for breakfast sounds delicious! I'll put the tent away first in case it starts to rain before we leave."

Martha suggested, "Could we stop for a coffee down the road somewhere?"

Richard and Martha cleared out the tent, and then Richard took it down, rolled it up, and stuffed it into its bag, and then placed it in the trunk of their car. He found his battery-operated shaver and stood at one of the outside mirrors of their car. Martha set the pumpkin pie on the table along with two plates. A minute later Richard opened his shaver and blew out the hairs. He had another look in the mirror and then put away his shaver.

Martha came over to him. "Mister Jack!" she declared as she ran her finger along the bristle above his upper lip.

"Mrs. Jack," he replied, "is the pumpkin pie ready for breakfast yet?"

When Richard and Martha drove past the office with the battered brown and white truck parked by the door, raindrops began to hit the windshield of their little car. They started along the gravel driveway towards the secondary road, and Richard switched on the wipers. Up ahead they could read what was printed on the back of the sign they'd seen when they had arrived. Martha read the words aloud. "'PLEASE COME BACK AGAIN'."

"Yes, we will," Richard promised, and he grinned at Martha who was smiling as well.

chapter eleven

about eight years later—Christmas 1977

The Night Before Christmas

"When are we leaving, Dad?" asked seven-year-old Timothy for the ninth time.

"When we're ready," Mr. Jack replied as he smoothed back his handlebar mustache, "and not a minute sooner." He glanced up at the hired man's clock as it began to strike seven o'clock.

"Jennifer," her mother called out, "don't get into those boxes of Christmas decorations. They're ready to go out to the car." She was about two years younger than her brother. A red bow on one pigtail and a green one on the other added to the festive season.

"Mom," Jennifer wanted to know, "do we have any little Christmas bells? I want to put one in each of my pigtails." She followed her mother into the kitchen, and Timothy looked over at her in exaggerated disbelief and then disgust.

His dad picked up the sleeping bag which had just rolled off the suitcase waiting by the front door. "Timothy," he warned him, "don't lean on that box. You might break what's inside."

Timothy knelt on the floor, opened the cardboard flaps, and peered in. "Just a bunch of Christmas lights and other stuff." He pulled on the end of the string of lights, stood up, and lifted it over his head. As he swung around, the lights snagged on the corner of the box, and it nearly tipped over.

"Timothy!" his dad scolded him. "Be careful, will you! You're going to break something. Put those back." Timothy lowered the lights into the box, and he tried to fold the flaps and close it the way he had found it.

"Timothy, I wish you'd leave things alone," Mr. Jack let out impatiently. "I haven't time to do the same job more than once.

Why don't you find something to do somewhere else and not get in the way here."

"Dad?" Timothy said as he stood facing him.

He answered, "What is it now? I'm pressured here, you know. Can't you see I'm busy with all this?" He scowled at his son. "Tim, is it important?"

Timothy took a step towards his dad. "Dad," he said, trying a second time, "I love you." With that, the boy turned and left for the living room.

The Jack family had had an early supper, and they were doing last minute tasks before the one hour drive from their rented house in town to Uncle Allan's farm. Mrs. Jack had made plans a week ago for their family to have Christmas at the homestead of this distant relative. Uncle Allan was to be picked up soon after supper at his second floor apartment in the next town, and then they would drive out to his unoccupied farm. They were planning to spend Christmas Eve there and stay until late Christmas afternoon.

Finally the Jack family piled into their car with their things and drove through town. As they traveled along the main street they enjoyed the colourful lights and other Christmas displays. "Let's count how many Santas we can see," Jennifer suggested with enthusiasm.

Timothy pulled off his blue stocking cap and said, "Mom, today I read five verses in my Bible. Yesterday I read four."

"That's good," his mom answered him pleasantly. "We should read our Bibles every day."

Mr. Jack commented to his wife, "We haven't seen your Uncle Allan since his wife died—must have been three years ago. The children say they don't remember him."

She answered, "I told them Uncle Allan isn't a Christian, and we should put on our best behaviour."

They left their town and headed for William Station, the next town thirty minutes away. As they moved along the highway, the full moon could be seen floating on the indigo sky beyond the trees.

The old man was waiting for them with his small brown suitcase. Going away for Christmas was exciting for the Jack family, but Uncle Allan said little as he joined them in the car. In the semi-darkness he looked depressed.

They were on their way once more through town, and the old man muttered to himself, "Did you ever see such displays of foolishness!"

During the silence that followed, Mrs. Jack thought, *Uncle Allan is sour. I sure hope he doesn't spoil it for the children. We've got to show him the love of Christ and the true meaning of Christmas.*

Mr. Jack decided, *Uncle Allan must have had an overdose of ugly pills. He's getting grumpy in his old age. I sure hope I don't get that way when I'm old.*

Timothy wondered, *Who is this old man, anyway! Why did we have to bring him. We should dump him off in a snowbank!*

Jennifer reasoned, *We need to take him back to his place until he behaves himself.*

They came to the outskirts of William Station, and Mr. Jack sped up along the main highway leaving the coloured lights of town behind. About twenty minutes passed, and they turned off at the recently plowed, gravel side road.

Five minutes later, Mr. Jack brought the car to a stop on the shoulder of the road at the snow-covered, tree-lined driveway to Uncle Allan's farm. In the light of the full moon, they could see the silhouetted shape of the deserted house where they were going to spend this Christmas, and the barn could be seen off to the right. The old man seemed even more melancholy as he viewed his property from the Jacks' car.

"Look, Mommy," Jennifer pointed out, "the moon followed us all the way to here where we're at now."

Mr. Jack stepped out to shovel an opening in the snowbank across the driveway to make room for their vehicle. After the car was parked, the four Jacks and Uncle Allan picked up as much as they could carry from the trunk and started through the snow, up the long driveway between the trees to the dark, cold house.

When they arrived at Uncle Allan's house, Mrs. Jack and the two children waited outside while Uncle Allan unlocked the door, and he and Mr. Jack entered the house with flashlights and went down into the basement to turn the power on. Several minutes later the kitchen was lit up, followed by the porch light coming on, and then the yard light.

Mrs. Jack and the children entered the house through the porch and stood in the kitchen. It was as cold inside the house as it was outside. Uncle Allan grasped the bowl of his pipe and said, "Make yourselves at home, Folks." It was clear he was putting out an effort to be cheerful.

Mr. Jack looked bewildered, but said nothing. Mrs. Jack stood there with her mouth dropped open. The old gentleman ran his fingers through his thick, white hair. "Well," he decided, "I'll go down to the basement and start a fire in the wood furnace." He promptly left the Jack family standing in the kitchen, and he shuffled off to the basement.

"Richard! What are we going to do? The place is a mess—a right, royal mess!"

"I don't know," he answered his wife as he shook his head and twisted one side of his mustache. "Children, keep your coats on—it's cold in here."

The kitchen table was cluttered with hand-tools and an assortment of nails and screws in glass jars and tobacco cans. There was a pile of newspapers on one end of the counter, and next to it was an electric drill whose cord was draped over dishes, cups and cutlery left to dry on the draining tray from months ago.

"I've got to cook Christmas dinner tomorrow for five people here in this muddle and junk!" Mrs. Jack lamented as she surveyed the large farm kitchen.

Jennifer's pigtails brushed the fur collar of her coat as she turned to her mother. "Mom, does Santa Claus know we're here and not at our place?" she asked.

Mrs. Jack tried to sound cheerful. "Yes, Dear, I'm sure he does."

"Jenny," Timothy informed her, "you should read your Bible every day, shouldn't she, Mom?" He squinted at his sister with his blue eyes, and he gave her a phony smile.

There was junk-mail scattered over the counter and on the burners of the electric stove. One of the cupboard doors was open, revealing on one of the shelves a toaster and a pair of binoculars. "I'm afraid to look in the fridge," Mrs. Jack muttered as she wandered around the spacious room with her clenched fists deep in her coat pockets. Everything they touched was cold, and some things were grimy.

"Have I been good enough for Santa?" Jennifer asked. Her mother, deep in thought, did not reply.

"No, you haven't!" accused Timothy. "You wouldn't share your candy with me after I pulled you on my sled." Mrs. Jack remained silent.

The two children left to explore the downstairs. "Don't get into anything," their mother called out to them. "How could they not get into anything!" she grumbled under her breath.

Uncle Allan could be heard in the basement, and soon wood smoke as well as tobacco were detected, drifting up the stairway and into the kitchen.

Several cardboard boxes in the corner of the kitchen were nestled together and a broom was standing near a little black and white television set on a chair. On the floor in front of the sink was a large piece of well-worn, corrugated cardboard.

The children returned. "We don't have the Christmas tree yet," Jennifer reminded her dad.

Timothy agreed. "We need a tree, Dad."

"Yes, I know. Uncle Allan said we could cut one the other side of the barn."

"Let's go now. We need a Christmas tree tonight. Tomorrow is Christmas!"

"Not just yet. I need to help your mother here first." Mr. Jack glanced around the room and scratched the back of his head. *This is not the way Christmas is supposed to be!* he told himself.

"I wonder what the living room is like," Mrs. Jack remarked. Her husband left to have a look, and the children followed him.

He promptly returned. "You don't want to know," he informed her casually.

"Oh, Richard!" she whispered loudly. "What are we going to do? This is going to be the worst Christmas ever! And what about the children? And Uncle Allan is bothered by something. I wish we hadn't even thought of coming here."

"Well, Martha, 'tis the season to be jolly. We'll just have to make the best of it," he replied. "The children don't seem to mind. Uncle Allan is probably a little sad because his house here brings back memories. What would the Lord want us to do?" He picked up the pile of newspapers from the counter and moved them across the kitchen and left them on the floor in the corner. "Would you like me to start tidying up here or should I leave to get the rest of the things from the car?"

"Oh, Richard, please don't leave yet! Can't you see I'm overwhelmed with all this?"

Uncle Allan could be heard coming up the basement stairs. He entered the kitchen puffing on his pipe. "I got out this here nativity scene for you. I thought you religious people would like to use it." He seemed genuinely pleased, and his bushy eyebrows shifted slightly as he carried the model into the living room.

Mr. Jack began to move the clutter from off the kitchen table, and Uncle Allan, when he returned, told him, "Just move things out of the way to suit yourselves. Lots of junk and stuff here, I'm afraid." He proceeded to his bedroom off the kitchen carrying his small suitcase. Mrs. Jack hunted around for dishcloths and towels.

The smoke was getting thicker. Mrs. Jack tried to open a window but found it was painted shut. *I wouldn't live here even if this place was given to me!* she determined.

"Maybe I should check the furnace," Mr. Jack suggested as he started down the basement stairs.

"Will there be any hot water?" Mrs. Jack called to him, and she shook her head. *And that smelly tobacco pipe of Uncle Allan's!* she concluded bitterly.

Several minutes later Mr. Jack came back. "There, that should be better," he announced cheerfully. "And I turned on the hot water, too." He returned to rearranging things in the kitchen, and ten minutes later he called Timothy to go with him to the car to bring the remainder of their things.

"Okay, Dad, let's vacate the premises!"

Mr. Jack and Timothy stepped out into the moonlight and tramped through the snow, retracing their tracks along the driveway. As they went, the moon cast their shadows across the snow at their feet. Overhead, thousands of stars could be seen in the clear sky.

"Dad, why is Uncle Allan's house so messy?"

"Well, probably because his wife died, and he lived there by himself for a while."

"Why didn't he keep it tidy?"

"He had no reason to—it's easier that way. He was by himself—he felt he had nothing to live for."

The shadows of the leafless maple trees lay across their path. Mr. Jack stopped and pointed to the stars through a gap in the trees on the side of the driveway and remarked, "There's the Big Dipper, Tim."

Timothy pushed back his stocking cap, looked up, and studied the stars. "Yeah," he agreed. "The handle of the Big Dipper is pointing almost down."

"Can you find the North Star?" asked his dad. "Follow the last two stars of the Big Dipper over to the left, and the North Star is that brighter one you see away up there."

Timothy said, "The North Star never moves, so it's always straight north. Right, Dad?"

"That's right. And do you know, the Lord has names for all those stars, and there's thousands and thousands of them." They then marched on in the moonlight and the snowy stillness.

"Dad, why do you and Mom let Jenny think there's a Santa Claus?"

"Because Jenny enjoys it."

"Yeah, but she thinks it's true. She believes you and Mom."

"We're only kidding."

"Yeah, but she doesn't know that. That's lying, isn't it?"

"Well, she'll find out sometime that Santa's not for real."

They arrived back at the car and gathered up the remainder of their things and started for the house which was now lit up and looked more inviting than it did earlier this evening.

"Timmy, you're right, we shouldn't tell lies even if we are teasing," his dad admitted. "We'll tell Jenny the true facts."

"Can I tell her, can I?" Timothy quickly offered.

"No, I think I better."

They arrived back at the house with their loads. "Well, it's warmer in here now," Mr. Jack pointed out as they carried the things into the kitchen.

"Richard, would you put the frozen turkey here in this large pail in the sink." Mr. Jack removed his coat and pushed the melting frost off his mustache. He washed his hands at the sink, shook them off, and dried them in the armpits of his bulky green and blue sweater. After he carefully lowered the turkey into the pail, Mrs. Jack turned on the water to cover it. As water surrounded the turkey and slowly filled the pail, Mrs. Jack told Timothy, "The Christmas tree decorations can go in the living room, and then come back for the sleeping bags."

When he returned, he asked, "Dad, when are we going to get the Christmas tree?"

"Well, I'm helping your mom right now," he replied. "How about later?"

Uncle Allan appeared and suggested, "Me and you could get a Christmas tree, Tim."

His dad replied, "Hey, Timmy, that's a good idea."

"Okay!"

The old man told the boy, "There's a saw in the porch."

Timothy followed Uncle Allan out of the house and onto the landing. The old gentleman paused in the moonlight, and before stepping off the landing, he turned his pipe over and tapped the bowl against the railing, spilling out its contents. He then pushed his pipe into the pocket of his coat, and he and Timothy headed through the snow in the direction of the barn. Timothy explained the Big Dipper and the North Star to the old gentleman, and then they saw a meteor.

"Did you see that, Uncle Allan?"

"Yes, I did!" he replied enthusiastically. They walked past the barn, and Uncle Allan thought, *The barn's still in pretty good shape, from what I can see in the moonlight.*

Timothy interrupted his thoughts. "There's Christmas trees over there, Uncle Allan." He pointed them out in the semi-darkness, and he and Uncle Allan tramped in that direction through the snow to the double row of spruce trees. "These are nice Christmas trees."

The old man explained, "These are special spruce trees I pruned to be used as Christmas trees." They selected a suitable one and walked around it to check its shape from all sides. "Looks pretty good—don't you think?" Uncle Allan placed the saw near the base of the tree and began to cut, causing the tree to quiver with each stroke of the saw.

"Uncle Allan, can I do it?"

"Well—yeah sure, Timmy." He handed the saw to the little fellow, and after getting the saw blade back into the groove, Timothy worked it back and forth.

"Make long cuts," Uncle Allan instructed as he pushed on the tree to prevent the blade from binding. Several minutes later the saw cut through the trunk, and Uncle Allan gave the tree a push, and it fell to the snow-covered ground. "There, Timmy, we did it!"

"Yeah! Hurrah!"

The old man reached into his pocket, removed something, and without looking he threw it as hard as he could towards the moon. "There!" he mumbled under his breath.

"What was that you chucked, Uncle Allan?"

"Oh, just something I needed to get rid of."

Uncle Allan picked up the butt end of the Christmas tree. Timothy adjusted his stocking cap, grabbed the other end of the tree, and they headed back past the barn and to the farmhouse. Outside the door to the house, they shook the tree to make sure most of the snow was gone from it.

"Tim, you can take the tree into the house. Carry this butt end first to get the tree through the door."

They entered the porch and into the kitchen, and Timothy announced, "Mom, me and Uncle Allan got us a Christmas tree!" She was washing dishes and other things they would need, and Mr. Jack was drying.

His mom turned and smiled, "Oh, that's a nice tree, Timmy."

"It looks like it's good and bushy," his dad added.

"Uncle Allan let me use the saw to cut it down," he announced proudly.

"Timmy done a fine job," Uncle Allan said to the boy's parents. "Okay, let's carry it to the living room now."

Jennifer spoke up, "I want to help decorate it." She followed them to the living room, and Uncle Allan returned to the kitchen.

"Come on, Dad, let's put the tree up!" Mr. Jack dropped the dishtowel on the counter and joined the children in the living room.

"Well, where do we start?" He moved the pair of tires from off the couch and stacked them behind one of the large stuffed chairs. "Timmy, you move those boxes of whatever to over there. And Jennifer, shove these newspapers under the couch."

"Are we going to sleep on the living room floor like we did last Christmas Eve at home?" Timothy wanted to know.

"Yeah, Dad, are we?"

"Yes, we're planning to," he answered. "Where can we put this dead something-or-other potted plant?"

"I know," Timothy answered quickly. "Inside the tires."

"Good idea."

Things were nicely rearranged in the living room, and Timothy asked, "Where are we going to put the tree?"

"I know," Jennifer suggested. "Over there between the couch and that big chair."

"I'll get the Christmas tree holder," volunteered Timothy. Soon the tree was up, and the two children and their dad were having a great time decorating it. Some of the decorations had been bought, and some were homemade.

"Hey, what's this?" asked Timothy. He was looking deep into the tree near its trunk.

His dad came over to look. "Why, it's a bird's nest!" Mr. Jack grinned. "Come check it out, Jenny."

"A bird's nest!" she repeated in awe as she held back her pigtails and leaned forward. "Don't hurt it—don't hurt it!"

They finished trimming the tree, and then, last of all, their dad stood on the arm of the large, stuffed chair and put the silver star on the very top. "Mom!" called both children at the same time when the star was in place. Mrs. Jack came in from the kitchen, and Uncle Allan followed.

"Well," their mom said with pleasure, "it's looking like Christmas here for sure!" Mrs. Jack straightened and secured the red bow on one of Jennifer's pigtails which was in danger of slipping off.

"Yes, it does seem more like Christmas," agreed the old man, looking pleased. He removed the shoe box containing junk from the top of the treadle sewing machine and replaced it with the nativity scene. "There's a record-player over there," he informed Timothy, "and the albums are in the box underneath. You'll find some Christmas records there somewhere, too." Timothy helped Uncle Allan set up the record-player, and Timothy selected a Christmas recording. Soon the sounds of a scratchy but joyous rendition of 'Joy to the World' enveloped the delighted group of people in the living room of the old farmhouse.

Jennifer grinned at Uncle Allan. "There's a bird's nest in our Christmas tree, Uncle Allan," she informed him. "Come have a look-see!" When the old gentleman came closer, Jennifer pointed it out to him.

"It's a robin's nest," he told her.

The fragrance of the spruce tree and the smell of hot chocolate floating in from the kitchen made each one feel more like Christmas. "Turn on the Christmas tree lights!" Timothy demanded in his excitement.

When the tree lights were on, Mrs. Jack announced, "Time for hot chocolate." It was a tradition for the Jack family to have this treat every Christmas Eve. Mrs. Jack served it in Christmas mugs used only for this occasion.

Timothy said, "The one with the snowman is mine."

"Mine's the one with the Santa," Jennifer reminded her mom.

"Which do you want, Richard," his wife asked, "the Christmas tree, the winter scene or the picture of the fireplace? Uncle Allan and I will take the other two." The old gentleman was visibly pleased to be included, and Mrs. Jack was relieved things were turning out so well.

Another family tradition was reading about the birth of Jesus from God's Word.

"Uncle Allan, would you mind if we read the Christmas story from the Bible?" asked Mr. Jack when everyone was served a mug of hot chocolate.

"Sure, go ahead, that would be nice." He smiled and moved to sit in the large armchair. When everyone was seated, Mr. Jack opened his Bible and turned to Luke Two. The melody of 'Silent Night' gently permeated the room.

"Timothy," his dad said, "get your Bible and follow along."

"I—I don't—I don't know where it is," he stammered and looked the other way. "I think I didn't bring it."

"How can you read your Bible every day when you didn't bring it with you?" Timothy did not answer. "Luke Two," Mr. Jack began. "'And it came to pass in those days that there went out a decree from Caesar Augustus that all the world should be taxed. And all went to be taxed, everyone into his own city. And Joseph also went up from Galilee, out of the city of Nazareth into Judea, unto the city of David which is called Bethlehem, (because he was of the house and lineage of David) to be taxed with Mary his espoused wife being great with child. And so it was, that, while they were there the days were accomplished that she should be delivered. And she brought forth her first-born son and wrapped Him in swaddling clothes and laid Him in a manger because there was no room for them in the inn.'"

Mr. Jack stopped and looked up. "Tim, do you know what swaddling clothes are?"

He answered, "They're like sheets, aren't they?"

"Yes, that's right." And then he turned to Jennifer. "And what's a manger, Jenny?"

"A feeding trough," she answered confidently.

"Right!"

Mr. Jack continued to read with feeling. "'And there were in the same country, shepherds abiding in the field keeping watch over their flocks by night. And, lo, the angel of the Lord came upon them and the glory of the Lord shone round about them and they were sore afraid.'"

They were all listening with interest, even Uncle Allan. "'And the angel said unto them, "Fear not; for behold, I bring you good tidings of great joy which shall be to all people. For unto you is born this day in the city of David, a Saviour which is Christ the Lord. And this shall be a sign unto you, ye shall find the Babe wrapped in swaddling clothes, lying in a manger." And suddenly there was with the angel a multitude of the heavenly host praising God and saying, "Glory to God in the highest and on earth peace, goodwill toward men."'"

Mr. Jack commented, "The City of David is Bethlehem, and Bethlehem means, 'house of bread'. The Lord Jesus said He was the bread of life."

Mrs. Jack added, "That last verse indicates that we need to give God the glory before there is peace on earth which will result in goodwill toward men."

"Yes, I agree," Mr. Jack said, and he resumed his reading. "'And it came to pass as the angels were gone away from them into Heaven, the shepherds said one to another, "Let us now go even unto Bethlehem and see this thing which is come to pass which the Lord hath made known unto us." And they came with haste and found Mary and Joseph, and the Babe lying in a manger. And when they had seen it, they made known abroad the saying which was told them concerning this Child. And all they that heard it wondered at those things which were told them by the shepherds. But Mary kept all these things and pondered them in her heart. And the shepherds returned, glorifying and praising God for all the things that they had heard and seen as it was told unto them.'" Mr. Jack rested his open Bible on his knees. He looked thoughtful and pleased.

"I like that story," declared Jennifer. "And it's a true story, isn't it Dad? Because it's in the Bible."

Mr. Jack replied, "The Bible is the truth, and it tells us about the Lord Jesus, and we were reading about His birth. The Lord

Jesus came to tell us the truth about God, His Heavenly Father, and we know God is everywhere at the same time."

Timothy interjected while looking at his little sister, "He is here right now as well as on the other side of the world at the same time."

"That's right," his mom answered. "And God knows everything, too. He knows all that we do, all what we say, and He even knows all our thoughts. No one else is like God. No one else knows all about us, what we do, what we say, and what we think."

Timothy added, "God is the only One who really knows when we've been bad or good."

Mr. Jack continued, "God loves us very much. He gave us His Son, the Lord Jesus Christ, and His mother Mary laid Him in a manger while the shepherds were in the fields looking after their sheep."

"Later," Mrs. Jack said, "the Lord Jesus told the people that He Himself was sent by God and those who believed on Him would be saved from their sin. The Lord Jesus loved us so much that He took the punishment for our sin on Himself."

Mr. Jack pointed out, "No one else loves us as much as God loves us. No one else can do what the Lord Jesus did for us. The Lord Jesus was the greatest Man who ever lived on earth. No one else even comes close to His greatness, not even Santa Claus. It is wrong for us to admire anyone as much as we should admire the Lord Jesus. He is God, and it's a lie for us to say that Santa Claus is like God when no one is like Him. At Christmas time we should be thinking about God's Gift to us, the Lord Jesus Christ. It is wrong to think Santa Claus brings gifts."

Mrs. Jack got up out of her chair. "How thankful we should be that we know the truth about God and about Santa," she remarked as she gathered up the empty mugs.

Mr. Jack announced, "Okay, Timmy and Jenny, roll out the sleeping bags." Uncle Allan stood up and left for the kitchen. Timothy and Jennifer laid their sleeping bags close to the Christmas tree, and they placed their parents' double bag back a bit.

When the two children were ready for bed and were in their sleeping bags, the lights were turned off except for those on the Christmas tree. Mr. and Mrs. Jack laid down on their sleeping bag to be with their children for a few minutes.

"This is turning out to be a good Christmas, isn't it!" Mrs. Jack stated to her family.

"Yeah!" both children replied. The coloured Christmas lights shone on their pleased faces as they talked with their parents.

And then Jennifer spoke up. "I don't want to believe in Santa Claus anymore. The Lord Jesus is true—not Santa!"

"Jenny," her dad answered, "your mommy and I are really glad you know the truth, and we're sorry we let you believe the lie about Santa Claus."

Then Timothy remarked solemnly, "I haven't been reading my Bible every day." He was almost crying. "I was lying. I wanted you to be happy that I was reading my Bible so much."

His dad interrupted, "Just like we wanted Jenny to be happy believing the lie about Santa." The Jack family was briefly silent.

Mr. Jack sat up and leaned on one elbow. "I think this would be a good time to pray," he finally said. "Our Heavenly Father, we thank Thee we know the truth. We confess we have lied. Help us to always tell the truth. We thank Thee we know the truth about Thy love for us, and giving us the best Gift—the gift of Thy Son. We thank Thee we can trust Thee for salvation through Jesus Christ."

No one spoke for several minutes, and then Mr. and Mrs. Jack stood up to leave.

"Good night, Timmy and Jenny," Mrs. Jack said to them. "And Merry Christmas."

Timothy replied, "Good night, Mom and Dad."

"Merry Christmas," Jenny added as she suppressed a yawn.

Mr. and Mrs. Jack quietly left their children and moved to the kitchen where Uncle Allan was sitting at the table.

"It's some nice to have you folks here to put some life into this place," Uncle Allan said pleasantly.

"We're glad we could come," Mrs. Jack replied as she pulled a chair from the table and sat down. "We like to do something special at Christmas, and this is special for our family."

Mr. Jack put his elbows on the table and added, "The children are really enjoying it here."

"Uncle Allan, would you like some fruitcake for a lunch?" Mrs. Jack cut several pieces.

Uncle Allan took a slice of cake. "I built this house soon after me and Elna were married. A lot has happened in these here walls. We had six children. They're all married now and have families of their own." He stopped and took a bite of the fruitcake.

"Where are they living now?" asked Mr. Jack as he helped himself to a second piece.

The old man did not reply for what seemed like a long time. But then he answered, "Oh, they're spread out across the country. Very busy, you know—all doing very well." His eyes dropped, and he fiddled with the edge of the tablecloth. "I didn't seem to have time for the children when they were young and at home here, and now they don't seem to have time for me." He paused, then continued. "When I was young, my father didn't spend much time with me and my brothers and sisters, but when he did, he would sometimes tease us. We'd never know if he was kidding or not." Mrs. Jack listened thoughtfully. She could see Uncle Allan's eyebrows standing out from his crumpled forehead. "Once he told my younger sister that there was little elves playing in the woods, and anyone could see them if they snuck into the woods just before it got dark. Well, that night she went missing, and some time after dark we could hear her crying in the woods. Ever since then she's been afraid of the dark and the woods. And I'm sure she's passed that fear on to at least one of her children."

"Yes," Mr. Jack commented, "we need to be careful what we say to children. They are, or they should be, trusting of us."

Uncle Allan continued. "When we all left home to get married and Mother died, none of us kept in touch with Dad, even when he lived handy to us." He paused again. Mr. and Mrs. Jack listened politely. "We never heard from him for a while, and we didn't have telephones back then, so I finally went over to check on him. It was winter, and when I stepped inside his house, it was right cold." The old man's voice dropped, and he stared at the fruitcake in front of him. "I found him in bed barely alive. He had been sick for about a week, and no one to look after him. I got him to the hospital, but he was gone a day or two later."

Mrs. Jack remarked, "That must have been some hard on you."

Uncle Allan nodded. "It's nice to see you're spending time with your children, Richard," he told him. "When they grow up and look back on their childhood, I'm sure they'll have happy memories of home and will remember their parents as being patient with them." He pushed back his chair and stood up to leave for his bedroom.

Mr. Jack rose to his feet. "Good-night, Uncle Allan, and thank you."

"Good-night and Merry Christmas, Richard and Martha."

"Merry Christmas to you, Uncle Allan," Mrs. Jack answered sincerely.

Mr. and Mrs. Jack did a few more things in preparation for Christmas day. Mr. Jack then turned out the lights except for the one over the kitchen stove, and he and his wife headed for the living room where their children were sleeping.

The house was dark, but not cold. It was silent except for hushed conversation from the floor of the living room. "It would be nice to have property like this." The man sighed. "This was a productive farm at one time. I'd like the children to live away from town and be in the country."

"Yes," his wife replied. "They've said they'd like to live in the country."

He responded, "There's no way we can do that right now and maybe never."

She concluded, "We need to let the Lord lead us as a family."

The man went on, "Somehow I believe He caused us to come here to Uncle Allan's place this Christmas."

"Uncle Allan nicely fits in with us, doesn't he?" the lady whispered to her husband. "And I like the way he gets along with the children."

"Yes. And I think he misses his family even when they don't make time for him. We should keep in touch with the old fellow more often."

They were silent for several minutes until the man whispered. "Merry Christmas, Martha—and good-night."

"And Merry Christmas and good-night to you, Richard," his wife replied, and she rolled over.

Soon they were both asleep, but not everybody was asleep in that tranquil house. The old gentleman was wide awake in the quiet darkness of his bedroom. He had never felt this peaceful since his wife passed away. *I didn't realize I missed my place here until I came back tonight,* he concluded. *The loneliness of town makes me some miserable, but I couldn't possibly live here in my house by myself, and none of my children want to live here, especially with me.* This made him feel sad again.

He took a deep breath and let it out slowly. *I know what I'll do!* He almost spoke aloud in his excitement. *In the morning I'll ask Richard and Martha if they would like to live here in this house. I'll stay here with them, and they can look after me as long as they can. I'll even change my will to leave them my house and property!* He suddenly realized he was smiling, in fact, he was almost laughing. He knew this was going to be his best Christmas ever.

chapter twelve

about two and a half years later—summer 1980

The Mystery of the Old House

"And, Timmy, be careful riding your bike on the highway," his mom reminded him as she brown-bagged his lunch and placed it in his hiking bag.

"Yeah, Mom." He shoved the last bite of toast into his mouth, glanced at the hired man's clock on the shelf over the refrigerator, and wiped his hands on his pale blue t-shirt.

"And take time to stop and eat your lunch—do you hear?"

"Yeah," Timothy answered again, and he reached for his red cap hanging from the hook by the door. "Bye, Mom. Bye, Uncle Allan."

"Timothy, not so loud! Don't wake up your baby brother," she told him before she returned the roll of waxed paper to the drawer under the counter.

"Bye," his younger sister Jennifer called from the kitchen table where she was playing checkers with Uncle Allan.

"Bye," Timothy answered, and he gave her a big, fake smile. He picked up his hiking bag and left the house for the barn where he kept his bike.

Overhead, the sky was deep blue with a few fluffy, white clouds, and the gentle breeze promised to make biking pleasant. Timothy put his foot up on a bale of hay and double-knotted his sneaker laces, and then he placed his metal pant leg guard around his right ankle. After he wheeled his bike outside, he glanced to the kitchen window where his mom was watching. He waved, and then he was off, pedaling down his long, tree-lined driveway to the gravel road.

Timothy and his friend were planning to bike to the river in the nearby valley. Mike was waiting with his bike at the end of his driveway several farms along the road. Timothy could see his buddy was wearing his favourite shirt, the blue and white one with several sports logos across the front. Both boys were nearly ten years old, and they had discovered recently their birthdays were only one day apart.

As Timothy approached, neither boy spoke, but they raced side by side along the wide dirt road for about fifty metres. A tractor pulling a wagon with a load of hay bales coming towards them prompted them to slow down and bike on the loose gravel on the shoulder of the road. Timothy and Mike returned the farmer's neighbourly wave, and then they were on their way once more. Cattle grazing in the field next to the fence eyed the two friends warily as they pedaled by.

"This old bike isn't going to do me much longer," Mike lamented. "Elliot pretty well wore it out before I got to it."

Ten minutes later the boys turned onto the paved highway. "This is better," Timothy remarked as he pedaled.

"Hey, Tim," Mike called back to him, "you know what a monkey is, don't you?"

"Well, sure," he replied as he came alongside his buddy.

"And you know what a donkey is?"

"Yeah," Timothy answered. "What do you think I am?" He gave him a phony smile as he squinted at Mike.

"Well then," Mike quizzed him, "what's a door key?"

"A dorkey?" he questioned in surprise. "I don't know." And he shrugged his shoulder.

"A door key is used to unlock a door." Mike giggled and pedaled ahead.

About two kilometres down the highway, the two boys left the pavement and biked along a gravel road which dropped into the valley. "I heard that the old guy lives in town but goes to the farmhouse by the river nearly every day," Timothy related as he skirted a line of potholes.

Mike added, "I've heard he never stays in the old house overnight." The dirt road with a couple of switchbacks, traversed the steep terrain of the woods and dropped onto the valley floor where the river slowly wandered by. "There's his place away over there." Mike pointed through the trees to a one and a half story house and a barn at the end of a long driveway which partially followed the curve of the river. When they pedaled along the road and closer to the property they could see a red pickup truck parked in the yard close to the old farmhouse.

"I'd like to know what he does there all day," Timothy wondered aloud.

"Let's go and find out."

"We can't just go up to the old guy and ask him what he does there all day," Timothy protested as he jostled over the washboard of the dirt road.

Mike suggested, "We can tell him we're lost and quickly take a gander around."

"Yeah, but we're not lost," objected Timothy as he glanced over sideways at his friend.

Mike had an idea. "Let's sneak up through the woods over there and have a look from there."

Timothy hesitated. "Well, I don't know," he replied and he pulled on the visor of his cap.

"Come on, Tim! Remember, I'm older than you. You have to respect me and do what I say."

"Yeah, but you remember, I'm taller than you by two centimetres. You have to look up to me," Timothy reminded him and he stopped his bike, jumped off and after removing his pant leg guard, he placed it over the handlebar. The two boys hid their bikes behind the alder bushes in the ditch and with their hiking bags on their backs, they entered the cover of the woods.

"We've got to stay back behind these spruce trees so he doesn't see us," cautioned Mike in a hushed voice. They hiked through the mixed woods and when they came alongside the old farmhouse as close as they dared yet still out of sight, they sat hidden in the tall ferns at the edge of the field and faced towards the house.

"The house looks okay enough, Tim."

"Yeah," he answered in a near whisper as he shifted his cap. "Maybe there's nothing to see after all."

The young fellows studied the house and yard for several minutes. When Mike began to lose interest, he dug out an apple from his hiking bag and bit into it. Timothy looked over at him. "Do you know what is worse than finding a worm in your apple?"

"No, what?" Mike replied as he took another bite.

Timothy snickered before he answered. "Half a worm."

Mike considered what Timothy had said, and then he suddenly stopped chewing. "Half a worm! Gross!" He made a disgusting face and quickly spat out the mouthful he had. He then cautiously turned his apple over to examine it more closely as Timothy snickered again.

Timothy tore open his chocolate bar, and when he faced the house again, he suddenly piped up, "I can see someone moving in that window!"

"Where? Oh yeah, that one over there."

"It's the old man, isn't it? What's he doing anyway?"

"Look," Mike pointed out excitedly, "he's moving something."

"Keep your voice down, Mike," Timothy warned. "He might hear you. It looks like he's moving a ladder."

"He must be working on something in there."

Timothy figured, "Maybe he's fixing up the place."

"Do you see something weird?" Mike asked as he tossed his apple core into a clump of wild raspberry canes nearby. "I can see movement in that lower window and that upstairs window at the same time."

"Must be two people in there."

"Maybe. But look, Tim, when the old guy moves the ladder, it can be seen downstairs and upstairs at the same time."

"Yeah, you're right," Timothy agreed as he bit into his chocolate bar again. The two friends continued to observe the old farmhouse for several minutes as they tried to determine what its strange occupant was doing.

"You know," suggested Mike as he leaned forward between the ferns, "if we went through the woods a bit and then came across the field over there, we could get right up to the barn without being seen from the house. If we did that, we would be a lot closer to the house than we are back here."

Timothy felt uneasy, and his eyes dropped. Mike jumped to his feet and took several steps away from where they had been crouching, and Timothy stood up and followed him. The boys turned back into the woods, and they quickly moved through the trees. When they figured the barn came between them and the house, they came out to the edge of the clearing. They left their hiking bags against a large rock near several pine trees and walked into the open, but out of sight of the old house. After climbing through the barbed-wire fence, they walked through the field of tall grasses straight towards the barn. Cautiously, Mike entered the empty barn by a door which had fallen from its hinges, and Timothy followed. They stayed away from the large, partially open, sliding door as they silently crept over to the side closest to the house.

Mike spoke in a hushed voice, "We can look through the cracks between the boards." Timothy rotated his cap, placing the visor at the back of his head and squinted between the barn siding. The two boys could see the old man working on something that appeared to be very large. It could be seen in the downstairs windows as well as the second floor windows.

"What's he doing!" wondered Mike as he stared with one eye through a wide crack.

"Can't tell for sure. The windows of the house are kind of dirty."

The old man went out of sight momentarily, but suddenly the porch door opened, and he stood outside on the large stone step, and then he came towards the barn in their direction. "Oh, no—he's coming!" Mike gasped. The boys dared not move, and Timothy held his breath. The old man tipped down the front of his white painter's cap, and he snapped one of his blue suspenders. He turned and walked over to the truck. After reaching into his pocket for the key, the old man stepped up into the truck, started the engine, put it in gear, and left the yard.

"He didn't see us!" Timothy responded with relief.

"Yeah!" Mike agreed, and then he said, "Come on—let's go have a closer look."

Timothy's mouth dropped open. "We have to wait 'til he's out of sight." The boys watched the red truck through the vertical spaces between the boards of the barn as it slowly moved along the driveway. They followed it as it turned onto the road and traveled up the hill out of the valley.

"Okay, now!" Mike shouted, and he ran to the large barn door and moved out into the sunshine. Now that they were out of the barn, the boys walked boldly towards the old farmhouse.

"Let's have a peek in here," Mike suggested, and he and Timothy stepped up to a window and looked in.

"Look at that, will you!" Timothy exclaimed in amazement.

"Yeah! Look at the size of it!"

"How'd he get that in there!"

"The old man must've built it inside," Mike figured. "Let's go in," he said as he stepped away from the window and glanced towards the porch door.

"No, Mike, we can't do that!"

"Why not? He'll never know." Mike walked towards the door and turned the knob. It was not locked. He grinned at Timothy who reluctantly joined him on the large stone step. The two boys moved into the old farmhouse and with trepidation they went through the porch to the partly opened door to the main part of the house. Mike slowly pushed on the door and they stepped into the kitchen. In the centre of the room they saw an old kitchen table with several chairs around it. An unwashed plate and mug were on the table. The counter had things on it indicating the kitchen was being used, and a saucepan was on the cold woodstove. A faded apron hung from a hook near the stove and several balls of wool lay on a rocking chair nearby. Timothy noticed a Bible text on the wall between the two windows. This kitchen looked like any of the old farm kitchens the two boys were familiar with.

"Come on," Timothy spoke nervously, glancing back at the door, "let's get out of here."

"No, I want to see the rest of the house," Mike insisted as he set out to open the door to the back part of the house. "Don't you want to see what's in here?" Timothy then followed close behind Mike who slowly pushed open the door.

They stared in amazement at what was before them. "I don't believe it!" Mike exploded as he entered the room. His mouth dropped open, and Timothy's eyes widened with astonishment.

Timothy answered, "I don't either—but there it is!" They took several more steps into the room.

"This is some unbelievable!" Mike blurted out. Most of the inside partitions of the house had been removed and a large portion of the downstairs ceilings and the second floor above were cut away. It was now one large room open to the ceilings of the rooms upstairs.

But what interested the two boys the most was what occupied the large space within the shell of the old farmhouse. "A boat!" Mike nearly shouted. "He's building a big boat! The old man is building a boat!"

"And look at the size of it!" Timothy added. "The old man will never get this out the door!" The boat was positioned diagonally and resting on large cradles. The area where the bow was located was at one time the living room and the stern was where the downstairs bedroom once was. The boat's cabin reached up through the downstairs ceiling and into what had once been the bedrooms upstairs. They could tell where each room had been by the different designs of the wallpaper which still clung on much of the remaining outside walls.

"How's he going to get this big boat outside!"

Timothy gasped, "And when he does get it out—it's way too big for the river."

Mike made a face. "He must be some crazy!" Timothy and Mike shuffled through the wood shavings and sawdust, and they made their way around to the other side of the boat.

"The boat is almost done," Mike observed as he nearly tripped over an electrical cord half buried in the shavings.

"Yeah. It looks like he only needs to finish painting it." Several cans of paint were sitting on an old bedroom door set up over a couple of sawhorses, and empty cans had been tossed in a corner nearby. Leaning against the side of the boat was a wooden ladder, and another longer, orchard ladder reached up to the second floor of the old house.

"I'm going upstairs, Tim." And Mike started up the ladder leaning against the exposed floor joists overhead.

"Hey, listen!" Timothy said in a coarse whisper. He faced the window and stared with a horrified look. Mike froze in mid-step on the third rung, the colour draining from his face. They could hear the sound of a vehicle in the driveway, and it was quickly coming closer.

"Run!" Mike shouted. He jumped from the ladder causing shavings to scatter from the spot where he landed. Timothy ran around one side of the boat and nearly tripped over the base of the cradle extending across the floor, and Mike ran around the other side. They collided in front of the kitchen door and tumbled to the floor creating a cloud of dust. When the two boys got to their feet, they could see through the grimy window that the red truck was now in the yard. "We can't go out there now!" Mike said.

Timothy retrieved his cap from the floor. "What are we going to do?" he groaned with a pleading look on his face. They heard the truck come to a stop just outside the house, and several seconds later the engine became silent, and then the boys heard one truck door slam followed by the other door.

"Quick! Hide over here," Mike commanded, and he ran behind a stack of several wooden crates. Timothy quickly followed, and the boys crouched down onto the shavings and sawdust scattered over the floor. Less than a half minute later they heard footsteps in the kitchen and the muffled voices of a man and a lady talking. Mike whispered, "I didn't think the old man was going to be back so soon."

"We can't hide here the rest of the day," Timothy replied in a very hushed voice.

Mike agreed, "I know. And soon I'll have to go to the bathroom something fierce."

How did we get into this mess? Timothy wondered to himself, and then he whispered, "Maybe we should just tell them we're Christians and that we didn't mean any harm." Mike did not answer, and he looked the other way.

Timothy thought to himself, *We can't say that. Christians don't go into other people's houses without permission. What are Mom and Dad going to think of me being here?* And then he remembered, *They're Christians, but I know I'm not saved.* He rearranged himself in the shavings and held tightly to his cap. *What is it that Dad says? "Be sure your sins will find you out." What if these people call the police, and Mike and I go to jail?*

He glanced over at Mike. He saw he had a bump on his forehead, but what caught his attention was that Mike's nose was twitching, and he had a very distressed look on his face. Next thing Timothy heard was, "ACHOO!" as his friend bucked in the dusty shavings. And then Mike sneezed once more, "ACHOO!"

"Oh no!" groaned Timothy, and Mike moaned and looked like he wanted to sink through the floor to the dark cellar beneath.

The kitchen suddenly became quiet, but not for long. The two boys heard the sound of a chair being slid back along the kitchen floor, and then they could hear a pair of heavy footsteps. Timothy felt himself shaking, and he glanced once more at Mike who he could see was trembling, too. They crouched even lower and then lay flat in the wood shavings on the floor behind the wooden boxes. The boys heard the door open, and the gruff voice of a man hollered out, "Hello!"

Timothy flinched. He could hear his heart pounding, and he imagined the old man must be able to hear it, too. And once more the voice demanded, "HELLO!", only a little louder this time.

Timothy thought, *What's the use? We can't hide, and we can't run*. He slowly stood up, revealing himself to the old man. Mike did the same. Both boys had wood shavings on their clothing and in their hair. The two fellows stood there with their heads bowed, staring at the floor in front of them. Timothy could sense the man's eyes boring into him, and he wanted to cry. He could feel Mike leaning against him slightly. In the silence that followed, the seconds seemed like hours.

"What are you two doing here?" the old man demanded with pursed lips.

"We didn't mean any harm, Mister," Timothy pleaded as he fidgeted with his cap he held at his waist. He glanced up at the old man who was standing there with his arms folded across his chest, staring at them over the top of his glasses. The man's graying hair lay flat on his head. Timothy saw a lady standing behind him at his elbow and looking at the intruders with a pleasant smile, which to the two boys seemed out of place at a stressful time like this.

The old man tapped one of his worn army boots on the dusty floor several times. "You can call me, Mr. Charles," he sternly informed them.

"Mr. Charles!" Timothy blurted out in surprise. Mike quickly looked over at Timothy beside him, and then at the couple in the doorway.

"Edmond! These boys are from the Chapel," the lady said warmly as she held the edge of her faded yellow apron. "We met their parents a couple of Sundays ago, remember? That one is the Jack boy, and the other is the son of the Fitzgerald's."

Mike spoke up, "We're sorry we came into your place when you weren't here, Mr. Charles."

"Yeah, we know it was wrong," Timothy quickly admitted. "I'm sorry, Mr. Charles. You're not going to call the police, are you?"

There was another long pause as Timothy and Mike studied the face of Mr. Charles which now at this close range did not seem so old. The stern look melted away and was replaced by a friendly grin. "Well, how do you like the boat I'm working on?" he asked enthusiastically, and he waved his arm in that direction. "Isn't it a beauty!" he remarked proudly. "I've been working on this here baby for nearly a year."

Timothy and Mike felt much relieved as they stepped away from the boxes and brushed most of the wood shavings off their clothing. "It's some neat!" Mike replied trying to hide his relief.

Mrs. Charles left for the kitchen. "I'll leave you fellows to visit," she said to them, and she closed the door behind her.

"I'm building this boat for a gentleman from the city," Mr. Charles went on, "and now it's almost complete." He once more waved his arm towards the large structure before them. "Come on, I'll show you." Timothy and Mike looked at each other and grinned. The three of them slowly walked around the boat as Mr. Charles continued to tell the boys about his project. To punctuate his animated talk, the old gentleman patted the boat's hull a few times. His blue suspenders made him look slim, but emphasized his slightly bulging abdomen.

"Why did you build this boat in the house, Mr. Charles?" asked Mike when he had the opportunity to say something.

"I built it in here so I could work on it all year round. There isn't much time left, you know."

Timothy asked, "How are you going to get it out of here?"

"Well," Mr. Charles began, "there is only one way to get the boat outside." He paused and looked at the boys.

"You'll have to tear down that end of the house," figured Mike as he motioned in that direction.

"That's right," the man replied, and then he asked, "And what's your name, Boy?"

"Mike. And this is my friend Tim."

"Mike and Tim," he repeated as he shook their hands.

Hey, this old guy's all right! Timothy decided.

Mrs. Charles opened the kitchen door and called out pleasantly, "Would you two young fellows like to join us for noon meal? We have enough for all of us."

"We brought our lunches," Timothy answered her. "We left our hiking bags in the woods."

Mike looked at Timothy and suggested, "If we left now we could be back in five or six minutes with our lunches."

Mrs. Charles smiled. "Okay, we'll wait for you fellows."

Timothy and Mike left through the kitchen and porch. Once outside they broke into a run past the red truck and barn. "Mr. and Mrs. Charles are some nice, aren't they!" Mike remarked as they trotted side by side.

"Yeah, for sure," Timothy replied. "But I wish we hadn't snuck into their house."

The two boys scurried across the field following the tracks through the tall grasses they had made earlier. After climbing between the barbed wires of the fence and crossing to the edge of the woods, they headed to the large rock where they had left their hiking bags. The boys were out of breath, but they grabbed their bags and started back to the old farmhouse and the friendly couple who were waiting for them there.

The two fellows felt much better about approaching the house this time. They crossed the yard without any guilty feelings, in fact, they felt excited as well as happy. They boldly opened the door and walked in. Mrs. Charles was in the kitchen making a pot of tea. "Oh, you're back already, Lads!" she welcomed, and she wiped her hands on her apron. "Come on in. We're almost ready."

Mr. Charles came into the kitchen and sat at the table. He removed his glasses and lowered them into his shirt pocket behind his left suspender. His wife sat on the chair opposite him. Timothy hung his cap over one of the chair posts of the two remaining chairs, and the boys sat down and held their bags on their laps. Mr. and Mrs. Charles bowed their heads, and the boys did likewise. Mr. Charles thanked the Lord for the food and then thanked Him for Timothy and Mike who were visiting with them today. Finally he thanked God for Jesus Christ and salvation through Him.

Timothy opened his hiking bag and reached for his sandwiches. He suddenly gasped and jumped up causing his chair to tip over backwards onto the floor with a crash. He dropped his bag and stepped back. "There's a mouse in my hiking bag!" he uttered with alarm.

Mrs. Charles laughed, "I hope you're not planning to eat him!"

"No," Timothy assured her, "but he probably ate some of my lunch."

Mr. Charles grinned and stood up. "Let's carry your bag outside, Tim. We can let the mouse get away in the grass."

Timothy carefully picked up his bag and carried it outside while the others followed. He laid the bag in the grass next to the dirt driveway and gently spilled out the contents. The mouse darted from his bag. "There he goes!" Timothy pointed as it disappeared into the tall grass and wildflowers. He examined his lunch and found that each of his peanut butter sandwiches had been sampled along with one of the oatmeal cookies.

Mrs. Charles said, "Tim, we would be glad to share our lunch with you."

Mike, who had brought his bag outside as well, searched through his lunch, but found everything as it had been before. "I guess mice don't like bologna sandwiches!" he figured.

Back in the kitchen, Mr. Charles grinned as he returned the chair to its feet. "You gave that little mouse quite a ride in your bag!"

"And a lunch, too," his wife added. "He'll have quite a story to tell his family when he finds his way home." She then offered Timothy buttered rolls, cheese, bananas, and donuts.

"Yes, thank you." He sat down again and reached for a sesame seed roll (his favourite) and a piece of cheese.

"You know, Boys," Mr. Charles said as he picked up a piece of cheese and laid it on his plate, "I was reading this morning in God's Word where it says, 'the wages of sin is death'. That means we have all sinned or broken the ten commandments, and we deserve death and separation from God. The Lord Jesus paid the penalty for our sin by taking our sin to Himself and giving His life by dying on the cross." He bit into his onion roll.

The boys listened politely as they ate. Mr. Charles continued, "The rest of that verse says, 'but the gift of God is eternal life through Jesus Christ our Lord.' And that means eternal life is free—we can do nothing to get it, we can only accept it. What do you do when someone offers you a gift?" He looked over at Timothy, and then Mike.

Timothy thought, *That sure is plain! But I'm not ready yet.*

Mrs. Charles moved to the side table where the hot plate was, and she poured tea for her husband. After she sliced more cheese, she broke off a banana from the bunch and placed it on the table in front of Timothy.

"Thanks."

Mrs. Charles sat down again and pointed out, "The Bible also says, 'God so loved the world,' and that includes each one of us here, 'that He gave His only begotten Son that whosoever believeth in Him should not perish but have everlasting life.' God loved us so much that He gave up His Son, the Lord Jesus Christ for us. When we believe in Him or trust in Him, we will not perish or be destroyed, but we will have everlasting life with Him. And that's the gospel, the good news."

"It sure is!" Mr. Charles exclaimed, and he dribbled a bit of milk into his tea. The two boys continued to eat in silence.

A minute later Mike asked, "What are you going to do with this house when the boat is out? You can't live here."

"I need to tear it down—the barn, too," he answered, and he sipped at his tea. "A hydro electric dam is being built down the river right now. This whole area is going to be flooded. The hydro electric people have bought up all this land."

Timothy and Mike had looks of amazement as they glanced at each other. Mike piped up, "I didn't know that!"

"Me neither!" admitted Timothy, and he took another bite of the banana.

"Yes," Mr. Charles continued. "Where we are right now will be underwater by this winter. I have my eye on another piece of property up a few miles."

"Oh, so that's why the boat's too big for the river as it is right now!" Mike realized.

Timothy added, "You'll be able to float it away then, no problem." He folded the empty banana peel and laid it down on the table.

"That's right. Would you fellows like to help get the boat outside in another week when I finish painting it?"

"Sure!" they both said at once.

Mr. Charles advised them, "You'll need permission from your parents first."

"We'll ask them tonight, and let you know Sunday," Timothy promised.

"First we need to tear off that end of the house." Mr. Charles nodded that way. "We'll build a ramp outside. I made arrangements some time ago for a bulldozer to pull the boat out and away from the house when we're ready for that. And then the bulldozer will be used to level this house."

Mrs. Charles interjected, "Help yourselves to the donuts, Boys."

"When you fellows are through eating," Mr. Charles told them as he lowered his empty mug to the table, "I want to show you inside the boat."

"That would be great!" Mike answered, and he reached for a jelly donut.

"Yeah," Timothy agreed as he grinned at Mike.

The two friends followed Mr. Charles into the large room where the boat was situated. They enjoyed visiting with him almost as much as he delighted in talking with his young visitors.

An hour passed quickly. "Mike, we should leave for home soon," Timothy reminded him.

"Yeah," he answered. "I'm supposed to be home in plenty of time for supper, and I have some chores to do, too."

Several minutes later they picked up their hiking bags in the kitchen. Mrs. Charles was sitting in the rocking chair and knitting a bulky sweater. "Mrs. Charles," Timothy told her, "thanks for the lunch."

"Oh, you're welcome! And thanks for coming. It was a nice visit from you boys. We don't have company here very often."

Mr. Charles came into the kitchen, and Mike said, "Thanks for showing us around your place, Mr. Charles."

Timothy nodded in agreement and picked up his cap hanging from the back of the kitchen chair. "Yeah. And thanks for showing us the boat," he added.

Mr. Charles smiled and nodded as he stood with both hands on his suspenders. "See you Sunday," he replied.

The boys left the house and walked briskly along the driveway towards the gravel road and to where their bikes were hidden. "I've never heard tell of a full-size boat that was built inside a house," exclaimed Mike to his friend.

Timothy nodded. "And the house needs to be torn down to get the boat out."

"Yeah, but the house needs to be torn down anyway."

"Mr. Charles sure knows what he's doing!" Timothy decided.

They retrieved their bikes from the cover of the alders in the ditch, and the boys wheeled them up and onto the road.

"That was some funny!" Mike laughed as he swung his leg over the seat of his bike. "You ran one way, and I ran the other, and then we smacked into each other."

"Yeah," Timothy agreed as he pedaled to catch up. They rode their bikes along the level road and soon started up the steep hill out of the valley. Before the boys reached the first switchback, they could pedal no more. They dismounted their bikes and turned to look back at the old farmhouse where they had just been.

"All that down there will be underwater soon," Timothy remarked as they surveyed the scene below them.

Mike added, "The yard where the house and barn are, and the driveway and all those fields over there." They walked their bikes the remainder of the way up the winding road. At the top they hopped onto their bikes once more and pedaled towards the pavement.

Suddenly Mike chuckled, and Timothy looked over at him. "What's so funny?"

Mike grinned. "Oh, I was just thinking of that mouse. You should've seen your face."

Timothy laughed, "When you carried out your hiking bag, you looked kind of grossed out."

Once the two boys reached the highway, they biked at a steady pace without conversing. It was not long before they left the pavement and were on their own familiar side road. Timothy reflected, *It's nice to have a buddy like Mike—we can have lots of fun together, but I better not let anyone, even a friend, talk me into doing anything I know I shouldn't do. Mom and Dad have told me I should stay away from friends when they are doing something wrong.*

Mike considered, *Tim's a good friend, but I shouldn't get him to do things that I know are wrong.*

Neither boy spoke as they biked along their road. Timothy was thinking of what he had heard this afternoon. Soon they came to the mailbox at the end of Mike's driveway. Mike turned in and started along towards his house as Timothy kept going. "See you," Mike called after Timothy.

"Okay. Hunky-dory," Timothy shouted over his shoulder. "Bye for now."

Timothy left his friend and pedaled fast for home. *Mr. and Mrs. Charles are right,* he remembered as he pulled his cap down snugly. *I'm a sinner and I'm not saved. But I want to be.* He stopped pedalling his bike to concentrate. *God gave His Son the Lord Jesus Christ, who took the punishment for my sin. Like the Bible says, salvation is a gift from God. All I need to do is accept His gift of the Lord Jesus.*

He allowed his bike to gradually coast to a snail's pace. *Lord,* Timothy prayed as he barely moved along, *I know I'm a sinner, and I'm sorry I've sinned against You. Thank You for sending Your Son the Lord Jesus Christ to take my punishment. Thank You for Your gift of salvation to me through His death on the cross. I now receive that gift of the Lord Jesus Christ. Thank You for giving Him for me.*

Timothy quickly sped up, and he suddenly realized what had just taken place. "I'm saved!" he said aloud. He stood up to pedal even faster. "I'm saved!" he shouted to the countryside and to the cattle in the field nearby. "I just got saved!" He raced along the dirt road next to his parents' property. *I'm going to tell Mom and Dad,* Timothy determined as he barely slowed down to turn in at his long driveway, and soon the last part of his trip for home was ended.

chapter thirteen

four years later—summer 1984

The Hay Bale Room

"Well, Timothy, that sounds like a great idea you have," his dad said to him after supper. "Go ahead, but be sure it's safe so it doesn't fall on you or your sister and little brother. And don't break any bales if you can help it. Mr. Holmns will be coming for most of them towards the end of summer."

"Okay, Dad, thanks." Timothy, who was nearly fourteen, grabbed his blue cap and started out the door. "I have it figured out how I want to build it."

"Don't let this project interfere with your jobs around here. We need your help," Timothy heard his dad say. He stopped, turned, and leaned against the doorjamb.

"Timmy," his mom reminded him, "we need raspberries picked tomorrow for the fruit and vegetable stand. Jennifer's going to help, too."

"And have a look for weeds," his dad added. "You decide if they need any attention."

Timothy grinned. "Well, I see the carrots are getting crowded out. I'll work on them in the morning." Mr. Jack nodded and turned away. "Dad, you'll come out to the barn, too, won't you?" Timothy questioned.

"Sure, I'd like to." Timothy's dad reached for his cap, and they both left the house. When they arrived at the barn, they entered the hayloft and crossed to the large pile of hay bales. The bales were loosely piled and stacked higher than their heads.

Timothy informed his dad, "I'd like my room to be over there in that corner where the window is, and I want the room to be hidden. And it'll need a tunnel with a turn." Mr. Jack grinned as he envisioned the room, and he nodded in reply.

Timothy liked spending time with his dad, and he could tell his dad enjoyed his company. They began removing bales from the area of the loft next to the window. After twenty minutes of strenuous work there was a large cleared area in the corner by the small window. Timothy removed his cap and plopped himself down on a bale of hay.

"Let's go, Tim," his dad said as he stood there breathing hard. "You have a good start here, but it's time for our family Bible reading."

Timothy found it difficult to concentrate this evening on what his dad was saying to the family. He was thinking, *It'll be too dark to work in the barn when we're through here.*

Later, Timothy showered and got ready for bed. As he drifted off to sleep he wondered, *How will I do the roof?*

It was late morning when Timothy returned to his project in the barn. He had moved several bales of hay when he heard a young voice. "What are you doing, Tim? Timmy, can I help?" His four and a half-year-old brother was wearing denim overalls with patches over each knee.

"No, Billy, you can't help; you'll just get in the way." And then Timothy remembered his dad said he used to want to help him, and he would let him even when it made it inconvenient for him. *"And look at you now," he would say. "You can do all sorts of useful things."*

"Okay, but these bales are kind of heavy for you, so you can watch for now, but there might be something for you to do later."

When Timothy moved several of the bales from the hayloft floor, he realized the window was going to be too high and the wooden floor was very rough. *I could put a layer of bales down for a floor, and when the walls are up, maybe I can put some planks across from that beam to hold the bales for the roof.* He wanted the room to be a little larger than his bedroom so he laid out bales for the floor accordingly.

Billy had grown tired of waiting so he silently slipped away and left Timothy to work alone.

After dinner at noon, Timothy returned to his work in the barn. The two walls were next. Mr. Jack had told his son at breakfast that morning to use three bales at the bottom and overlap them in both directions to make the walls sturdy. Timothy decided to have a narrow, low doorway on the longer wall. He kept the bales flush on the inside of the room to make a smooth surface and he built up the walls until they were almost level with the top of the barn beam.

Mr. Jack had granted Timothy permission to use some of the planks which were stored on the other side of the loft. He carried a few over and began to lay them from the beam to the longer hay bale wall. Next, bales of hay were laid on the planks and when the last one was in place, Timothy hurried down and crawled into his room. *It's sure quiet in here,* Timothy discovered. *The hay makes it sound soft here—and I like the smell, too. I'll make a bed out of bales and spend the night here.* He dragged in four bales and laid them side by side against the hay bale wall, and he laid down on the bed he had just assembled.

Mrs. Jack blew the whistle, but Timothy did not respond. Next thing he knew his dad was sitting on his hay bed next to him and surveying his room. "You need two beds, Tim," he announced. Timothy blinked several times, sat up and swung his feet from the bed of bales and onto the hay bale floor.

"What do you mean, Dad?" he asked.

"You and Brian could sleep out here."

"Brian's coming?" he asked in surprise. He retrieved his cap from the floor and planted it on his head.

"Yeah. Day after tomorrow." It had been a couple of years since Timothy had seen his cousin Brian who was a year or two older than him. "I like your room, but Mom's called us for supper. Let's go."

As they jogged to the house, Timothy determined, *I'd like to get the room finished before Brian comes.*

When they reached the house, Timothy's dad told him, "You could use that long electrical cord hanging next to the stable door. Plug it in just inside the door and run it up into your room. Be sure the bulb is hanging free and away from the bales."

The next day when he was free to work on his hay bale room, Timothy dragged in four bales of hay and laid out a second bed on the long wall. He then brought in three more bales. He set one beside the head of each bed and the third against the long wall near the window. *Now for the electrical cord,* Timothy decided. He placed the outlet end of the cord behind the bale near the window. He knew where he could get a wall lamp, and his tape-player could go on the hay bale by the window.

At the house, Timothy pulled out his sleeping bag from the back of his closet, and he gathered up, from his dresser, his tape-player along with several tapes. He found the wall lamp in the basement, and after putting these things in place in his hay bale room, he thought it was now looking like a room which could be identified as his.

Timothy was anxious to build the tunnel. It was to extend straight out allowing him to detect anyone coming through and into his room. He wanted the other end to have a right angle turn so anyone discovering the entrance would not see the length of the tunnel. It would be four bales high from the barn floor, necessitating a step up into his hay bale room. After the hay bale tunnel was completed he tried it out, going back and forth several times.

Then Timothy loosely scattered bales of hay over the outside of his room and up as high as the planks, making sure all the plank ends were covered. To disguise its flatness, he casually threw several bales along the edge of the roof. Other bales he positioned on both sides of the tunnel and a few on top and two leaning against the entrance. He stood back from what appeared to be a large pile of loose hay bales in the barn loft, and he studied it from several positions.

Jennifer suddenly appeared. "Hey, Tim, what are you doing?" She held the ends of each of her long, blonde braids.

"Oh, nothing."

"When are you going to start your room?" she asked as she scuffed at the loose hay on the barn floor with her sneaker.

Timothy repressed a grin. "What room?" he asked innocently.

"Mom says you're making a room out here. So, where's it at?"

Timothy gave her a fake smile. "See if you can find it."

Jennifer glanced over the large pile of bales but turned to leave. She thought, *I'd like to see it, and I know it's in that big pile of hay bales, but I'm not going to search for it and look dumb for his satisfaction.*

"Keep up the good work!" she put in with false enthusiasm as she headed for the large barn door.

"But you haven't even seen it!" Timothy stared at her and concluded, *Boy, she sure gives up some easy!*

Jennifer stopped and turned. She decided, *I'll make him show me.* Then she muttered, "Your room is probably a mess just like your bedroom." She knew this was not so; his room was usually neat, and when he made something it was well done.

"The room I made is not a mess!" he declared hotly. "Wait'll you see it!"

"Well, I don't think I want to see it." Jennifer spun around on one foot and headed outside and into the sunshine.

While his sister was walking away towards the house, Timothy moved over to the pile of bales.

Oh well, thought Timothy as he removed the two bales leaning against the entrance. *She nearly had the privilege of being my first guest. Too bad—she blew it.* He stooped and entered into the tunnel's opening, and then he turned to reach for the bales to pull them to their closed position.

"I'm back!" Jennifer suddenly shouted out, and Timothy lurched in surprise and then froze in his bent-over posture.

"Where are you going?" she asked simply, holding a braid in each hand as she eyed him.

Timothy did not answer, but he left the two bales where they were and disappeared into the dark tunnel. As he crawled along, he could hear Jennifer following not far behind. *Got outsmarted by my little sister!* he realized with disappointment. *But I can't wait for her to see my room!*

Timothy emerged into the light of his room and sat on the sleeping bag on his hay bale bed. Jennifer came to the end of the tunnel and looked up into the room, and her mouth dropped open. She slowly crawled in, stood up, and surveyed the two walls of hay bales, the floor, and then the ceiling. "It's big in here," she exclaimed in surprise. "You have two beds and night tables and another table over there and a lamp and your tape-player, too!"

"Yeah, well, I might want to listen to a tape," he replied casually, and he tossed his cap onto the bale next to his bed. He made an effort not to smile.

"Tim, this is some neat!" she stated as she continued to survey the room. "And there's your Bible verse from your bedroom, 'In all thy ways acknowledge Him and He shall direct thy paths'. You've hung it up here on that wall—and you even have the campfire painting Grandpa Palmer gave you."

Several minutes later Mrs. Jack blew the whistle, and Timothy and Jennifer jumped up to leave. After grabbing his cap, Timothy crawled along the tunnel, and his sister followed. When they emerged, Timothy replaced the two bales.

During supper Jennifer told her parents about Timothy's room in the hayloft. "It's really neat!" she related to them. "We should all go see it after we eat."

"I'd like to see it," agreed Mrs. Jack. "It sounds just great!"

While they were eating raspberry pie for dessert, Mr. Jack commented to his wife, "I heard Mr. Charles say that he and his wife plan to use their new property for Christian camping."

She answered in surprise, "There's nothing there but that old house and a barn. And part of the property is flooded."

Right after supper, Timothy, his dad, and Billy left for Timothy's room in the barn. Timothy crawled into the disguised tunnel first. "Wait for me, Timmy!" pleaded Billy as he followed close behind him. "It's kind of dark in here."

"I'm right behind you, Billy," assured his dad. "Keep going. Just follow Timmy." When they scrambled up into the room, Timothy sat on one bed, and his dad, with Billy, settled onto the other.

"You've done an excellent job, Tim. And the way you did the light's a good idea."

Billy suddenly announced, "I hear Mom and Jenny coming." He jumped up and moved over to the door. "Mom, we're in here."

When Mrs. Jack and Jennifer were almost at his room, Timothy ordered, "Take off your boots before you come in here."

"That's quite the tunnel!" Mrs. Jack exclaimed. "And look at this room—it's a good size, too!" She sat on the bed with her husband, and Jennifer settled down with Billy on the bale near the window.

"Tim, are you going to sleep out here tonight?" asked his sister.

"Well, yeah, I guess I could." He squinted and gave her a big phony smile.

Billy jumped up. "Mom, can I sleep here with Timmy, too? Can I Mom, can I?" he pleaded.

"Not this time," his mom answered him. "Maybe another time." He plopped himself down beside Jennifer. "Hey, what's that you have there, Billy?" His mom stared at the young boy's hands.

Billy held the object up for her to see. "I found it in the grass on the far side of the barn."

"Why, it's an old smoking pipe!" Mr. Jack noted as he leaned over to reach for it. "I wonder why it was at the far side of the barn?"

"Hey!" Timothy said excitedly. "I think I know where that came from. Remember that Christmas we spent here before Billy was born? Well, Uncle Allan and I came out in the moonlight and cut down a Christmas tree on the other side of the barn. After we chopped it down, Uncle Allan chucked something as far as he could. He wouldn't tell me what it was."

"That must've been seven years ago," Mrs. Jack figured. "Uncle Allan tried to be a Christian by giving up smoking. We explained to him that we're saved only by trusting in the Lord Jesus. We can't become or even stay Christians by our own efforts. The Lord has done everything that can be done. The Bible says that we are His workmanship."

Jennifer's face lit up. "And he did get saved," she remembered, "just before he died."

"You can keep the pipe, Billy," his dad informed him, "in memory of Uncle Allan who trusted in the Lord near the end of his life." He returned the pipe to the young fellow and ruffled his hair.

His mom added, "It's not a toy. Keep it with your other things in your treasure box."

The Jack family sat quietly, and Timothy laid back on his sleeping bag.

"I hear a car," Mrs. Jack said, glancing towards the window.

Billy jumped up and peered out the window. "It's going over to the house, Mommy," he informed her with his nose pressed against the glass.

Timothy crossed to the window and looked over Billy's shoulder. "I don't recognize the car," he told them.

"Quick, Timothy, go see who it is," his dad told him. Timothy crawled along the tunnel, left the barn, and trotted across the yard towards the house.

The car was now parked near the porch, and a man stepped out when Timothy approached. "Hello. Are your parents home?"

"Yes, Sir," Timothy replied as he ran his fingers through his hair.

A lady came around from the other side of the car and asked, "Was your mother's name 'Palmer' before she married?"

"Yes," Timothy informed her. "Mom and Dad are in the barn. Would you like to see them?" He started in that direction, and the man and lady followed. He led the couple into the barn and through the tunnel and into his hay bale room where his family was waiting.

"Hello," the man greeted as he stood up in the hay bale room. "My name is Lionel Reid, and this is my wife, Marg." Mr. Jack rose to his feet and introduced himself and his wife and children.

"We're born again Christians," Mr. Reid reported to them.

"So are we," Mr. Jack replied.

"Perhaps we should visit at the house," Mrs. Jack suggested with a giggle. "We do live in the house. This is our son's room. Well, that is, for the summer."

Mrs. Reid replied, "No, this is fine. I like it here." She sat down on the hay bed and glanced around.

"You have a great room, Timothy!" Mr. Reid grinned at him as he settled down next to his wife. "You built this?"

"Yes, I did." Timothy smiled, and he dropped beside Jennifer on the bale near the window. Billy moved over to his parents and sat between them, holding his pipe.

"It must be nice to sleep out here!" Mrs. Reid responded. "The smell of the hay is sweet especially with the clover in it." Timothy could see she was also studying his campfire painting.

Mr. Reid turned to Mrs. Jack. "Martha, we would like to get in touch with Brent Palmer," he said with interest. "I think he could be your brother. Can you tell us where he lives?"

The colour drained from her face, and she did not reply. Mr. Jack answered quietly, "Martha's brother Brent was killed in a car accident years ago."

Mrs. Reid looked shocked. "Oh, we're sorry to hear that."

"Yes," Mr. Reid added. "I was hoping to see how he was getting along."

There were several awkward seconds when no one said anything. Martha stared at the floor and tightly folded her hands on her lap. Billy stood up and put the pipe in his pocket. Mr. Reid broke the silence. "Richard, how long ago was he killed?"

"I was nineteen at the time," Mrs. Jack answered as she thought it through, "so that makes it twenty years ago." She ran her fingers through Billy's hair.

"It was about twenty years ago that I attended a Bible conference down country from here," Mr. Reid recalled. "I was single then and hitch-hiked both ways. Martha, your brother Brent picked me up on my way home. He told me his parents were Bible-believing Christians and his sister was too, but he said he tried to discourage his younger brother from living for the Lord."

"Yes," Mrs. Jack replied sadly as she bowed her head. "Brent died without having salvation."

"What!" Mr. Reid gasped as he faced her. "Are you sure?"

She nodded her head. "He never showed any interest in spiritual things."

"I explained the gospel to him plainly, and I was sure he had agreed that he was a sinner and that he had accepted the Lord there in his car as we were driving along. When he stopped to let me out, he said he was anxious to tell his family he had seen the truth and that he had put his trust in Christ."

"He said that?" Mrs. Jack questioned in surprise as she leaned forward to face Mr. Reid. "Then he must've gotten saved at the time he was with you. When did he pick you up, Lionel?" Timothy and Jennifer listened with interest, and Billy stared at Mr. Reid.

"It was the long weekend in May," he remembered.

Mrs. Jack added excitedly, "It was the long weekend in May he had the accident!" She took a deep breath and leaned back.

Mr. Jack quickly reasoned, "The accident which took Brent's life must have occurred right after he gave Lionel the ride and before he arrived home and could tell his family he was a believer now."

"And we thought all these years," Mrs. Jack exclaimed to her husband, "that Brent died without ever knowing the Lord. Wait 'til I tell Mother and Dad!" She turned to Mr. Reid. "Then, you, Lionel, were the last person to talk with my brother. Thank you for speaking to him about the Lord."

About fifteen minutes later, Mr. and Mrs. Reid stood up to leave. Mrs. Jack and Jennifer returned to the house, and Mr. Jack, Timothy, and Billy left to check on the garden to see what needed to be done the next day.

After the family Bible reading, Mr. Jack gave Timothy the household flashlight, and his mom handed him a large jar filled with an assortment of plain cookies. When Timothy closed the door behind him, he turned on the flashlight and headed for the barn. He entered the tunnel, closed the bales behind him and crawled along and into his hay bale room. After he switched on the wall lamp, he laid his Bible and flashlight on the bale next to his bed, and the jar of snacks he placed beside his tape-player. The room was cozy and quiet, but he decided he wanted a couple of bales to cover the doorway leading to the dark tunnel. These he borrowed from the second bed.

Timothy removed his cap and boots, and he glanced over at his copy of the biography of George Müller. His parents selected this book for his reading over the summer. *Mom and Dad don't want any books around that have any wrong in them. There are a lot of good, wholesome books out there that will benefit us. There are biographies and autobiographies of missionaries and other Christians. Mom says it would be better to buy worthwhile books for us to read than to redecorate the house when it really isn't necessary to do so. She says that ten or twenty years from now the good we got from the books will still be with us, but any good we might have received from redecorating the house will be long gone. Mom and Dad want a wholesome environment, a safe place all the time for us—not necessarily a stylish place. That's why we have Scripture texts on the walls in all the rooms of the house—even the bathroom, as Uncle Drew likes to point out.*

Timothy picked up the book and lay back on his sleeping bag. He was nearly halfway through reading the biography.

He enjoyed learning how other Bible-believing Christians lived. *Does anyone live like this today?* he wondered. *If not, why not? We have the same God today as back then in George Müller's day. Mr. Müller himself said he wasn't special—any believer can live by faith as he did.*

After a quarter of an hour he found it difficult to keep his eyes open. He turned off the wall light, undressed, and slid into his sleeping bag. Brian comes tomorrow, he remembered as he closed his eyes.

It was daylight when Timothy awoke and for the brief few moments before he opened his eyes, he could not remember where he was. Suddenly he realized he had spent his first night in his hay bale room in the barn and he smiled as he quickly scanned his room. After he closed his eyes in prayer, he reached for his Bible. After reading a portion of Scripture and thinking about what he had read, he prayed he would please the Lord that day.

After his breakfast, Timothy picked peas and shelled them on the porch steps. Before he and his family ate at noon, he hauled out his bike and rode down the driveway to the family's fruit and vegetable stand, and while there he emptied the money box. In the afternoon he spent time in his hay bale room reading and listening to Christian tapes. While there, he started a letter to a young man in a detention centre.

Late that afternoon, Mr. Jack decided it was time to go to the town of William Station for Brian.

"Wait for me!" called Billy as he and his dad and big brother climbed into the family's red, compact car and left to pick up Brian from the bus drop-off. Brian's parents would come for him the following week. "I don't remember him," Billy said as they traveled along the highway.

They drove to the restaurant where the bus had already unloaded and was now pulling away. "There he is," pointed out Timothy and then added, "He may be older than me, but I don't think he's any taller."

"I don't remember him," Billy said once more when Mr. Jack had parked the car. The young boy stared out the window at Brian.

Mr. Jack called out, "Brian. Over here."

"Hi, Uncle Richard," Brian answered with a wave of his hand. "Absolutely gorgeous!" he added. He tossed back his head to flip away his hair from off his face. He grinned as he approached the car with his bags.

"I don't remember him," Billy put in as he continued to check him over.

Timothy and Brian exchanged 'Howdies', and then Brian asked as he looked at Billy, "Who's the big guy?"

"I don't remember him," Billy whispered to his dad.

When they arrived at the Jack's property, Brian headed for the house, and Timothy informed him, "Hey, Brian, you sleep in the barn."

"What?" he squealed. "No way, Man!" He shifted his weight from one foot to the other.

"Sure you will. That's where my room is and where I sleep."

"Yeah, sure. Tell me another one."

"Tim's right," his dad agreed seriously and winked at Timothy. Brian stopped and put his duffel bag and sleeping bag down in the grass. He lifted the bottom of his extra long, black and burgundy striped top and shoved both hands deep into his denim pockets.

"Come on, Brian," Timothy responded with a grin. "It's hunky-dory. I'll show you."

As they were on their way to the barn with Brian's things, Billy could be heard informing his dad once more, "I don't remember him."

In the hayloft, Timothy paused for about ten seconds and then walked up to the large pile of hay bales. He carefully pushed aside the two bales to reveal the entrance to the tunnel. "I'll take your sleeping bag," Timothy offered.

The two fellows crawled through the tunnel and up into Timothy's room. "Hey, this is neat!" Brian exclaimed. "Absolutely gorgeous!" He lowered his duffel bag to the hay bale floor and sat on the bed meant for him. After examining the room, he spread out his sleeping bag. Five minutes later, Jennifer blew the whistle for supper, and the two fellows left for the house.

After supper, Timothy and Brian returned to the hay bale room. Brian saw Timothy's Bible on his bed. "You still read the Bible?" he asked in mock amazement. "And you even have a Bible verse hanging up there." He snickered as he looked over at his cousin. "Isn't that just a bit much?"

"Well, I try to read my Bible every day."

Brian crossed over to the window. "We're taught evolution at school, and that disagrees with the Bible."

"Yeah, I know, but I'd like to inform you—in case you didn't know—that evolution is not a proven fact," Timothy told him as he sprawled out on his bed and faced up at the planks of the ceiling. "The Bible's been around for thousands of years, it's never been proven wrong and that includes what it says about scientific facts. And it's a well-known fact that science over the years has been wrong many times including modern science in the past half-century. Evolution has never been proven right, and science has never successfully proven anything in the Bible to be incorrect. In fact, real science states that evolution could not have possibly happened."

Brian ignored him. "Scientists are still looking for the missing link," he stated as he faced the window. "They think they have just about found it."

"The missing link!" Timothy blurted out. "What missing link?"

"The missing link, you know—the missing link that proves we descended from the primates."

"Well, let's look at the undisputed, true facts," Timothy suggested as he stretched his arms up over his head. "We have plenty of fossilized remains of the primates, and there are plenty of living people around today to examine, but we have none of the thousands of missing links or stages in between which are needed to prove evolution from primates to humans. And those are the correct, without error, proven facts."

Brian swung around. "Yeah, but we have proof for the missing links and all the stages in between. I saw a picture showing a monkey or a gorilla or something on the left side and a modern guy on the right and all the evolutionary steps in between."

Timothy sat up and swung his feet onto the floor. "Oh yeah! I've seen that picture. It's neat!" he agreed. "It's well done, it's colourful, it's interesting, but if you read the small print—if they didn't neglect on purpose to put it there—that picture is from the scientists' imagination, and it's also an artist's rendition. They just made all that up—that's what they think happened. It's a neat picture, but that doesn't make it true. That picture doesn't show proven facts."

Timothy picked up his cap and ran his fingers along the brim. "Besides that, all the fossilized remains of the primates aren't much different from the living primates we see today, yet we're a lot different from their fossils. How is it we've evolved so much but the living primates today haven't changed any in the last ten thousand years or so?" Brian shrugged his shoulders, and Timothy added, "Evolutionary scientists spend much of their time trying to prove their theories, but the Bible just states the facts. It doesn't need to prove anything. The Bible is the truth."

Brian sat on his bed and leaned back against the hay bale wall. He drew his feet up close, and his knees partly hid his face. "Well, if the Bible is the truth, why don't the scientists just read it to get the facts?" he mumbled.

Timothy answered, "Scientists have spent a lot of time and money on their brilliant theories, and they take pride in their many accomplishments, and we have great respect for them. Do you think they could swallow their pride and admit they were wrong? I doubt it! Their lifelong careers are bound up in their research. If they were proved wrong, we'd never trust them again. Their very lives would be at stake! Yeah, your question is a good one. So Brian, why don't you read the Bible and get the facts for yourself?"

"Well, I don't like to read the Bible," he admitted.

"Why not?" Timothy faced Brian who had pulled some hair over one of his eyes.

"The Bible talks about sin," Brian mumbled.

"And what do you have against that? It's the truth." Brian did not answer. He got up, shook his hair from his eyes, and went over to the window again. "It's because you're a sinner," Timothy told him, "and you don't want to admit that fact."

"Well," Brian snapped as he turned and glared at Timothy, "I'm not as bad as some people are."

Timothy grinned and replied, "Yeah, you're a nice guy and all that, and there sure are a lot of bad people in the world these days, but even good people sin once in a while. Everyone has sinned, so all are sinners before God." He planted his cap on his head. "But those who are trusting in Jesus Christ—He took their sin onto Himself, shed His blood, and died for them—they are righteous before God or are free from their sin."

Brian shrugged his shoulder again, and then he reached for the jar of cookies. After removing the lid, he pulled out a peanut butter cookie and bit into it. "Can I have one of these?"

"Sure," Timothy answered. "Throw one to me, will you, Boy." Brian tossed him the one he had sampled, and he took an oatmeal cookie from the jar.

Timothy carefully examined the bitten cookie. "If I eat this, I might die a slow, agonizing death before sundown." He quickly checked his watch but then confidently bit into the cookie. "But I'll take my chances."

Later that evening at the family Bible reading, Mr. Jack asked, "Do you know what would happen if you put a frog into a pan of water on the stove and slowly heated it up to boiling?"

Brian responded, "The frog would jump out when it got too hot for him."

"That's what you'd think, Brian. But the frog would stay in the water, and it would eventually cook to death. The water would heat up slowly, and the frog wouldn't notice that it was getting hotter and that he was in a life-threatening situation."

"Absolutely gorgeous!" Brian exclaimed, and he looked over at Timothy with a grin. "Hey, we should try it, Tim. Are there any frogs around here in these parts?"

"That's awful!" Jennifer protested in disgust. "Don't let them do it, Dad."

"Don't do it, Gentlemen," Mr. Jack informed them sternly. "The purpose of this interesting fact of nature is to demonstrate how sin can creep up on us unawares, and we don't even know what's going on. We might not be aware of the dangers of sin to ourselves until it's too late. Sin is a real problem for all of us. But listen! Jesus Christ the sinless One became our substitute to take our place because of our sin." The hired man's clock in the kitchen struck eight o'clock, and Mrs. Jack silently prayed Brian would take this in, realize his need, and trust in Christ.

After prayer, Mrs. Jack served a lunch of raspberry pie.

"Hey, Tim!" Brian said as he pushed his fork into his piece of pie. "Did you hear about the guy who burned his lips on the tailpipe of a car?"

Timothy looked over at Brian who sat there with a silly grin on his face. "Okay," Timothy chuckled, "why did the guy burn his lips on the tailpipe of the car?" His little brother listened with concern.

Brian took a bite of pie. Timothy watched him as he slowly and thoughtfully chewed it and then swallowed before answering. "He'd been hired by a gang to blow it up."

Timothy laughed but Billy had a blank look on his face. His mother told him, "He tried to blow up the car like a balloon."

By the time the two guys finished their lunch, it was dark outside. They left for the barn and crawled into the hay bale room. "You people are so religious!" Brian muttered as he turned on the light.

"No, we're not," answered Timothy with determination. "We're not religious at all. Someone who's religious does things like going to church, reading the Bible, praying and singing hymns to make them feel good. And they need rules to feel secure. We're not religious, we already feel good, we're happy and secure, and we like to meet with others who know the Lord, and we actually enjoy reading the Bible, praying, and singing hymns."

"Well, I think people like you are kind of weird, and you really don't know what's going on." Brian sat on the edge of his bed and continued. "I don't think God cares about us, and I think death ends all."

"You're entitled to your opinions, but your opinions don't change the facts," pointed out Timothy. "It's a free country, Brian. You have the right to be wrong."

Brian commented, "I didn't know your dad had a tattoo."

"Dad usually wears long-sleeves when out in public to hide his tattoo. He got it before he became a believer. He doesn't want people to think he isn't a Christian by his looks." Brian sighed deeply; he said no more, and both guys were soon in their sleeping bags and asleep.

At daylight, the fellows awoke, and as they left the barn to return to the house for breakfast, Timothy remarked, "I like your t-shirt, Brian."

"Yeah, absolutely gorgeous!" Brian replied. "Dad thinks it's great, but Mom wasn't impressed." Timothy glanced again at Brian's shirt which was flesh-coloured with bulging muscles, a tattoo and chest hair printed on it. Brian told him, "You should see people gawk at me when I walk through the mall." He laughed, and Timothy joined him. "Timothy, you should get a t-shirt like this. Absolutely gorgeous!"

After they had eaten breakfast, Mrs. Jack said, "Timmy, you and Brian can load up the car with everything out there on the landing, and take it down to the fruit and vegetable stand. Put it all on the table, and bring back what's there now. And please handle those raspberries carefully."

Timothy and Brian loaded the car, and Timothy took the keys from the drawer next to the phone in the kitchen. He climbed into the car, started it, and beckoned for Brian who was hesitating, to get in on the other side.

"You drive?!" Brian asked in surprise. "Absolutely gorgeous" He got in next to Timothy, who put it in gear and drove down the long driveway to the stand.

After unloading what they had brought and putting the other things in the car, Brian suggested, "Let's drive down the road a bit."

"No, we can't do that." Timothy sat behind the wheel and started the engine.

Brian climbed in the other side. "Why not? No one will ever know," he protested as he closed the car door. "We could drive to that next farm, turn around, and come back. Just like that. What harm is there in that?"

"Maybe they won't know, and maybe there's no harm in it, but it's still wrong." He put it in gear and started up the driveway to the house.

"You're chicken, Tim," Brian sneered at him.

"No, I'm not! I'd like to drive along the road, too, but it takes guts to do the right thing. A chicken is someone who's afraid, gives in, and does the wrong thing. You're all mixed up, Brian. Besides, my parents trust me. I earned their trust by being trustworthy." Timothy parked the car, and after they unloaded it, he returned the keys to the kitchen.

That afternoon in the hay bale room, Timothy organized himself to write more of his letter. Brian tossed his book on the table made from two bales. He said, "This book about having fun is no fun." He jumped up and grinned at Timothy. "Hey, I dare you to walk along that high beam out there."

"No, I've other things to do," he replied as he worked at getting his pen to write. Brian continued to grin. "You're just a chicken."

"Well, I'd rather be a chicken than a dead duck. I could fall and get injured or even get killed."

Brian sat forward, put his elbows on his knees, and his chin in his hands. "Is writing letters fun or exciting? Who are you writing to, anyway?"

"Writing letters is not fun nor exciting, but then everything doesn't have to be fun or exciting." His pen was finally working. "I'm writing to a guy in a detention centre. He's about our age."

"What's a guy my age doing in a detention centre?"

"I don't know. I wasn't told," Timothy answered him. "I'm telling him about my hay bale room here. I've even mentioned you. Is 'dead duck' a hyphenated word?"

The next afternoon when Timothy and Brian had finished their chores, they retreated to the hay bale room to have their lunch. Mrs. Jack had given them a plate of freshly baked biscuits with jam, and they each had a mug of milk.

"Hey, Tim, have you ever smoked a cigarette?" Brian asked as he bit into his biscuit.

Timothy looked over at him. "No, I haven't."

"Why not? Everybody has."

"Hey, wait a minute, Brian, you're wrong," Timothy protested as he struggled to keep from spitting out his lunch. "Everybody hasn't, because I haven't." He took a swallow of milk.

Brian brushed the hair off his cheek and hooked it behind his ear. "Yeah, well, you're different anyway."

"Thanks for the compliment," Timothy responded sincerely. "I'm different, and I'm proud of it. But I'm still included in everybody, you know."

"Well, Mr. Different-and-Proud-of-it, cigarettes are cool."

"Yeah, you're right, cigarettes are cool; cool as death."

Brian reached for another biscuit. "Come on, what's wrong with cigarettes?"

"What's wrong with them? What's right with them, besides being cool? Cigarettes are addictive. Do you know of anyone who found it easy to quit? Do you know anyone who has smoked for years and is glad he's hooked? Have you ever heard anyone say, 'I'm hooked on cigarettes, Man, and I'm some glad cigarettes control me!'" He paused, squinted, and put on a big, make-believe smile for Brian, and then he sipped his milk and added, "Cigarettes are a health risk. And don't eat more than your share of the biscuits."

"I left that one for you, Tim. It's the one that dropped from the plate on our way here. It rolled across the grass and onto the dog dirt. Lots of healthy people smoke; besides, who wants to be healthy?"

"Yeah, thanks!" Timothy replied as he picked up the biscuit and blew it off. "How come I didn't know we had a dog? Some healthy people might smoke, but they don't stay healthy. I want to be healthy and stay healthy all my life-long. I want to enjoy life without shortness of breath and without a lot of poisons all through my body to drag me down. Tobacco brings an early death. They aren't called 'coffin nails' for nothing, you know. I can't imagine why anyone would put a bunch of rolled up, dry weeds between their lips, set them on fire, and then blow the smoke out their nose. Beats me!"

"Okay, okay, you've made your point," Brian responded, and he belched loudly to distract from the subject at hand. "That was a message from the interior," he informed Timothy.

"Besides they stink," Timothy continued without any mercy for his cousin. "They stink up the air we breathe and our clothing, too. And smokers have chimney breath." Timothy paused to add his belch and asked, "Would you like to have chimney breath, Brian?" He gave him his fake smile again.

Brian ignored his question but noted, "Nice milk-mustache you have."

Timothy wiped his mouth on his sleeve. "Someday I'll have the genuine thing," he boasted. "Like a man."

After supper, Timothy and Brian returned to the hay bale room, and several minutes later Billy joined them. "Mommy says I can be with you guys for a while," he said to them when he had crawled into the room.

"Okay, Billy," Timothy answered his brother sharply, "but you have to do what I say and leave when I tell you to. And don't get into anything."

"Yes, Sir!" Brian added looking through his hair. He turned to the little fellow. "Billy, you can sit here on my bed." He looked over at Timothy. "I don't mind."

The three of them sat in silence for about a minute, and then Brian muttered, "I seem to have something in my eye." He looked like he was trying to work it out. "I guess I'll have to remove my eye and wash it off." Timothy and Billy watched Brian as he dug hard at his eye with his finger for several seconds.

"There, I got my eye out!" Brian cupped his hand and looked at Billy with one eye, the other eye held tightly closed. Billy stared at him looking very concerned. "Where can I rinse off my eye?" Brian asked as he quickly glanced around. Then he fumbled with his hands. "Oops, almost dropped my eye!"

When he recovered, he looked at Billy again with one eye and told him, "I know—I'll wash it off in my mouth." He put his cupped hand up to his mouth, and after closing his lips but spreading his jaws, he pushed his tongue first against one cheek and then the other, working his tongue back and forth. Billy stared wide-eyed with his mouth open, and Timothy tried not to laugh.

Suddenly Brian made out he was going to choke, and he leaned forward and gagged, but he quickly regained control and sat up straight. "Just about swallowed my eye," he mumbled with his tongue between his back teeth. Timothy laughed, but Billy looked shocked and kept his eyes on Brian who then leaned over and pretended to drop his eye into his cupped hand. "Now, Billy, I need to get my eye back in the right way," he stated firmly. "Sometimes this can be tricky, so please don't move and please be quiet."

Billy did not seem to hear his brother laughing. "Okay," the young boy agreed in a hushed voice.

Brian put his hand to his closed eye and worked at it for several seconds as Billy watched anxiously. "There, I'll try that." And he opened his eyes and looked cross-eyed at Billy. The young boy lurched back in surprise.

"Oh, no!" Brian uttered disappointedly. "I'll have to adjust it a bit." He gently pushed all around his closed eye as Billy looked on intently. When Brian opened his eye again, he blinked a few times, looked at Billy, and decided, "There, that's better! Absolutely gorgeous! I can see you much clearer now." Billy was relieved and looked over at Timothy who was still laughing.

Several days later, Brian's parents came for him after supper. "Do you know where they made me sleep?" Brian asked his parents as soon as they emerged from the car.

"Probably out in the barn where you belong," his dad replied with a chuckle. "You make any trouble, Boy?"

"Come on," Brian answered as he looked towards Timothy. "We'll show you." The two fellows, Billy, and their dads headed for the barn as the two mothers and Jennifer visited in the garden. Brian proudly showed his dad the hay bale room in the loft of the barn.

"I think you had a good time here, Brian," his dad decided.

"Absolutely gorgeous!" Brian nodded and tried not to smile.

Mrs. Jack served a lunch before Brian and his parents left for home. Later, outside, just before Brian opened the car door, he turned to Timothy and grinned. "You're weird," he informed him, "but you're alright, Tim!"

Timothy looked at him and replied, "I was just thinking the same about you. You know, you have longer hair on your head than any of the primates ever had. And you need to cut your hair regularly. As for the primates—their hair never grows long."

Brian shrugged his shoulder, and he became solemn. "I can't accept the theory of evolution. It's too far-fetched to take seriously."

Timothy answered, "It takes more faith to believe evolution than it takes to believe what the Bible says about creation."

Brian did not reply, but he beckoned for Timothy to come closer. "Thanks," he whispered as his hair swung across his nose, "I'm not going to smoke anymore." Timothy grinned at him and nodded.

When Brian's dad started the engine, Timothy's cousin told him, "I left something on your bed for you." Soon they were on their way down the driveway. "Absolutely gorgeous!" Brian shouted from the open window of the moving car.

The next afternoon, Timothy was reading in his hay bale room about wilderness survival when his dad crawled in through the tunnel. "Mr. Holmns just called on the phone," Mr. Jack said to him as he lowered himself onto the other bed. "He plans to come tomorrow afternoon to take the bales of hay."

Timothy did not respond immediately, but when he did, he told his dad, "I'll move my things out in the morning."

Mr. Jack pointed out, "This would be Billy's last opportunity to spend the night out here with his big brother. It would mean a lot to him."

"Okay, Dad, I'll talk to him."

That evening before dark, Timothy's friend Mike biked over to visit with him. "Remember three summers ago?" Mike remarked as he leaned back against the hay bale wall. "We rode our bikes over to the river in the valley."

"Yeah," Timothy grinned. He tipped up his cap and scratched the top of his head with the visor. "That was peachy! We should go again. I'd like to see how high the water is now that the river's damned up."

"Yeah," Mike answered. "How about tomorrow?"

"Okay. I'm free tomorrow afternoon."

Later that night, Timothy lay in the darkness in his sleeping bag on his hay bale bed. He could hear his young brother on the other bed breathing peacefully in his sleep. There were no other sounds except for crickets in the tall grasses next to the barn indicating summer was more than half gone.

Suddenly, off in the distance, he heard a long, high-to-low grunt. *What was that!* About a minute later he heard it again. *Must be a porcupine,* he decided. *It's much clearer out here.* And then he remembered that the grunts of the porcupines are heard in the late summer and early fall.

Time goes so quickly! I built this room about six weeks ago with dad's help, he reminisced, *and I've slept here every night since. No one would know this room was here—even disguised the entrance. But my sister tricked me into showing her the tunnel. Our family was here when Billy showed us the tobacco pipe he found. And then I remembered that that must have been what Uncle Allan had thrown away that Christmas Eve years ago when we visited here.* Timothy rolled over in his sleeping bag. *And that couple came looking for Mom's brother Brent. We thought all along Uncle Brent had died without being saved. But we found out he became a Christian just before he was killed. Mom was some pleased! Dad wrote a note in his Bible beside Uncle Brent's name: 'Saved May 25, 1964'.*

Brian came to visit. We talked about evolution and about smoking. And he was surprised I drove the car. He gave me his muscle t-shirt. Dad said not to wear it off the property; Mom said I was to change if any company came to visit. Timothy turned his head to face the darkened corner of his room. *Over there is his fun book—he nailed it to the post. Didn't want me to forget him, he said. What a rig!* Timothy realized he was smiling. *That was funny!* he recalled, and he snickered out loud. *Billy believed Brian had really pulled out his eye, and we had to convince him it was just a trick.*

That old farmer's seat I found on the other side of the barn—if I had a base for it, I'd have a nice seat for my bedroom. I'd paint it red—bright red.

I finished the book about George Müller. I'm glad Dad wanted me to read it. It isn't the Lord's will that all Christians run orphanages like Mr. Müller did, but the Lord does want all of us to be dependent on Him in every way. The Lord's presence is real to those who trust Him with their daily circumstances and expect Him to work in their lives. Dad's been telling us about some 'Jim Elliot' guy he's reading about. Sounds interesting. I'd like to read that book next.

And now, this is my last night here in my hay bale room. I'm glad Billy can share it with me; he'll remember this. I want to be the kind of big brother to him the Lord wants me to be.

Tomorrow Mike and I'll be away for a while on our bikes. I'm glad I won't be around when my room here is taken apart. It's been a good summer, concluded Timothy, and he began a prayer of thanksgiving to the Lord, but he did not finish because several minutes later he was fast asleep.

chapter fourteen

one year later—summer 1985 to summer 1986

The Fireplace

"It would be fun to go to a summer camp," Timothy remarked to his sister Jennifer as they picked peas in the family garden.

"Yeah, it would," she replied without looking up. "They do lots of fun things there." She tossed one of her long, blonde braids behind her back.

Timothy said, "Like sports and swimming."

"And handcrafts and nature lore," Jennifer added, and she emptied the peas from her small bucket into the large pail at the end of the row. The topic of camping had come up because they had heard that Mr. and Mrs. Charles had said the Lord was calling them to start a Christian camp in their area.

Timothy was nearly fifteen, and his sister was a year and a half younger. Their job this summer was to look after the garden and take the produce to their fruit and vegetable stand by the road at the end of their long driveway.

Jennifer began to pick peas again, and she called over to Timothy on the next row and farther along, "I wonder why Mom and Dad wouldn't let us go to the camp on the other side of William Station? It's a Christian camp."

"Probably costs too much," he figured as he stood up and shifted his cap to shade his eyes, "or maybe they didn't like that camp for some reason."

"Why wouldn't they like a Christian camp?" she exclaimed in surprise. Timothy had no answer, and they continued their work in silence. Several minutes later Jennifer glanced over at her brother. "We're supposed to pick until five," she reminded him. "What does your watch say?"

Timothy stood up, faced his sister, and put his watch to his ear. "My watch says, 'tick, tick, tick'."

At the supper table that evening Timothy asked if they had heard any more about the camp Mr. and Mrs. Charles wanted to have. "Well, they plan to remodel the barn into a lodge," answered his dad, "and cabins will be built for the campers. Pass the potatoes along this way."

"Would you like bread, too, Richard?" Mrs. Jack asked him.

"What's a lodge?" questioned six-year-old Billy.

"We already have a camp in the area," Timothy pointed out, ignoring his younger brother. "Why would we want another one?"

"No, this is fine, Martha," Mr. Jack answered her. "What do you know about the other camp?"

"Well, it's a Christian camp, and they do fun things there like swimming and sports and nature lore and handcrafts." He helped himself to more peas. "And they have Bible study, too."

"Anything else?"

"Jenny," her mom asked, "would you plug in the kettle, please."

"What's nature lower?" asked Billy, looking over at Timothy.

He replied, "I've heard they raid other cabins at night." Jennifer crossed to the counter and said, "Sue told me that one of the boys threw a snake at her."

"Jennifer, be sure there's enough water in the kettle."

"That's just a part of camp," Timothy laughed. "Camp is supposed to be fun."

"Sounds to me," Mrs. Jack spoke up, "like they do things at that camp that aren't such a good idea. Who wants pie?"

"I do," Timothy quickly answered. "What kind is it?"

"Raspberry—again," Jennifer informed him, and she returned to the table. "What do you think?"

Timothy told her, "I'll have a piece of raspberry-again pie."

Mr. Jack replied, "Things that are called 'Christian' aren't always Christian."

"But it's a church run camp, Dad. What can be wrong with that?" And that is how the conversation went one summer evening at the supper table of the Jack family.

Several days later Mr. Jack joined his wife in their living room with two mugs of coffee. Before he placed one of the hot drinks on the arm of the chair where his wife sat, he raised his knee and dragged the bottom of the moist mug across his pants. He did the same with the second cup then sat on the stuffed chair opposite his wife. Behind her on the wall hung the 'whatsoever' verse from Philippians.

Mr. Jack began, "Mr. Charles has requested a meeting tomorrow night at the chapel to explain what he has in mind regarding his camp."

"Are you planning to go?" she asked as she crossed her ankles over the rug.

"Well, I don't know. I suppose I should in order to be polite and show an interest in what he has to say. I hear the elders approve of this meeting." Mr. Jack slowly ran his finger along the handle of the mug. "I don't think our children should take the time to go to a camp when there's so much to do around here. When they help out, we can get some of the extras we want. We haven't gone on a family vacation for a long time, and that costs something. Timothy is talking about a better bike, and Jennifer would like some good nature books, Billy's not fussy though, he'll settle for just about anything."

The next evening Mr. Jack attended the meeting. After a hymn and prayer, Mr. Charles proceeded to the platform. "As most of you know," he began, "my wife and I were missionaries for many years until the Lord brought us to this area about five years ago." He looked out over the top of his glasses and then removed them and placed them on the pulpit.

"When I was a boy, my parents sent me to a summer camp. I had a lot of fun at camp, but it was there that I heard the gospel clearly and saw it lived in the staff members. I soon realized I was a sinner, and I put my trust in Christ at camp that first year, and each year following I was encouraged and challenged at camp to allow Him to work in me and through me. After eight summers as a camper, I took the staff training and became a junior counselor. That first summer was difficult for me, but the Lord was with me, and the encouragement from others on staff was a big help. The next summer I was a senior counselor. I lived and breathed camp all year round even when I worked at the boatyard. Over the winters I made plans and prepared for camp. I could see the benefits and potentials of Christian summer camping. Eventually I became the assistant camp director for two years, and then I was asked to direct camp."

He paused a few seconds and brushed his hand over his graying hair. "It was at this time that I met a young lady who had come to help in the kitchen." He smiled shyly. "She came back to camp the following summer, and at the end of that camp session I felt the Lord directing me to ask her to be my wife." He took on a look of surprise. "I thought this was rather bold of me—I barely knew her. But when the Lord directs, we need to be bold. Much to my pleasure she said, 'Yes,'! She told me she felt the Lord was telling her that I was the young man for her. We could hardly believe it!"

He grinned and continued. "The following summer we were married, and we joined Mary's parents to help them on the mission field. Our involvement at camp and the experiences we gained there were an asset to the Lord's work on the mission field, along with my boat-building experience."

Mr. Charles became serious, and he continued emphatically as he tapped the pulpit several times, "I was saved at camp. I grew spiritually at camp. I received training for leadership at camp. I served the Lord at camp. And at camp I met the young lady who became my wife." He paused again and resumed, "Many people who are in the Lord's work abroad today and even at home here in local churches have had experiences at Christian camps either as campers or as staff members, or both."

He glanced over those before him and went on, "My wife and I now feel the Lord would have us develop and run a Christian summer camp on our land. He has given us a suitable piece of property which can be developed as a campground. He has given us the desire and some ability, but we can't do it all on our own. This labour needs to be shared, and the blessings as a result of this labour of love will be shared—no!—multiplied."

Then he spoke earnestly. "The most important reason for having a camp is that it be to the glory of God. Therefore everything is to be done to honour Him, and nothing is to be done copying the ways of the world. We must be careful to draw them to Christ because He is the One who bore their sin so they could be saved from the wrath and condemnation of God." And then he scanned the people before him and asked, "Are there any questions regarding this venture?"

Mr. White raised his hand, and when he was acknowledged, he asked, "What do you plan to call this camp?"

"I suggest it be called 'Camp Bethlehem,' which you know means, 'House of Bread.'"

Someone asked, "A work like this costs a lot of money. How do you plan to finance Camp Bethlehem to get it started and to keep it going? None of us are by any means wealthy."

"This is the Lord's work," replied Mr. Charles with conviction. "He has lots of money—He owns the cattle on a thousand hills, and He keeps His money in the pockets of His people, so finances should be no problem. The actual difficulty is in getting the Lord's people to see the value of Camp Bethlehem which in turn will cause them to support it abundantly."

Then he spoke again with emphasis. "When the Lord's people see He is honoured in all things at camp, and that it's a testimony to Him, they will gladly help out. When the Lord's people see their children and young people are getting saved at camp, they will give. When the Lord's people see their children and young people are growing spiritually because of camp, they will give of their time and money and possessions. When the Lord's people see their children and young people are being trained and given the opportunity for Christian service at camp, they will support it wholeheartedly."

Mr. Jack stood and asked, "How will this camp glorify the Lord? Many camps are called Christian camps, but they are a disgrace to the Lord's Name."

"What causes them to be a disgrace to His Name?" replied Mr. Charles, and then he answered his own question. "It is how the camp is run. Staff members are the most important commodity at any camp. The weather can be bad, the grounds in poor shape, the food unappetizing, but properly trained staff members who want to honour the Lord will make all the difference. Camp is to be a safe and wholesome haven where our children and young people will come to know the Lord and will grow to appreciate Him without any harmful, worldly influences to distract them and stunt their spiritual growth."

He paused, then continued. "Before the Lord will allow us to work for Him, we must allow Him to work in us. All potential staff members for Camp Bethlehem will be carefully screened and selected. They will be required to take a course on staff training with refresher sessions every year. Staff training begins in the early spring, and Bible studies for staff members during camp will be geared to help and encourage them while at camp. All this is designed to ensure we honour the Lord in every possible way."

Mr. Blair asked, "Will there be some means in place allowing any parents who wish to send their children to Camp Bethlehem but can't afford it? It would be too bad if some children and young people do not experience camp who want to go."

"Good question," Mr. Charles replied. "Do we charge children and young people who attend our Sunday school? Do we charge people who come to chapel dinners and other get-togethers? This camp, Camp Bethlehem, is the Lord's work—we cannot charge for our service—our ministry of the Lord to them. Opportunities will be given for anyone to contribute at any time for the expenses of camp. In this way, any who can't pay will not be denied the Lord's blessings at camp, and those who are financially blessed by the Lord can give richly as He leads them."

"Can gifts be given tonight?" someone wanted to know.

"I haven't made arrangements to receive gifts tonight." He was taken back by surprise. "But perhaps we could borrow the collection box and leave it at the back of the room for this time. I believe that a gift, no matter how small, even a quarter, when given in the right spirit and received in the right spirit will be used in a great way rather than a larger gift given or received in a wrong spirit. I should say at this time that the gifts towards camp should not take away from our regular giving to the Lord on the first day of the week."

Mr. Charles continued. "The Lord has given me several abilities to be used for Him, but I can't do everything. Besides, I want to share this exciting work with others—with you folks here. I suggest we have a committee of experts. We need someone to organize each different phase of construction such as electrical and plumbing. Someone needs to take on finances and other legalities. My wife is willing to organize meals. Besides a few advisers, I would like at least one other elder on the committee. I ask that each of you pray about this work, and if the Lord leads you, let me know. We need lots of willing workers."

After the meeting was over, and twenty minutes later when everyone had left, Mr. Charles picked up the money-box and slid back the lid. He could hardly believe his eyes. There were tens and twenties, a fifty, and folded several times was a hundred dollar bill. He trembled as he gathered them up. *Thank You, Lord, for all this money.* As he folded the bills together, a quarter fell to the floor and rolled under a chair near the door. *And thank You for this twenty-five cent piece. May it, too, be used for Thy glory.*

The following Sunday, Mr. Charles wore his small lapel pin which read, 'For me to live is Christ.' After the meeting, he shook hands as usual, with all who were there. Several people left money in his hand which he slipped into his pocket without looking. When he returned to his car, he found a five dollar bill draped over the horn ring of the steering wheel.

Mr. Charles now had four hundred and sixty-three dollars and twenty-five cents. It was a good start and the beginning of tens of thousands of dollars needed and yet to come. He knew he would have to look to the Lord for every cent, and he knew it would not come all at once. This continual dependence on Him would cause him to seek the Lord's will each step of the way, and it would guarantee the Lord's will was done and done in His way.

Joshua Palmer, the grandfather of Timothy, Jennifer, and Billy, volunteered to organize the carpentry projects. Mr. Charles immediately began the work of remodeling the barn by ordering some building supplies. His policy was to spend only the money he had and to pay cash immediately for products and services. He felt this method was honouring to the Lord, and that the Lord would honour him in return.

Money steadily came in and sometimes from unexpected sources. Mr. Charles received two hundred dollars from an elderly couple whom he thought had no time nor patience for children. They informed him, "We feel that the Lord wants us to give this money towards reaching children and young people for the Lord."

"Thank you for your generous gift," Mr. Charles replied as he shook their hands. "And I thank the Lord for people like you who are sensitive to His leading."

Whenever possible, materials were purchased on sale, but they had to be of good quality. "No junk for the Lord, please," he would say.

Mr. Charles located some good quality windows that were at a discount. They were end-of-line, and some were odd sizes. These windows were installed soon after the roofing was complete.

In a pile of metal at a Saturday yard sale, Mr. Charles found a length of steel rod. *This could be made into a triangle to call campers to the barn for meals and meetings,* he realized, and he carried it over to the lady in charge.

"How much for this?" he enquired as he held the rod with one hand, and with the other he grasped one of his red suspenders.

"How about a quarter?" He reached into his pocket and removed the twenty-five cent piece he had received the evening he presented Camp Bethlehem at the meeting place.

"Sounds good to me," he replied as he handed the coin to her. "I can almost hear it now." He turned, and as he walked to his car, she stared after him looking puzzled.

"So that's how the quarter is going to be used," he said aloud as he laid his purchase on the backseat.

Sometimes men came to help during the week, usually in the evenings, and on Saturdays there were always work-parties of at least a dozen helpers including young people. When there were enough workers to start, they would assemble together, and someone would pray, committing themselves to the Lord and asking that His greatness would be evident to them today.

Each family brought a dish of something to eat which was served at noon by the ladies. After dinner, they sang a chorus or two, and one of the men brought a short devotional from God's Word.

Mrs. Charles was finding it difficult to find enough of her plates to go around for everybody. One of the young ladies suggested they start a collection of kitchen things. "We should bring from home anything extra we aren't using," she suggested as she helped set the table, "dishes and cups, knives and forks, pots and pans, and stuff like that."

Someone laughed, "But they wouldn't match!"

"They don't have to match, as long as they're good quality and not cracked or chipped. There's a high-class restaurant in one of our big cities which uses unmatched fine china."

"That's a good idea," agreed Mrs. White who was filling the salt shakers, "and we could be looking for things at yard sales, too."

One of the ladies received the contents of her late aunt's kitchen. She had no use for any of it and passed it all on to Mrs. Charles. Mrs. Jack gave some things which Uncle Allan had left. Several people brought mugs they were tired of, and others donated incomplete sets of tableware. One person gave a kettle.

Mrs. Boates took on the important job of organizing a camp library. She and her helpers read books which were donated, to make sure the contents were suitable, and several people gave money for the purchase of new books. All stories were to be wholesome and were to encourage children and young people in the Lord. Other books collected were biographies and autobiographies of Bible-believing Christians and were intended to show what the Lord can do through those who trust Him and follow in the ways He leads.

At the midweek meeting, Mr. Charles mentioned the moneys that had been received recently, and he told briefly how things were progressing with the work at the barn. "Let's thank the Lord we now have enough money to purchase the rest of the plywood to finish the flooring."

After the meeting, Mr. Charles approached one of the young ladies at the back of the chapel. "Here's a counselor application for you, Elizabeth."

A look of shock came over her face. "But, Mr. Charles!" she sputtered.

"But what?" he answered calmly as he continued to hold out the paper to her. "You're a born again believer, aren't you!"

"Yes—but!"

"I know about you," he smiled and continued. "Your desire is to please the Lord and to live the way He wants you to live."

"Yes," Elizabeth protested, "but I hardly qualify!"

"You get along well with children," Mr. Charles insisted.

"But what about Amy?" she asked in a near whisper.

"Pray about it, Elizabeth. If the Lord directs you, your daughter can come as a camper. You're a trophy of His grace. You're a good influence on children and young people, Miss Johnson."

Mr. Charles wanted to complete the fireplace before the cold weather came. Mr. Jack organized the construction of a concrete base to go on top of bedrock under the barn. The hearth was made from flat fieldstones.

The mild days of late summer were past, and the leaves on the trees in the woods nearby were turning colour and fluttering to the ground. "Hey, Jennifer," Mr. Charles said when they headed with his wheelbarrow towards the old stone wall, "did you hear about the man who broke his arm raking leaves?"

Jennifer looked over at him. "How could he do that?" she asked in surprise.

Mr. Charles grinned. "He broke his arm when he fell out of the tree." Jennifer giggled, and Mr. Charles dropped the wheelbarrow and laughed with her.

They arrived at the old stone wall bordering the field next to the woods and began to load the wheelbarrow with rocks to haul to the barn for the fireplace. "Don't scratch yourself on these raspberry canes," Mr. Charles warned her. "And we should be careful not to damage the new canes. We can have fresh raspberries next summer."

"Hey, Mr. Charles, what are you doing?" called Mr. Cunningham as he hurried over to join them. "Hold on! I live just down the road a bit. I'll get my tractor and wagon." When he returned, several men and two young fellows helped load the wagon with suitable stones.

The fireplace was only thirty centimetres deep and the opening was a metre wide and just as high. "That won't heat very much!" someone commented to no one in particular. Mr. Jack was the organizer for the construction of the fireplace and chimney. He followed Mr. Charles' plans although he was not familiar with this particular design. The narrow smoke opening was as wide as the opening of the fireplace but only ten centimetres deep from front to back.

"That'll make the room fill up with smoke right quick," someone mumbled to several others nearby.

"Maybe it's only for small fires."

"Then again, maybe it's just for looks. It does look kind of cute, don't you think?"

Two weeks after the chimney was completed up to the ceiling, Mr. Charles announced they needed no more stones.

"But we need the chimney to continue outside up above the roof," someone reminded him.

"We'll put an insulated metal pipe outside," he explained. "In that way none of the heavy fireplace will extend from inside the barn to outside, causing the heat to migrate outside."

At the next midweek meeting at the chapel, it was announced there would be a get-together the following Friday evening at Camp Bethlehem to officially light the fireplace for the first time. "Bring a plate of finger food for an evening lunch."

Friday evening when people arrived at the barn, they found the fire had been set up and was ready to light. The evening air was cool and everyone kept their coats on. People were talking quietly. "It looks like it's going to be a big fire for that shallow fireplace."

"And look how far the wood is set out this way into the room."

"Yeah, and you should see the small opening for the smoke to go up!"

"Mr. Charles is going crazy," hissed one of the young people. "Or maybe he is already!"

Mr. Charles asked Jennifer to strike the triangle a few times to call any who might be outside. When all were present in the barn, it was evident a good number had come. The evening program began with singing several praise hymns followed by prayer. Mr. Dodge thanked the Lord for all the willing help which was received for the work so far.

"And now," Mr. Charles announced with a flourish, "the moment we've all been waiting for!" He removed a match from his pocket and held it up. He grinned and looked around at those assembled there. "But first." He paused as he lowered the unlit match. "This fireplace could be an object lesson for us. Scripture says we who are believers are living stones, and we make up the Church, the Body of Christ. Each stone here is needed. If one went missing, it would be noticed."

He glanced up the face of the chimney and went on. "We are built on Christ the solid rock. We can't see the rock this fireplace is built on, and we can't see Christ with our natural eyes either. But we know there is bedrock deep in the ground under this fireplace, and we know we have Christ the solid rock as the author of our salvation."

Mr. Charles again scanned the fireplace from its hearth up to the six-metre-high ceiling. "What holds all these stones together?" He turned to face the crowd before him. "It's the mortar between them. It's the Holy Spirit who binds us together, and without the Holy Spirit we would be ineffective for the Lord."

He continued. "This fireplace was designed and built according to plans. As a result we have a beautiful structure before us—also very functional, as you will soon see. The church was designed and is now being built by the Lord, and it is beautiful in His eyes as well as it being functional. And often people don't understand the church just as this fireplace is not understood by everyone."

Mr. Charles once more held up the match. "Who would like to light the fire for us?"

Mrs. Taylor who stood off to the side and towards the back of the crowd, coughed nervously.

"Mrs. Taylor! Would you like to do the honours for us?"

"Oh no! I'm not the outdoorsy type," she protested, stepping closer to her husband.

Mr. Charles noticed young Henry who was holding his baseball cap and standing next to his dad in the crowd. "Henry!" Mr. Charles said as he looked directly at the red-headed boy, and then he spoke distinctly. "Would you like to light the fire for us?"

Mr. Blair smiled, nodded his approval, and gently pushed his son forward. Mr. Charles beckoned to Henry, and as he came to him, he pointed to where the lighted match was to be placed on the paper under the kindling and wood. The boy put his cap on, grinned, took the match, and knelt on the hearth. After he struck the match, he placed it where he had been instructed.

The fire blazed up nicely, and Henry continued to grin as he returned to stand with his dad.

A small puff of smoke drifted into the large room, and Mrs. Taylor coughed again, but soon all the smoke stayed at the back of the fireplace and ascended out of sight up the chimney.

"Hurrah!" two or three people called out, and several stepped closer to the fire.

"My, I can feel the heat from here already!"

"And there's no smoke at all!"

Mr. Charles removed his coat. His red suspenders could not be missed over his long-sleeved, pale blue shirt. He commented, "We'll need to install a couple of ceiling fans, I think, to push the warm air down towards the floor."

As people wandered about and visited with others, a lunch was served. "These squares are some delicious!" Mr. Charles exclaimed as he reached for a second one. "Who made them?"

"My wife did," George proudly informed him.

"Tell Elizabeth," Mr. Charles said with a grin, "that I'd like these squares to be served at the party—I mean the fellowship following my funeral."

Work continued in the barn all winter. There was much to be done. The main room was insulated and covered with vertical pine boards, the kitchen needed cabinets and worktables, and two washrooms were installed. One of the men offered to do the backhoe work for the disposal system when the frost was out of the ground in the spring, and that was also the time to start the cabins. Mr. Joshua Palmer organized the construction of the two cabins on both sides of the barn.

Several old apple trees in the field between the barn and the lake were starting to blossom when the training for staff members began. Mr. Dodge was to be the camp director, and four young men and four young ladies were accepted as counselors. Others who wanted to help out occasionally, but were unable to commit themselves to being on the camp grounds twenty-four hours a day were also present.

These dedicated people met weekly on the camp property at the home of Mr. and Mrs. Charles. The purposes of camp were reviewed, and they discussed how the program was to be run in order to bring glory to God. "We'll have good, wholesome fun at camp," Mr. Charles told them, "but we'll also have activities to encourage personal growth and activities which will give satisfaction and enjoyment. We'll encourage the young people to be helpful and to be responsible, and they'll soon find out that this is fulfilling to them." He paused to let that sink in.

"Let's not forget," Mr. Charles informed the group, "that most believers came to the Lord when they were still children or young people. Statistics show that more people were saved as children than as adults."

Camp was to demonstrate to others that believers enjoy the things of the Lord and that they like to sing hymns and choruses. "And," Mr. Charles insisted, "we need to get across to the children and young people the great truths of our faith not just the beauty of the music. The Lord created music—He designed it to be used to praise Him and to tell of His greatness. In addition to that, the early church was told to use singing to instruct believers and to encourage them."

One of the young men commented, "In that case, Christian rock music sure isn't appropriate for believers to use."

"Yes," Mr. Dodge agreed. "Christian rock music is a contradiction. It tries to mix that which brings glory to the Lord with the self-centered ways of the world. And rock music can be sensual in an improper way."

The young man added, "I've heard that some hymns use bar tunes."

"'Bar tune' is a musical term which refers to the form the music was written in," Mr. Dodge stated as he glanced over the group. "It does not refer to music used in a bar or a pub. I can't imagine a godly hymn-writer applying a tune associated with a drinking establishment. Occasionally a tune of a secular folk song was used, but there again, the hymn-writer would be very careful to use a tune which was appropriate for the words. No way would the hymn-writer want the tune to be connected with anything which was contrary to the things of the Lord."

Many passages of Scripture were read and applied to camp situations. Mr. Charles encouraged others to contribute to the staff meetings, and sometimes the group stopped to ask the Lord for guidance about something.

A daily, private, quiet time with the Lord was explained by Mr. Dodge. "It's a personal time between us and the Lord," he pointed out. "We need to first confess any known sin in our lives. First John One tells us that, 'when we say we have no sin we deceive ourselves.'" They looked up the passage, and one of the young ladies read it. Mr. Dodge also said that we must not allow sin to control us by thinking we are hopelessly entangled in it. We are not bound in sin, for Christ has given us the victory over sin—we are saved from sin.

"Next, we ask the Holy Spirit to speak to us as we read God's Word. The Holy Spirit who authored the Bible is the One who speaks to us as we read it. We must not use God's Word only as our guide; we must use it as instructions for us to obey."

"Prayer follows," Mr. Dodge continued. "Pray for yourself. Ask the Lord that you'll be the person He wants you to be this day." He paused to let them think about that and then said, "Pray for anything and everything you are led to pray for. And don't be bound by a prayer list—that would in effect prevent us from being led by the Holy Spirit. When we pray we acknowledge our dependency on our Lord, and we seek His will for us, His servants. And remember, the Lord answers those prayers which bring Him glory."

"Meditate on or think throughout the day about what you have read in His Word," he told the group. "The Holy Spirit will speak to us as we meditate on what we have read but He'll not speak to us when we are not actively listening."

Mr. Charles was pleased at how things were developing in preparation for camp. Work continued on the grounds with the property being made ready, and staff members were excited as the Lord became more real to them and as they grew more dependent on Him. It was clear the Lord was working in the lives of His people, even those who were not directly involved with the camp operation. The Lord was being glorified even before Camp Bethlehem was scheduled to begin in another month and a half.

"Any more gravy?" Timothy asked at the family's dinner table, and when he was handed the pitcher, he slopped some over his potatoes.

"Jenny, please pass the carrots to Billy," Mrs. Jack said.

Timothy asked, "Are we having raspberry-again pie for dessert? It's my favourite, especially when we have ice-cream with it."

"Tim, Jenny," Mr. Jack announced when he had the opportunity to speak, "how would you two like to go to Camp Bethlehem this summer?"

"Yeah!" Timothy exclaimed as he sliced his meat.

Jennifer spoke up, "I'd love to!"

"Can I go, too?" Billy wanted to know, looking towards his dad.

"But don't you need us around here to help with the garden?" Timothy asked his dad as he loaded his fork.

"You're too young, Billy," his mom answered him, "but next summer you'll be old enough."

Mr. Jack replied, "Yes, we do need you here to help with the garden. But your mother and I feel that when we send you to camp, the Lord will give us the things we need, not the extras we want. If Tim really needs a better bike and if Jenny really needs some good nature books, the Lord will somehow provide them for you two—just trust Him. And we don't really need a costly family vacation. Some day-trips should be satisfying to each of us."

"We approve of Camp Beth," Mrs. Jack stated. "We know it is honouring to the Lord and not just having fun for the sake of having fun."

"We want the Lord's best for you children," Mr. Jack added as he looked over at each of them.

"I like sports," Timothy grinned. "I hope there's lots of sports and swimming."

"And I like handcrafts," Jennifer added as she flipped back one of her braids, "and nature lore in the woods, the fields, and in the water."

chapter fifteen

about two and a half years later—late winter 1989

The Three Wise Men

"Okay, Tim, slow down," instructed Stanley from the backseat, "and pull over close to that big, funny-looking, pine tree there." Eighteen-year-old Timothy quickly geared down and then parked his small, red car on the shoulder of the gravel road.

The three fellows stepped out. "I'll unlock the trunk for the shovels," Timothy said as he stroked his scanty mustache and made his way around to the rear of his car. Joel and his friend Stanley grabbed the two shovels and dug into the snowbank. Several minutes later the two young men had cleared a suitable area on which to park the car on the woods road just off the gravel road. Timothy relocated his vehicle, and the three fellows retrieved their things from the trunk.

"It looks like it's going to snow," Joel figured. "Check out the sky over there."

The three young men put on their hiking bags and began their long walk into the mixed woods along the old logging road. Timothy carried a thermos of tea as well as bologna sandwiches and some date squares his sister had made the day before. Tucked away in a side pocket was his small Bible.

Thirty metres into the woods, the fellows came to the ruins of a stone house several metres off the path. Two walls and part of a third wall were still standing, and towering up into the trees was a huge rock chimney. When they approached the ruins, they could see a few trees and bushes were growing inside the remaining walls where the living room had once been.

Stanley brushed back his shoulder length hair from off his face. "My grandparents lived here until they were burned out," he explained. "My great-grandfather built this house using stone from this property."

The young men circled the rock shell and tried to determine where the different rooms would have been. "That low part over there is where the cellar was under the kitchen."

"Let's go, Guys," Stanley urged. "We go a mile along this road and then about a half mile along a side path." Timothy took off his glasses and pushed them into his coat pocket. The fellows set off again and plodded along in the deep snow of the woods road parallel to an old stone wall.

"Used to be a cleared field here," Stanley informed his companions, "and this stone wall was made from rocks gathered from the field. The field's grown over now and has returned to woods."

Several minutes later the fellows came to another stone wall perpendicular to the wall they were following, indicating they were at the back end of what was once a large field. They passed through a wide gap near the corner where the two stone walls met. The wooden gate was long gone.

A few flakes of snow began to fall as they entered the shelter of the deep woods. "Let's take turns taking the lead," suggested Stanley when about twenty minutes had passed since leaving the car. "You go first, Tim, and we'll follow in your tracks." Timothy stepped ahead of Joel and Stanley who remained a dozen paces behind.

Joel whispered to Stanley, "Why did we have to invite him? He's no fun."

"He's the one with the wheels."

Joel called ahead to Timothy, "What are you carrying in your bag, anyway, Tim? We aren't staying overnight at the cabin, you know."

"Just my noon meal, and I have an extra pair of socks, too."

Joel muttered, "You need another pair of socks like a fish needs a bicycle—like a hen needs a toothbrush."

"That's cute," Timothy uttered as he struggled to get his hood up over his head. "I'll have to remember that one."

By now the snow was coming down thicker. The wildlife had taken shelter from the impending snowfall, and there was no sign of animal tracks, and no birds could be seen nor heard. The young men stopped their chitchat, and the only sound came from their heavy breathing and their clothing as they trudged through the deep snow.

Sometime later Stanley offered to take over as leader. The road followed the gentle up and down slopes of the wooded hills. It curved around large, old, poorly shaped pine trees unsuitable for the logging operation which had been in the area many years previous.

The woods road here passed between several huge boulders the size of large trucks. Timothy remarked, "That one looks like a dump truck with a full load of something or other."

The road now sloped down steadily. The fellows eventually came to a narrow low clearing where the large flakes of falling snow were more evident in the open. The road here was level and straight, for it had been built up nearly a metre. A now frozen-over brook meandered through the meadow, and the young men paused on the sturdy wooden bridge. Out of sight under the ice and snow could be heard the faint gurgling of the stream.

"Some hard to believe now, but in the summer it can be hot and humid when we come here for brook trout," Stanley recalled.

Timothy realized he should not be bitter towards Joel. Instead, he silently confessed his attitude towards Joel as sin, and he asked the Lord that he would have the opportunity to show kindness to him.

They continued across the meadow and plodded up the hill and into the woods on the other side. The guys had been on the old logging road for nearly an hour, and they had changed leaders several times. Joel was eating one of his jam sandwiches for a lunch, when they came to a large spruce tree lying across the road. "Looks like it blew over just recently," he decided, and he paused to have a look. "Probably during that storm last month."

They marched on single file for about a quarter of an hour without saying much. Each fellow carried freshly fallen snow on his head and shoulders. "Hey, look at this, will you?" Timothy stopped to examine an old, rusty chain wrapped a half dozen times around the trunk of a large pine tree. The chain was imbedded in the thick bark of the tree, indicating it had been there many years.

"Oh yeah, that's where we turn off the road and go along the side path," Stanley told him. He had been in the lead and now retraced his steps. "In the summer we can drive to here and park over there by those cedars. This woods road continues on to Cow River. Cabin's about a half mile from here." With the deep blanket of snow on the ground, there was no sign of the narrow path, but they could see the lower branches had been trimmed back from some spruce trees to allow a clear path for walking. "Looks different in the winter," Stanley admitted.

The walk was difficult, and the three fellows breathed deeply as they moved through the woods. Stanley mumbled, "I'm glad we're almost there because my knees are wet through."

"That's nothing!" Joel lamented. "I have snow in my boots." They trudged on in the deep snow and peered through the trees and the falling flakes searching for the cabin.

"There it is!" Stanley finally announced as he grinned at his companions. The cabin could easily be missed for it was partly hidden by thick, bushy spruce trees. There was about ten centimetres of snow on the roof, and the snow on the ground was halfway up to the windows. The bright red door, the only cheerful colour in sight, seemed to welcome them to come inside. The young fellows were finally at their destination, and they made their way over to the cabin with renewed energy. It had taken them about an hour and a half to hike in from Timothy's car.

"Oh, no, Guys!" Stanley groaned when they reached the door. "I forgot the key."

Timothy and Joel stopped brushing the snow from their clothing. "What? You didn't!"

"Just kidding." Stanley promptly unlocked the door and walked in, with Timothy and Joel close behind.

"I'll light the fire." Stanley went over to the woodstove, lifted the lid and as he held back his hair, he scanned its dark interior. "All ready to light." He removed a match from the glass jar left on the stove and set the burning match against the birch bark.

"Whenever possible," Stanley explained, "the fire's left ready to be lit next time we're here. We keep matches in this glass jar. I've heard of cabins going up in smoke in the dead of winter and with no one around. Probably from mice chewing on the matches."

"Could be a hot time for the mice," Timothy agreed with his phony smile.

The sound of the crackling fire was a promise of heat to come, and the smell of the burning wood reminded the fellows they were far from civilization and the comforts they were accustomed to.

"I like your cabin, Stan," Timothy said as he released his hiking bag and lowered it to the couch. He glanced around and grinned as he contemplated, *Dad would love a place like this.*

Stanley told him, "My old man built this cabin back before he met Mom. He and my grandfather logged this neck of the woods. My grandfather built and operated a mill on Cow River years ago, and Dad and his brother built this about that time. The main part here was built first, and then the bedroom was added several years later, and I think it was the following summer Dad put the backroom on." Stanley nodded towards the room. "They hauled everything along the road on the back of a pickup and then carried it all in to here. They had no power tools or nothing."

As the cabin gradually warmed up, Timothy and Joel checked out its interior. Six wooden chairs surrounded a chrome kitchen table. An enamel sink with its faucet was mounted in the countertop, and there were cupboards above along one wall. Between the kitchen area and the living room was the woodstove which was used for both heating and cooking. Timothy tried to visualize the heavy stove and bulky couch being carried along the narrow path. The couch had a matching stuffed chair and there was one scruffy, unmatched chair, all from the 1950's. Several pieces of worn linoleum covered parts of the floor.

The bedroom had two single, iron beds and an old bureau. A large braided rug lay over most of the floor between the beds. Four or five patchwork quilts were folded and placed at the foot of one of the beds. Another kitchen chair was set in the corner. A blue-gray, army blanket served as the door to the bedroom, and it was hooked over a large nail to keep it open.

Off the kitchen was the backroom which was used for storage. A good supply of dry firewood was stacked next to a tiny room with a pit-toilet.

All the windows of the cabin were large sizes but none matched. The curtains were homey with colourful patterns, indicating a woman's touch. There were candles and oil lamps on the shelves which were mounted on each wall in the main room.

A stuffed owl, perched high on a shelf in the corner, glared down with its large brown eyes at the intrusion of these unexpected winter visitors. "We call her Miss Barred Owl," Stanley explained to the fellows.

By the bedroom door was a windup clock which showed three twenty-seven.

"Look what time it is!" Joel called out in mock surprise.

"That's not the right time," Timothy scolded him. "The battery's probably frozen."

"Hey, Guys, don't knock my clock. I'll have you know, it tells the correct time twice a day."

The young men stood around the stove to dry and warm themselves as they ate their lunches. "The old man drinks tea," remarked Joel when he glanced over at Timothy.

Timothy wiped his mustache and said nothing, and Joel pulled a can of pop from his bag, and with a flourish he yanked off the tab. After he took a slurp, he asked, "Anybody want my piece of cheese? I don't like cheese. I told her not to give me cheese." He looked at Stanley and then Timothy.

"Don't leave it for the mice," Stanley informed him. Joel returned the cheese to his lunch container, bit into one of his donuts, and had several swallows of his soft drink.

Stanley commented, "It's finally warm enough here to take off my coat."

"Yeah, now I can remove my boots and stick my cold feet in the oven," Joel expressed, and then he belched loudly.

Timothy replied, "Now you know why I brought extra socks." Joel ignored him, and he removed his coat and tossed it over to the couch. On the front of his fleece pullover was a silly cartoon of a cow's head.

Stanley glanced out the window between the stuffed chairs. "We could get a fair bit of the white stuff," he said.

"Maybe we should leave soon," Timothy hinted. "Driving could be a challenge."

"But we just got here!" Joel barked, and he squeezed his empty pop can causing it to crumple in his fist. "Besides my socks are still damp." When he turned, the back side of his pullover revealed the hind end of the same cow.

Stanley grabbed his knees. "That's nothing!" he put in. "My pant legs are still wet." And then he suggested, "We could stay another hour or so."

Timothy searched through his coat pockets. "Oh no, I can't find my glasses," he exclaimed, and then he checked through his pockets a second time.

Two hours later when the fellows were dried out and warmed up, they decided it was time to leave. Before they left the cabin, Stanley put five or six pieces of firewood in the wooden butter box with some kindling and paper and left it by the woodstove. Since Joel's socks were still damp, Timothy tossed his extra pair to him and said, "Like a fish needs a motorcycle. Like a hen needs a toothpick."

"Thanks," Joel admitted. He changed socks and dropped his damp ones into his hiking bag. "My sister will be surprised to find these in here."

The three young men put on their coats and picked up their hiking bags. "Vacate the premises!" Timothy ordered.

After the door was made secure, they left the cabin and walked through the steady falling snow. *I'd like to have a cabin just like Stanley's,* Timothy pondered as they tramped along. *Camp Beth could have a great cabin away back there in the woods behind the barn. It could be used for outings and camp-overs and stuff like that.*

When the fellows reached the woods road, they moved single file along the route they had made coming in. Their tracks were now nearly filled in with fresh snow. The young men came to the fallen spruce tree across their path, and after a while they descended the hill and crossed the meadow. Although it was not snowing as hard now, there was no sign of the trail they had made coming in that morning. None of them spoke until about an hour after leaving the cabin they came to the large, snow-covered rocks.

"Your dump truck has an even bigger load now, Tim," Joel observed. The fellows changed leaders and continued through the woods.

The snow had stopped falling by the time they came to the opening in the stone wall at the back of the old field. Several minutes later they passed by the ruins of the stone house with just a quick glance in that direction and without slackening their pace. "We're almost there, Guys," Stanley cheerfully announced. "The car and the road are just up ahead."

"Good!" Timothy replied with enthusiasm. "Soon I can sit down."

Joel replied, "Good! Soon I can warm up my feet." It was late afternoon when the three weary fellows arrived back at Timothy's car.

Stanley walked past the car. "Oh no!" he exploded, breaking the silence of this remote location. "The road hasn't been plowed!" He glanced one way and then the other along the snow-covered road.

Joel gasped, "I thought you said this road was well traveled."

"Well, it is in summer."

"Well, it's not summer now, you know!" Joel snapped at him. "What are we going to do? Snow's too deep to drive through."

Stanley shrugged one shoulder and pushed his hair back. "We'll just have to wait it out here for the plow."

"Wait for the plow!" Joel shouted. "That could be tomorrow."

"Guys, we can't hunker down here in the car all night," Timothy admitted, trying to sound calm. "We'll freeze. And I have less than a quarter tank of gas."

"Great!" Joel muttered in disgust. "I suppose then we go back to the cabin."

"That could be a good idea," Timothy said, looking at Stanley. "At least it would be warm there."

"Yeah," Joel complained, "but my boots are full of snow, and my feet are cold. Besides it's getting dark—we'll get lost for sure."

Timothy and Stanley talked it over while Joel mumbled something about hypothermia being a right dandy way to end it all. They reluctantly decided they had no choice but to hike back through the woods to Stanley's cabin. Timothy silently prayed, then he searched in his car and found a part of a package of cookies under the front seat and a chocolate bar in the glove compartment. "Look what I found, guys! We have some supper."

Joel still carried his piece of cheese, and Stanley had a small bag of potato chips.

"That might do for supper," Joel said with a scowl, "but what about breakfast? I don't take any delight in skipping breakfast."

Timothy answered with his overdone, cheerful smile, "I'll have bacon and eggs, please—sunny-side up. And toast with marmalade on a side plate, and tea in a glass mug. Thanking you in advance, Sir."

The sky was beginning to clear in the west, and the low setting sun cast a warm glow on the distant hills. Stanley looked off into the darkening woods. "We better move along," he said.

Timothy told them, "I'll call my parents on the CB and ask them to call your folks."

It was noticeably darker as the young men entered the woods this time and the temperature had dropped a degree or two since the morning. "We have to do it all over again!" Joel muttered to himself.

"It won't be so bad," Stanley pointed out as they passed by the ruins of the stone house. "We can easily follow in our tracks." They did not glance over to look.

Timothy could sense Joel was feeling uncomfortable. When he tried to make conversation, the fellow sputtered in annoyance. Timothy prayed he would have the opportunity and the wisdom to react in the proper way.

The young men followed the stone wall and moved through the opening at the far end of the grown-over field. Rabbit tracks now crisscrossed the woods road, and deer tracks followed the road for a short distance. The quietness was shattered when a partridge flew up from under a spruce tree two metres from Stanley. "Major heart attack!" he exclaimed.

By the time the young men came to the large boulders, the sky was a dull gray shade. Nearly black were the trunks of the spruce and pine trees as well as their evergreen boughs, and the fresh snow on the forest floor appeared drab. The peeled back bark on the occasional birch tree revealed a washed-out, pale pink colour.

Stanley was ahead, and Joel suddenly admitted to Timothy he had a problem. "I have a phobia—a fear of the dark." Timothy didn't know how to answer him. "I can't get over it, and it really bothers me."

Timothy prayed once more for wisdom. Then he answered, "A phobia usually starts with a fright or scare from something in our past, but our on-going fear which follows the fright is sin and can become a phobia. Our sin needs to be confessed and forsaken. I suggest you tell the Lord you have sinned by still fearing the dark and ask Him to remove that fear. It's as simple as that, Joel." The young man did not respond, and Timothy wondered if he had made him feel worse.

It was still fairly light in the open area of the meadow, but when they reentered the woods, it became noticeably darker. About a quarter hour later, they skirted the large, fallen spruce tree. Towards the top of a nearby tree, a porcupine could be seen silhouetted against the darkening sky. As the fellows moved closer, the animal slowly climbed even higher. Even though it was too dark to make out its beady eyes, they knew it was staring down nervously as they passed below.

Finally, in the dim light, the young men could make out the pine tree with the chain buried in its trunk. They turned off the old logging road and trudged farther along in their earlier tracks. They were exhausted but forced themselves to go on through the thickening darkness.

"Finally," Joel stated when they neared their destination. There was barely any light in the sky, and even from a short distance away, the cabin was not distinguishable from the spruce trees surrounding it. The bright red door was now nearly black, and from the outside the little building appeared uninviting.

Timothy opened the door and entered the dark, cold cabin. They cautiously felt their way across the floor. "I found a candle!" Timothy exclaimed. "Where are the matches?"

Stanley replied, "Should be matches in the jar on top of the firewood next to the stove."

"Have the matches here, Tim," Joel called out in the dark. He struck one against the sandpaper glued to the top of the jar lid. The room instantly took on a warm glow.

Timothy quickly pushed the candle towards the burning match Joel was holding out to him. When the candle was lit, Joel shook out the match. Suddenly Joel threw back his head and laughed. He looked over at Timothy who immediately laughed with him.

"What's going on?" Stanley demanded. "You guys got the giggles?"

Joel laughed again and then said, "I'm not afraid of the dark!"

"What! What do you mean?"

"I used to have nyctophobia, but I don't any more. I confessed it as sin and asked the Lord to take away the fear, and now the dark doesn't bother me." Timothy could feel himself grinning as he gathered up four or five candles and lit them one by one.

The cabin was as cold as it had been that morning when they first arrived. Stanley built a fire in the woodstove, and Joel closed all the curtains. The cabin took on a cozy atmosphere after dark although the warmth from the stove could not be felt yet by the young men.

"I'm freezing!" Joel said as he stood close to the stove, hugging himself with his arms around his shoulders.

"That's nothing, I'm tired!" Stanley put in. He let his head drop, and his hair fell forward.

"That's nothing, I'm starved!" Timothy added as he placed his cookies and chocolate bar on the table. "Let's eat!" Stanley dug out his potato chips, and Joel left his place by the stove to contribute his piece of cheese.

The cabin was soon warm enough for them to remove their coats, and the guys sprawled out on the couch and the two stuffed chairs.

"You catch any mice while we were away, Miss Barred Owl?" Joel called up to the bird. "I think you're already stuffed." When the owl did not respond, he stretched out his long length and closed his eyes. "We've had a hard tramp—a total of four and a half miles through deep snow, if I figured the math correctly." Joel groaned and took a deep breath. "No wonder I have jelly-legs! And my get-up-and-go has got up and gone."

"We should sleep well tonight," Stanley said, stifling a yawn. "There's some quilts in the other room."

And then Stanley suddenly looked thoughtful. He sprang up from his comfortable chair and marched over to the counter in the kitchen; he lit another candle and began to search through the cupboards. "Hey, look what I found, Guys." He lifted down a large glass jar half full of something which he placed on the counter. "Oatmeal," he announced. "We'll have porridge for breakfast."

"And how are we going to have porridge for breakfast when we don't got no water?" Joel wanted to know without making the effort to open his eyes.

"Could melt some snow," Timothy suggested, and then he reminded them, "but I was hoping for sausages and eggs, sunny-side up. And white toast with marmalade on a side plate. And don't forget the tea in a glass mug, if you please."

"This cabin has running water," Stanley remarked. He dragged back the large mat which was lying on the floor in front of the sink, and he removed a trapdoor. Timothy came over, and Joel, relaxed on the couch, opened his eyes, sat up, and joined them at the trapdoor. They held candles over the opening and peered into the deep hole. The space below was a little more than a metre by two metres, and it was two metres deep with concrete walls and a gravel floor.

"This is our fridge," Stanley told them as he lowered himself through the opening using the ladder inside. There were shelves along one wall suspended from the floor joists above.

Timothy and Joel watched as Stanley closed the valve at the end of a plastic pipe coming through the concrete wall, and then he opened the valve in the same pipe but next to the concrete wall. Between the two valves was another pipe which passed up through the floor to the faucet over the sink.

"Any water yet, Guys?" Stanley called up to them. Several seconds later a small stream of water splashed into the sink. The sound of running water seemed out of place in this remote cabin.

"Leave it running to get fresh water," Stanley said as he climbed up into the cabin. He replaced the trapdoor and positioned the mat over it and then explained the water system. "This cabin is lower than the water above the falls. A pipe from the river slopes down to here underground below the frost line. The drain from the sink goes through a pipe to a gravel bed buried several yards away on the lower side of the cabin."

"Well, that's quite the system," remarked Timothy as he glanced again at the water coming from the faucet over the sink.

A few cooking pots hung from nails along one wall in the kitchen area, and the cupboards contained other things they would need for breakfast.

After several minutes, Stanley closed the faucet and then crossed over to the window. He parted the curtains and stared out into the darkness. "It's pitch black. Can't see a thing out there, no lights or nothing. Well, I'm wrong—there's a few stars there the other side of that maple or whatever." Then he turned around and said, "You guys are religious. My grandmother was very religious. She went to church almost every Sunday most of her life. I admired her for her religious living. Maybe religion is a good thing."

"We're not religious; we're born again Christians," Timothy informed him.

"Yeah, I've heard of being born again. What does that mean anyway?"

"To be born again means to be born into God's family. We're not good enough as we are. The Bible says, 'all have sinned.'"

"Yeah, but I'm not all that bad," Stanley said. "I figure that religion will cover any wrong I might have done."

"You're right, you're a nice guy and all that, but no one can say they've never done anything wrong—we've all broken at least one of the ten commandments in our lifetime. We've all sinned before God, and He won't tolerate sin."

"Yeah, but I've done more good than bad," Stanley protested. "My good far outweighs any bad I might have done in my life."

Timothy gave him a quick nod. "If a guy who was charged with murder stood before the judge, and the guy argued he had killed only one person of the thousands of people he had come across in his life, and he said it wouldn't be fair if he was punished for that one murder—would the judge let him off for being a good person?" Timothy could see his friend was beginning to look uncomfortable, but at the same time, he was interested in what he was saying.

"So, what can we do about it?" questioned Stanley after he had sat down on one of the large chairs.

Timothy told him, "There's nothing we can do."

"We can be religious, can't we?"

"No. That wouldn't help any," Timothy pointed out. "God gave us His Son the Lord Jesus Christ, who paid the penalty of our sin by dying on the cross. The Bible says, 'the wages of sin is death'. The Lord Jesus became our substitute—He took our place by dying for us—He's our Saviour."

"So you're saying that there's nothing I can do to clean up my life?"

"Right! Nothing but admit your sin to God and accept the Lord Jesus as your substitute—He took the penalty of your sin. To try to do anything else is to reject what God has already done for you."

The cabin was beginning to cool down, and Stanley fed the stove another stick of wood. Joel sat up and pulled off his damp socks. He hung them over the back of a kitchen chair which he then pushed closer to the stove. After he took his place once more on the couch, the three fellows sat in silence.

Several minutes later Timothy dug out his little Bible and brought a candle to the chair where he was sitting. He placed the candle on one of the large flat arms, and he leafed through his Bible. "I wish I had my glasses."

"Why don't you pray about it?" suggested Joel who looked over at him with one half-opened eye. "Where are you reading from?"

"The Proverbs. There are thirty-one chapters in the book of Proverbs. That's one chapter for every day of the month. This is the third of the month, so I'm reading Proverbs three. Thousands of people are reading this chapter today, and there are probably many around the world reading it right at this very moment." Joel closed his eye and grinned.

"Listen to verses four and five, 'Trust in the Lord with all thine heart and lean not unto thine own understanding. In all thy ways acknowledge Him and he shall direct thy paths'. That means we are to trust in the Lord completely and not try to do anything our own way. We should also acknowledge the Lord or give Him the credit for what happens in our lives as a result of trusting in Him. And then look at the promise that follows; 'He shall direct thy paths,' or the Lord will show us what to do, or He will cause circumstances in our lives."

Timothy looked up another passage in his Bible. "My grandpa pointed out to me a couple of verses in the New Testament which go along with the ones in Proverbs," he told Joel. "'Be careful for nothing but in everything by prayer and supplication with thanksgiving let your requests be made known unto God. And the peace of God which passeth all understanding shall keep your hearts and minds through Christ Jesus.'"

"It sounds so simple and yet so reasonable" admitted Joel.

The cabin fell silent once more. A mouse darted across the floor and scurried into the pile of firewood in the backroom. The candle on the shelf by the bedroom door was burned down to nothing, and it flickered and went out. Soon Joel began to snore quietly.

"Your belief and trust in God is real," Stanley declared thoughtfully. "It's personal—something you really believe as fact—not just something to do religiously." He put more wood into the stove then went to the bedroom and returned with a quilt which he covered Joel with. "It's three twenty-seven," he said to Timothy.

Stanley lit a tall candle and placed it on the shelf by the bedroom doorway. He snuffed out the remaining candles and then removed his damp pants and draped them over a chair close to the woodstove. Timothy was lying on one of the beds in the bedroom when Stanley came in. "Good night."

"Good night."

Timothy silently prayed, thanking the Lord for being with them today and that they were comfortable here in the cabin. He thanked the Lord he could talk with both Joel and Stanley about spiritual things. He then prayed he would find his glasses although it seemed unlikely he would see them again. He thanked God for the Lord Jesus Christ and salvation provided through Him. Timothy could sense Stanley was wide awake, and before he himself drifted off to sleep he prayed for his salvation.

Sometime in the night Stanley put more wood in the stove, and at daybreak he was up again to attend to the fire. He lifted down a saucepan and ran some water into the pan and added the oats and salt.

Joel stirred on the couch and sat up. "Good morning!" He retrieved his dry socks from the back of the chair by the stove and opened the curtains to let in the morning light. "It's going to be a sunny day," he noted.

Timothy came out from the bedroom, tucked in his shirt, and stood next to the woodstove. "What can I do to help?"

"Get some bowls from that shelf over there. You might need to dump the mouse dirt out of the top bowl. The mice use them as toilets, you know. Why don't you make us some tea, Tim.

There's a kettle there on the counter, and you'll find a jar of tea bags somewhere. Just poke around."

The porridge and tea were ready in about twenty minutes. Stanley refilled the kettle and put it back on the woodstove. Joel found a jar of brown sugar and some spoons.

"Sorry I don't have no milk," Stanley said, and then he added as he glanced over at Timothy, "Or bacon and eggs."

Joel grinned. "I didn't expect to have a hot meal like this, this morning!"

Then Stanley asked, "Tim, would you pray?"

"Our Heavenly Father, we thank Thee for being with us during the night, and we thank Thee for this day, and we thank Thee now for this food provided for us. Most of all we thank Thee for Thy Son the Lord Jesus Christ. May Thy presence be known to us today. And we pray in the Name of the Lord Jesus Christ our Saviour."

The young men ate in silence for a few minutes until Joel spoke. "This tastes pretty good, but then Donald says anything can taste better back in the woods."

"And we're back in the woods all right," added Timothy. "Even tea without milk is hunky-dory back here."

After a short pause Stanley said, "Last night I accepted the Lord as my substitute—my Saviour. I believe He died for me because of my sin, like the Bible tells us, and now I am trusting in Him for taking away my sin." He spoke thoughtfully, and as he pushed back his blonde hair, a slight smile spread across his face.

"Hey, Stan, that's great!" exclaimed Timothy.

Timothy broke into song, and Joel joined in. "'Thank You, Lord, for saving Stan's soul. Thank You, Lord, for making him whole. Thank You, Lord, for giving to him Thy great salvation so rich and free.'"

"Let's pray again," Timothy said, and he placed his spoon down. The three young men bowed their heads, and Timothy prayed for Stanley, thanking the Lord he was now a believer. He prayed he would have a close relationship with the Lord and grow as a believer. He prayed Stanley would read His Word every day and look to Him to guide him in all areas of his life. And he prayed he would recognize the goodness of the Lord day by day in his life and that others would see the Lord through him. And then he said to Stanley, "Hey, Brother, you can use my little Bible until you have one that's more suitable for you."

After they had finished eating, the pot, bowls, mugs and spoons were washed in warm water from the kettle. "How does the Lord guide us in our lives?" asked Stanley as he stacked the clean bowls on the shelf.

"He guides us when we read His Word every day. That's just as important as eating every day. We should first pray that He will speak to us through His Word, and then we read until we have something that is meaningful or useful to us. We should think about what we have just read and then pray that what we have read will help us that day."

"I don't read my Bible every day," admitted Joel, "but I know I should."

Timothy wondered, "How would you like it if you could eat only as much and as often as you read your Bible?"

"I'd be just skin and bones," Joel admitted. "Well, I guess that would make me a skin-and-bones Christian."

Timothy continued. "God's Word is the Truth, and the Bible is the most valuable possession we have. It helps us to know and appreciate the Lord, and it teaches us how our attitude should be and how we should live, and it tells us how to get along with others."

"We could read now, couldn't we?" Stanley proposed. He flipped through the little Bible Timothy had lent him. The three fellows moved to the couch and stuffed chairs.

"Let's ask the Lord to guide us as we read." Timothy prayed they would read something that would benefit them that day.

Stanley handed the Bible to Timothy and he turned to First Peter, chapter three. "Let's start at verse eight and read down to the end of verse twelve."

Timothy handed the Bible back to Stanley who read the passage of Scripture thoughtfully. "Now let's look at these verses and see what they tell us," he began. "Verse eight is simply saying to be nice to each other, and verse nine says we shouldn't try to get back at those who have wronged us. In fact, we should bless them."

"How do we bless someone?" asked Stanley looking up from the Bible.

Joel answered, "We bless them by making them happy or by adding to their wellbeing in some way."

Timothy nodded and continued, "Verse ten simply says that we will have a good life when we don't say things which are meant to hurt others. Verse eleven tells us to eschew evil, which means we are to turn away from doing evil. The last part of that verse says we are to do good and seek peace. In fact, we are to ensue it, which means we are to run after it."

Joel decided, "That sounds like we're to put out a real effort to make or cause peace." The sun shone through the large window between the two stuffed chairs, flooding the room with light and giving some warmth as well.

"Verse twelve has a warning for us," continued Timothy. "It says that the Lord sees the righteous and hears their prayers, but He is against them that do evil. We as Christians are capable of doing evil as mentioned in the previous verses."

"Such as saying nasty things," Stanley added as he ran his fingers through his long hair. "I wouldn't want God to be against me."

Joel said, "Just quickly reading verses from the Bible doesn't do the words justice. We need to think about what the words mean." The young men continued their discussion for several minutes, and then Timothy suggested they pray. He thanked the Lord for this helpful passage of Scripture and that they would be able to apply it to their lives. He concluded his prayer by again thanking their Heavenly Father for giving His Son who died for them.

The young men sat thoughtfully, and then as Stanley stood up to put the Bible into his hiking bag, he glanced at his watch.

"What do you guys want to do? You want to stay all morning and have porridge for dinner or do we leave?"

Joel jumped up. "Let's go!"

Timothy glanced at the windup clock on the shelf. "Look, it's three twenty-seven. We better get going."

Stanley pulled back the floor mat, lifted the trapdoor, and climbed down into the fridge. He closed the valve on the pipe coming through the concrete wall and opened the valve at the end of the pipe. After returning up to the kitchen and replacing the trapdoor and mat, he opened the faucet at the sink allowing the water in the pipe to drain back down and into the gravel in the little room. Then he carried a container of antifreeze from the backroom and carefully poured a little down the sink drain to settle in the trap under the counter. Timothy put firewood, kindling, and paper into the wooden box by the stove and placed the jar of matches on the wood. Joel folded the quilts and laid them on one of the beds.

"Well, that seems to be everything," Stanley said.

"Vacate the premises!" Timothy barked as he grabbed his hiking bag.

The young men put on their coats and hiking bags. "So long, Miss Barred Owl," Joel called up to the owl. "We hope you stay stuffed."

Stanley made sure the cabin door was securely closed, and the three young men were on their way through the spruce trees. Although they had been along this path three times already, everything appeared new in the bright sunlight. Hundreds of sparkling diamonds could be seen in the freshly fallen snow of yesterday.

The young men came to the old pine tree with the chain imbedded in it, and they turned and marched along the logging road. In the distance, crows could be heard calling. "Did you know that a group of crows is called a murder of crows?" Timothy questioned his companions.

Joel took the lead and replied, "Did you know crows keep their mates for life?"

"That's more than we can say for a lot of people," added Stanley.

"Many Christians are like that," Timothy put in. "The Bible says those Christians who are friends with the world are adulterers and adulteresses and are enemies of God."

Stanley asked, "What does it mean to be friends with the world?"

"To be friends with the world is to be interested in the lifestyles—the fads and fashions of those who don't belong to the Lord. The Bible also says the Lord Jesus gave Himself for our sins that He might deliver us from this evil world with its fads and fashions and self-centeredness."

Then Stanley said, "Why would anyone want to get saved from sin in the first place if he didn't want to live like he was saved from sin? That's like wanting to be married to one woman and then being unfaithful to her."

"Caw, caw!" agreed Joel.

The young fellows came to the spruce tree lying across the road, and they skirted around it. Timothy said, "Believers should be baptized." He paused and then added, "Peter the apostle commanded the new believers to be baptized right away. Baptism is something the new Christian experiences for his own benefit. He is demonstrating to himself that he has died to his old sinful life and that he is risen with Christ who now lives within him. 'We are buried with Him by baptism into death, that like as Christ was raised up from the dead by the glory of the Father, even so we also should walk in newness of life.'"

"Well, then," Stanley said, "I'd like to be baptized. I'm a different person, and I'm starting to live my new life."

The young men began the gentle descent towards the meadow. Through the trees ahead they could see the brilliant sunlight on the snow in the clearing.

"Prayer is important," Timothy pointed out. "Prayer is communicating with God. The only ones who have the privilege of talking to God are those who belong to Him, and only they have the right to call Him their Heavenly Father. We can talk to the Lord at any time, and the Holy Spirit will guide us how to pray when we rely on Him."

They crossed the bridge in the meadow without slowing down, and they tramped on, single file, squinting in the bright light reflecting off the snow. None of the young men spoke as they moved up the slope through the trees. They could hear, as they marched, the faint musical call of the chickadees in the trees around them, and a gentle breeze could be heard in the upper boughs of the taller pine trees. Occasionally, snow cascaded from the overloaded spruce and pine boughs above their heads.

As the young men walked between the large boulders topped with thick blankets of fresh snow, Timothy commented, "The Lord has saved us in order for us to praise Him for what He has done and to worship Him because of who He is."

"Worship?" questioned Stanley who was in the lead. "Tim, that sounds religious to me and even kind of weird. I've heard of people getting together to worship and having a good time or even an exciting time of worship."

"Well, Stan, worship is simply acknowledging the worthiness of the Lord. It's appreciating and loving Him. Our worship of Christ focuses on Him, not on us nor what we can get out of the activity like having a good time or trying to generate an emotional experience. Worship isn't for our benefit—it's for the Lord's benefit. It's Him receiving our praise and adoration."

"Well, in that case," Joel contemplated as they traveled through the woods, "we don't have to worship only on Sundays and only in a place of worship, nor do we have to worship with other people. Neither do we need a worship leader to get us into the mood."

The young men changed leaders once more, and they hiked on without speaking. Rabbit tracks crossed their path several times. Joel saw a rabbit bounding away, but by the time he pointed it out to the others, it was out of sight. Eventually they passed through the wide gap in the stone wall and they were now in the area which was once a field. When they came to the ruins of the stone house, Timothy walked over to have a final look, and Joel and Stanley followed. They looked again through the window openings and where the door had once been.

"I hear the snowplow, guys," Joel announced.

Timothy said, "Let's get the show on the road and the road on the show." He swung around and brushed a spruce bough heavy with fresh snow causing most of it to tumble off the branch as he passed by.

Joel was right behind him. "Hey look, Tim!" he exclaimed excitedly as he reached down into the snow.

Timothy turned. "My glasses! You found my glasses."

Joel handed the glasses to Timothy and said, "The Lord must have directed us here—to where they were and caused us to find them." And then added, "I'm glad I prayed about it."

"I'm glad I prayed, too," Timothy remarked grinning at Joel.

Stanley replied, "I wish I had prayed about it."

Timothy wiped the snow from his glasses. "We can thank the Lord for answered prayer." He carefully lowered them into his pocket as he silently thanked Him for showing them where his glasses were.

Several minutes later the fellows could make out Timothy's car ahead through the trees, and they could see, as they got closer, that the road had been plowed in both directions. They reached the car and began to clear the snow from the roof and hood.

Timothy looked over at his friends. "I'd like to thank you guys for including me on your trip to the cabin. I've had a great time."

"Yeah, I've had a good time, too," Joel admitted, "even if we did walk six miles in deep snow."

"I'm glad I could share the cabin with you fellows," Stanley answered them, "and I got to know you guys better, too."

As the young men reopened the snowbank, Timothy started the engine and turned the heat on full. When the snow removing job was completed, the shovels were returned to the trunk, and the guys climbed into the warm car.

After Timothy pulled ahead and onto the gravel road, Stanley spoke up. "There's a difference between being religious and being a Bible-believing Christian," he acknowledged as he pushed his long hair off his face, "in fact, I'm now a genuine Christian."

Joel remarked, "I can see that living for the Lord is real and that I need to confess my sins regularly. Also, I need to read my Bible every day so I won't be a skin-and-bones Christian."

"I need to trust the Lord more," Timothy admitted, "and I need to acknowledge Him in all situations." He shifted up and increased his speed.

Joel concluded, "The three of us are wiser now than when we first hiked to the cabin yesterday morning."

Stanley pointed out, "That makes us the three wise men." And Timothy and Joel grinned in response.

chapter sixteen

about a half year later—summer 1989

Roots

"Okay, Tim, this is the last one. It's heavy—it has our food in it." Ten-year-old Billy leaned over the side of the wharf and lowered the bag to his brother standing about two metres below on the deck of the fishing boat.

"Got it." The bag was added to the heap of two tents, four sleeping bags, the canvas bag with the cooking-pot and the frying pan. Other knapsacks were there as well which contained extra clothing and other personal things the fellows wanted with them.

"Can me and Henry come now?" Billy called down to Timothy.

"Yeah, come on," he replied as he shifted his cap. "Be careful on the ladder, Guys." The two younger boys climbed down the wharf ladder to the open, fish-smelling deck of the boat. They joined Timothy and his friend Stanley who were both in their late teens.

The diesel engine which had been idling as the captain checked things over now sprang into life. The captain's helper untied the mooring ropes and the boat with its passengers glided away from the wharf. *We're finally on our way!* Timothy realized as he slipped into his blue jack-shirt. With his thumb and forefinger, he brushed his scraggly mustache and glanced over at his brother Billy and his red-headed friend Henry. Both boys were grinning and were clearly excited as they tried to take it all in. None of them had been on a fishing boat before, and this was the first time Timothy and Billy had gone camping without their parents.

The water was calm as they headed into the early morning dense fog. They stayed clear of Fearful Rocks on the port side, and the village of Rogers Cove was slowly shrinking and becoming absorbed by the fog. Soon all they could see was the boat they were on, the water close by surrounding them, and nothing but gray fog beyond that. *But there is some blue sky above us,* Timothy discovered when he tipped back his head.

In the cabin at the wheel was Captain Rafuse, a fourth generation captain and fisherman from Rogers Cove. He peered out the window and periodically glanced at the radar screen.

Stanley, who was wearing a red and blue jack-shirt and his wide-brimmed felt hat, came over to Timothy. "It's a good thing the water's as calm as it is, or we'd be feeding the fish." He spread his feet to steady himself and shoved his hands into the back pockets of his denims and returned to his humming.

"Feeding the fish! What do you mean?" Timothy frowned as he looked over at his friend. "Oh, I get it." He grinned at Stanley. "Never mind!"

Henry pointed over the water. "A seagull!" Billy called out as he rolled down the sleeves of his heavy, red and white striped, pullover shirt—the one he called his 'lighthouse shirt'. Henry dug into his knapsack and removed his bird field-guide. After flipping through the section on water birds, he grinned at his friends and pointed to the illustration showing the herring gull with its flesh-coloured legs. The large white bird accompanied them briefly, disappearing and then reappearing, looking for a snack from those on the boat.

Billy and Henry knelt at the side of the boat and leaned against the gunnel, facing out over the water. Timothy and Stanley made themselves comfortable by sitting on the rolled up sleeping bags in the centre of the boat.

"I was reading recently," began Timothy, resting his elbows on his knees, "that there are three ways to know the will of the Lord. First, what does the Bible say? It's never the will of the Lord for us to disobey God's Word. When we don't know which way to go—keep to the right—what the Bible says."

"Makes sense," added Stanley. He pulled off his wide-brimmed felt hat and ran his fingers through his short blonde hair. "It will never be the Lord's will for us to marry non-Christian girls because the Bible makes it clear we are not to be unequally yoked."

"Yeah," Timothy replied. "Next, what would Jesus do? We should be like Him or conduct ourselves as He would." Stanley nodded in agreement and slipped his hat on.

"And thirdly," Timothy continued, "what do the circumstances dictate? The Lord places us in situations, and opens and closes doors for us. And we should ask if we would allow ourselves to be led by Him, or are we filled with ourselves and what we want to do."

"Good points, Tim. And we need to ask for and expect wisdom from Him as well."

"That's right. And I thought of another point. We should ask ourselves, would this make any difference or be any benefit ten years from now, or will it bring glory to the Lord? Maybe we could be doing something else that would have some spiritual impact on us and others."

"Well, what about us going to Bunchberry Island?" questioned Stanley. "Will we see God's goodness and His greatness during this outing?"

"I think we will," replied Timothy thoughtfully. "I felt I should spend some time with my young brother and he with his buddy. I wanted to do something nice for Henry, and I wanted to visit or have fellowship with you. Those things could have spiritual benefits and show that the Lord is good."

Timothy glanced behind him at the two boys, and he suddenly jumped up. "Billy! Henry! Get back!" Billy quickly knelt down again, and Timothy grabbed Henry and hauled him back. "You guys are not to lean over the side," he scolded as he tightly grasped their clothing and looked sternly from one to the other, "even if you are wearing life jackets."

Timothy sat down once more beside Stanley and looked back at the boys. "Those guys would wrestle on deck if we didn't stop them," he said to Stanley. Timothy could see Henry raise the hood of his brown pullover and eye him sideways as he made an effort not to grin. He prayed silently, *Thank you, Heavenly Father for keeping them safe. And help us to do the right things today, and I ask that You overrule when it's necessary.*

Timothy turned to Stanley again and said, "Something else I thought of. We shouldn't decide what we want to do and then ask the Lord to bless our plans."

"That would be silly," Stanley agreed. "That's like making plans to do what we want to do and then trying to talk the Lord into going along with our ideas when He already has other plans for us."

Timothy nodded and reflected, *Stanley has grown spiritually the past few months. Thank You, Lord, for guiding him and causing him to get the Scriptural teaching he needs at this time in his life.*

It was about mid-morning when the boat decreased speed, and there ahead in the fog and a bit to the left could be seen a faint silhouette of trees and cliffs. All eyes on board turned in that direction. "Bunchberry Island," Timothy said aloud. "I can trace my roots to this place." The boat moved closer to the island and drifted slowly along the shore for a hundred metres until they came to four or five weather beaten timbers sticking out from the smooth stones of the beach. They could see the tide was nearly in.

Timothy stood up. "Must be the remains of the old wharf." He pointed in that direction. The boat gently rocked in the shallow water about five or six metres from the dry stones soon to be submerged beneath the advancing tide.

The fisherman's helper untied the lifeboat and slid it over the gunnel of the fishing boat. The fellows made two trips using the dory to carry themselves and their camping gear to shore. Several minutes later the four campers hauled their stuff up the short distance of the stony beach to the flat area just beyond the high-tide line. This grassy area was lined with large pieces of driftwood.

"See you tomorrow morning about ten o'clock," Timothy called as he waved to the captain and his helper. "Thanks, Mr. Rafuse. See you, Cam." The fishing boat sped off and was soon dissolved by the fog, and the diesel engine could be heard gradually diminishing in sound. And then Timothy could hear nothing but the gentle waves lapping the stones several metres away. He prayed silently, *Thank You, Heavenly Father, for the good trip over in the boat.*

"We're on our own now," Stanley announced breaking the silence of this isolated place, "miles from everyone and miles from everywhere." The island was deserted; visitors seldom came, but there was some evidence of others picnicking or camping last year or maybe the year before.

Billy grabbed his sleeping bag and scanned the foggy landscape. "Is this where Grandpa Palmer grew up!" he asked in surprise.

"Sure is—and his brother Bobby, and their parents did as well," Timothy answered. "They lived on top of the island, but no doubt they spent time down here on the beach where the boathouse and wharf were."

Billy looked thoughtful but soon said, "Hey, let's set up camp over here." He and Henry were standing on a flat area with a couple logs nearby. This grassy location was close to the high-tide line and where a campfire had been built some time ago.

"What do you think, Stan?" Timothy asked as he picked up the folded blue tent.

Stanley briefly interrupted his humming. "Looks good to me." The two excited boys gathered up their belongings, and Timothy and Stanley carried over the remaining luggage. *I wish Mom and Dad could be here,* Timothy thought. *They'd love this for sure!*

Billy and Henry quickly erected the two tents. Timothy and Stanley had the larger one, and the orange pup tent was for the two younger guys. As the boys worked at their campsite, Timothy and Stanley made their way along the beach to gather firewood.

"Well, I believe the fog's beginning to lift," Timothy said when he returned with a load of driftwood. He dropped the wood behind the large log near their fire area and brushed off his jacket sleeves.

Stanley removed his felt hat, placed it on the top of one of the logs, and replied, "Yeah. We can now see the cliffs better and the trees over there and down that way to the point." Henry was arranging stones to contain the fire.

"Man, I'm some starved!" Billy made it known as he picked up an empty orange coloured crab shell from the smooth stones. "When are we going to eat?"

"It's not eleven o'clock yet. But let's have a bite to eat now, and then hike up to where the lighthouse and Grandpa's house used to be." Timothy looked over at the spruce trees and tried to determine where the only access to the top of the island and the light tower was. "First we need to find the path," he stated.

They dug out their lunches and sat on the silvery-gray logs. Henry removed his pullover and tossed it towards the orange tent. "Let's give thanks before we eat," reminded Timothy, and he took off his cap, and Billy stretched over to Henry to get his attention. Timothy thanked the Lord for the safe trip over to the island and then for the food. He then concluded by thanking the Lord for His Son Jesus Christ.

"Are your hands clean, Billy?" Timothy quizzed him as the boy grabbed a sandwich.

"Clean as a surgeon's," he answered, and then he bit into his sandwich. "Why does Mom always give me peanut butter!" he muttered, screwing up his nose.

"She doesn't always give you peanut butter," answered Timothy. "Besides all little kids love peanut butter. Especially when it's peanut butter on raisin bread like you have there. When you get to be big like me, you can have bologna sandwiches like I have." Timothy looked pleased as he pushed the heels of his work-boots into the gravel and took another bite of his sandwich.

"I'm not a little kid," Billy protested.

"Well, in that case, you can have a couple of these, Sir." Timothy handed him the package of bologna sandwiches and added, "And save some of those delicious peanut butter on raisin bread for me, will you." He squinted and gave him a phony smile. "And then both you and I will have peanut butter breath."

Henry suddenly exclaimed and pointed out to a hundred metres over the water. The others followed his gaze. Billy whispered, "There's something moving in the water!"

"It's a seal," decided Stanley. They watched the creature as it watched them, and then it sank beneath the surface of the water. "Probably he's never seen people before."

"I read somewhere that seals can stay underwater for five minutes," explained Timothy to the others.

After a while it resurfaced. "There it is again!" Billy pointed to it. "And look! There's another one over there!" The fellows thought there might be four seals altogether. Henry grinned as he pointed out the marine mammals whenever they surfaced.

Two peanut butter sandwiches and three bologna sandwiches later, Timothy stood up and stretched. "Who wants to go up to the light tower?"

"I do!" Billy shouted. He packed the last of his sandwich into his mouth and wiped his hands on his red and white shirt. Henry grabbed an apple.

The four fellows started over to where they figured the path was. Billy and Henry raced the last half distance ahead of the two older guys and pushed their way through the thick alders. Timothy pointed to a foundation of large weather beaten beams resting on flat stones near the beach. "Must be the remains of the boathouse."

"The path is here, Guys," hollered Billy from the cover of the alders, and Timothy and Stanley followed behind the two boys. Henry beckoned them to come, and once they entered the bushes it was easy to see that the path was where the old road used to be, and it went up the steep hill at an angle. Billy and Henry quickly scampered up the path ahead of Timothy and Stanley. The woods here was mostly cat spruce with some maple and birch.

"Look at the way this road was built!" exclaimed Stanley as he proceeded up the steep incline. "The side of the hill was dug into, making the road level side to side. Must be over twelve feet wide in some places."

"And it was all done by hand," Timothy exclaimed. "No heavy equipment here."

They stepped over several trenches which crossed their path. "You can see that there was a ditch at one time on the uphill side of the road," Stanley pointed out, "but over time it got filled in at several places and the runoff crossed the road and caused these here gullies."

The boys were well ahead and out of sight by now. The young men found that the path gradually leveled out, but the alders became thicker, causing the path to become narrow. Timothy observed, "These alders are some thick. We couldn't get off the path and into the woods even if we wanted to."

Stanley added, "Even a snake would have trouble moving through these alders."

They eventually emerged from the woods to a level field of waist-high grasses and wildflowers. The path through the alders simply ended here, and the two boys could not be seen, but the freshly trampled grasses indicated they had been here. Overhead they could see puffy streams of fog gently flowing through the upper branches of the taller spruce trees.

"We're at the top of the island, and this must have been one of the fields for sheep," Timothy figured as he took off his cap and scratched the back of his head with the visor. "We haven't come to the light tower yet, and I don't see the boys." A suppressed giggle came from the tall grasses, and Henry's red head of hair could be seen slowly rising as he sat up and looked through the thick vegetation towards the two young men.

"There's Henry," remarked Stanley, and then Billy stood up followed by his buddy who was munching on his apple.

"We were just waiting for the old men," Billy giggled. He yanked on a green timothy flower.

Old men, Timothy contemplated. *The last time I was called an old man was last winter when Joel said I was an old man for drinking tea.* Timothy lowered himself into the grass near Billy. *We had hiked into Stanley's cabin for the day but ended up staying overnight. That was when Stanley admitted he was a sinner, and he first began to trust in Christ.* He looked over at Stanley now lying in the grass with his hands behind his head and his wide-brimmed hat on his chest. *He doesn't seem like the same fellow. Not only is Stanley saved, he is converted as well, as evidenced by his new lifestyle. He says no one pressured him to cut his hair, and he didn't feel he needed to conform to the group. He had his hair cut because he felt his long hair was unnatural, and he now wanted a man's hairstyle.*

When Henry finished his apple, he hurled the core with all his might, and it splattered against the trunk of a large birch tree five or six metres away. Billy picked a daisy and placed its stem under his nose, balancing it on his upper lip. He turned to Henry who grinned at him. Billy giggled, and the daisy dropped into the tall grass. Timothy slowly shook his head and remarked, "Billy, you sure know how to have a good time!"

Stanley sat up and looked across the overgrown field. "The old road must continue over there the other side of this field where those alders are." He rose to his feet, pressed his hat onto his head and started to wade through the tall grasses, and the others followed him.

Timothy could hear Stanley singing as he went, and he grinned as he considered, *Stanley has changed his interest in music as well. He now appreciates wholesome music and the empty, irreverent stuff is foreign to him.*

"This is like exploring undiscovered land," declared Billy as he walked with his arms extended out from his sides, and brushing the higher vegetation.

"Yeah, you're right. No one has walked through this grass this year up until now. That means we have been the only ones up here this summer." The four fellows rejoined the path in the trees, and several minutes later came out at a large clearing of high grass dotted with scrawny spruce trees. And there, about fifty metres along in the slow-drifting fog and reaching up over the surrounding trees was the light tower.

"We're nearly there," called back Stanley who was still in the lead. The guys made their way across the old field. Although they could not see the top edge of the cliff, they knew it was on the other side of the thick alders and spruce trees. The trees were slowly taking over the land which at one time was a productive island farm.

They stepped up to the site where the house and lighthouse once were located. The buildings had been destroyed by fire over fifty years ago, and all that remained now were the foundations. Patches of dull orange coloured lichen grew on some of the squared stones lining the cellar cavity which was now littered with debris including pieces of rusted lighthouse mechanism. Several spruce trees were growing up through the junk.

"Is this where Grandpa Palmer's house was when he was little?" Billy exclaimed.

"Hey, Billy," Timothy recalled, "remember that old photo we saw of this place when the buildings were still here? That square foundation over there was where the tower was, and it joins this here where the house used to be."

"Yeah. And over there where the stones are lined up but no cellar must be where the woodshed was," Billy replied. "That's where the hired man got the firewood just before he dropped dead."

"Yeah, you're right, and it was in that woodshed where our great-grandmother kept his body until our great-grandfather who was the lighthouse keeper came back from Rogers Cove nearly a week later. Mom says that we're Bible-believing Christians today partly because the hired man told our great-grandparents about the Lord."

Billy added, "So, it was right here where Grandpa Palmer was born seventy-two years ago this past March. I bet Mom would love to be here and see all this."

"That's right, and it's here that we have our roots," Timothy agreed, staring into the old cellar. "It was this hired man who gave our great-grandparents his clock because he didn't like to hear it ticking in the night after he went to bed—it reminded him of his home on the mainland before his wife passed away."

"That's why we call it the hired man's clock," Billy recalled.

Stanley and Henry had gone over to a raised wooden platform, and Timothy and Billy joined them there. The decking was about six metres square and had a large, red circle painted on its surface which was just below the tops of the surrounding high grass. Old, dried raspberry canes were poking up through the planking as well as last year's canes with ripe berries which Stanley and Billy were munching on.

When Timothy approached, Henry looked up at him, frowned, and pointed to the platform they were standing on. "Helicopter landing pad," Timothy said clearly, and he attempted to imitate one with his arms spread out and spinning around once. Henry grinned and nodded. Billy laughed and rotated around several times, mimicking his brother but with more exuberance. Henry did the same, and then both boys spun across the landing pad. Timothy stepped aside to avoid a collision.

"Excuse me—coming through," Billy warned him. He flew off the side of the deck, tumbled to the ground, and rolled against a wild rose bush causing Henry to burst into laughter.

"Crash landing!" his brother responded. "Where'd you get your pilot's license?"

Timothy yanked off his jack-shirt and dropped it to the platform, then made the wailing sound of a siren. He jumped off the side, and as he picked up the giggling boy, his cap tumbled into the tall grasses. Timothy cradled Billy in his arms and quickly laid him out on his jack-shirt at the edge of the platform. He then gave him a chop-chop from his head down to his feet.

When Timothy was finished, Billy grinned, sat up, and swung his legs off the side of the deck. He looked over at the tower. "I'm going to climb up that ladder to the top."

"No you won't, Boy—better not."

Billy studied the tower. "What's that blue thing up there?" he wanted to know.

"Looks like a solar panel to power the light at night," Stanley answered him. It was mounted on the south side about halfway up the metal structure.

Billy and Henry waded through the tall grasses to the alders a stone's throw away to have a look around. Then Billy called out, "Hey, there's some old junk in the bushes here. Come have a look-see." Timothy picked up his cap and tramped over to where Billy was pointing into the thick alders. Stanley followed, and they peered into the bushes where they could see pieces of rusted metal.

"Looks like old farm equipment," Timothy decided. After pushing their way farther into the tangle of alders, they realized they were tramping over rusted tin cans and glass bottles hidden under the new vegetation.

"Look at all these old glass bottles!" Stanley exclaimed, picking up one. "This was the household dump." He straightened his wide-brimmed hat which had been nearly bumped off by the thick alders.

"Yeah," Timothy replied. "No weekly garbage pickup here. Grandpa says it was his job to chuck the garbage out towards the cliff beyond the house."

"Hey, here's a broken chimney from an oil lamp." Billy held it up for the others to see. "I wonder if we can find anything that belonged to Grandpa Palmer."

"I doubt it," answered Timothy from his crouched position. "They left the island for the mainland when he was about your age. Besides, there was another family here after the Palmers left who stayed a few years until the fire wiped them out."

Several minutes later, Timothy crawled out from the mass of bushes. He returned to the helicopter landing pad and sat down, and Billy came over to him. "Can me and Henry go back to our camp now?"

"You mean, Henry and I?"

"No, me and him," he insisted with a scowl.

"Yeah, okay," Timothy answered. Billy waved to Henry to come, and the two boys started back along the path. "Billy," Timothy called to him. "You and Henry stay in sight of the tents, will you." And then he added, "You could cut us some sticks for the wiener roast for supper. And be careful with that knife." Billy waved in reply.

Stanley came over to Timothy and sat in the grass facing him. "Well, Tim, this is alright—it's so quiet here."

"Yeah, sure is," he answered. "And I'm glad the boys are enjoying it. They're having a right-royal picnic."

Stanley added, "Those two have a picnic wherever they are and whatever they do." He removed his hat and lowered it to his knee.

Timothy looked out across the grown-over field. The fog had left the island and they could see the water in the distance, but the mainland farther away could not be seen yet. "I reckon Rogers Cove is over that way." He pointed with his chin. "At one time they could see the fishing village from here. But now, even if it wasn't foggy, I doubt that we could see it because the trees have grown up so thick."

Stanley faced that direction and agreed. Then he turned to Timothy and said, "Tim, Christians don't swear, but what about words that aren't really swear words?"

Timothy paused before answering. "Well, we shouldn't use words that are vulgar or rude even when those words are commonly used today." He reached for his jack-shirt and flung it over his shoulder. The two young men moved along the path skirting the foundations of the house and lighthouse.

Timothy had more to say. "We shouldn't use words which some people might consider to be polite substitutes for rude words. Words like 'shoot'. Neither should we use any substitutes for the name of God, like 'gee'. And we shouldn't use substitutes for words that are mild curses, like 'darn'." Stanley had to agree; he was several steps behind Timothy as they followed the path away from the deserted homestead and into the dense alders.

Stanley added, "The way we use and handle our language shows what kind of people we are, whether we are respectable or not, and when we have respect for others they more likely will have respect for us."

"That's right," agreed Timothy as they walked along.

Stanley grinned. "That eliminates a lot of words from our vocabulary," he realized.

"But we don't need those words," interjected Timothy. "We should be able to adequately express ourselves without using inappropriate words. Jennifer likes to say, 'Those people have a limited vocabulary.' And Christians shouldn't lose control and get upset which leads them to using words which aren't appropriate."

The two young men crossed the field and took to the path in the woods on the other side. The hike through the trees, back to the beach was mostly downhill. Timothy and Stanley emerged from the alders at the bottom of the hill where the boathouse on the beach once had been. Timothy looked over to their camp and then beyond. "The boys are farther along the beach near the point," he said. "I see Billy's red and white shirt."

The fog was now burned off, and the sky was mostly clear. The mainland and Rogers Cove could be seen across the water with Bennys Bump rising up over the far side of the village. "The tide's on its way out," Timothy noted. "Let's go down to the point and see what's around the other side of the island. Jennifer wants me to collect some beach stuff so she can make a couple of Bunchberry Island beach plaques."

The young men approached the boys who were constructing something using logs and boards they had gathered from along the shore. "We're building a fort," Billy informed them as he carried one end of a pole and Henry held the other.

"Yeah, I can see that," Stanley replied as he tipped down the brim of his hat. He walked into the open area inside. "I like it. This should keep the bad guys away."

"Are you going to put a roof over it?" Timothy wanted to know.

Billy glanced over at his buddy. "Yeah, we should."

"Guys, we're going around the point to the other side of the island," Timothy informed them as he held the plastic container for the shells, stones and fishing debris Jennifer wanted for her beach plaques. "Want to come?"

"No, we're going to work here," Billy answered as he leaned a weathered plank against the structure. "Aren't we, Henry?" Henry moved over to Timothy.

"Better come too, Billy."

On the other side of the island, the cliffs were jagged and almost vertical. There were many large pieces of rock on the beach which had fallen from the cliffs over the years.

"Look at that rock there!" Billy shouted out, pointing to a rock balanced on its smaller end, rising about three metres above the beach. "It looks like a giant head. See his funny nose and messy, long hair?" On one side of the head, strings of knotted-wrack were hanging loosely.

Stanley pointed farther along. "And look at that huge rock over there at the base of the cliff. It's the size of a small house."

Timothy studied it and figured, "Must have stayed in one piece because it fell on that huge pile of smaller rocks which cushioned its fall. I've heard that a couple of men were at the base of a cliff somewhere on the mainland; there was a large rock-fall that killed them. Because of the remote location and the amount of rocks, it wasn't possible to retrieve the bodies."

Stanley looked up, "You can see where it came from, up there." The four fellows moved away from the base of the cliff and continued along the beach.

Many of the rounded, football-size stones at their feet were covered with green, hairlike seaweed. "We're stepping on the heads of a lot of green-haired men," Billy giggled as he hopped from rock to rock. "They just got out from swimming."

"We need to be very careful tramping on wet seaweed," Timothy cautioned the others. "It can be very slippery—like walking on spaghetti."

"I've never walked on spaghetti before," Billy said. "Stanley, have you ever walked on spaghetti?"

The four fellows found that the hike along the beach was fascinating even when it was difficult going. Timothy had placed in his container over a dozen small stones and a few shells. About thirty minutes later, he said, "I better get back to start the fire for supper."

"Can the rest of us keep going, Tim?" Billy wanted to know. "I want to see that little cove just up ahead there." He pulled on a short piece of blue nylon rope which was snagged between two large stones.

"Yeah, if Stanley is with you." When Timothy had Henry's attention, he asked him, "What do you want to do?" The boy glanced at Billy, but moved over towards Timothy.

Part way back to their campsite, Timothy stopped to examine the many, pinhead size, red insects roaming over the face of a large rock. Henry picked up an empty sea urchin shell with its many tiny green spines and looked up at Timothy.

"That's a sea urchin shell, Henry." Timothy held out his plastic container for the boy to put it in. "Thanks," and then he asked, "Are you glad you came to Bunchberry Island with us?" Henry grinned shyly and nodded. Timothy replied, "I'm glad you came, too."

Back at their campsite, Henry set up the wood for the fire and looked to Timothy for his approval.

"You know how to do it, don't you." Timothy dug out the box of matches and gave it to the boy. "Here, you can light it now," he said to him. "But no more than two matches," he added as he held out two fingers.

Henry knelt down by the wood and dragged the match along the fly of his pants. After the fire was burning nicely, he returned the matches to Timothy and held up one finger.

"You lit the fire with just one match?" Henry nodded, and then Timothy asked, "Did you and Billy get the roasting-sticks?" Henry nodded again and brought the sticks out from behind one of the nearby logs. "Five, six, seven, eight, nine!"

Timothy counted. "Why so many?" Henry grinned at him and shrugged his shoulders.

Stanley and Billy came into view down at the point, and about five minutes later they were back.

"Look what I found!" Billy held up a white buoy with a florescent orange stripe surrounding it.

Fifteen minutes later the fire had produced some good hot coals and was just right for roasting wieners. Stanley gave thanks, and the hungry fellows gobbled up the hotdogs.

"Henry," Timothy said as he held out the last two wieners, "would you like one of these?" Henry grinned, took one, and pushed it onto his roasting stick as Timothy did the same with the remaining wiener.

"Hey, Tim," Billy wanted to know, "can I open these donuts?"

"Okay. And offer them to Stanley, will you."

Timothy and Henry turned their wieners frequently as they roasted them over the hot coals. When the wieners were done, the young fellow put his in a bun and applied plenty of mustard, ketchup, and relish. Billy placed several more pieces of wood on the fire to build it up, and Henry laid his hotdog on the log he had been sitting on and reached for his pop. When he sat down, his hotdog toppled from the log, and the wiener spilled onto the sand. He first looked horrified, then disappointed, and finally embarrassed. He squirmed as Timothy reached over, picked up the bun and wiener, and tossed them into the fire. He then faced the boy, grinned, and reached for a knife. He cut his hotdog in half and handed one of the halves to him.

"Did you know you can boil water in a paper cup?" Timothy asked the others as he filled his cup with water to a half inch from the brim.

Billy protested, "You can't do that. The paper cup would burn, and the water would leak out." Timothy said nothing, but he carefully set up in the fire the paper cup filled with water. Henry came closer to watch as he finished his half hotdog.

Less than a minute later the brim of the cup began to burn. "See, I told you!" Billy announced proudly as he glanced over at his brother.

Timothy ignored him, and Billy stuffed the rest of his donut into his mouth. Several minutes later Henry jumped up from his crouched position by the fire and pointed excitedly at the paper cup in the fire.

Billy joined him and exclaimed, "It's boiling—the water in the paper cup is boiling!"

"Sure it is," Timothy agreed knowingly. "The water keeps the paper cup cool so it doesn't catch fire." And then he reached for the donuts. "Billy! You ate nearly half the donuts!" he protested with a frown.

"Oink, oink!" Billy answered with his big, make-believe grin.

After the fellows had eaten, the two boys returned to their building project a short distance down the beach. Timothy and Stanley remained at the fire. "Stanley, I hope you'll pray about being on staff at camp next summer."

Stanley poked at the fire with the end of his wiener stick. "I don't have the qualifications nor the experience to be a camp counselor."

"That's right, you don't," Timothy agreed, "but if the Lord leads you to be on staff, you'll be able to do it. The Lord doesn't give us jobs to do without giving us what we need in order to do those jobs. And there's good staff training in the spring."

"Yeah," Stanley objected, "but I need to work next summer to get money for college." He removed his wide-brimmed hat, held it by the edge of its brim, and let it hang down between his knees.

Timothy looked over at his friend. "If the Lord wants you at camp, He will supply the money you need. The Lord tells those of His people who are sensitive to Him that guys like you have a financial need and they will give."

"Why would anyone give me money!" Stanley exclaimed looking at Timothy with disbelief. "I wouldn't have value at camp like others on staff - besides I need a lot of money."

Timothy answered, "Those helping at camp are not paid according to their value, but according to their need. Folks know the value of Christian camping, both to the campers and to those who help out there, so there's money available for those like you who have a need."

A couple hours later it began to get dark, and Timothy pulled out his whistle and blew it. Billy immediately looked back towards his brother who signalled for them to come. Billy beckoned to Henry, and the boys left their work.

"You guys want a lunch?" Timothy asked when the boys had returned. "There's some cookies, and I found some cheese."

The tide was about halfway in, and the moon was high in the sky over the island. Billy and Henry put more wood on the fire, and Timothy dug out his jack-shirt. "It's going to be cool tonight," he decided. "The sky is nearly clear." He shielded his eyes from the light of the fire and surveyed the navy blue sky in the direction of the light tower. "I was hoping we would see the light of the beacon," he remarked to Stanley. "Guess the trees up there are too tall and too thick to see it from down here."

Stanley nodded in agreement, and then he faced out over the water and announced, "I see the north star away up over there." He called to Billy, who with Henry was throwing stones towards the dark water. "Billy, you know how to box the compass?"

"Box the compass?" Billy stooped and picked up a pebble the size of a small egg. "Sure. You want to hear me?" He threw the stone out over the rocky beach to the water beyond. He listened for the splash and then began by pointing north and rotating counter-clockwise as he quickly rattled off, "North, north north-west, north-west, west north-west, west, west south-west, south-west, south south-west, south, south south-east, south-east, east south-east, east, east north-east, north-east, north north-east, north."

"Hey, that's pretty good," Stanley exclaimed as he buttoned up his jack-shirt.

"You want to hear me say it again starting with 'south south-west' and go in the other direction?"

"Yeah, okay," decided Stanley.

When Billy was done, he picked up another stone and pitched it as hard as he could over the water and into the blackness. "North north-west," he shouted after it could be heard plopping into the water.

It was daylight when Timothy awoke in his tent set up on the grass just above the high-tide line. He could hear the crackling of the campfire, and when he rolled over in his sleeping bag, he saw that Stanley had left the tent. He dressed, planted his cap on his head, picked up his Bible, and opened the tent flap which Stanley had left unzippered.

After he had crawled out and stood up, he buttoned his jack-shirt, and then he pushed his feet into his boots. He could see that this morning was as foggy as it had been the day before when they had arrived on the island.

Stanley was wearing his wide-brimmed hat and sitting on the log by the fire reading his Bible. "Morning," he greeted.

Timothy nodded and replied, "Morning, Sir." He sat on the other log and opened his Bible. He prayed first, asking the Lord for guidance, and after he read, he talked to the Lord concerning the passage. Finally he prayed for himself that he would be sensitive to the Holy Spirit that day and recognize the Lord's goodness. He stood up, and as he stretched, he held his Bible high in the air. "Let's start breakfast, and then call the guys."

Stanley dug out the large frying pan and the grill, and Timothy located the carton of eggs. "There's a package of bacon here someplace, too," Timothy said as he rooted through the food box. "Probably wrapped in this newspaper." He removed the paper from around the bacon. Stanley set up the grill over the fire, and Timothy covered the bottom of the frying pan with pieces of bacon which soon began to sizzle.

"Bacon smells great over a fire like this," Stanley exclaimed as he crouched down to attend to the bacon.

Timothy smiled and then faced the boys' orange tent. "Billy. Henry," he called. "Time to get up." Henry was already at the door of the tent. The boy grinned at him through the screen. "Tell Billy to get up, Henry."

Henry backed into the tent, and a few seconds later Timothy and Stanley heard a loud groan and Henry giggling.

"Hey!" Billy exploded, "I was asleep, you irresponsible rooster!" Henry could be heard laughing.

"Almost breakfast time, Billy," Timothy advised him.

The well-done bacon was placed on a paper plate, and the fellows gathered around the fire, and Timothy gave thanks. As the eggs were frying, they ate the crispy bacon with their fingers.

"Don't run off after breakfast, Guys," Timothy informed the two boys. "We're going to read from God's Word first."

When they were finished eating, Timothy turned to Romans twelve in his Bible. Henry sat facing him and watched him attentively. "First we'll pray." Henry kept his eyes on Timothy while the others bowed their heads.

"I'll read verses one and two," Timothy began. After reading he said, "The word, 'beseech' means plead. So what these verses have to say to us Christians is very important." Timothy spoke distinctly. "We are to give our bodies fully to God. It says, 'living sacrifice', which tells us we are to be active Christians not just hanging on for the ride to Heaven. And the word 'holy' means dedicated or devoted only to the Lord and to be pure for Him." He paused as he glanced at his three listeners. "The last part of that verse means that this should be the normal thing for us to do." He could see Stanley nod in agreement. "Verse two tells us not to copy the ways of the world, but we need to allow the ongoing leading of God to change our outlook or attitude, and this will show what is 'that good and acceptable and perfect will of God.'" Timothy looked over at Stanley. "Do you have anything to add, Stan?"

"When we realize," Stanley observed, "that the will of God is 'good and acceptable and perfect,' we will not want to be 'conformed to this world.'"

"Good point," replied Timothy.

After Timothy prayed again, he stood up and said, "Let's take down the tents and pack up before we do anything else. And we need to douse the fire."

Twenty minutes later the four fellows carried their things along the beach to where they had come ashore the previous morning.

"Can me and Henry go now?" Billy wanted to know.

"Yup," he replied, "but stay in the area of your fort, down along the point where you can hear the whistle."

"Did your fort ward off any bad guys?" Stanley wanted to know.

Billy grinned. "Sure did! Not even one got inside our fort."

"Tim," Stanley told him, "I'm going to hike along the beach this side of the island for a short ways. Want to come?" He pulled his hands out of his pockets and shifted his felt hat.

"No. I think I'll return to where we camped." Stanley left to go along the shore, and the two boys scurried off to their project.

Timothy stood near the luggage and watched his young brother leave with his buddy. *Thank You, Heavenly Father for Thy presence with us here. I thank Thee that Billy and Henry are getting along so well together. Work in their young lives, I pray.* Timothy turned and faced in the opposite direction to where his friend Stanley had gone, now barely visible in the thick fog. As he disappeared into the white mist, he could hear him singing a hymn of consecration. *And I thank Thee that Stanley and I have had good talks which have been an encouragement to both of us. May he be led by Thee in the things he's to do.* Timothy slowly walked back towards their deserted campsite. *Heavenly Father, I pray You would continue to mould me and make me suitable for Thy service and that I would know of Thy goodness and greatness in my life.*

Their campsite was now lifeless, and the fire was out. Two areas of flattened grass marked where the tents had been. Timothy sat quietly on a log staring out over the water. About ten minutes later he was startled when someone leaned on his back and threw his arms around his shoulders. He could see Henry's red head of hair on his shoulder and he reached up to touch him. And then the boy pulled away and was gone. Timothy did not turn to observe him leave, but he put his elbows on his knees and bowed his head into his hands. *Thank You, Heavenly Father for Thy great love for me. And thank You for working in my life and using me to accomplish Thy will.*

Soon the distinctive rumble of the fishing boat's diesel engine could be heard although the boat could not be seen in the fog. Timothy stood up, removed his cap, and ran his fingers through his hair. He then blew his whistle for Billy and Henry and started for the luggage where Stanley was waiting. The four fellows stood together on the beach above the high-tide line, looking into the fog. Their visit to Bunchberry Island where Timothy and Billy had roots was about to come to an end.

chapter seventeen

a year later—summer 1990

A Day in the Life of Camp Beth

"Okay, Guys, there's the triangle," announced Timothy Jack who was nearly twenty years old. "Time to wake up, and get out of your sleeping bags. There's a light drizzle, and the grass is wet. Might want to wear your rubber boots if you have them." He shoved his hands into his back pockets and quickly glanced around at his campers.

"I hate the rain!" mumbled Chord as he lay on his back and stretched his arms up towards the bunk above him.

Matthew spoke up solemnly. "He's allergic to the rain, Sir."

"How's that?" Mr. Jack asked. He removed one hand from his pocket and smoothed back his mustache. "What's it do to him?"

Matthew snickered. "The rain gets him wet!"

Mr. Jack grinned and replied, "Yeah, I guess it would, but everything's hunky-dory. We're not going to let any rain bother us, are we, Guys?"

"Hey, these are my golf socks," Jonathan said to the others as he sat on the floor with his socks in his hand.

"Your golf socks?" Noah replied with a frown. "You don't play golf, Jon."

"Yeah, I know, but they're my golf socks because there's a hole in one." He held it up for all to see.

The campers were soon dressed when Stanley Clark, the second counselor arrived at the cabin. "Where were you, Mr. Clark?" asked Harry accusingly as he tied his sneakers laces.

Mr. Clark ran his hand over his short brush-cut and grinned at Harry. "I was having my private time with the Lord—like I do every morning."

Camp Bethlehem was situated on what was once farmland. The kitchen of the old house was now used for handcrafts, the ping-pong table was in what had once been the large dining room, and sports equipment was stored in what used to be the downstairs bedroom. The staff made use of the living room for meetings and for their Bible study. The rooms upstairs were used during camp by Mr. Dodge, the camp director, and his wife and young child.

The barn had been renovated into a lodge. From the outside it still looked like a barn except for its many windows. The inside was finished but had a few reminders indicating its earlier farm use. The posts and beams could be seen with their wooden pegs holding them in place. The main room of the barn was used as the dining area and for Bible classes for campers, and the kitchen was off to one side. The chimney of the fieldstone fireplace extended to the six-metre high ceiling. The barn was winterized making it useful all times of the year.

The cabins and barn formed a semi-circle. Some of the cabins were partly in the field and partly in the trees. They were standard frame construction, but the walls were covered with canvas which made the campers feel closer to the outdoors without exposure to the elements.

The level, grassy field beside the old house was used for sports. The large clearing near the barn where the cabins were situated sloped gently down to the lake which was called 'New Lake' because it was formed ten years ago when the hydro electric dam several kilometres away was constructed. The field had patches of daisies and buttercups, and the raspberries along the edge of the field were ripe for picking during children's camp. Off to one side close to the lake was the campfire circle.

Mr. and Mrs. Charles lived in a recently built, small house near the driveway. Next to their dwelling was a large vegetable garden in which the campers often helped. Mr. Charles took the campers' Bible class, and his wife was the head cook.

Several metres away from the main entrance to the barn was the flagpole, and beneath the Canadian flag was the Camp Beth flag designed by one of the ladies of the meeting place.

The drizzle had just about ended this morning when the campers assembled on the damp grass by the flagpole. Flag raising time this morning was shorter on account of the dampness. The camp song would be sung in the barn after breakfast.

After flag raising, some of the counselors entered the barn to help set the breakfast tables. The remaining counselors returned to their cabins for a time of Bible reading with their campers. The readings were designed to demonstrate how our daily, personal, private time with the Lord should be conducted.

"I can't find my Bible, Mr. Jack," Matthew notified him as he searched through his things.

"We'll wait until you find it before we begin to read." Campers were encouraged to follow along in their Bibles whenever possible. This made them realize the value and the authority of God's Word, and it helped them to concentrate on the lesson. It also caused them to be more familiar with the Bible and to know where to find particular passages.

"We need to read our Bibles everyday," Mr. Jack had explained to his campers the first day of camp. "It's like eating. We need to eat everyday. If we didn't eat everyday we would be just skin and bones. When we don't read our Bibles everyday, we become skin-and-bones Christians."

The gospel was presented during each of the cabin Bible reading times. "But I already know all this, Tim," complained his brother Billy.

"Hey! You call me, Mr. Jack, even when I am your brother. And that goes for what you call Jennifer, too—I mean, Miss Jack. Maybe you do know all this, Billy. Don't you like to hear good news over and over again? And please remove your cap when we're reading the Bible. Now, where were we?"

Mr. Jack grinned, and he continued. "The gospel is the best good news there ever was. I like to hear it over again, and I like to share the good news with you guys, too. There are some here who aren't saved. Just because we're from Christian families doesn't mean we know the Lord. When I was nine, I first began to trust in Christ as I was riding my bike along the road."

"Here it is—found it." Matthew had located his Bible under his blue pullover sweater on the floor next to his bunk. He balanced it on his knees as he sat on his sweater and leaned back against the bunk.

Mr. Jack looked around at the boys. "On our first day at camp," he reminded them, "we looked at Romans 3:23—'All have sinned.'" He glanced at the texts printed out with felt markers and taped to the wall. "What did we say that meant, Noah?"

"It means we're all guilty of sin," the dark haired boy answered.

"Yes, that's right. Yesterday we read John 3:18, where it says, 'He that believeth not is condemned already.' And we said that means those who aren't trusting in what Christ has done for them are condemned and heading for hell. This morning let's look at Romans 5:6." He waited until all the boys had found the passage. "It says here in the Bible, 'Christ died for the ungodly.' Peter the apostle said, 'the Just for the unjust.' The Lord Jesus is the Just One, and we are the unjust ones. That means the Lord Jesus took our place—which we call substitution. When we put our trust in Him, we become just, and we receive His righteousness. Having His righteousness is the only way we are saved from His wrath. And that's the good news."

"Can I put that verse up?" asked Chord.

After the verse was secured to the wall, Mr. Jack asked who would like to thank God for giving His Son the Lord Jesus Christ who took our sin. No one was pressured into praying; it was voluntary participation.

After prayer time the campers had an early start on cabin cleanup. Each cabin had a broom and a dustpan as well as a garbage can.

"There's the triangle for breakfast." Mr. Jack started for the door and barked, "Vacate the premises." The triangle was made from a length of steel rod which Mr. Charles had paid a quarter for at a yard sale. It was set up near the main entrance to the barn, suspended by a metal ring.

By now the sun was beginning to show through the dissipating mist. The campers lined up near the veranda of the barn, and the counselors came out and joined the group assembled there.

"What's for breakfast, Mr. Clark?" Rachel called out to him.

He tipped back his wide-brimmed felt hat and looked over at her. "Grilled peanut butter and mustard sandwiches."

Rachel replied sadly, "I was hoping for fried slugs with pine syrup."

Mr. Clark found it strange to be addressed as 'Mister'; he was only eighteen. But there were a lot of changes in his life since he had begun to trust in the Lord two winters ago. He was now living for Him and reading His Word and praying everyday. He had new friends who shared in his interest in spiritual things and in his desire to bring glory to the Lord. His former friends spent much of their time in things which now seemed to him frivolous. He wanted to be involved with worthwhile activities like being an influence for Christ on children and young people by helping at camp. His life now had real purpose and satisfaction. He had resolved to not return to the world's lifestyle.

When everyone was inside, a hymn of praise was sung, and one of the young men gave thanks. He thanked the Lord for camp and for the rain in the night. Counselors were in the habit of thanking God for the Lord Jesus Christ every time they led in public prayer.

"Please pass and pile your plates," instructed Mr. Dodge, the director, when everyone had finished eating. "Mr. Clark and Miss Knott will lead us as we sing some hymns before we're dismissed for cabin cleanup." The time of singing was concluded with the camp song.

On their way back to their cabin, Chord walked along with Mr. Clark. "Why do we have to sing so many hymns?" he grumbled. "I like songs that are fun."

"Christians like to sing hymns," Mr. Clark informed him. "The words are beautiful, and the meaning of the words is important. They remind us of God's love for us, and when we sing, it's our way of showing our appreciation for Him. I love to sing hymns."

On the other side of the barn, Barbara asked Miss Knott, "Why is this camp called 'Beth'? That's a funny name for a camp."

Miss Knott grinned. "Beth is short for Bethlehem which means 'House of Bread'. And we have good meals here, don't we? But more importantly, the Lord Jesus is the bread of life, and we learn more about Him here."

Cabin cleanup consisted of tidying the interiors of the cabins and sweeping the floors. The garbage pails were to be emptied, and there was to be no litter on the ground around the cabins. Dry clothing and towels on the clotheslines were to be put away. The kitchen staff inspected the cabins during Bible study, but a surprise inspection could be anytime.

The Bible study for campers was held in the dining area of the barn. The campers moved the tables out of the way, and the benches were arranged in a semi-circle which promoted better singing. The campers liked to help whenever their help could be used.

A separate Bible study for counselors and other staff members was led by Mr. Dodge and occurred at the same time in the living room of the old house. Their theme this summer was taken from First Corinthians 10:31, 'Whatsoever ye do, do all to the glory of God.' It was explained that this means everything we do is to demonstrate that we are living for the Lord. We show the Lord's goodness and His greatness by our lifestyle. Practical examples in everyday life were discussed such as putting the interests of others first before our own and not arguing with the campers but being calm and gentle yet at the same time being firm.

Miss Knott composed a suitable tune to accompany the words of First Corinthians 10:31, and the staff members sang this simple song each day at their Bible study. The counselors' study took a short time which allowed the remaining minutes to be used for preparation of camp activities and for personal time away from the campers.

This camp offered a good time to the children and young people, but was careful to draw them to Christ because He bore their sin so they could live for Him as they acknowledge His goodness in their lives day by day.

Group activities at Camp Beth were swimming, boating, sports, handcrafts, and nature lore. Swimming classes were supervised by a qualified instructor. "Today we are going to practice treading water," she announced to the girls.

"Will we have time to play water tag later?" one of the girls inquired.

"Yes, Vanessa, we probably will."

Sports activities were played on the large field when the weather was suitable and the grass was dry. Good sportsmanship and fun were the emphases rather than winning at any cost.

Today the boys were playing soccer. "Kill him!" shouted out one of the players.

"Thomas! You can get thrown out of the game for disrespectful talk like that," Mr. Taylor told him. "Then your team will lose for sure."

"I was only kidding!" He kicked hard at a dandelion clock causing its seeds to float gracefully away in the gentle breeze.

The grass was dry when Jean arrived at the kitchen of the old house where handcrafts were worked on. "Jean, you're wearing rubber boots, and I can tell you're not wearing socks," Miss Johnson said to her.

"That's because I got my sneakers and socks wet this morning," the girl responded and then asked, "How can you tell I'm in my bare feet?"

"I can tell by the squeak, Girl." Jean looked down at her boots and then back at Miss Johnson who continued, "You wear sneakers when it's wet out and rubber boots without socks when it's dry."

"I live an exciting life, don't I!" replied Jean, grinning broadly.

"Well, yeah, I guess having blisters on your feet can be exciting."

A minute later Jean suddenly called out with alarm, "Oh look, Miss Johnson that's disgusting!" Two boys were outside facing in through the window with crossed eyes and pressed-up noses against the window glass, stretching out their nostrils. Miss Johnson appeared startled, and the boys giggled and backed away. Billy and Henry soon entered the handcraft area, and they were still giggling when they came over to the table where Miss Johnson was standing.

"I like the way you're doing your work," Miss Johnson said to Henry when she could see the boy could read her lips. He and Billy began working, and Billy could be heard softly whistling a three-note tune between his slightly parted lips.

At handcrafts, the campers were expected to follow the directions given for technique, but they were encouraged to work on their projects using their own personal style.

Nature lore was usually a walk into the fields and forest to examine plants, animals, birds, and insects. Today they were on the two kilometre trail which Miss Jack was developing. The path was through the woods behind the barn, and it looped around and returned to the field near the volleyball court.

"What kind of tree is this?" Miss Jack asked her little group as she tossed her long, blonde hair back over her shoulder.

The group paused next to the tree, and Amy spoke up. "It's a pine tree."

"How do you know it's not a spruce tree?"

Noah immediately responded, "Because it has long needles. Spruce trees don't got long needles."

Stephen pushed back his cap and remarked, "I know what kind of pine tree it is, Miss Jack."

"Okay, Stephen, tell us."

"It's a white pine because it has bundles of five needles."

"Yes, that's right."

Amy added, "The word, 'white' has five letters—same as the number of needles."

Miss Jack and the group of campers strolled farther along the path into the mixed woods. "This big fly sure is making a nuisance of himself!" protested Amy as she tried to shoo it away. "He's after the top of my head."

"Yeah, there's one bothering me, too," Noah blurted out. He batted at it, ducked down, and ran ahead. When he stopped several seconds later he moaned, "He's still after me!"

"I'll show you what we can do," Miss Jack informed them. She picked a bracken fern and planted it upside down on her head. "There, that should do it."

Several of the campers giggled. They broke off ferns and set them on their heads, too. "Hey, it works!"

"Yes, it does. Do you know why?"

"The flies don't like the ferns?"

"That's right. They can't get at your head very well, and there's another good reason. The ferns have a natural insect repellent in them."

Before the little group turned around to retrace their path, Miss Jack surveyed the woods around them. *I wish we could build a cabin somewhere in this area,* she contemplated as she adjusted her fern head-wear. *A cabin could be useful for camp activities.*

Free time gave the campers a choice of individual activities or small group events with counselor supervision when necessary. Counselors who were not involved directly were visible and on the lookout for campers who might be left out, lonely, or troubled.

Thomas and Chord saw Mr. Taylor sitting on the cabin steps, and they started through the daisies to him.

"When I grow up," Thomas began as the boys approached the counselor, "I want to be an airline pilot."

Mr. Taylor lowered the book he was reading. "That would be nice," he replied to the boy.

Chord quickly put in, "Did you know that when my great-grandfather—Dwight Harriston was his name—well, when he was in his teens he ran away from home, and he, well, he never ever went back home to his parents?"

Thomas continued, "My dad says that I need good grades in school to fly an airplane."

"No, Chord, I didn't know that about your great-grandfather," Mr. Taylor answered him as he slammed closed his book on a mosquito in mid-air, and he added, "Yes, Thomas, good grades would come in handy for flying an airplane."

"He never got in touch with them again, and they never found out where he was at or what happened to him."

Thomas asked, "Why would I need good marks just to fly an airplane?"

Chord said, "My grandfather says his father tried to find his parents later but couldn't find them nowhere—they had moved away to somewhere else." He shrugged his shoulders.

Mr. Taylor responded, "Airplanes are kind of complicated to fly."

"Maybe instead I should be a dairy farmer like my uncle."

"That's a sad story, Chord," Mr. Taylor answered. "That might be a good idea, Thomas. We need good dairy farmers." He was becoming skillful at multiple conversations at the same time with nine and ten year olds.

The triangle was sounded indicating there was another fifteen minutes to finish up a game, put things away, and get ready for dinner. After lining up and then entering the barn, a hymn of praise was sung followed by giving thanks.

At the end of the meal, the plates were passed and stacked. "Would anyone like to lick off these pickle forks?" Mr. Jack asked the campers at his table. When he got no response, he flashed a phony smile around to all his boys.

There was nothing gross nor disrespectful about the fun-songs after the noon meal, but they were intended to be fun for everyone.

"Clubs today will be as follows," Mr. Dodge announced. "The sports club will play volleyball. Mr. Two Rivers will demonstrate to four people only, how to change the wheels of his car. The ever-popular self-defense club will meet at the usual place. And those who would like to join the hiking club—where are they to meet, Miss Jack?"

"At the flagpole," she replied and nodded in that direction.

Mr. Dodge continued. "Mr. Charles will have his gardening club as usual. Mrs. Charles told me that she will hold a cake-baking club for boys only. Meet here in the barn. A visitor will be here this afternoon to have an archery club for four campers only. Meet at the back end of the playing field. Mr. Taylor will have a campfire club to set up for the campfire for this evening's program. Sign up for one club only immediately after you are dismissed from here. First come, first served. You can change clubs tomorrow but some clubs will be for one day only. Any questions?"

Rob's hand shot up. "Will there be a fishing club today?"

"I was hoping you'd ask, Rob. Yes, and we'll have room for one other fellow in the boat."

Since there were no more questions he said, "As soon as we're dismissed, it will be our hush-time. I need to remind you that hush-time is the time we have quiet activities. Please, no noise. Some people are resting and some sleeping. There are board games over there you can borrow. Bring them back at the end of hush-time. This would be a good time to go over your memory work by yourself or with a friend."

The hiking club was well attended. The little group moved across the field and entered the old apple orchard the other side of the campfire circle. A couple of crows flew up from under a tree to its top branch and squawked at the intruders as they passed beneath. "Those old crows!" Stephen protested as he searched for something to throw at them. "I don't like the noisy pests."

"I like crows," Miss Jack reported to him as she looked up at them against the bright sky, and then she sneezed. "They're a beautiful black colour—and they're very intelligent, too."

Susan said, "Crows are alright, I guess, but I like blue jays. They're so pretty."

"Stephen," Miss Jack enquired of him, "what bird do you like?"

Stephen pushed aside an apple tree branch and turned to face her. "What bird do I like? I like chicken of course—fried chicken. Some delicious!"

The group left the orchard and followed the path into the woods.

"Hey! Come have a look-see at this!" shouted Stephen who was ahead on the path. "A snake swallowing a frog! Neat!" He leaned over with his hands on his knees.

"Gross!" exclaimed Rachel, and she cautiously came up behind Stephen. "Miss Jack! Stop the snake from hurting the frog!" she demanded as she grabbed the arm of Miss Jack. "The frog's going to die."

"No, let him be. The snake needs his supper, too. Besides snakes are beneficial creatures." Miss Jack steered Rachel past Stephen and the snake on the path.

"Let's stay and watch!" suggested Stephen as he squatted down on the ground to get a closer look.

"Gross!" Rachel expressed again as she continued to stare at the snake with the frog's long back legs protruding from its jaws.

At the garden club, the campers pulled enough carrots for supper. "Can I help wash the carrots, Mr. Charles?"

"Yes, Nancy," he replied, "but let's first break off the tops and save them for the compost."

At the campfire club, three boys and a girl showed up. "Where's Harry?" Mr. Taylor asked the little group. "He wanted to join this club."

"Harry?" Chord repeated. "He went to the bat room, Sir."

"The bat room? Okay, he won't be long."

When Harry arrived, Mr. Taylor told his club members they would first go to the woodshed where the five of them each picked up a piece of firewood. After they carried the chunks back to the campfire area, they entered the woods nearby and gathered up small, dry branches from off the forest floor.

Mr. Taylor instructed them, "Don't remove any live branches from the trees. They don't burn well, and the trees won't look nice either."

"Let's get some of the loose birchbark from off this tree here," suggested Vanessa.

"No, don't rip off any bark from the trees. Birchbark burns very well, even wet birchbark, but maybe we can find some on the ground. We don't need much."

"Here's some, Mr. Taylor."

"And there's some more on the ground over there."

Back at the campfire area, they placed in the circle what they had gathered, and Henry picked up a piece of firewood and positioned it in the fire ring. Then he put the strips of birchbark next to it on one side, the smaller twigs on top and the larger sticks leaning on top of it all.

"Henry, where did you learn to do that?" asked Mr. Taylor looking pleased. The boy laid the other pieces of firewood, tepee fashion on top of everything. He grinned and looked around at the others. "Henry knows how to do it," Mr. Taylor remarked.

Mr. Dodge, Noah, and Rob dug for worms near the compost pile in the garden. Five perch were caught between the three club members, all too small to keep.

"That was fun!" Noah responded as he helped pull the dory out of the water. "Can we fish again tomorrow, Mr. Dodge?"

"We'll see," he answered as he removed his life jacket.

There was another free time before supper. Mr. Clark showed Stephen how to make a moose call from a tin can and a piece of string. The unusual sound coming from the area of the old apple trees soon attracted six or seven more children.

"Can I try it now?"

"No, I'm next."

"But it's my turn."

"No, it isn't."

"How come I never get a turn?"

"Hey—no shoving," Mr. Clark hollered at the children.

Miss Fraser who was close by began to hum, "'Whatsoever ye do, do all to the glory of God.'"

Mr. Clark acknowledged her hint and said gently but firmly, "Okay, Guys, wait your turn, but don't take a long turn. That sounds good, Vanessa. Let Harry try the moose call now. Thomas, why don't you and Noah go to the kitchen and ask Mrs. Charles for more tin cans. Don't forget to thank her. And would someone get us some more water to wet the strings?"

"Mr. Clark," Vanessa asked, "will these moose calls really bring a moose to here?"

He replied, "I don't think there's any moose handy to here."

Vanessa look puzzled. "So, why are we calling them?"

Meanwhile, Nancy had made it on stilts from her cabin to the barn. "I made it! I made it!"

"That's nothing," Billy informed her. "Anybody can walk on stilts."

"Okay, you do it." Nancy handed the stilts to him. He stepped up onto them and took several wobbly strides. "Stand back everyone," she warned, "he's going to fall!"

Billy snagged a tuft of grass and dropped the stilts. "It's harder than it looks," he had to admit as he picked up his cap from the grass.

The supper triangle sounded, and at the lineup Susan muttered, "My mosquito bites are really itching me!"

"What is this—show and tell!" demanded Benjamin with a sour grin.

Chord quickly jumped in, "Thank you for that exciting announcement, Susan."

Soon everyone was present near the entrance to the barn. They filed in and stood at their places to sing before Mr. Clark gave thanks. During supper Mrs. Charles announced, "Keep your forks for dessert, Everyone."

After supper was finished and the tables were cleared, they sang a few choruses.

Free time this evening included canteen. A group of campers was congregating near the door of the barn eating their snacks when Billy mentioned casually, "I think I have something in my eye." He stood up and let his bag of potato chips drop to the ground, and other children began to look his way. He rubbed his eye, and it looked as though he was trying to work something out. "Guess I'll have to take out my eye and wash it off."

More campers now looked over at Billy as he dug with his finger at his eye. He nearly knocked off his cap. Rachel told him, "You're crazy, Billy! You can't take your eye out."

Billy ignored her. "There, I got it." He cupped his hand, brought it away from his face, and with one eye tightly closed and his other eye open, he looked at Rachel and then around at the others. All the campers nearby stared at him now, and some were looking concerned.

"Where can I rinse off my eye?" Billy demanded as he quickly glanced around again. Then he fumbled with his hands. "Oops, almost dropped my eye!" Jean, who was sitting nearby, gasped. She stood up and stared at him uneasily.

When Billy recovered, he looked with his one eye at Harry and suddenly decided, "I know. I'll wash it off in my mouth." He put his cupped hand up to his mouth and after closing his lips but spreading his jaws, he pushed his tongue first against one cheek and then the other, working his tongue back and forth.

Jean watched him wide-eyed with her mouth open and clutching her partly eaten chocolate bar. "Gross!" She quickly glanced around to see if any adults were aware of this critical state of affairs. Chord tried not to laugh.

Suddenly Billy made out he was going to choke, and he leaned forward and gagged, but he quickly recovered and sat up. "Just about swallowed my eye," he mumbled in alarm with his tongue between his back teeth and his one eye still tightly closed. Chord laughed, but some of the other children looked shocked as they kept their eyes on Billy. He then leaned over and with his cupped hands at his mouth, he pretended to drop his eye into them.

"Now, everyone," he announced sharply with a scowl, "I need to get my eye back in the right way. Sometimes this can be a bit tricky, so please keep still, and please be quiet." All eyes were fastened on Billy. With his free hand, he turned his cap, putting the visor to the back. He put his cupped hand up to his closed eye and then worked at it for several seconds. Harry and Barbara watched him anxiously.

"There, I'll try that." He opened his eye and looked around cross-eyed at the others. "Oh, no!" Billy moaned disappointedly. "I'll have to adjust it a bit." He gently pushed all around his closed eye as the group watched intently. When he opened his eye again, he blinked a few times, looked at the campers, and said with satisfaction, "There, that's much better. I can see all of you much clearer now." He sat down, turned his cap around, and picked up his bag of potato chips. Harry and Barbara were much relieved, and Chord was still laughing.

Camp operated on standard time during the summer which made dusk arrive one hour earlier. Flag lowering was attended by the campers and those staff members who were available. The camp song was sung again at this time followed by the camp cheer.

When everyone arrived at the campfire area, the fun-to-serious evening program began. Mr. Taylor beckoned to Henry, and when he came forward, he handed the young fellow a match and pointed to the firewood the boy had set up this afternoon. Henry dropped to his knees next to the wood and struck the match against the fly of his pants. After the fire was going nicely, its heat caused the small amount of smoke to rise up into the air away from those sitting around the fire. It would later be suitable for the marshmallow roast.

As the sun slipped down behind a stand of spruce trees, one of the campers begged, "Tell us a ghost story!" Several other children quickly agreed.

"No, we're not going to tell any scary stories," answered Miss Fraser firmly. "It's wrong to enjoy things which frighten us. The Bible tells us what things we should think about. It says, 'Whatsoever things are true, whatsoever things are honest, whatsoever things are just, whatsoever things are pure, whatsoever things are lovely, whatsoever things are of good report; if there be any virtue, and if there be any praise, think on these things.'"

Mr. Dodge added, "The devil uses ghost stories to have an effect on some of the people who hear them. Real ghosts are actual evil spirits or demons, and we don't want to help the devil by enjoying evil. Our purpose here at camp is to glorify the Lord."

After the program, the campers prepared for bed. One counselor from each cabin stayed with their campers. The campers' time in their cabins began with discussing the good things that happened that day and then thanking the Lord in prayer.

"I like the club periods," Harry said to his cabin group. "They're fun, and we do neat things."

Chord related, "I'm having a good time at this camp."

"What do you like about camp, Chord?"

"Well, the counselors are nice. They care about us and make sure we have a good time."

Thomas spoke up, "I can see that there's a difference between religion and living as a Christian."

Mrs. Boates who organized the camp library had a collection of books of missionary stories and biographies as well as Christian fiction. These books were borrowed by staff members and campers. The counselors promoted calmness at bedtime, and they discouraged rowdiness. Usually they read to their campers at this time.

When the campers had settled down and most were asleep, the counselors quietly slipped out to join the staff meeting in the living room of the old house. At the meetings, the events of the day were analyzed, and plans were made for the following day.

"This is going to be our best camp session yet," Mr. Dodge shared with the group.

"There's a good spirit, and the campers get along nicely. Children and young people are coming from a distance as our reputation spreads."

Mr. Two Rivers related, "At the beginning of camp, it looked like we were going to have problems with Chord, but when we were firm with him yet showed him respect and insisted the campers show him respect, he was alright."

Mr. Dodge nodded, and then he glanced around at the staff members in the room. "How do you people feel about having a whisper meal tomorrow noon?" he asked.

"A whisper meal," Miss Knott repeated as she leaned back on the couch, crossed her ankles, and closed her eyes. "What's that?"

Mr. Dodge whispered, "A whisper meal is a meal when no one is allowed to speak above a whisper all during the meal." The others looked at him and grinned. Miss Jack and Miss Knott giggled, and then he returned to his normal voice. "We'll give thanks outside before we go into the barn, but then once we get inside there's to be no talking except by whispering."

Mr. Two Rivers stretched his arms up over his head. "A whisper meal sounds like a great idea," he agreed, and then he placed his hands behind his head and slouched lower into the chair. "It can get pretty boisterous in the barn at mealtimes. And the campers will enjoy the fun, too."

There was a lull in the conversation in the living room of the old house, and Miss Jack fingered the ends of her long hair. "That sure was a strange sound coming from the apple orchard," she told the group, and then she looked over at Stanley. "I was impressed with your moose call, Stanley." He grinned back at her.

The staff meeting concluded with a short devotional, and praise and prayer to the Lord. Lights-out time was about twenty-five minutes later. Mr. Clark retrieved his wide-brimmed hat from the top of the library bookcase, and he planted it on his head and left with several other staff members. Outside, they gazed up at the stars in the clear, black sky.

"There's millions of them!" exclaimed Mr. Taylor.

Miss Knott added, "And the Lord has names for all of them."

"Look," Mr. Jack pointed out to the group, "there's a falling star—or meteor as Jennifer would insist. 'Stars don't fall.'"

Mr. Clark and several other staff members accompanied Mrs. Charles to the barn for a quick bite to eat, but Mr. Jack returned to his cabin.

"Tim," a young voice whispered through the semi-darkness of the cabin as he quietly closed the door behind him.

"What is it, Billy?" Mr. Jack replied in a hushed tone. "Can't you get to sleep?" He crossed over to Billy's bunk, stepping over the pair of denims abandoned in the middle of the floor.

"I got saved tonight!"

Mr. Jack knelt on the floor beside his young brother in the lower bunk. "What!" he responded in a surprised whisper. "I thought you got saved several years ago."

There was a pause before the boy answered. "I thought I did, too. Back then I knew Mom and Dad trusted in the Lord, and you and Jenny did, and lots of other people were saved, so I thought I should get saved, too."

Mr. Jack could barely see Billy in the dark. He leaned a little closer and touched his shoulder. "What made you realize you weren't saved?" he asked, sitting back on his heels.

"Back then when I got saved—I mean when I thought I did—I wanted to be just like you guys. And I know now that's not the reason to get saved. I know that trusting in the Lord isn't what we do so that we can belong to other Christians. It's not a club that we're joining."

"That's right, we don't get saved just to continue the family tradition or to be like other people," Mr. Jack agreed. "Well, how do you know you're saved for sure now?"

The boy partly sat up in the dim light and rested on one elbow. "I'm really saved now because I know I was a sinner, like the Bible says, and I don't want sin in my life anymore. The Lord Jesus paid the penalty for my sin, and I know I'm saved because I accepted the gift of salvation—and I now have His righteousness just like the Bible says. That means I'm righteous just as Jesus Christ is righteous. I understand it now, Timmy," he nearly spoke aloud.

"Yes, you're really a believer now." The two brothers looked at each other in the near darkness for several seconds. Mr. Jack bowed his head. "Our Heavenly Father, we thank Thee for our Saviour the Lord Jesus Christ who shed His blood and died for us that we could be saved from the penalty of our sin. We thank Thee that His righteousness has been given to us, unworthy sinners that we once were. And we thank Thee Billy is now one of Your children and he can know You as his Heavenly Father."

He paused, and Billy continued. "Thank You, Lord Jesus for dying for me and saving me from my sin. My Heavenly Father, help me now to live for You, the way You want me to live."

Billy stopped, and his brother concluded, "We pray in the Name of Thy Son the Lord Jesus Christ."

Mr. Jack stood up to leave. "Good night, Brother Billy," he said.

"Tim," Billy exclaimed in a whisper, "aren't you going to sing 'Thank You, Lord, for Saving My Soul'?"

"Let's do that tomorrow morning when you tell the others you're now trusting in the Lord."

"How about when we're at the barn for breakfast?" the boy answered, and he snuggled down into his sleeping bag. "Good night, Tim."

Five minutes later Mr. Clark entered the cabin he shared with Mr. Jack who was now settled in his sleeping bag, but still wide awake. After Mr. Clark climbed into his bunk, both counselors, unknown to the other, silently prayed for each of the campers in their cabin by name, for salvation for some and spiritual growth for the remaining boys. And then each young man silently prayed for his friend and fellow-worker with whom he was sharing the cabin.

chapter eighteen

two years later—summer 1992

The Sea Creature

It was a cloudy morning in late summer when Timothy Jack parked his car on the shoulder of the road close to the Rogers Cove wharf. "I thought there'd be more vehicles here than this," he commented to Stanley as he released his seat belt.

His friend opened the car door and paused his humming. "There's been several tides," he replied. "Maybe it's washed away by now." The young men emerged from the vehicle, and Stanley stepped through the swath of asters between the road and the ditch. He joined Timothy who was tightening the laces of his boots.

Timothy and Stanley scanned the shore of the cove from left to right. "There are some people away over there to the north," Timothy pointed out, "just this side of Indian Head."

Stanley shaded his eyes with his hand. "Maybe that's where it is."

"Let's go," Timothy said. He reached back into the car and grabbed his camera, and Stanley put on his wide-brimmed felt hat. The fellows climbed over the large rocks placed on the beach for a breakwater next to Sawmill Road.

"Some guy from around here said on television it was a sea monster," Stanley related as they walked along the stony beach, "but the scientist who saw a video of it said it was only a large basking shark."

"A basking shark," Timothy repeated with a grin. "I've never seen a basking shark before. Like to see one."

The tide was about halfway out. As the young men hiked along the high-tide line, they stepped over several clumps of knotted-wrack, an old board, and a couple of plastic containers the recent tides had deposited on the beach.

"Basking shark or no basking shark," Timothy decided as they moved along at the base of the bluff, "it looks like it's a fair size from what I can see from here." Stanley grunted in agreement, and Timothy came down on an empty, green, sea urchin shell causing it to crumble under his boot. The fellows now stepped from rock to rock as they moved along at the base of the cliffs toward Indian Head.

"I think I got a whiff of it," Stanley said when they were nearly at the large carcass. "The wind's blowing this way."

"Yeah," Timothy agreed. "We'll have to stay upwind when we get to there."

When Timothy and Stanley approached the little group of people standing near the body of the enormous creature lying on the rocks, an older man greeted them with, "Howdy." Timothy and Stanley nodded in reply and then studied the carcass along with the other curious people there.

"That's some strange creature!" a lady exclaimed.

"Sure is," the person beside her agreed.

"It's a sea monster for sure. Look at the size of it!"

Someone stated, "It's a basking shark."

Neither Timothy nor Stanley said anything as they stood among the onlookers. Timothy waited for a fellow to move aside before taking an overall photograph. The fellow said, "I've never seen nothing like this before."

"Maybe it's one of those prehistoric animals," another man stated. "You know, that's supposed to be extinct—lived a million years ago."

"That scientist on TV said it was a basking shark."

Timothy estimated the carcass to be about twenty feet long. "But the creature had been much longer," Stanley pointed out to him. "See the tail there, Tim? It's only about three feet long, but where it's broken off, it's about five inches in diameter. The tail was probably at least a good ten feet longer—don't you think?"

Timothy took a photograph of the tail section and then moved along to what was left of the head. "Small head compared to the rest of the body," he noted. "Looks about two and a half feet long on that long, skinny neck." Stanley smiled in agreement.

"Those must be the eye sockets there," Timothy continued. "About three inches in diameter on either side of the head which is about a foot wide, I'd say." Timothy took a photograph of the head, and he grinned and imagined, *Wouldn't Jennifer love to see this!*

Stanley pointed to the head of the creature and noted, "Must be nostrils there—see? And look at these things, Tim. They're about six inches long with knobs at their ends. Strange!"

"Like catfish feelers," Timothy suggested, "only larger—much larger."

Timothy and Stanley could hear others talking. Someone questioned, "How long's this thing been here on the rocks?"

"Some guy that lives handy to here said he first seen it nearly a week ago."

A woman answered, "I heard tell that that Rafuse fellow saw it a month ago—out there, halfway to Bunchberry Island."

"Ugh!" someone piped up. "The wind's shifted."

"Well, don't stand there so close, Honey," the older man advised her. "Get back to over here where we're at."

"Don't smell like rotten whale any. Smells like rotten fish, I'd say."

"Stan," Timothy told him, "I'd like to get a picture of one of those long fins. You mind getting close for scale? You might want to hold your breath. Okay, that's good. Put your hand out toward it, will you. Okay, thanks, I got it."

"You know," Stanley exclaimed when he stepped back, "Jennifer would find this fascinating."

Other people were arriving at the scene and someone brought over what looked like a jawbone about two feet long. The fellow laid it down next to the head of the creature. "Hey,

I saw another one of those over that way," a man commented. He left the group and carefully stepped from rock to rock to retrieve it.

Before the man returned with the other half of the jawbone, another man wearing a gray cap spoke up. "We can tell by just looking at this carcass that it's not a whale," he stated with authority as he glanced around at the people. "The spine is situated towards the top part of the body rather than through the centre which is typical for whales." The man pointed to the top of the carcass.

A man in the growing crowd wearing dark glasses called out, "It's a basking shark."

The man with the gray cap ignored him. He asked another man who accompanied him, "Get a picture of me holding these jaw pieces." And then he addressed a young lady, "Write in your notes that there's no evidence of this creature having teeth." He pushed his hands into a pair of surgeons' gloves and then dragged his fingers along the edges of the jawbones.

When the man looked around at the people congregated there, Timothy could see on the front of his cap, an outline of a fish. The man declared, "Sharks have teeth. This creature did not have teeth." He motioned back to the body of the animal. "And this creature has a large chest and abdomen as you can see. Sharks are slim—they are streamlined."

"If it's not a whale or a shark," someone in the crowd asked on behalf of everyone else, "then what is it?"

"I don't know yet," he admitted. "But it might be a plesiosaur." He returned to his examination of the carcass. The man with him took several more photographs, and the young lady continued to write in her notebook.

Timothy edged a little closer to the man with the gray cap. He waited for him to notice him and when he looked his way, Timothy could see that the outline of the fish on the front of his cap had letters printed inside.

"Excuse me, Sir," Timothy began. "May I ask who you are and who you represent?"

The man grinned slightly. "My name's Harold. Harold Roop, and I'm with 'Science and the Bible'."

Timothy's mouth dropped open. "You're Dr. Roop from 'Science and the Bible'! We get your monthly newsletters." He looked down at Dr. Roop's hand in the surgeon's glove. "My name is Timothy Jack. I wish I could shake hands with you." They exchanged grins, and Timothy looked over at Stanley. "Hey, Stan, come here. This is Dr. Roop from 'Science and the Bible'." Stanley promptly came over and stood beside Timothy. "This is my friend Stanley Clark. We're glad you're here, Dr. Roop," Timothy informed him.

Stanley added, "I have several books and a couple videos from you people. Nice to meet you, Dr. Roop."

Dr. Roop grinned and nodded, and Timothy quickly examined his cap. *Hey,* he remembered, *didn't I see that fish design years ago on the bumper sticker of Mom and Dad's old car? It means 'Jesus Christ the Son of God'.*

Dr. Roop returned to his work, and Timothy and Stanley stepped back.

Someone in the crowd commented, "Well, I never thought we'd see a sea monster around these parts—right here in Rogers Cove."

"Maybe it's a dinosaur," someone joked, and others giggled in response.

"Scientists don't know for sure what it is. Maybe it's a missing link from millions of years ago." Several people joined in laughter.

Dr. Roop stood up from his crouched position near the tail. "No, it's not a creature from millions of years ago," he said loud enough for all to hear. "The earth is only seven or eight thousand years old."

A man asked him doubtfully, "Are you a scientist?"

"Yes. I have two degrees in science and one in education. I used to teach evolution and all that goes with that subject, but gradually I began to see that evolution and millions of years did not make sense. They were not good science, in fact I could see that evolution and millions of years were bad science." Timothy was pleased to hear what Dr. Roop was saying, but he sensed some disbelief among the people there.

Dr. Roop continued. "I'm giving a talk this evening in the Hannah Community Centre on the subject of dinosaurs past and present. There's no charge for admission. Please come—we'd like to see you there, and there'll be opportunity to ask questions later."

"Are you going to talk about this creature here?" someone asked. "What is it anyway?"

"I don't know what this creature is," he admitted once more as he checked his watch. "It's not a whale, and I don't believe it's a shark. I'm coming back this afternoon to dissect the body of this creature. No doubt we'll then have more clues as to what it is, and we'll be able to establish what it is not."

Timothy glanced over at Stanley who was now looking his way. Neither fellow said anything. Timothy concluded, *I'd like to be here, and I know Jennifer would, too.* He stepped closer to Stanley. "Let's get a move-along," he said to him. "It'll be nearly noon by the time we get home. I'd like to come back this afternoon. And I can think of several other people who would like to be here and see this. We could get a whole carload for sure."

Timothy and Stanley headed back to the Rogers Cove wharf where the car was parked. As they moved along they again stepped from rock to rock near the high-tide line.

"Tim, did you see what that girl back there was wearing?"

"Was wearing?" he questioned as he glanced over at his friend. "Or do you mean not wearing?"

"Yeah, that's the one. Sure hope she doesn't catch a cold."

"How could I not notice how she was dressed—or not dressed!" Timothy answered.

"I know how guys think," Stanley acknowledged as he stepped over a clump of knotted-wrack. "They'll look at a girl like that, but they won't respect her; they can't."

Timothy added, "Most girls don't realize to what extent their appearance can affect a guy. A fellow will get wrong or harmful thoughts because of the way some girls look, and he'll have improper feelings even when he doesn't let his feelings show. And those girls who do know what they're doing to a fellow are disrespecting him, and they are harming him in the long run."

"Girls like that turn me off," Stanley disclosed, "or I turn myself off by ignoring them."

"Yeah, me too," Timothy admitted, "but sometimes it can be difficult for me to avoid being tempted to look or think."

"You, Tim!" Stanley questioned in surprise. "You're affected by the way girls can look?"

"Well, sure I am," he replied to him in no uncertain terms. "I'm a normal guy. I have all the natural instincts God gave to men, but this isn't the time in my life to use all of them. So in the meantime with the Lord's help, I'll avoid temptation and keep my mind clean." And then Timothy said thoughtfully, "I want to be attracted to women who not only look pleasant but are wholesome in their personality—women who are nice to be with and are not overly occupied with themselves." He smiled as he added, "Oh, and I look forward to having a woman who is comfortable being the person she is. I want her to be practical and know how to support me in my goals, be feminine, and be my best friend, too."

The fellows crossed the stony part of the beach and soon arrived back at the car. Stanley removed his jacket and felt hat, and Timothy put his camera on the backseat before sliding in behind the steering wheel. Timothy started the engine, turned around, and drove up the hill and through the village of Rogers Cove.

"Well, Tim, that sure was interesting. A large, unidentified sea creature washed up on the beach and close to our part of the world. Thanks for driving out here to see it."

"Thanks for telling me about it," Timothy said to his friend. "We didn't have the television on last evening."

Stanley stretched out his legs. "I'm sure glad someone like Dr. Roop is examining that carcass. He's not going to insist it's a basking shark or anything else when evidence proves otherwise. Scientists who believe in evolution will not admit that this creature here today in Rogers Cove was something they assumed became extinct a million years ago. Even if the facts prove this creature was one they thought became extinct many years ago, they will manipulate the facts to fit their own point of view."

"Yeah, you're right, Stan," Timothy told him as he slowed down and signalled to turn onto Shortcut Road.

Stanley shook his head. "I can't believe I used to think evolution was correct," he related in amazement. "It can't be proved—all they can do is repeat their assumptions. Evolution just doesn't make sense—millions of years ago. Right! 'Excuse me, Sir, were you there?'"

Timothy grinned and nodded as he shifted up. "It's sad," he added, "when intelligent people kiss their brains good bye." And then he quickly added, "Well, to be fair, we better not be too hard on the scientists. They're intelligent people, they've accumulated a lot of knowledge, and they've done a lot of good. Some scientists only repeat what they've been taught, and they do a lot of assuming. They don't realize that it's incorrect information they have and are passing on to others." Stanley nodded in agreement as he listened.

"Many people put their trust in modern science including evolution," Timothy continued as he drove along the road, "and they don't trust the creation bunch because of the variety of conflicting religious views they hold. Also scientists need to see things and put their hands on things, but religious people live by faith—what they believe in. Not very scientific, those religious folks. So we can't blame these science-people."

Stanley took a swallow of water from his pop bottle, and he added, "And then there's the scientists who have invested their lives in their chosen fields of study, and they don't want to admit even to themselves that they could be wrong. What would people think! Their reputation would be at stake as well as their very lives." He laughed.

"And finally," Timothy concluded when he glanced over at Stanley, "there's the group of scientists who want millions of years of evolution which would discredit the Bible and therefore exclude God, rather than believe in the creation account which includes God. Because, if the Bible is right about creation, then there must be a God who created all things, and consequently He has a claim on everything including them, and that doesn't suit them. So it's easier to deny creation and believe in and promote evolution. Besides, who wants to be associated with creationists who are a bunch of narrow-minded religious nuts?" He snickered. "I don't blame them."

After they rode in silence for several minutes, Timothy questioned, "You think your brother Colin would like to come with us this afternoon? I know he's not on good speaking terms with you or even us since you became a Christian, but you could ask him." Without pausing his humming, Stanley shrugged his shoulder and then pushed his wide-brimmed hat over one knee.

After Timothy dropped his friend off at his place, he checked his watch again and then headed home. He parked the car near the porch and entered the house where Jennifer met him at the door. "Tim, why didn't you invite me?" she asked expressing her disappointment. "Mom said you went to Rogers Cove to see a dead creature on the beach. I'd like to see it, too, you know."

Timothy grinned at his sister. "You mean the monster or the basking shark?" he teased as he left for the kitchen where his mother was at the stove preparing the noon meal.

Jennifer followed him. "Tim, you know I don't believe in monsters," she retorted with a scowl. "And the picture in the newspaper doesn't show anything like a basking shark." She reached for the plates in the cupboard. "You were actually there, and you saw the creature! I wish I hadn't missed it. Why didn't you tell me you were going?"

Timothy viewed the table to see if dinner was nearly ready and then asked, "There's a picture in today's paper?" He glanced over at the place where the newspaper was usually kept, and he could see it was opened to an article with the headline, 'Monster Found on Local Beach.' He picked up the newspaper and studied the photograph of the carcass. "Yup, that's what it looked like," he informed his sister and then added, "This picture's in black and white." He gave her his big fake grin. "I took coloured photos."

"Tim," his mother interrupted, "we're going to eat in three minutes."

Jennifer asked, "Are you going to let me see your pictures or are you keeping them to yourself and your friends?"

Timothy's jaw dropped in mock surprise. "Well, I'll have you know, it was one of my friends who said that you, Jennifer Jack, should see the body of this creature when we go back this afternoon."

Jennifer looked at him in astonishment. "You're going back this afternoon! Tim, you're going all the way back to Rogers Cove this afternoon to see the monster—I mean the creature!"

"Well, yeah," he replied calmly as he shrugged one shoulder. "Stanley and I plan to be there this afternoon when Dr. Roop from 'Science and the Bible' is returning back again to the site."

Jennifer was even more amazed. "Dr. Roop! From 'Science and the Bible'! What's he doing in Rogers Cove?"

Timothy tried not to grin. "Well," he answered seriously, "he told us he's going to dissect the creature this afternoon right there on the beach in Rogers Cove. Jennifer, you want to come? You're invited this time." He gave her another big phony grin.

Twelve-year-old Billy entered the house and came into the kitchen. "What's up?" he asked, and then he turned to his brother. "Hey, what did the bug say after he was splattered on the windshield of the car?"

Timothy looked over at Billy and replied, "The bug said, 'If I had the guts, I'd do it again.'"

Billy looked disappointed. "You knew that one?"

"You'd be surprised what I know," he informed him. "I'm nearly twenty-two years old. I first heard that one when you were still in diapers."

Their mother said, "Billy, wash your hands—dinner's almost ready."

Early that afternoon, Timothy again parked his car on the shoulder of the road in Rogers Cove. "There are more cars here now than this morning," he said after he switched off the ignition. He and his passengers emerged from the car, and Stanley planted his wide-brimmed hat on his head.

Jennifer looked over at the group of people standing together on the beach just this side of Indian Head. "Don't forget the camera, Tim," she reminded him, and then she removed an apple from the lunch bag and snapped it in two.

"Mom, can I have a swig of that water?," Timothy asked before she returned the bottle to the canvas bag and left it on the floor of the car.

Billy was wearing his t-shirt with lettering printed across the front, 'I'm smarter than I look'. As he left to go ahead by himself, he could be heard saying, "Nice day if it don't rain." Colin lit a cigarette before the little group climbed down over the breakwater to the beach below.

Several minutes later as they moved along the shore, Mrs. Jack commented, "Your grandpa has painted several pictures of this cove. I don't think I've been along this beach even this far, and I know I've never been to Indian Head."

"Oh, I come here fairly often," Jennifer replied. "I was here about three weeks ago when I brought a group from camp to see the little creatures in the tidal pools at low-tide. And this is where I collect some of the things for my beach plaques." She tossed her apple core towards the water.

Timothy glanced back along the shore in the direction they had come. "That looks like Dr. Roop coming now," he reported to the others. "And there's a few other people with him."

When the four Jacks and the two Clark brothers reached the body of the sea creature, Jennifer inspected the carcass beginning with the skull. "Look at this creature!" She then slowly moved along the length of the body to observe the different features down to the broken-off tail. When she returned to stand with her mother and brother, she remarked, "This is fascinating! I'm so glad I came." She turned and looked over at the body. "This creature—whatever it is—doesn't appear to be a whale nor a shark. Its head isn't broad enough for either, and its neck is long and narrow and doesn't match the head of either one. Also, the tail is too heavy beyond the end of its abdomen to be a whale or a shark. I don't see any blow-hole for a whale nor any gills for a shark." She looked over at Timothy. "Tim, did you get photos of this?"

Timothy nodded. "Five or six. Maybe seven."

Dr. Roop came to the group of curious on-lookers standing around near the carcass. He was carrying a small corrugated cardboard box and a tree-pruning saw. He and two of his helpers took surgeons' gloves from the box and put them on and then, grasping his saw, he climbed onto the carcass of the creature and faced the people there. The crowd became silent as everyone looked his way expectantly.

"We don't know what this creature is because it's quickly decomposing," he began, speaking loud enough for all to hear, "but I'm standing on its body to prove that it's not so rotten that it's falling apart." Most people stepped over the rocks a little closer as he spoke.

The man with the dark glasses was back. He called out, "The scientist on TV said it was a large basking shark."

Dr. Roop did not acknowledge the remark. "I'll cut into this carcass and we'll see evidence which will point to what it might be, and we will hopefully prove what it is not. It might be a plesiosaur, but we might never know for sure what it is."

He turned and stepped off the body of the creature onto the rounded beach rocks.

Dr. Roop positioned his saw against the chest of the animal and began to cut into the flesh. Several people came closer to watch, and a few moved back. A woman commented, "It's going to stink even more when it's cut into."

Jennifer exclaimed, "This sure is interesting. I'm glad I could be here." She took several steps closer and balanced herself on a rock just large enough for her two feet.

As the flesh opened up, Dr. Roop explained, "You can see the blood is still red. This indicates to us he died a short time ago—not more than a few weeks at most."

A young man asked, "Could he have died thousands of years ago and froze and then floated in to here in an iceberg?"

"Good question," Dr. Roop answered him. "But we can tell by the consistency of the blood that it's never been frozen."

"Just a large basking shark," the man with the dark glasses again insisted.

"It might not be a basking shark," Jennifer got across to him with her hands on her hips. "It doesn't have the shape of a basking shark, and it hasn't deteriorated to the extent that parts of the body have fallen off. It's still pretty well the shape it naturally should be except for its obviously missing long tail. It looks like a plesiosaur." The man pursed his lips and rolled his eyes in disbelief but said nothing more.

Dr. Roop made a long cut the length of the chest and with the help of his assistants they peeled back the thick flesh. "Look at the size of this liver!" he exclaimed when the organ became exposed. "It's five feet long." The heavy flesh fell away completely. "No," he corrected himself, "it's about eight feet long - it can't be a liver. It must be a lung."

Dr. Roop cut into the abdomen and uncovered another organ similar to the first but much smaller. "This must be the liver here," he decided. Colin grinned and stepped closer to have a better view.

"This sure is interesting," Jennifer said to Timothy. "This creature here could be a plesiosaur. We could be looking at a plesiosaur right here at Rogers Cove."

Timothy grinned and nodded. He tried to position himself to take a photograph of the internal organs of the sea creature, but because Dr. Roop and his assistants were working close to the body, it was not possible to have a good clear view. *I wish I could get a little higher from where I'm standing,* he determined. He raised the camera high over his head. "Jennifer, tell me when the camera is aimed at the lung and liver, will you."

"Down—tip it down a little more. Stop! Up slightly. That looks good right there," she told him. "Take it now." Timothy took the picture and then stepped over the rocks to stand with his mom.

Dr. Roop put his hand on the large lung, and with the pruning saw he cut it in two. It was several feet wide and about a foot thick. He stood up and addressed the watching people. "The size of this lung tells us this creature had the ability to remain underwater for very long periods of time."

Jennifer looked around for the fellow with the dark glasses. "The basking-shark fellow is gone," she decided with disappointment. "Too bad. He might have learned something—but then maybe not. Some people don't want to learn anything, and some people don't want to be corrected."

"Is it male or female?" someone in the crowd wanted to know.

"Another good question," Dr. Roop replied as he relocated himself next to the body. "I'll try to determine that next." He made several more cuts with his saw into the lower abdomen of the creature. "It appears to be female," he finally announced.

"A female," a lady repeated thoughtfully. "I wonder if her mate is still out there somewhere." Several other people along with the lady looked out beyond Rogers Cove to the open water this side of Bunchberry Island.

And so it went that eventful day in late summer, but now, several months later, the circumstances of that time were far from Timothy's mind as he drove his car up his long driveway on this unusually cool day and parked it next to the house. He had other exciting news he was anxious to share with his family.

Several large wet snowflakes slowly floated down from the mouse-gray, October sky as Timothy stepped from the vehicle. He closed the car door and headed for the house. As the flakes landed on the hard-packed ground near the porch, they promptly melted leaving small wet blotches.

Timothy entered the kitchen where his mom was preparing the evening meal. *Smells good!* He glanced over at the weekly newspaper which was open on the counter, and he abruptly halted in his tracks.

"What!" he exclaimed, and he picked up the newspaper. He read the headline aloud. "'Experts lay sea monster rumours to rest.'" As he began to silently read the article, he moved over to a kitchen chair at the table and settled onto it.

"Supper's ready in five minutes, Tim," his mother reported.

Jennifer came in from the living room, opened the cutlery drawer, and gathered up the forks and knives to set the table. She said nothing as she worked around her brother who leaned the newspaper against the edge of the table as he concentrated on his reading.

"Huh!" Timothy blurted out. "How do they know that?" He then went on with his reading. "What! That's not what we saw, and I have photos to prove it," he said. His family remained silent. "Aw, come on, that's not right," he burst out without looking up from the newspaper. "How can it be a basking shark?" When he had finished the article, he stood up and dropped the newspaper with disgust onto the counter. "What do those expert guys know? They weren't even there."

Timothy could hear Jennifer giggle, and when he glanced over at her, he saw her grinning at him. "The experts say it was a basking shark," she reminded him. "That's what the article says. You've read it."

Timothy leaned back against the counter and looked over at his sister. "Whose side are you on?" he demanded, glaring at her. "I thought you thought it was a—what's it called—a plesiosaur."

"Well, I'm not on your side," Jennifer answered, still grinning. "I'm on the side of truth." She stepped aside to allow her mother to drain the potatoes into the sink. "Tim, you're not an expert," his sister informed him. "You don't even know the difference between a dinosaur and a plesiosaur."

Timothy stared at her. "Yeah, but—" He shifted his feet.

"Jennifer," her mother told her, "tell Dad and Billy that dinner's nearly ready."

Jennifer backed out of the kitchen and headed for the living room. Timothy called after her, "But Jennifer, what about that large lung we saw? I have a photo of it."

"Dad, Billy," she called, "supper's ready."

When Mr. Jack and Billy arrived in the kitchen, Billy was holding several sheets of paper. "You see this yet?" He held it out to his brother. "Came in today's mail."

Timothy could see it was the latest newsletter from 'Science and the Bible.' He took the papers, and when he glanced at the second page, he saw a sketch of a basking shark superimposed over a sketch of a plesiosaur, and there was an article entitled, 'East Coast Sea Creature not a Plesiosaur after all.' Timothy started to read the article in the newsletter but laid it on the counter when he heard his dad say, "Okay, let's sit down for supper."

As soon as Mr. Jack had finished giving thanks, Timothy looked at his sister across from him and began. "So what about that huge lung we saw? You can't say it was a liver. A liver wouldn't be that big."

Jennifer reached for the bowl of vegetables and advised him, "If you check the diagram in the 'Science and the Bible' newsletter, you'd see that a basking shark could be larger than a plesiosaur, therefore the basking shark would have larger organs. What we thought was a lung could have been a liver of a large basking shark and what we thought was a liver could have been some other smaller organ."

"Well, maybe so," Timothy replied, "but if that's the case, why isn't the rest of the basking shark there? Dr. Roop stood on the body to prove it wasn't rotten to the extent that it was falling apart."

"Tim," his mother reminded him, "help yourself to the potatoes, and pass the bowl to your dad."

Jennifer explained, "The parts of the basking shark that weren't there were soft body tissues. As the carcass rotted, they fell away, making it now look like a plesiosaur. We know it had been in the water at least several weeks, probably more."

Billy was seated at the end of the table. "Pickles, please," he asked.

"Jennifer, you sound just like the experts," Timothy said to her accusingly. "You sound like the scientists who deny it was a prehistoric animal. I can't believe that my sister would fall for that trick. You're taking the easy way out and saying that the rotting carcass on the beach was a basking shark. You sound just like one of those scientists or one of those other so-called experts."

"Please pass the pickles, Tim," Billy said again.

"Well, thanks for the compliment," Jennifer replied as she grinned at her older brother, "but I'm not an expert yet. I'm very open-minded, but not so open-minded that my brains are in danger of falling out." Timothy was not amused. He stared across the table almost glaring at his sister.

Billy stood up and reached across the table for the pickles between Timothy and Jennifer. "Excuse me, please," he said as he sat down.

Timothy admitted, "I was hoping that the dead creature at Rogers Cove was one of the animals that the evolutionists say became extinct millions of years ago. I wanted the evolutionists to be proven wrong, and the creationists proven right. That rotten carcass which we saw being carved up on the beach could have proved that the experts aren't so expert after all and that the creationists know what they're talking about. It would give us some credibility."

"Well," his sister expressed, "we shouldn't stretch or manipulate the facts in order to enhance our views or to support our cause. Neither should we present information which might be possible as though that information was indeed accurate, indisputable facts. I agree with you, we need credibility, but our credibility is based on truthfulness even if it appears to be to our disadvantage in that it doesn't support our cause. We don't have to be afraid of the truth, do we? Neither should we be afraid to admit we were wrong. Let's not kid ourselves; it doesn't matter what anyone believes, their beliefs won't change the facts, and the truth will always win out in the end." And then she added with a grin, "Anyway, I must say that dissecting a washed-up carcass on the beach was an interesting experience, don't you think? We saw the rotten body sliced into, and its internal organs removed and spread out on the rocks so we could examine them. I'm glad I was there to see all that. In fact, I loved it!"

"Excuse me!" Mr. Jack suddenly interrupted. "We're eating!" He had an exaggerated distressed look on his face. "Do we have to talk about dissecting rotting carcasses on the beach at mealtimes?"

"Yeah!" Billy interjected as he scowled at his brother and sister. "It's not fair! How come you two can talk about gross things when we're eating but I'm not allowed to—even when we're not eating?"

"Dad's right," his wife agreed as she laid down her fork. "I'm afraid I've just about lost my appetite. There must be something better to discuss at mealtime."

It was silent around the supper table for nearly a minute until Billy took on a phony, pleasant look. "Nice pickles," he commented to his family. "Delicious! Want some, Jennifer?" He pushed the jar towards his sister as he continued to grin.

"I have a request to make," Mrs. Jack said in order to change the subject. "Would everyone please make sure the hot water tap is turned off after you use it. I found it dripping again today."

Jennifer told Billy accusingly, "Don't you know that a dripping tap can lose up to a full tub of hot water in one year?"

Billy quickly answered, "I'm willing to give up one bath a year. Aren't you, Tim?"

His sister looked at him in disgust, and his dad snickered.

Timothy cleared his throat. "Oh, I almost forgot," he stated. "I was talking with Stanley today. He told me his brother Colin was saved yesterday."

"He was!" his mom exclaimed, and she smiled at Timothy. "Isn't that great! I've been praying for him regularly."

Mr. Jack added, "Yes, so have I. That's good news for sure."

Jennifer quickly put in, "Stanley came to the Lord first, then Betty, and then their mother," she recalled. "Mr. Clark was saved soon after, and now Colin is saved. That's the whole family. You must be pleased, Tim. Stan was saved when you talked to him when you guys had to stay over at his cabin because of the unexpected snowstorm."

Their mother asked, "Did Stanley give the circumstances of how Colin came to the Lord?"

"Well, it was partly due to the before-mentioned subject which I won't identify by name, but I'm sure you already know what I mean," Timothy revealed to his family. "Colin began to see at that time that evolution didn't make a whole lot of sense, but creation did make sense. And he also realized that although the Bible's been around for thousands of years, it's never been proved incorrect and that includes what it says about scientific facts. And it's well-known that science over the years has been wrong many times including modern science in the past century. The Bible has an excellent record of being reliable in all areas."

Timothy's family listened with interest, and he continued. "Stan told me Colin was reading his stuff from 'Science and the Bible', but more than that, when Colin spent time with us, he could see we were genuine and that our Christianity affected all areas of our lives in practical and beneficial ways. But most of all, when he realized he was guilty before God because of his sin and Jesus paid the penalty for his sin by dying on the cross for him just like the Bible says—it was then that he accepted the gift of salvation for himself."

Mr. Jack grinned. "That's just great! I'm glad Colin is now saved. We need to pray for him that he will grow in the Lord and he would know the Lord's greatness in his life."

The following Saturday morning, Timothy parked his car on the shoulder of the road next to the Rogers Cove wharf. After he stepped from his vehicle, he flipped the camera strap over his head, and then he closed the car door. "I like these sunny, late autumn days," he said. "No flies."

His brother Billy came through the tall, dry grasses lining the edge of the road, and then he scanned along the beach to the north. "I'm going over to Indian Head," he said. "I want to see what the tide brought in." Timothy nodded, and the fellow trotted off, and when he reached the beach, he hopped along from boulder to boulder.

Jennifer reached into the backseat of the car, picked up the model creature she had made, and carefully drew it out through the open door. "Now, where's a good place?" she asked as she moved to the edge of the breakwater next to the road. "I'm glad the tide's just right—about halfway in."

Timothy and Jennifer climbed over the large rocks and stood at the high-tide line on the beach. "How about over there, Jennifer?" Timothy pointed with his elbow. "Your creature will look good on top of that smooth rock there."

"The carboniferous one?" she asked.

"Yeah, whatever."

Jennifer placed her model on the rock and situated it facing away from the water of the cove. "There, how's that, Tim? I want it to look like he's coming from the water and heading for the land." She pushed her long hair behind her shoulder, stepped back, and stood near her brother. "Be sure to get close enough to clearly see the creature, yet we need to see its environment, too."

"Yup," Timothy agreed as he switched on the light-meter and then squatted down next to a bunch of seaweed.

"He should be looking directly at us," she instructed Timothy.

"Yup," Timothy said as he focused his camera on the creature.

"Do his front legs show up nicely?"

"Yup."

"How about his back flippers? Can you see them okay?"

"Yup."

"Does the water show in the background?"

"Yup," Timothy replied once more, "and I have the horizon level, too." And then he took the photograph. "Got it," he told his sister and he stood up.

"Good." And Jennifer grinned with satisfaction. "Let's move the creature and take another shot." She picked it up and lowered it to the smooth stones scattered over the beach.

After Timothy took the second exposure, Jennifer decided, "Two pictures should be enough, don't you think?"

Timothy rose to his feet and switched off the light-meter. "Yup," he agreed. He returned the lens cap onto the front of the camera lens and then looked off in the direction their younger brother had gone. "Billy's away over there this side of Indian Head," he could see. "We'll be here a while. That's all right; I like it here, and we aren't in a hurry anyway."

Timothy shielded his eyes from the bright sky as he surveyed Bunchberry Island to the west. Jennifer picked up a mermaid's purse tossed in by a previous tide.

"That's a strange looking animal," a man's voice behind them declared. Timothy turned to see who had spoken, and Jennifer faced towards the bright sky from her crouched position and sneezed. They saw a man scrutinizing Jennifer's model. "I was walking along the road up there and saw that animal down here and couldn't figure out what it was." He grinned, looking from the model and then to Timothy and Jennifer.

Timothy smiled and gave a quick nod. "My sister made it."

"Sure is life-like." The man leaned forward and stared at the creature several metres away. "Could have sworn it was real." Jennifer smiled broadly, stood up, and slowly ran her fingers through her hair.

The man then remarked as he looked more closely, "Strange animal, I'd say. It has two front feet and two hind flippers. I've never heard of anything like that before." He laughed. "What is it, anyway?"

"It's the missing link," Jennifer informed him.

"The missing link!" the stranger exclaimed as he came closer.

"Yeah," Timothy revealed. "He's part marine animal and part land animal. He's evolving from one kind of animal to another."

"Yeah, but—" the man hesitated. "He couldn't survive in the water or on the land like that. He's a dud." He glanced over at Timothy with a questioning look.

Timothy and Jennifer said nothing. They stared at the man and grinned, waiting for him to respond. Slowly, a thoughtful expression came over his face. "You've made a good point," he told them seriously. "I never could figure out how those transitional steps from one kind of animal to another worked out as they say they did. The animal wouldn't survive as it was changing from one kind to the other."

"We agree with you," Jennifer said to him. "It couldn't live in either environment."

Her brother added, "Makes about as much sense as this here animal. God didn't create nor use any monstrosities like this."

"God?" the man questioned abruptly. He pulled his hands from his front pockets and placed them on his hips. "I don't know if there's a God or not—I'm not religious. We're free to choose any religion we want. If you don't like one—choose another. They're all the same. For me—I have to see it to believe it, and I haven't seen any God nor any evidence of one," he flatly informed them. "Let's leave science to the scientists and religion to the religious bunch," he continued with an air of superiority. "You can't mix religion and science. Religion is what you choose to believe—science is fact. I think it took millions of years or so for animals to evolve. The scientists don't know for sure how long it has taken for animals to change to where they are now." He crossed his arms over his chest.

"Well," Timothy replied as he faced him, "I agree with you on one point anyway. We're free to believe whatever we want. God has given us the ability to think, to reason and to choose. But just because we choose to believe something—we can't alter any facts to suit whatever we've decided to believe."

The man ignored Timothy's remark as though he had not heard him. He peered out across the water to Bunchberry Island and then glanced towards Sawmill Road. "Got to go," he stated. The man walked away, and Timothy and his sister watched him until he reached the boulders of the breakwater below the gravel road.

"I've noticed," Jennifer remarked solemnly, "when someone denies obvious facts, that it's at that point their ability to reason leaves them. What they say about the subject doesn't make any sense, and they don't seem to realize it. If it wasn't so sad, it would be funny." She stood up and scanned along the beach to where Billy had gone.

Timothy bowed his head and slowly shook it. "Why would anyone choose to ignore or even deny the truth!" he exclaimed in exasperation. "Why would anyone choose to believe what they know is incorrect!" He raised his head and stared after the man who was now nowhere to be seen. "Well," he reminded himself, "they did not like to retain God in their knowledge so God gave them over to a reprobate or corrupt mind, and they just can't think straight on subjects on which they refuse to admit to the obvious facts."

His sister nodded in agreement and then continued the thought. "The reason they don't want any knowledge of God," she said frankly, "is because of sin in their lives. The knowledge of God interferes with the sinful lifestyle they want to hang onto. Or, even if they didn't want that kind of lifestyle, they are unable to shake it off on their own. They are powerless to change themselves, and they don't want to submit to a Higher Power."

There was a gratifying look on Timothy's face. "But the good news is," he declared, "that when a person believes what God has said and he admits to his sinfulness and he trusts God, God saves him from His wrath and condemnation." He paused and grinned. "And not only is the penalty of his sin now gone but when he believes and trusts what God has said, his sinful lifestyle will be gone, too—unless he purposely hangs onto it."

Jennifer smiled in agreement and added, "Salvation is simply wonderful as well as wonderfully simple."

Several minutes later Billy returned from his hike along the beach. "What's up?" he greeted his siblings.

"Ready to go, Billy?" Timothy asked him.

Jennifer picked up her model creature and inquired of Billy, "What did you see along the beach?"

"I saw a bunch of those lobster tags. And there was one sneaker washed in—medium size, and I saw a few plastic forks from the Red Roof, that fast food place up the road from here."

Timothy, Jennifer, and Billy moved up the beach towards the car. "Did you see any creatures, Billy?" his sister wanted to know. "Any marine life?"

Billy faced his sister. "Oh, yeah, almost forgot," he replied seriously. "There's a dead seal over there. It's pretty well mangled up. Looks like the road-kill we sometimes see on the side of the highway with its insides hanging out. You know what I mean? You can see the seagulls and crows had a real picnic on the beach with the dead creature." Billy quickly scampered up the large rocks which lined the beach along the road, and then he turned to his brother and sister. "I know you two would really enjoy examining the battered carcass—guts and all. It would set your bells a ringing," Billy informed them with exaggerated pleasantness. "You have a real interest in such gross, vulgar, disgusting things." He gave them a big, fake smile very similar to the ones Timothy was known to display on occasions.

Timothy and Jennifer were momentarily speechless as they stared at their younger brother. They climbed onto the road where he was, and Timothy said, "Come on, let's go home."

chapter nineteen

about two and a half years later—January 1995

The Weather Radio

"Hello," Timothy heard his dad downstairs say after the first ring. He wondered, *Who would be calling us so early on a Saturday morning!* He rolled over, opened one eye, and looked at the clock on his dresser. The glow of the red numerals told him it was six, fifty-six.

"Anybody hurt?" Mr. Jack demanded into the phone.

Timothy was now wide awake, and he pushed back the covers and sat up. *What's going on?* As he swung his bare feet to the cold floor, he could see the pale light of the early morning, winter sky between the closed drapes of his bedroom window.

"That's good," Timothy heard his dad answer, and after a pause his dad said, "Uh-huh." Timothy rose to his feet, crossed over in his shorts, and stood at his open bedroom door next to the painting of a campfire his grandfather did many years ago. "Uh-huh, yes," he heard from downstairs.

After a half minute of silence, Timothy could hear, "Okay, Mr. Charles, I'll be over right after I finish my breakfast." Timothy moved to his red-painted farmer's seat where he had dropped his clothes the night before, and he slipped into his heavy shirt and blue denims. Just as he left his room, his clock changed to one minute past seven.

Timothy studied the faces of his parents as he stood just inside the kitchen. He heard the hired man's clock in the living room give seven strikes. "It's completely destroyed," his dad informed his mom. "Nothing's left."

"How could such a thing happen!" she exclaimed as she dropped the eggshells into the compost pail by the door.

Timothy remained silent. He looked anxiously from his mom to his dad who replied, "We can't say at this time how it started." Mr. Jack quickly glanced over at his son before putting two pieces of bread in the toaster.

"What's going on?" Timothy demanded. His dad did not look up from the toaster, and his mom made no reply. "What's happened?" he asked again looking from his dad to his mom.

Mr. Jack slowly turned to face Timothy who was searching his dad's sober face. "The old house was destroyed by fire," he answered somberly. "Burned in the night."

Timothy's mouth dropped open as he stared at his dad. "The old house? At Camp Beth? Where we keep the sports equipment and stuff? It's all gone?"

His dad gave him a little, quick nod. "Mr. Charles says it's completely destroyed."

Several minutes later, Jennifer and Billy joined their parents and brother in the kitchen.

"How could the old house catch fire!" Jennifer exclaimed. "Nobody's living there and the woodstove was taken out ages ago."

Billy added, "I know I turned off the power last fall." The fifteen-year-old stood with his hands on his hips.

"It's hard to believe that lovely old house is no more," Mrs. Jack related. "Get me another frying pan, will you, Jennifer. There's more people for breakfast than I had anticipated."

After a hurried breakfast, Timothy, his dad, and Billy left to drive to Camp Bethlehem about twenty minutes away. When they had traveled about half the distance, Billy pointed ahead. "Look! Smoke in the air."

Timothy geared up as he accelerated from the stop sign. "No wind to blow it away."

About ten minutes later they drove over the brow of the little hill, and Timothy geared down. It seemed strange not to be driving onto the camp property as they were accustomed to.

Timothy brought the family car to a stop on the shoulder of the road behind a truck belonging to a volunteer fireman. There were several other vehicles parked along both sides of the road, and a fire truck and a tanker were in the driveway.

But what held the attention of Timothy, his dad, and brother was the smoldering ruins of the old house. Apart from the emergency trucks, the scene reminded Timothy of a familiar, friendly, smiling face, but now its front teeth were missing.

They left the car and moved over the well-trampled snow between several groups of people talking quietly. "Richard," a voice called out. Mr. Jack turned to face the elderly man who was coming their way.

"Mr. Charles," Mr. Jack responded, and he extended his right hand.

"Timothy. Billy." Mr. Charles nodded, and they shook hands. As the four fellows stood together under one of the two large, leafless maple trees, they stared silently at what was left of the charred building.

Mr. Charles spoke. "We never know what's going to happen from one day to the next, but the Lord knows, and nothing takes Him by surprise." He smiled as he glanced at Mr. Jack and his sons. "The Lord doesn't allow anything into our lives which isn't somehow for our good and for His glory, and He doesn't give us trials which are too much for us to bear." He turned and glanced at the burned out shell.

Mr. Jack stood with his hands in his pockets. "How's your wife doing?" he asked as he faced Mr. Charles.

"Oh, she's in the barn feeding some of the volunteer firemen and others who are still here."

"Mom sent a dozen eggs," Timothy remembered as he looked over to their car at the side of the road. He headed back for the eggs, and Billy moved to closer to what was left of the old house.

"Do they know yet how the fire started?" Mr. Jack asked Mr. Charles.

"Well, the first firemen who arrived told me they saw fresh footprints next to the building. And one of the windows over there on that side was open."

A look of shock came over the face of Mr. Jack. "Someone must have set fire to the old house just for the fun of it. There was nothing in it of any great value."

Mr. Charles looked concerned. "Yes," he agreed. "Some people have fun at the expense of others."

Timothy entered the barn and made his way past a line of tall rubber boots. He placed the carton of eggs on the counter and asked, "Can you use these eggs, Mrs. Charles?" He opened his jacket and let it hang loose.

"Why yes, Timothy, we can. I was running short of food to feed these hardworking men, but the Lord knew you dear folks would help. Thank you for your kindness." As she lifted the coffee pot from the burner, she gave him a smile. "Would you like a cup of coffee? Oh, I'm sorry, you're a tea-drinker, aren't you. I should make a pot of tea. Somebody else might want a cup."

"No thanks, Mrs. Charles. Maybe later." He turned and surveyed the main room of the barn. He saw a half dozen or so firemen gathered around a table eating breakfast, and Mr. Dodge was sitting with them and joining in on their conversation. Heaped across another table nearby were their heavy coats. Mr. Clark was at the fireplace adding more wood to the fire, and he and Timothy exchanged nods from across the room. Timothy could see Mrs. Charles had help in the kitchen, and he was not needed in the barn.

Timothy zippered up his jacket and returned outside where he joined Billy, Stanley, and Colin who were peering into the ruins of the house. "Hi, Stanley, Colin," he greeted.

"Looks like someone purposely set it on fire," Stanley remarked. "What did they think they were doing? I'd like to punch his lights out."

Billy commented, "Whoever they are should be made to pay even if it takes them the rest of their lives. That's only fair."

Colin added, "Even when insurance covers the cost of replacements, the persons who set fire to the old house should pay for their wrong. Insurance doesn't excuse anyone from the consequences of their actions." Timothy, Billy, and Stanley nodded in agreement as they stared into the charred mess of the old house.

"People donated good sports equipment and other stuff," Stanley remarked with disappointment. "We bought new legs last fall for that wobbly ping-pong table."

"And all those books in the library are lost," Timothy realized with a frown. "We can't just go out and buy the same ones again—not as simple as that. And that weather radio we bought last spring is gone, too."

Billy shook his head in frustration. "The rooms upstairs were used by some staff people. Where are they going to sleep now? It's not going to be easy to replace all that furniture—beds, dressers, and things. And the handcraft stuff is all gone, too."

Most of the bedroom floor above the living room was tipped sharply down and was resting on top of the floor beneath. The twisted metal frame of a bed poked through part of a wall which had collapsed into the house. "What a mess!" Colin said under his breath.

"Timothy, Billy," their dad called to them. "Ready to go? We need to get a move-along."

Twenty minutes later Timothy pulled into their yard and parked the car near the house. Before the three fellows reached the steps, the porch door swung opened. "Is the old house really gone and everything in it?" Jennifer asked, already knowing the answer. "How are the two large maple trees out front? Are they damaged any?"

Her dad did not reply. He entered the porch and passed through to the kitchen closely followed by his daughter.

"Mom and I have been thinking," Jennifer began as she glanced over at her mom at the sink, "and we have some ideas." She grinned confidently and waited nearly half a minute for her dad and brothers who were removing their boots to respond to her statement.

"Well?" her dad finally inquired as he pushed the bootlaces down into his footwear.

"Well, we think a sports storage building could be built more central to the playing field and the volleyball court. And a building a little larger than the size of one of the cabins could be built for handcrafts. It will need a sink and running water of course."

Mr. Jack nodded in acknowledgment, and Jennifer continued. "A staff meeting room could be built closer to the cabins so that the counselors would be handy to the campers."

Her dad nodded once more, but with a slight grin. Her brothers stared at her. "And," she said enthusiastically when she glanced around at her family, "on the site where the house is—or was, could be a welcome centre, an office where visitors register and other stuff like that. A second room behind could be used as a library."

Mr. Jack nodded his approval, and Timothy shrugged one shoulder. "Those are good ideas," Mr. Jack admitted. "I'll think about them and present them to the committee."

"Perhaps Grandpa Palmer could lend his expertise for the construction of the buildings," Jennifer added.

The next day being Sunday, there was much talk in small groups before, between, and after the two morning meetings, regarding the fire. Mr. Charles was concerned the conversations could be more detrimental than helpful, so he made arrangements to address the gathering that evening before the speaker gave the message.

"Friends, the Lord is in control," he began as he looked out over the people. "Saturday night about one-fifteen, my wife and I were awakened by a crackling and roaring sound and an orange glow coming through our bedroom window. Upon investigation, we discovered that the old house was on fire. I rang the fire department immediately. The building was nearly engulfed in flames before they arrived. There was nothing the firemen could do except contain the fire to prevent it from spreading to our little house."

Mr. Charles looked over the top of his glasses. "We're grateful to the Lord that the damage was not greater—the fire did not spread to other buildings. It's now certain the fire was deliberately set, but we have no idea who started the fire nor why. The sudden loss of the building was a surprise to us, but it didn't take the Lord by any surprise. All things are in His hands and under His control, and He permits circumstances for our good and ultimately for His glory." He removed his glasses and continued. "How this setback can be for our good and for His glory is beyond us at this time. All we can do is trust Him; He knows what's best. And when we do trust Him in all situations, He will give us peace, and He will cause us to see and know His glory in the situation. And that's what we can experience now at this time. The Lord can change tragedy into triumph."

He stroked his thinning hair and said to the people before him, "We must not be bitter nor revengeful because of the wrong we have suffered. Revenge springs from hatred in our hearts, and we aim it at those who have wronged or hurt us. We want to hurt them just as they have hurt us. I'm thankful the Lord didn't treat us in that way because of our offences towards Him. He was merciful and gracious towards us when we were still in sin and under His condemnation."

Mr. Charles paused and then began again. "This situation is in the Lord's hands. Let Him work it out for His glory. I feel sorry for the persons who are responsible for the loss of the old house—they don't know the Lord. To them, destroying property is entertainment or a diversion to block out their misery. These people will never know their need of the Lord and will not be attracted to Him if we don't show forgiveness to them. To forgive them is to not have ill-feelings towards them, but to have only goodwill."

Timothy bowed his head and listened as Mr. Charles said, "How can we do this? It's just not in us. But we're able to forgive those who have wronged us only through Christ who strengthens us. If we have been bitter or revengeful, we must confess it as sin. After we have done so, let's pray for those who have damaged our property—the Lord's property. Pray that they will see their need of Christ and put their trust in Him; and then wait and watch the Lord work out His purpose in this situation for His glory and for our good." Mr. Charles quickly surveyed the people and told them, "The Lord is in control; I believe He has plans for us. May the Lord bless you as you wait on Him. I'll sit down now—thanks for your attention."

As Mr. Charles took his seat, several people said, "Amen," and then there was about a half minute of silence before the speaker proceeded to the pulpit to deliver the evening message.

Later that week, what had remained of the old building was bulldozed into its cellar. Several loads of dirt were dumped in the cavity, and the site was leveled making it tidy as well as safe. After the snow had melted in the spring and the frost was out of the ground, nearly two hundred small spruce and pine trees were dug up from the edge of the woods. These saplings were transplanted to areas beside the driveway beginning at the public road along to where the welcome centre and library would be built close to the two large maple trees. This border of green trees would make Camp Bethlehem property a little more private. A winding dirt road was laid out through the spruce woods to the parking area behind the barn. This secluded roadway caused the main building, the barn, to be a retreat from the outside.

I love the smell of the earth, Timothy reflected one mild spring Saturday as he worked in the garden near the house. He pushed the spade into the damp, dark ground and lifted out a clump of rich soil and flipped it over.

"Timothy," his mother interrupted as she called from the porch of the house. "Phone. I think it's Stanley."

Timothy left the spade standing upright in the garden, and he walked over to the house. After removing his dirt-caked boots outside the door, he entered and dropped onto the chair by the phone. When he picked up the receiver, he recognized Stanley's humming.

"Hello," Timothy said to his friend.

"Hi. How are you?" Timothy heard as he leaned back and stretched out his legs.

Timothy waited several long seconds before answering. "I don't divulge personal information about myself to callers who don't identify themselves," he said accusingly, and then he snapped, "Who's speaking, please."

"Hey, it's me. How's it going? What are you up to?"

"Hi!" Timothy answered cheerfully. "Doing fine here. Working in the garden. What's up?"

"Found the weather radio," he heard Stanley announce.

"The Camp Beth weather radio?" Timothy demanded. "How's that, Stan? It was lost in the fire."

"Well, Tim, I just saw it at a yard sale here in William Station. When I removed the battery, I saw 'Beth' scratched inside. It's ours alright."

"Yeah, I scratched it there just after we bought the weather radio." He slid his sock-feet under the chair. "Did you say anything, Stan? Did you buy it?"

"No, I didn't say nothing. But some other people were looking around so I quickly bought it," he said. "Hey, Tim, the guy who sold me the weather radio could be the one who set fire to the old house."

"Hey, yeah, probably so," he had to agree. "Stan, where are you now?"

"I'm at the phone booth outside the drugstore just over from the yard sale."

"Stay handy to there," Timothy quickly advised him. "I'll call Mr. Charles and see what he wants to do." He stood up and stretched.

"Okay," Stanley answered him. "Let me give you the phone number here."

After Timothy finished talking with Stanley, he phoned Mr. Charles who said he would call the police and get back to him. About fifteen long minutes later Mr. Charles called Timothy back.

"Timothy, I talked to the police officer, and then I called Stanley," he told him. "He and I will meet the police officer outside the drugstore and return to the yard sale and confront the fellow who sold Stanley the weather radio." Before they hung up, Mr. Charles told Timothy, "Please pray that the Lord's will would be done and that we have the right attitude in our thinking and in what we say and do."

The next day being Sunday, Mr. Charles addressed the people gathered at the meeting place. "Brothers and sisters, the Lord is good," he reported to them as he glanced over the audience. "Yesterday before noon, a young man was taken into custody for the possession of stolen goods and attempting to sell them. This man also admitted to breaking and entering, and also to destroying the old house on Camp Beth property." Everybody in the room listened with interest. "Mr. Dodge and I, and several other men of the camp committee met last evening with the police officer who is handling this case. The young man in question was also present. We were told this fellow has a police record and has served time for about a year in a detention centre when he was a young teen."

He paused several long seconds before continuing. "The other men on the committee and I have decided to drop the charges against this young man." There were many surprised and startled looks, and Mr. Charles told them, "But only if certain conditions on his part are met. The police officer is cooperating and working with us on this as he is sympathetic to the work of Camp Bethlehem."

He hesitated once more as he scanned the group over the top of his glasses, and Timothy thought, *Mr. Charles is a master of suspense. What are the conditions? Tell us!*

Timothy watched as Mr. Charles slowly removed his glasses and placed them on the pulpit. "The conditions which this young man is to comply with are as follows," he finally began to reveal to the people seated before him. But he halted again, picked up his glasses, and dropped them into his front pocket. "He must work two hundred hours on Camp Beth property under the supervision of Mr. Dodge, between now and the end of June. Second, he must attend the family Bible hours each Lord's Day starting next Sunday until the end of June. And thirdly, he must accept the invitations from us for every Sunday noon meal in our homes." Mr. Charles looked out over the surprised people before him and grinned slyly. "This young man has agreed to these terms, and he has agreed that any violation of these conditions will result in him being charged with breaking and entering and theft, and the more serious charge of arson, resulting in him having a police record." Mr. Charles then looked seriously at the people and said, "We need to pray for this young man. His name is Jeff—Jeff Bell."

Timothy stared at Mr. Charles. *Jeff?* he wondered. *I knew a Jeff who was in a detention centre in his early teens.*

Mr. Charles reminded the people, "He needs the Lord. The Lord has brought Jeff to us so we would point him to the Lord."

Timothy was thinking, *I wrote to a guy named Jeff who was in a detention centre. He was about my age. I wasn't told his last name.*

Mr. Charles continued, "Be friendly with Jeff. Forgive him—don't have any hard feelings towards him. Pray for him, and put your prayers into action. Welcome him here at this meeting place, and welcome him into your homes Sunday noon. Perhaps Jeff will become a brother in the Lord. Let's pray right now for Jeff Bell, and let's pray for us, too, that we will react towards him as we ought to. The Lord is good," he reminded them again, and he returned to his seat.

After Mr. Charles sat down, one of the men stood up to lead in prayer. He was promptly followed by two additional men in turn. They asked that they as a group and as individuals would show the love of God to Jeff and they would have forgiveness towards him and that they would show kindness and goodwill as well.

The next morning, Timothy busied himself by looking over the building supplies recently deposited at the site of the new welcome centre. When he heard a vehicle coming along the camp driveway, he looked up to see Mr. Dodge's car approaching, and he could see an unfamiliar passenger in the front seat. *Now I'll get to meet the guy who set fire to the old house and caused us all this trouble,* Timothy concluded as he purposely stood tall and pushed his shoulders back.

Mr. Dodge parked near a stack of lumber and emerged from his car. "Morning," Mr. Dodge greeted pleasantly as he walked over to Timothy.

"Morning," he answered.

Timothy heard the car door close, and he turned to face the stranger. *So this is what an arsonist looks like. He doesn't look any different than some of the other punks I've seen around.*

"Jeff," Mr. Dodge said to the fellow who was now leaning back against his car with an unlit cigarette in his mouth and a match in his hand, "I'd like you to meet Timothy."

As Timothy walked towards Jeff, he tried to smile. "Hi," Timothy said when he extended his hand. Jeff lit his cigarette and then tightly folded his arms across his chest. Timothy decided, *I didn't want to shake hands with him anyway.* And then he wondered, *How am I supposed to not have bitter feelings for this jerk?*

Timothy then returned to where Mr. Dodge was standing. "Jeff," Mr. Dodge called to him, "bring that hammer from the floor of the backseat will you. Let's get started." Jeff brought the hammer and stood with disinterest several yards from Mr. Dodge and Timothy.

"Okay," Mr. Dodge said to his two workers, "Let's pray before we start." Timothy saw a look of shock come over Jeff's face which quickly turned to scorn. Mr. Dodge and Timothy bowed their heads, and Mr. Dodge asked for safety, wisdom, and skill as they worked. After Mr. Dodge finished praying, Timothy could see without looking directly that Jeff was blankly gazing off towards New Lake.

Two hours later the three men walked towards the barn for a lunch put together by Mrs. Charles.

"Did you receive mail," Timothy asked Jeff as they went along the roadway, "about eleven years ago, from a guy named Timothy Jack?"

Jeff did not answer right away, but when he did he snapped, "How am I supposed to remember who I got mail from eleven years ago!" He did not look directly at Timothy. "Besides, I didn't agree to disclose personal information about my past."

Timothy dropped the subject. *I won't mention it again,* he decided as he moved along. *If he's the Jeff I wrote to years ago, he'll bring it up.* He bounded up the steps and across the veranda to open the door for Mr. Dodge and Jeff.

To Mr. Dodge, Jeff seemed to enjoy the work more each passing day that week although Jeff tried not to show it. He did not allow himself to get close to Mr. Dodge and Timothy, nor to Mr. and Mrs. Charles, and he did not contribute to any conversation other than what was necessary in their work on the camp property.

The next Sunday morning just before the family Bible hour, Timothy saw Mr. Dodge come into the meeting place after returning from picking up Jeff. Jeff was not with him but Mr. Dodge did not seem to be concerned. As they stood to sing the first hymn, Timothy quickly turned to scan the back of the crowded room. *I don't see him,* Timothy said to himself, but when he looked at Mr. Dodge, the man grinned and nodded.

Timothy prayed for Jeff several times during the meeting, and after the last hymn was sung he went looking for him. He found him standing by Mr. Dodge's locked car at the far end of the parking area.

"Jeff," Timothy greeted pleasantly. "Nice day." Jeff puffed on his cigarette and stared at him suspiciously but said nothing. "I like the drizzle," Timothy informed him with his fake smile. "It makes everything look clean and bright."

"Clean and bright. Whatever," Jeff answered with a scowl. "I don't fit in with that clean and bright crowd." Timothy could see he was wearing denims and a patterned shirt.

When Jeff glanced at Mr. Dodge's car, Timothy asked him, "You going to the Dodge's for noon meal?"

"What's taking him so long!" Jeff sputtered impatiently as he looked back at the meeting place.

"Come on," Timothy suggested, "let's stand under the canopy over there out of the rain."

"I'll wait here." Jeff glanced again at the meeting place and blew out a stream of smoke. "Hurry up, Tom," he muttered. "Cut out the chit-chat and the quack and jabber."

"You'll like it at the Dodge's," Timothy told him. "Tommy has a large collection of walking sticks." Jeff looked over at Timothy in disbelief and then rolled his eyes. "Tommy finds sticks in the woods and turns them into works of art. Each walking stick is unique. He supplies walking sticks to stores all across the province and even to some stores farther away." Jeff rolled his eyes again.

* * *

Work was progressing nicely at the welcome centre and library building. "Having problems, guys?" Mr. Dodge asked as he came up to Timothy and Jeff who were searching through the grass between the tool shed and the new handcraft building.

"Yeah. We've lost the chuck key for the electric drill," Timothy informed him. "I must have dropped it after we left the tool shed. We'll never find it in all this tall grass and stuff." He stood with both hands on his hips as he glanced along the trampled grass and new dandelions. Jeff continued to stoop over as he combed through the vegetation.

"That chuck key will be hard to find," Mr. Dodge agreed. Timothy and Jeff paused and waited for him to decide what to do. "Let's pray about it," Mr. Dodge suggested, and Jeff looked over at him in astonishment. As Mr. Dodge began to pray aloud, Jeff shifted his feet uneasily, then he moved away and resumed his search through the grass. When Mr. Dodge was finished, he and Timothy hunted in the other direction from Jeff.

Less than a minute later, Jeff called out, "Here it is." He leaned over in the tall grass, took hold of the chuck key, and held it up. As he approached Timothy and Mr. Dodge, he tried to hide his surprise that it had been found, and also found so quickly. But he said nothing.

"Good," Mr. Dodge stated. He looked pleased but unimpressed at what had just taken place. "Now you fellows can get back to your building project." Just as he was about to leave, he saw Jeff staring at him in amazement with his mouth dropped open. Mr. Dodge grinned at Jeff who promptly turned away.

One afternoon, Timothy and Jeff were working in the spruce thicket. Timothy quickly glanced along the fifty metre length of the shallow trench which lay between the trees. With his foot, he drove the blade of his shovel into the long mound of earth and then dropped the clump onto the plastic pipe in the trench. He and Jeff did not speak as they worked, and Timothy grinned as he imagined the purpose of this buried pipe.

About ten minutes later, Jeff, without slowing his pace, said almost sneeringly, "You guys talk about getting saved and being saved. Saved from what?"

Timothy tossed another shovelful of earth onto the pipe before answering. "Being saved means being saved from the wrath or anger of God because of our sin. And the only way we can escape His wrath or be saved from it is to be righteous before Him or to be free from our sin." He tramped on the earth over the buried pipe to help it settle into the floor of the woods.

Jeff stopped and leaned on his shovel as Timothy said, "Jesus Christ the Son of God, the only sinless or righteous Man that ever lived, took our sin in our place when He died on the cross. This is how He is able to offer us salvation." Jeff said nothing, and he had a scowl on his face. Timothy then told him, "When we believe as fact that He died in our place, and we respond by trusting in Him, we receive His righteousness. Because we are now free from our sin, we are saved from His wrath."

"Yeah, well," Jeff replied, and then he said, "Fifteen minutes to break-time."

The building for staff meetings was to be known as the House of Prayer. It was here the Lord's will and guidance would be sought regarding things related to camp. The building was being constructed in an area where most of Camp Beth could be seen by those in the building, causing them to pray and plan more realistically. Also when people on the grounds saw the building, they were made aware that prayer and relying on the Lord was a big part of Camp Beth, and it resulted in them expecting great things from Him.

Every day following his walk on the grounds, Mr. Charles would join the work parties. "Good day," he greeted one morning as he came up to Timothy and Jeff who were nailing down the floor of the sports hut. "I'm thankful that the black flies don't eat me alive anymore than they do." He grinned at the young men. "I have a question for you, Timothy. What is greater than God and worse than Satan? And dead people eat it and if we eat it, we will die, too."

Timothy was perplexed. He looked at Mr. Charles blankly, and then he picked up another nail and positioned it on a floorboard ready to strike. "I—I don't know," he answered uneasily.

Mr. Charles grinned for several seconds. "Nothing!" he finally revealed to Timothy. "Nothing is greater than God. Nothing is worse than Satan. Dead people eat nothing, and if we eat nothing, we will die, too."

Timothy grinned and nodded. "Yeah, you're right, alright," he said with relief, and he drove the nail into the board with four heavy blows.

"Gentlemen, what can I do to help here?" Mr. Charles asked.

Mr. Jack drove his family home Sunday after the two meetings of the morning. As they turned off the road and onto their long driveway, Timothy thought he detected a slight look of interest on Jeff's face, and as they moved along the driveway, Jeff turned his head to study the barn.

Mr. Jack parked the car near the house, and everyone climbed out. As the others were heading for the house, Jeff hesitated by the car, and Timothy turned to face him. Their eyes met for several seconds until Jeff turned and walked towards the barn. Timothy said nothing, but he caught up to him, and the two young men walked along the path up to the barn and through the partly opened, large door of the hayloft.

They stood on the bare floor, and as their eyes adjusted to the dim light, Jeff looked around the interior of the nearly-empty loft. He peered into the corner where the little window was and stepped towards it. Timothy watched him and smiled. Jeff turned to face Timothy, and he returned the grin. Timothy suddenly realized, *This is the first time I've seen him smile.* He could see Jeff trying to imagine how the hay bale room had been.

Jeff peered into the darkened corner of the barn. He soon noticed the book fastened by several nails to the post near the window. "There's the book that belonged to your cousin, What's-His-Name." He stepped closer to it. "'Fun, Fun, Fun,'" Jeff read the title aloud. "'How to have Fun with Watermelon Seeds, Toothpicks, and Drinking-straws. And Much, Much, More.'" Jeff grinned and looked at Timothy. "Your cousin must be a real fun-guy."

"Well, he tries to be," Timothy answered as he gently thumped his thigh with his Bible. "But then he's matured somewhat since that summer he was here."

Jeff shuffled his feet. "He a Christian like you guys?" He looked up at the roof of the barn with a smirk on his face.

Timothy briefly shook his head. "No," he answered, and when he glanced at Jeff, he could see a look of satisfaction as well as smugness.

The two young men stood silently, and then a sharp whistle could be heard in the distance. Jeff grinned again, looked over at Timothy, and concluded, "That's the whistle for dinner."

"Yeah," Timothy agreed as he turned. "Let's go."

Later that afternoon after Jeff thanked Mrs. Jack for the dinner, he and Timothy left for William Station. As Timothy pulled onto the road, he realized that today Jeff had been more sociable than he had ever been before. And Timothy again remembered, *This is the first time I've seen him smile.*

They rode in silence for several minutes until Jeff spoke. "Your mom fixes a good meal." Timothy nodded in acknowledgement.

"I see your dad has a tattoo," Jeff remarked after a while. "I thought Christians didn't do stuff like get tattoos—Christians are so clean living."

Timothy did not detect any arrogance coming from Jeff. "Yeah, well, Dad got the tattoo years ago before he was saved - before he trusted in the Lord." Timothy could see out the corner of his eye that Jeff was mystified and he quickly explained. "Dad didn't come from a Christian family. He became a Bible-believing Christian when he was in his mid-twenties after he already had the tattoo."

Jeff shifted his feet. "Is being a Christian something you just decided one day to believe in whether it's for real or not? Like, it's your personal belief."

"Oh, no!" Timothy quickly answered as he kept his eyes on the road. "Being a Christian or being saved is real, it's not something we decided to believe in or to follow because it appealed to us, neither did we stay with the family religion only because we grew up with it. It's really real."

Jeff shifted his feet once more, and he stared out the front window. "Yeah, but how does anyone know all that stuff is really real?" Jeff suddenly turned to face Timothy, and he glared at him. "How can anyone be sure the Bible's true, like you say? There's so many different religions in the world. Even those people who say they believe the Bible don't agree with each other. How can the Bible be reliable truth if the Bible-believers can't agree to what it means? So, who's right?"

Timothy quickly glanced over at Jeff. "It's not a case of who's right, but what's right. The Bible is right—it's the truth. Those religious people just have to read the truth for themselves. Don't trust what anyone says—trust the Bible. Don't believe anyone or even any religion—just believe the Bible."

"Yeah, but how do you know the Bible is right?" Jeff demanded. "It's full of contradictions."

"Contradictions?" Timothy questioned as they traveled towards William Station. "Like what?"

"I don't know. I just heard that the Bible has lots of contradictions."

"Yeah, I heard there's lots of contradictions, too," Timothy admitted. "But when I've carefully, and even casually, looked at them, I can see that most of the contradictions are statements taken out of context."

Jeff asked, "How do you know the Bible is as accurate as you say it is?"

"The Bible was written by over forty different men over a period of fifteen-hundred years, and none of them disagree with any of the others. That's pretty amazing, don't you think?

And science has never been able to prove the Bible wrong even when the earliest writers lived away back about thirty-five hundred years before today's modern science. Also, history and archaeology have never proved the Bible wrong; in fact archaeology, independently carried out by non-Bible-believers, confirms what the Bible says. And here's something even more amazing—everything predicted in the Bible did in fact come to pass. All of them came to pass - some of them were prophesied hundreds of years before. The only ones that didn't are those which were prophesied for later than we presently are now in history."

"Yeah, that sounds impressive," Jeff mumbled as he put his elbow on the edge of the window and rested his head in his hand. "How do you know all that?" Timothy could tell it was not a question he was expected to answer.

Jeff leaned against the door and looked the other way, but several minutes later he said defiantly, "I'll be glad when my time with that religious bunch is up. I've had more than enough of you people. I have one more day of work, and then I'm through—that's it, I'm out of there." Timothy knew he should say no more, and the young men rode the remainder of the distance in silence.

Ten minutes later they drove into William Station, and Timothy brought the car to a stop in front of the house where Jeff was renting an apartment. Jeff released his seat belt and stepped onto the sidewalk, and Timothy called out to him, "See you tomorrow."

"Whatever," Jeff answered with a scowl, and he promptly closed the door and marched up to the house.

The next morning the sky was gray, and the weather forecast called for rain, heavy at times, during thundershowers. Timothy felt discouraged. He sat at the table as he waited for his mom to finish preparing breakfast. "This is Jeff's last day with us," he reminded himself and his mother. "Still no sign of him coming to the Lord. I feel like all the time and effort we put in has been for naught."

Mrs. Jack put the boxes of cereal on the table. "We've done all we can," she told him as she started the toast. "Just continue to pray for him, and don't neglect to pray for yourself." Timothy ate his breakfast in silence. Raindrops began to splatter the kitchen window and run down the panes of glass. His mother reminded him, "The Lord is more interested in our attitude or our response in any situation rather than in what we actually do or what takes place." As he left the house, the hired man's clock struck the half hour.

Mr. Dodge organized inside jobs for this wet morning. Timothy and Jeff worked at painting the inside walls of the welcome centre. Timothy did not have much to say, besides Jeff was in no mood to talk. It seemed to Timothy that Jeff checked his watch every few minutes.

"Five minutes to ten." Jeff spoke for the first time. He crossed to the paint can on the floor and laid his paintbrush across the lid next to it.

Timothy tried to sound pleasant. "Break-time," he answered. With his foot he carefully pushed the paint tray close to the wall, and he left the roller in the paint and its handle leaning against the wall. Although there was a temporary let up in the rainfall, Timothy walked briskly towards the barn. Jeff made no attempt to keep up to him, and Timothy thought it best to not slacken his pace.

At the barn, Mr. Dodge joined the young men for a lunch, and Mr. and Mrs. Charles also sat with them. Timothy felt the conversation around the table this morning was as dull as the weather outside, and the others seemed to speak only because that was the proper thing to do, not because they actually wanted to say anything.

When Jeff had finished his lunch of bannock bread with jam and coffee, he hunched over his empty mug and slowly rotated it, studying the last dark drop of coffee as it slowly circled the bottom, leaving a wet, pale brown trail. Several minutes later he suddenly pushed his mug aside, rose to his feet, and left for the outside without saying anything or waiting for Timothy. The four at the table stopped their talk and looked over at the door as it closed behind Jeff. From where Timothy was seated, he could see the fellow step off the veranda and into the drizzle and go out of sight along the path beyond one of the cabins.

Timothy glanced over at Mr. Dodge. "He's sure been miserable!" he said to the little group as he fingered the handle of his mug. "Hardly said a thing all morning."

Mrs. Charles answered, "The poor man is deeply distressed." She looked over towards the closed door of the barn.

"Jeff desperately needs the Lord," Mr. Charles reminded the group. "I think he knows he needs the Lord, but he's running from Him."

Mr. Dodge looked thoughtful. "Only when a person admits he's a sinner, and he gives up on himself and surrenders to the Lord will he experience His mercy and grace, and he'll have peace as well," he said with assurance and a knowing smile.

There was a long moment of silence, and then Timothy told the others, "I've been praying regularly for him."

"So have I," Mrs. Charles added. "I think we all have."

Mr. Charles suggested, "Let's pray again for Jeff right now." The group around the table in the barn bowed their heads. One by one each prayed for Jeff, and they prayed for themselves that they would be as they should with the Lord's help. And they prayed that the Lord's workings would be obvious to them at this time.

When they had finished speaking to the Lord, Timothy found he was smiling, and when he glanced around at the others, he could see they were grinning with him. "Well," he exclaimed, "finally I have some peace today about Jeff." He rolled his shoulders and then stretched his arms up high above his head and wiggled his fingers.

Mr. Dodge looked around at the group. "Let's sing something," he proposed to them.

"How about, 'Tis so Sweet to Trust in Jesus,'" Mr. Charles answered, and he smiled as he leaned back with his hands behind his head.

Several minutes later, Timothy dashed through the rain and up to the welcome centre. He laughed as he closed the door behind him and lifted his wet shirt off his shoulders.

"Sure is raining!" he told Jeff. "I should have left when you did." There was no answer. "Jeff?" Still no reply. Timothy then realized he was alone in the building, but he was puzzled concerning the whereabouts of Jeff and what was going on with him, yet at the same time he was at peace. The heavy rain could be heard as it beat down on the roof of the building, and Timothy sang as he returned to his work. He continued with the roller and then finished Jeff's job using the paintbrush.

A sudden flash of light made Timothy look towards the large window. It was followed by a faint rumble in the distance. "I hope you're under cover, Jeff," he said as he drew the paintbrush along the inside corner of the shelf. "Because, Boy," he snickered, "the rain's coming down something fierce. You're going to get drenched for sure."

There was another flash, but brighter this time. It was quickly followed by a crack of thunder. Timothy crossed over to the window carrying the paintbrush. He could see the sky over New Lake was dark gray and the surface of the water was being stirred up by the stiff wind. He noticed the trees around the property were showing their undersides as the branches were tossed about, and then Timothy observed the House of Prayer standing firm in the storm. *I'm glad we closed in that building last week,* he told himself.

Timothy glanced down at the paintbrush in his hand and then back through the heavy rain to the House of Prayer. He then stared intently at the window of the building and slowly leaned forward until his nose bumped the glass of the window where he was working. There was another flash of lightning in the distance followed by a rumble of thunder as Timothy continued to study the window of the House of Prayer. *There's someone in there,* he could tell. *Who would be there, and why is he looking this way and waving?* he wondered as he squinted through the pouring rain.

"It's Jeff!" he suddenly realized. "Strange!" He frowned and waved back, and then Timothy returned to his work. "You better stay there out of the rain, Jeff."

Over the next few minutes the thunder and lightning and the wind slowly abated, but the downpour increased. *The rain sure is loud on this here roof,* he stated to himself. Timothy decided to returned to the window to watch the weather. *It's almost too much rain for ducks—it's pouring buckets!* As he stood there with the paintbrush in his hand, he could see the torrent of rain drops bouncing off the surface of the lake. And when he looked towards the House of Prayer, he saw Jeff was no more in the window.

Suddenly, a figure could be seen coming from the building. *It's Jeff!* he determined, *What's he doing out in this heavy rain? Couldn't he wait until the rain let up a bit?* Timothy leaned forward until his nose again bumped the glass. *You're going to get wet, Boy—real wet.* He studied Jeff as he walked towards him at the welcome centre, and when Jeff was about halfway, Timothy dropped his paintbrush into the paint tray on the floor. He crossed to the door and yanked it open. As he stood in the entrance, he watched Jeff coming his way through the falling rain. He could see that Jeff was in no hurry, yet at the same time he seemed to be anxious to reach him.

"Tim," Jeff called out to him as he plodded through the rain-soaked grass and splashed along the flooded path. Timothy could only stare at him. He could see Jeff's shirt was soaked and sticking to his body, and his denims were thoroughly wet, but he could also see the guy was grinning. "Tim," he heard him say again, and he saw Jeff raise his hand in greeting. Timothy's mouth began to drop open as he came closer, and he stepped aside to let the drenched fellow enter the welcome centre. Jeff stood just inside the little building, and he continued to grin at Timothy. As he shifted his feet, the sloshing of his footwear could be heard.

There was a noticeable decrease in the sound of the rain on the roof as Jeff began to speak. "I want to tell you," he said as the water dripped from his cap onto the floor. "I prayed to God," he said hesitantly. "I told Him—I was a sinner—and needed to be saved—from His condemnation." He took a step farther into the room leaving a wet area on the floor. "I believe Jesus died for me—in my place—that's what the Bible says, and I now trust in what He did for me—and I accept His forgiveness."

Timothy grinned broadly at Jeff, and he reached out and placed his arm along his wet shoulder. And when he glanced beyond him and through the open door, he could see the sky was beginning to clear. In fact, there was a strong hint of sunlight in the southern sky over New Lake.

chapter twenty

two years later—June 1997

So Be It

Timothy, who was in his mid-twenties, leaned back in his chair, stretched out his feet under the seat in front of him, and stared down towards the floor of the barn between his dress shoes. He could hear the rustling movements of families and friends as they came in and sat down. Without looking up, he could sense that the spacious room of the barn was quickly filling with people. *Hope there's enough chairs for everyone,* Timothy thought over as he fingered the edge of his Bible. *Billy and I rounded up all the chairs we could find. Even borrowed a few from the meeting place.* He pushed back his left cuff. *Eighteen minutes to two,* and he let his cuff slide back over his watch. Timothy did feel sad, but he had peace. *We sorrow not, even as others which have no hope. We sorrow, but we don't despair. How good it is to know the Bible says to believers, 'absent from the body and to be present with the Lord.'*

Timothy lifted his eyes and looked through the array of heads and hats of the people in front of him. On the mantel of the fieldstone fireplace were several bouquets of flowers. When he leaned to the right, he could see on the small wooden table, the arrangement his sister Jennifer had put together that morning. He smiled as he considered her contribution. It was composed of deep blue lupines, pure white daisies, and a profusion of sunny-yellow buttercups all gathered from the Camp Bethlehem property.

Timothy recalled what Mrs. Charles had said when Jennifer brought the flowers to her. *"Oh, Jennifer, what a beautiful arrangement! Edmond would have loved it. He always appreciated what you did around the property here to cause so many wildflowers to grow. Thank you, Dear, for your thoughtful and lovely bouquet."*

When Timothy leaned in the other direction towards his brother Billy, he could see the open coffin which held the remains of Mr. Charles. He knew the well-worn Bible under the hands of the old gentleman was open to First John 1:9. *I have seldom seen that Bible closed,* he recalled, *and it's fitting now that it'll never be closed again.* Timothy could see a single pink rose lying on the chest of Mr. Charles.

When Timothy first viewed the body of Mr. Charles, he was pleasantly surprised as well as comforted to see his elderly friend and encourager even in death had a slight smile on his kindly old face. Timothy could feel a smile come over his own face now as he again thought of Mr. Charles.

Timothy was deep in thought, but he was now aware of music coming from the old piano on the far side of the large room in the barn. *I didn't know that old piano could sound so good,* he pondered as he shifted his feet, and then he remembered, *That must be the granddaughter of the Charles's. She was to play the piano before the funeral was to start. My, she plays beautifully!* He turned his ear in that direction. *I wonder when she'll find out that one of the notes doesn't play.* Timothy listened as she played, 'Blessed be the Name of the Lord.' He remembered, *That was one of Mr. Charles's favourite hymns. But then he would say, "Most of the hymns are my favourites—they're all good."* Mr. Charles couldn't read music, and he didn't sing well, but he knew the value of good Christian music and the influence it had on those who sang and those who listened. "The Lord created music," Mr. Charles would explain. "He designed it to be used to praise Him and to bring Him glory."

When the young lady started the chorus, Timothy turned his head to face her, and he leaned back slightly to see beyond Jennifer. The girl at the piano had her back to him. She was wearing a navy blue mantilla covering most of her long auburn hair. Timothy could feel his eyebrows give one quick, sudden twitch, and his chin involuntarily dropped a fraction of an inch. He slowly faced forward and stared at the back of the seat in front of him. He had a strange feeling in the pit of his stomach. Timothy figured she was a bit younger than him, but it was hard to tell without seeing her face. *I wonder if she's the girl the Lord has prepared for me. Lord, may Thy will be done. I don't know this young lady or even her name—she might be already spoken for or even married for all I know.*

The young lady at the piano began to play, 'Jesus Loves Me', another favourite of Mr. Charles. When she started the third verse with yet another variation, Timothy turned his head once more and leaned back. He stared at her for several seconds until Jennifer looked his way. He quickly faced forward and dropped his eyes to his Bible on his lap. *What's going on? I've never felt like this before.*

It was during the next piano selection that the missing note was evident. Timothy whispered, "Oops." He stared straight ahead and thought, *We'll have to get that fixed somehow.* The young lady played several more verses, but there was no sign of the missing note.

Timothy thought he could tell which verses were being played on the piano without hearing the words. *Not only is she playing the notes,* Timothy determined, *but she is making the piano sing the words.*

The young lady played several more selections on the piano, and just before two o'clock she stopped and turned to face the front. Mr. Green, one of the elders, stood and thanked everyone for coming and supporting Mrs. Charles and her family. After thanking the Lord for the love and concern Mr. Charles had had for the Lord's people and that he had put that care into action, he thanked the Lord for Christian fellowship at difficult times like this.

The people who were gathered in the barn stood to sing a hymn without the accompaniment of the piano. A grandson of Mr. Charles walked to the front to recite Psalm Twenty-three, followed by his older sister reciting First Corinthians Thirteen. As the next hymn was coming to an end, Timothy gave his mustache a quick stroke, and he moved to the front. He stood next to the coffin and faced those who had come, and then he waited for everyone to sit down.

"I personally met Mr. Charles and his wife when I was nine years old," Timothy informed them with a slight grin as he looked out over his audience. "My friend Mike and I biked to the valley a few miles over from where we live. We had heard that some strange things were going on in an old house there, and we wanted to check it out. An old man was seen going to the house nearly every day, but he never stayed overnight. As my buddy and I descended the hill into the valley on our bikes, we could see the house and a barn at the end of a long driveway in a large open area. The old man's pickup was parked between the house and the barn. How were we going to get up to the house to have a look?" Timothy paused and grinned.

"That's easy for two adventuresome nine year olds. We simply hid our bikes behind the alders in the ditch and snuck into the woods next to the field." Timothy could see his family and others grinning as well as Mrs. Charles, who he noticed was holding a single red rose.

"When Mike and I got as close to the house as we could and still be hidden in the woods, we scrutinized the house. Sure enough we could see the old man moving around inside doing something. What was he doing?" Timothy took on a look of inquisitiveness, and he quickly glanced over at the young lady at the piano. She was listening intently with a half smile and an expression of suspense on her face.

"After sneaking into the barn so we could get a closer look at the house without being detected, we could see the old man come out from the porch and climb into his truck and drive off. We then came out of the barn and looked in the windows of the house." Timothy stopped and then addressed several children who were sitting nearby with their parents.

"What we did was wrong," he explained to them. "It's wrong to go into buildings which belong to other people; and it's wrong to do anything we don't want anyone else to know about. We mustn't forget that God knows what we do even if no one else does. And when we do something a little bit wrong the first time, we probably will do even more wrong like my buddy and I did next. We went into the house through the porch and into the kitchen. We knew what we were doing was not right, but we had come this far and didn't want to stop now. That's the way it is with sin."

Timothy could see all the chairs in the barn were occupied, and some people were standing along the far wall. *It's a good thing we didn't have the funeral at the meeting place,* Timothy noted. *There'd be a lot more people standing, and some outside, too, no doubt.*

Timothy continued, "Mike and I opened the door, and we went into the other part of the house. We couldn't believe our eyes. The old man had a boat in there—a real boat—about the size of the fishing boats we see at Rogers Cove and around Bunchberry Island. The ceiling of the house and second floor above had been removed as well as most of the wall partitions. It was one very big room. We spent several minutes looking around, but then suddenly we heard a vehicle approaching." Timothy looked over at Mike who was grinning and knew what was coming next.

"We panicked," Timothy exclaimed. "We ran and then hid behind some boxes. Soon we could hear the old man and a lady in the kitchen. We were trapped—what were we going to do? I thought we should just tell them we were Christians and didn't mean any harm. But I knew that wouldn't go over very well. Christians don't go into other people's houses without being invited. Besides, I wasn't a believer, and I knew it." Timothy looked at Mrs. Charles in the front row. She was smiling at him and nodding.

"Several minutes later, because of the dust and wood-shavings we were lying in, Mike sneezed." Timothy heard several people giggle. He looked over and saw the young lady at the piano was amused as well.

Timothy grinned and continued. "We didn't have long to wait before we heard the old man come into the large room where we were hiding. He hollered out, 'Hello!' We were in for it now! We couldn't run for it, and it was useless to try to stay hidden." Timothy heard chuckling throughout the room. He was beginning to wonder if this humour was out of place at a time like this, but he could see Mrs. Charles and her family were enjoying his story.

"Mike and I slowly stood up." Timothy looked out over the people. "I started to explain to the old man that we didn't mean any harm. I looked over at him and saw a frown on his face, but I couldn't help noticing the lady with him—she was smiling at us, and I was immediately drawn to her." Timothy turned to face Mrs. Charles. "She's been smiling at us ever since, and we're still drawn to her."

Timothy addressed the crowd. "Mrs. Charles then told her husband that we were sons of people from the meeting place. We told him we knew it was wrong to come into his house, and we were sorry." Timothy paused and then interjected, "I must say at this time that the Lord sometimes takes the wrong we have done and turns it into good and causes it to be for His glory."

Timothy then continued his story. "The frown the old man had on his face quickly disappeared, and from this close distance, he didn't look so old, and he turned out to be very friendly after all. He was a real gentleman even to us boys; and Mr. Charles has proven through the years that he was a godly gentleman and a real friend. He shook our hands and then showed us the boat he was working on. Mike and I knew we had been forgiven."

Timothy took on a look of relief, and then he continued. "Mrs. Charles invited us to eat with them as it was nearly noon. As we sat at the table in the kitchen, Mr. and Mrs. Charles talked to us about two Bible verses: 'The wages of sin is death but the gift of God is eternal life through Jesus Christ our Lord,' and 'For God so loved the world that He gave His only begotten Son that whosoever believeth in Him should not perish but have everlasting life.' Our new friends didn't condemn us nor pressure us. They just explained the good news of salvation. Later that afternoon, Mike and I took off on our bikes for home. We had a new perspective for this gentleman now that we knew him. He wasn't a mysterious old man after all." Timothy turned and looked down at the lifeless body in the coffin.

"After I left Mike at his driveway," Timothy told the people assembled before him, "I biked towards home and thought about what Mr. and Mrs. Charles had said to us—to me. I knew I was a sinner and that the wages of sin is death. I knew I couldn't do anything to make myself right before God, and I knew the Lord Jesus took my place—took my sins upon Himself, the Just for the unjust - me, and that He received the wages of my sin and died in my place for me. I knew the gift of God is eternal life through Jesus Christ our Lord, and for me to have the gift, I had to receive it. Right then and there as I biked, I responded. I told the Lord that I was receiving His gift, and I thanked Him for it. Suddenly I realized what had happened - I had put my trust in Christ. I shouted out, 'I'm saved, I'm saved!' And I remember the startled cows in the field lifting their heads and eyeing me as I pedaled by." Timothy paused and turned to face Mrs. Charles who was smiling broadly.

"I thank the Lord for people like Mr. and Mrs. Charles who took an interest in young guys like Mike and me. And I thank the Lord for the Charles's who continued to encourage me in the things of the Lord through the Word of God." Timothy smiled and nodded at Mrs. Charles. "Thank you, Mrs. Charles, for the evidence of your love for the Lord and thank you for your encouragement to us." Timothy crossed over to her and touched her hand, and then he returned to sit with his family.

Mr. Green stood and thanked Timothy for sharing one of his experiences and some of his thoughts of Mr. Charles, and then he led the people gathered in the barn in another hymn.

As the people were sitting down, Mr. Dodge walked up to the front and stood next to the coffin. "It has been my privilege to know Mr. Charles and his wife since I was first associated with Camp Bethlehem twelve years ago," he began as he placed his right hand on the coffin. "Brother Edmond J. Charles has been gone from us about three days now. We'll never see him again in this life. If he could send a message back to us, what would he say?"

Mr. Dodge briefly scanned Mrs. Charles's family. "He would first say to his family and loved ones, 'Don't weep for me—I'm having a great time here. I'm with the Lord whom I've loved and served for more than half a century.' Mrs. Charles told me that several times in his last days that her husband had said, 'I was glad when they said unto me, Let us go into the house of the Lord.' Mr. Charles has been known to say more than once that he'd like our first response to the news of his death to be, 'He's finally where he's always looked forward to being—at home with the Lord, face to face in His presence.'"

Mr. Dodge took one step forward, and with a smile on his face he continued. "Mr. Charles would then have something to say to the Lord's people. 'Don't be discouraged, Believer—it's well worth it here. Keep living for the Lord even when it's hard going—and even when it means suffering for Him.' He would say, 'Our light affliction which is but for a moment, worketh for us a far more exceeding and eternal weight of glory.' Mr. Charles often said if he had a thousand lives to live, he would live them all for the Lord."

Mr. Dodge moved in front of the coffin and looked out over the people. "Mr. Charles then would have something to say to those who are not born again," Mr. Dodge told them. "He would say, 'admit you are a sinner, and then believe on the Lord Jesus Christ, and thou shalt be saved.' He would tell you, 'You can receive the righteousness of the Lord Jesus and stand uncondemned before God. You can experience the broken power of canceled sin in your life. And you can have the leading of the Holy Spirit of God through His Word in every area of your life.' Mr. Charles reminded us just two Sundays ago that the Lord Jesus gave His life that we might have life—life abundant, both now and for eternity." Mr. Dodge smiled and added, "And that's the gospel, the good news."

After the family and friends of the Charles's stood to sing another hymn, the coffin was closed and carried out to the waiting hearse. The hearse slowly traveled along the dirt road and through the thick spruce woods on the Camp Bethlehem property. It would take nearly an hour to drive to the cemetery several kilometres the other side of William Station.

After the Jack family was well on their way in their car, Timothy related what Mr. Charles had told him several months previously. "He and his wife went into a store to buy some things for Camp Beth," he reported to his family, "and there was loud, jarring music coming over the intercom. The manager happened to be standing there so Mr. Charles told him what he wanted to buy—came to several hundred dollars easily—and the manager said he would be happy to help them make their selections. Mr. Charles then told the guy he wasn't going to buy anything as long as the music was on. The manager quickly left and turned it off and then led them to where the stuff was they wanted. So, ten or fifteen minutes later when they had made all their selections, the manager pushed the shopping cart for them up to the cashier and said, 'Have a good day,' and then he disappeared."

Timothy began to grin. "Just as the cashier smiled at them and said, 'Hello there. How are you today? Did you find everything you wanted?' the obnoxious music came back on. So Mr. Charles just pointed to the ceiling where the music was coming from." Timothy laughed and told his family, "And then he and his wife left the things in the shopping cart and walked out."

Timothy's family laughed with him, and Jennifer added, "Yeah, that sounds just like something he'd do."

Mr. Jack slowly drove along the narrow roadway inside the perimeter of the cemetery. The tall grasses and daises brushing the underside of the car could be heard as they passed over them. There were several vehicles between the Jack family and the hearse, and there were many cars behind.

"There's the burial site over there," Mrs. Jack noted as the hearse turned off the main dirt roadway within the grounds and stopped close to the large mound of earth covered with green carpet. Mr. Jack pulled over and parked in the shade of a large oak tree next to the woods.

Jennifer stepped from the car. "This is a beautiful cemetery," she said as she put her hat on. "There are pine trees and spruce trees as well as maple, birch, and some oak over there, too."

Billy came around from the other side of the car. "Nice day if it don't rain," he decided. He and Timothy walked over to the hearse and waited for the rear door to be opened. When the other pallbearers arrived, the coffin was drawn out and carried to the burial site. It had been the wish of Mr. Charles that the coffin lid be left open during this service, allowing the sun or the rain to fall on his cold, still face.

Timothy and Billy returned to their family who was quietly standing nearby. The group of friends was gradually and silently becoming larger as others arrived and joined the assembly. A dozen plastic chairs were placed several metres from the coffin for Mrs. Charles and her family and any people who wished to sit. Mr. Knott waited next to the coffin as Mrs. Charles and her family sat down. Sitting next to Mrs. Charles was the young lady who had played the piano and immediately behind them stood her parents and family. Stanley Clark placed his large tape-player near the hearse and then he stood with his family. Several minutes later, all the friends were present in a large group surrounding Mrs. Charles.

Timothy waited with his head bowed, and his hands clasped behind his back. He heard a muffled gasp, and he quickly looked up, and then he heard several louder gasps. "Skunk!" a lady exclaimed from behind the row of plastic chairs. "A skunk!" The animal had just crawled out from a fold of the green carpet covering the mound of earth. It blinked sleepily in the bright sunlight and looked bewildered as it sniffed the air.

"Skunk! Skunk!" several people repeated in loud voices. "Move! Get out of here!" Two or three parents grabbed their children and hurried them to their cars nearby. Timothy could hear someone praying aloud, and he silently prayed as well. The skunk raised its tail as it passed between the coffin and the people who remained trapped and seated on the chairs. They appeared to be frozen in place.

"Just keep quiet," Jennifer calmly called out above the commotion, "and don't move suddenly or quickly." Some people crouched behind nearby tombstones. The ladies tightly clutched their purses and hats, and others moved back cautiously followed by the sound of the thumping of running feet. "Don't make any noise," Jennifer called out again as she slowly walked forward in her dark blue skirt towards the skunk, "and don't move quickly. Just slowly step aside if he comes your way, and let him pass by."

The skunk hesitated, not knowing which way to go, his tail waved slightly, and then the skunk moved towards the ever-widening gap in the crowd. "That's right, people," Jennifer instructed. "Don't make any sudden moves or make any racket." She followed the skunk, keeping back several metres as it slowly made its way through the crowd and beyond. "That's good, Sweetie," she gently told the skunk, "just keep going." She giggled nervously, but then the skunk began to waddle towards the stand of thick spruce trees fifty metres away. When it reached the edge of the woods, it stopped, turned to face the crowd, and sniffed the air once more.

Mrs. Charles stood up beside her plastic chair watching the skunk. "That's good, Sweetie, just keep moving," she called after the skunk. She then turned to the young lady beside her and said, "Your grandpa would have loved this; it sure was exciting!"

The skunk pushed its way through the ferns and into the thick undergrowth of the woods. "Hooray!" a chorus went up.

Mrs. Charles laughed and sat down. "Thanks, Jennifer, you did an excellent job, Dear."

People began to return from the vehicles parked along the roadway. Others brushed off their knees as they came from their crouched positions next to the tombstones, and several ladies straightened their hats or put their mantillas back on. Mr. Knott came around from the far side of the coffin and stood at attention, looking relieved and with a slight grin on his face. Some people were talking excitedly with others, and some were chuckling or giggling and glancing over to where the skunk had retreated into the woods.

A minute later when it was somewhat quiet, Mr. Knott raised his hand and said to the group, "We thank the Lord for those who prayed, and we are grateful to Him for Jennifer Jack who used her God-given knowledge and skill as well as her leadership abilities for the good of the Lord's people here this afternoon." Timothy glanced over at Jennifer. She looked startled at this public acknowledgment, but then grinned shyly at those who were looking her way.

After the hymn, 'When We All Get to Heaven', was sung, Mr. Knott shared two thoughts regarding Mr. Charles. "As you know," he began, "our brother loved to talk about the Lord and the things of the Lord. No doubt he had talked to each of you folks here over the years—adults, young people and children, too."

Mr. Knott took several steps to the side and rotated a bit. "Mr. Charles made spiritual things interesting as well as relevant, and he made the Word of God alive. He could talk on and on, and hold our attention." Several listeners smiled and nodded. "And Mr. Charles had the ability to listen as well - he was interested in what others had to say. And Mr. Charles was a true shepherd or pastor in the Biblical way in that he counseled people in their personal circumstances."

Mr. Knott looked out over the crowd of people and continued with his second thought. "Mr. Charles was a praying man. He prayed as though he was talking to the Lord not just repeating words or saying words into the air or for the benefit of other people. But isn't that what prayer is - actually talking to the Lord?" The people standing and others sitting, listened knowingly.

Mr. Knott continued, "Mr. Charles never insisted that archaic words be used when addressing the Lord. In fact he used archaic expressions only when they didn't interfere with the smooth flow of his thoughts. Since he'd find it difficult to talk to his friends or even his wife using archaic language, how could he talk to the Lord in a meaningful way using those formal words? When he spoke with others about the use of archaic words, he'd say that when he got to Heaven and talked to the

Lord Jesus face to face, he wouldn't be using archaic expressions at that time either."

When Mr. Knott had finished speaking about Mr. Charles, he prayed for Mrs. Charles and her family members. He then made this announcement: "We are about to commit the body of this man to the ground, the body of Edmond James Charles, husband, father, grandfather, great-grandfather, friend, brother in the Lord and encourager to many. At his request, the 'Amen' chorus of 'Handel's Messiah' will be broadcast during the internment." Stanley stepped forward to the tape-player on the ground next to the hearse. After pressing the 'play' button, he returned to his family. Those seated at the chairs stood up.

The recorded music began with a chorus of amens, introduced with dignity by the deep voices of men accompanied by cellos. Other men's voices then added their amens with overlapping melodies. Soon the distinct sounds of the ladies blended in with the men, and together they repeatedly exclaimed, "Amen!" Timothy could see family and friends of Mrs. Charles standing at attention and being drawn to the majesty of this joyful proclamation.

Mrs. Charles with her two children stepped up to the open coffin, and they stood with their heads bowed. As loud amens blanketed the group and spread out over the cemetery and into the woods nearby, Mrs. Charles reached out and picked up the pink rose from the chest of the body of her husband and replaced it with the red rose she had been holding. She returned to her large, extended family and stood holding the pink rose close to herself with both hands as the lid of the coffin was closed for the last time.

Presently violins only were heard. First one tune and then two tunes intertwined. The voices of men and the voices of ladies returned, and with blended melodies they sounded forth many more joyful amens, and the coffin was slowly lowered into the ground. Timothy could sense people all around enveloped by the triumphant music. They stood motionless around Mrs. Charles as the sound of the different voices of the singers was punctuated by the brass instruments.

The chorus of amens accompanied with drums began to slowly descend, and then suddenly for an intense second there was a dynamic silence which penetrated the listeners. Some in the crowd held their breath as they waited motionlessly. The final amens then rang out with the blast of drums and brass instruments, and then the chorus of amens quickly and finally faded away. A great, thoughtful hush flooded over the group of people assembled there, and then from the far end of the cemetery could be heard the song of a robin.

After a short pause, Mrs. Charles and her family moved into the throng where they exchanged greetings with friends who had come to give them support. There were handshakes and hugs and kisses, and there were smiles as well as tears.

Five minutes later Stanley retrieved his tape-player. And before long the Jack family left with several others to set up for a lunch in the barn and to give opportunity for the Lord's people to have fellowship with others.

Some of the chairs in the barn were quickly placed along the outside walls of the large room, and others were spread out in groups. Chairs were also set up outside on the veranda. Three or four tables were placed end to end down the centre of the room, and finger foods which had been left in the kitchen earlier were put on the long table, buffet style.

Before all the food could be laid out on the table, people began to arrive. Soon long lines were forming and moving down both sides of the table. Mr. Jack rang a small bell before giving thanks, and then people returned to serving themselves and to visiting with friends and old acquaintances.

When Timothy could see there was nothing more he needed to do, he decided to wait until the food line was shorter before he joined it. Mrs. Charles and the granddaughter, who played the piano before the funeral, had not yet arrived, but Timothy could see one of the brothers of the granddaughter. The young fellow was making his way along the line at the buffet table and was nearly at the end where the punch was situated. *Maybe I can get some pertinent information from him,* Timothy reasoned hopefully. He casually positioned himself so the fellow had to pass by near him. Before long he came towards Timothy with his plate loaded with sandwiches, cheese, and a bunch of grapes. His tie was loosened around his neck, and his top shirt button was undone.

"Hi," Timothy greeted with a grin as the youth came closer to him.

Without stopping, the young man slurped on his full glass of punch, glanced at Timothy, and gave him a quick, "Hi."

"You must be one of the grandsons," Timothy stated pleasantly.

The young fellow was now an arm's length away. "Yeah," was his brief answer as he attempted to squeeze by Timothy.

Timothy leaned back to let him pass. "You been in these parts before?" he promptly put in.

The fellow paused for a fleeting second and looked sideways over at Timothy. "Nope." And he took another swallow of punch before moving on.

Timothy turned towards him. "Who's that girl who was with you?"

"My sister," the young fellow replied over his shoulder without stopping."

"Yeah, but what's her name?" Timothy questioned as he took a step towards the retreating fellow who reacted as though he had not heard him. Timothy could see him pull in his elbows to maneuver through the crowd. *A wealth of information he is!* Timothy figured as he watched him back through the door and join other young people on the veranda. *But this one thing I know,* Timothy concluded, *although the guy doesn't talk in sentences, he is able, on occasion, to say two words in quick succession.*

Timothy then joined one of the lines to the buffet table. Less than a minute later he heard behind him, "How old was Mr.

Charles when he passed away?" Without turning, he knew it was Mrs. Copton.

"He was eighty-two last month," Timothy heard his mom answer, and he took a step forward towards the table as the line advanced.

"He didn't seem that old," Mrs. Copton replied. "I thought he was younger than that."

Mrs. Jack said, "Well, he was very active physically. Nothing slowed him down until this past winter."

Timothy turned to face the two ladies and informed them, "Mr. Charles would take walks on the camp property here nearly everyday." He took another step in the line, and the two ladies followed.

"I have seen in the past that Mr. Charles was mentally active as well," Mrs. Copton stated. "He would read a lot—he proofread many of the new books in the camp library."

Timothy turned again. "That's right. He kept abreast of things which were going on in the community and across the country and around the world, too," he said, looking from one lady to the other. "And often on Sundays he would give a talk with a practical as well as spiritual application based on something he had read or heard about during the previous week. Mr. Charles would warn us of any hidden dangers related to what's currently going on in our lives."

Timothy reached the table and picked up a plate from the stack. "He was also active spiritually," he told his mom and Mrs. Copton. "He read his Bible throughout the day, and he meditated on God's Word and studied it thoroughly." Timothy placed a salmon sandwich and an egg sandwich on his plate and related, "He prayed a lot, too. He would pray while he was working or walking." Timothy put a piece of cheese into his mouth and two on his plate.

"When his wife found him," Mrs. Jack said, "he was sitting in his favourite chair with his Bible on his lap. He had been reading or praying when the Lord called him home."

Timothy slowly moved along the buffet table. "Mr. Charles was a pastor or shepherd," he reported to the ladies. "He often asked me what the Lord had shown me recently in His Word. That caused me to be positive in my reading and to be focused in what I was studying, and as a result I gained a lot more from God's Word." Timothy could see his mom was pleased. He added, "Mr. Charles asked me once: if the Lord revealed a truth to me in His Word, would I accept it, practice it, and share it with others even when that truth was contrary to the beliefs of my family and friends. Now that's a good question!"

Mrs. Copton picked up a half banana and several segments of tangerine, and then she reached for a blueberry muffin.

Timothy checked over the desserts and added, "Mr. Charles sometimes referred to people ten or even fifteen years younger than himself as 'old'." Timothy chuckled. "And then he'd say he hoped he'd never be as old as they are."

George looked over at him from across the table. "Try one of them squares, Timothy," he grinned. "Elizabeth made them. They're some good!" And then George added, "Mr. Charles requested some time ago that we serve them today."

"Okay, thanks," Timothy replied as he made room for a chocolate square on his plate.

Timothy could see Mrs. Charles and her granddaughter had just come in. The older lady was wearing the pink rose, and he could see her granddaughter's long auburn hair now hung loosely down her back. *I don't want to rush anything or interfere,* Timothy determined. *I'll let the Lord lead.*

Timothy wove his way through the crowd and over to the fieldstone fireplace where Chord was standing alone. "Hi, Chord," he greeted.

Chord, who was in his late teens nodded and placed his glass of punch on the concrete mantel behind him. "Nice funeral," he stated. "I like the way us Christians have funerals."

Timothy grinned as he set down his punch near a bouquet of flowers on a small table nearby. He took a bite of his salmon sandwich and glanced back over the crowd of people.

"Tim," Chord asked hesitantly, "have you ever doubted your salvation?" The young man shifted his feet uncomfortably.

"I have a few times," Timothy admitted as he picked up his glass of punch, "back before I understood what salvation was really all about."

Chord informed him, "Sometimes I go through times when I'm not sure whether I'm saved or not." He put a piece of cheese into his mouth. "I invited Jesus into my heart the winter following my first summer here at Camp Beth, the summer when I was in your cabin. That winter some guy at the church near where we lived led me to the Lord in the Sunday school there. But sometimes I don't feel saved, and I even get depressed over it." He shrugged his shoulders. "I want to be saved; I want to go to Heaven. But did I really get saved back then?"

"Lots of people doubt their salvation at some time or another." Timothy paused to sip on his punch. "But there's no need of doubting. You say you want to be saved. Your concern shows you are sincere. I think you recognize Christ as your Saviour but the question is, Chord," he faced him squarely as he spoke, "are you trusting Him as your Saviour?"

"Well, yes," Chord replied impatiently, "of course I'm trusting Christ as my Saviour. I just don't know when I got saved. Doesn't there have to be a definite time that I'm well aware of when I got saved?" He frowned at Timothy who was now reaching for his egg sandwich. "I don't think I got saved back then in the Sunday school when I asked Jesus into my heart. I didn't understand back then that I needed to be saved because of my sin. And I haven't gotten saved since." He paused and then added, "But now I think of Jesus as my Saviour from the penalty of my sin. But, Tim, am I really saved? And when did I get saved? Do I have to go through that process all over again to get saved?"

"To be saved," Timothy reminded him, "means we're saved from the wrath and condemnation of God because of our sin. But He loved us so much He gave us His Son to be our Saviour from our sin. We received salvation at the time we first began to believe or trust in Him. That's what God's Word tells us."

"Yeah, I know all that," Chord told him abruptly.

Timothy started to grin, and he slurped on his punch before continuing. "Trusting in an experience doesn't assure us our salvation, but trusting in Christ alone gives us salvation. Salvation does not depend on an emotional experience we can remember and can tell a convincing story about. Therefore, when and where or how we got saved is not the actual proof of our salvation." Chord's frown was now gone as he carefully listened to Timothy. "If right now we believe and are trusting in Christ as our Saviour, that alone is the proof of our salvation." He then plopped a whole slice of cheese in his mouth.

"Well," the young man replied as he thought it through, "I know Jesus bore my sin when He died for me, and I can say that I'm trusting Him right now as my Saviour. So," he concluded thoughtfully, "that means I'm saved." He grinned at Timothy. "Without any doubt I'm saved; how could I not be saved! I'll never doubt my salvation again."

Timothy nodded and reached over and gave Chord's shoulder a squeeze. "And another thing," Timothy added, "since believers are saved from the wrath and condemnation of God, they are righteous before Him, and that makes us worthy to have and know Him as our Heavenly Father, and we are worthy to be His children. And because we are now worthy and are His children, we have the privilege and indeed the right to come into His presence at any time. That's what God's Word tells us."

Chord looked surprised and then thoughtful, and then a grin spread across his face. "Well sure," he had to admit, "that's right."

"Brother," Timothy addressed the pleased young fellow, and then he raised his glass and drained the last of his punch.

An hour and a half later, Timothy was alone in the large, now silent, room of the barn. He sat on a wooden chair and stretched out his feet ahead of him. He could hear coming from the kitchen, the muffled voices of those who were cleaning up there.

Although Timothy could barely hear Jennifer, he could tell she was relating the story of their neighbours whose dog had met up with a skunk. The husband who had lost his sense of smell, let the dog into the house, and several hours later his wife came home. When she opened the door, she was met with the very strong odor of the skunk, and she soon found that the scent was now all through the house. Even when they left all the windows open overnight, the smell lingered for several days. Timothy grinned as the sound of much laughter came from the kitchen.

Timothy noticed out the window that Billy was returning the small table to the House of Prayer. *I miss Mr. Charles already,* Timothy pondered as he took a deep, full breath and quickly let it out. *It won't be the same either here or at the meeting place. But we must not rely heavily on others. The Lord knows what's best for us. So be it.*

Timothy glanced at the fireplace, and his eyes followed up over the mantel to the large, colourful painting of a sunny field. *It's going to be a busy summer here at Camp Beth,* he figured as he thought ahead. *Things going on continuously throughout July and August. I'm thankful to the Lord that He's going to use me here to serve His people for their good and for His glory. So be it.* He bowed his head and stared down at the floor between his heels.

When Timothy looked up, his eyes fell on the piano against the far wall. *We need to get that note fixed. Equipment in poor condition detracts from glory which belongs to the Lord.* He smiled as he thought of the granddaughter of Mrs. Charles. *She plays the piano well,* Timothy reasoned, *and that helps the Lord's people to praise Him. Her abilities could be used for the Lord's glory here at camp.* And then he wondered, *How should I be praying regarding her? What's the Lord's will? So be it.*

Timothy touched his mustache and then folded his arms over his chest. *What are the Lord's plans for me beyond this summer? I know the Lord's immediate will for me, but I must keep in constant touch with Him. When I pray, I need to acknowledge my dependency on Him and seek His will for me. Through prayer, I will know the mind of the Lord as well as His way and will, and that will cause me to pray more effectively and to truly pray in His Name. I want to be a tool to be used so others will be attracted to Him. So be it.*

"Ready to go, Timothy?" his dad interrupted his thinking as he stood in the doorway.

Timothy nodded and stood up. As he crossed the room, he prayed, *For Thy glory, Lord. So be it.*

chapter twenty-one

two months later—August 1997

Family Camp

Timothy Jack lowered his nearly empty tea mug to the table, smoothed back his mustache with his fingers, and stood up. "Ladies and Gentlemen and Young People," he called out as he held one hand high above his head, "could I have your attention, please."

Timothy, who was in his mid-twenties, stood tall and straight as he scanned the group of families seated at the breakfast tables. When the din in the barn died down, he began. "I would like to give you the announcements regarding the activities for the day."

Timothy and his sister Jennifer had been campers that first summer eleven years ago when Camp Bethlehem had come into existence. The following summers Timothy was first a junior counselor, then senior counselor at children's camps, and now this summer was his first experience at running family camp for the month of August. The purpose of family camp was to have meetings which would glorify the Lord and encourage His people to grow spiritually. There was opportunity to fellowship with others of like-precious faith, and family camp provided activities suitable for families to participate in together and with other Bible-believing Christians.

Timothy was enjoying his responsibilities, and he was thankful for each of the others who were working with him. Jennifer was in charge of the nature walks, and she helped in the kitchen. Stanley led the singing, and he also organized sports activities. Kathleen, the granddaughter of Mrs. Charles, played the piano, and she worked in the kitchen as well. Timothy's younger brother, seventeen-year-old Billy, helped out where needed. And then there were Mrs. Charles and the ladies in the kitchen.

"The ministry meeting this morning," Timothy spoke to the group, "will be in about three-quarters of an hour here in the barn." He glanced down at his notes. "Right after that, Jennifer will conduct a nature walk. For those who would like to come along, meet out by the flagpole."

Timothy could not help but notice the blonde-haired boy sitting with his parents who had arrived the evening before. He was slouched down in his chair, and he had a scowl on his face which was clearly visible beneath the visor of his red cap. He was obviously demonstrating his displeasure in what was going on. Timothy could see the boy's parents were uncomfortable with the situation, but they were trying to show an interest in the activities at family camp.

Timothy shoved one hand into his back pocket and continued. "There are three dories which can be used for rowing, and we have about a dozen life jackets of various sizes." Timothy pulled his hand from his pocket and pointed in the direction of the volleyball court. "Stanley will organize a volleyball game, and see him for other sports equipment." Timothy was glad the fieldstone fireplace close to his back was not in use at this time. Over the mantel was his grandfather's large painting of a gently rolling field blanketed in colourful wildflowers and bathed in warm sunlight.

"Dinner will be served at noon. The ladies in the kitchen tell me they need to know how many people will be here. I think they need to know how much water to add to the soup, so please let them know your plans as soon as possible this morning. They'll probably ask you to show identification and sign your name to a piece of paper." Timothy could hear Kathleen giggle.

"Mrs. Sonnet has volunteered to help us brush up on reading the music in the hymn book. Do you remember or know what all those funny marks are that go with the words in the hymn book?" Kathleen giggled once more, and Timothy gave his fake smile. "Mrs. Sonnet will go over it all for us." And then he said seriously, "She has asked me to remind you that the best kind of Christian music is that music which all believers can sing together. And then we use that music to praise God, and as the Bible says, we use singing to instruct and encourage other believers."

Timothy paused and then made the next announcement. "The afternoon ministry meeting will be at four o'clock and supper will be at five-thirty." He glanced over the people seated at the tables as he continued. "Please pray regarding the ministry meetings. First, that the Lord would be glorified, that is, His greatness and His goodness would be evident to us. Pray for each speaker that the messages would be from the Lord and would be what we need at this time in our lives. Pray that each of us would be prepared to receive what the Lord would have us hear, and come to the meetings expecting to be encouraged in Him."

"At this evening's program at the campfire area, or maybe we'll have it here in the barn depending on the weather, we will have a singsong followed by a talk on the folly of evolution. Dr. Roop from 'Science and the Bible' has studied the controversy for many years and has all the helpful facts we need to know."

The boy with the scowl had sunk even lower, and he was now making what Jennifer called a duck-face. *What can we do to help him?* Timothy wondered. "We have a library in the backroom of the welcome centre," Timothy went on. He tried to make things sound more interesting. "You might want to borrow a book or two. We also have books and other items for sale. Don't feel you have to be involved with any of the planned activities, just relax and have fellowship with others." And then he thought, *That won't sound very interesting to a ten year old boy!*

"We would appreciate some help clearing the tables, and we need dish-washers. And would several men help Billy move the tables out of the way and set up the chairs for the morning ministry meeting." Timothy glanced out the large window of the barn. "Other families will be here for the day. They'll be arriving shortly, and they're anxious to meet you."

Before he sat down, he said, "While we finish up here, let's sing some choruses. We'll begin with the piece Stanley taught us last evening, 'I'll follow in the way He leads.'" Stanley stood up, and Kathleen moved over to the piano and played the introduction.

Some of the local Christians arrived, and they dropped off food to contribute to the meals. After the last breakfast dish was wiped and put away, Stanley gave the triangle several good strikes signifying the meeting would start in another ten minutes. Kathleen sat at the piano and began to play a lively tune. People who were in small groups outside moved into the barn and sat on the chairs which were arranged in a semi-circle before the portable pulpit. Kathleen continued to play, but slowly over the next ten minutes, changed the style of music to reflect dignity and reverence.

Timothy sat off by himself with his Bible on his knees. When he looked up, he could see the mother of the boy who had the scowl, talking earnestly with Stanley. When Stanley looked over at him and beckoned, Timothy moved across the room to them.

"It's Mitch, our son—we can't find him," the mother blurted out to Timothy. "He's run off, and Robert's still out looking for him."

"He can't get very far from here," Timothy said to her. "Is Mitch likely to hurt himself?"

"Oh no, he's probably hiding. Mitch didn't want to come here. He wanted something more exciting—you know how boys are. I'm really sorry for the trouble we're causing."

"There's lots of places to hide around here," Stanley admitted glancing at the mother and then Timothy.

Billy came in from outside, approached the little group, and listened attentively. And then he asked, "The blonde-haired kid with the red cap? I saw him go along the path into the woods."

"You did!" the boy's mother exclaimed. "Will you show my husband which way he went?" Billy did not reply. He rushed out the door and onto the veranda where he dropped his Bible on one of the twig chairs. He sprang off the edge of the veranda and over a clump of flowering chives. As he ran towards the trail, he prayed for wisdom and ability to handle this situation.

"Billy will find him," Timothy assured the mother. "Why don't you get your husband and join us here for the ministry meeting. Mitch'll be all right, he can't go far."

Billy jogged along the trail through the mixed woods. The two kilometre trail was recently developed by Jennifer and was used for nature study and for pleasant walks. It passed through a variety of terrain and returned to the far side of the barn.

Several minutes later, Billy could see up ahead, a boy's red cap moving through the trees. He slowed down to a noiseless walk and studied the young fellow from a distance. The boy kicked at a twig on the path, walked a few more metres, and glanced over at a large, old, pine tree. He scratched his arm, and then a minute later the boy stopped to observe a chattering squirrel. Billy stayed back, causing the youngster to be barely visible through the undergrowth. A half minute later Billy picked up a stick and snapped it in two over his knee. The boy immediately spun around, and Billy allowed the young fellow to see him for a split second before he dropped to the ground out of sight.

After everyone had arrived at the barn, Stanley moved to the pulpit and led in the singing of two praise hymns. "Before our first speaker comes," he said, "let's stand to sing another hymn—number four, forty-nine, 'To God be the Glory.'"

After the last verse was sung, and the people were seated, Timothy came to the pulpit and laid his open Bible on it. He spoke for about twenty-five minutes from God's Word. His message was from First Samuel chapter three. Timothy explained that the Word of the Lord was precious or rare which resulted in no open vision. He told those before him in the barn, "This shows that when we have a lack of God's Word, we will have no vision—no direction nor instructions from the Lord and no sense of His presence." Timothy also said, "Eli's eyes were dim so that he was in danger of allowing the lamp of God to go out in the temple of the Lord. When our spiritual eyes become dim because of a lack of the Word of God, our light, our testimony, will go out, and we might not even notice that we have lost our testimony."

The thud-thud sound Billy could hear from his flattened position on the trail told him the boy was running along the path and farther into the woods. Billy jumped to his feet. He knew that a hundred metres ahead was a narrow side path on the left which led to the cabin which was used for overnights. Billy charged into the woods and noisily ran along on the boy's right. The young fellow heard him and then saw him crashing through the underbrush, so when the boy came to the narrow path on his left, he quickly changed his direction onto it, and disappeared, running from view beyond the thick spruces.

Billy made his way back to the main trail, and he grinned when he could see several crushed ferns on his left where the narrow path began. He tucked in his shirt and then walked along at a leisurely pace towards the cabin clearing. When he came to the edge of the small open area, he stopped and stood with both hands on his hips. The boy was nowhere to be seen, but the freshly trampled grasses indicated he had gone into the cluster of spruce trees near the outhouse under the large single pine tree.

About a minute later Billy heard a muffled giggle coming from just beyond the base of the pine tree. He boldly strolled up to the dark green cabin, and he sat in the sunlight on the small landing and took a deep breath. He did not face where he knew the boy was crouching, but he watched out of the corner of his eye, then he leaned back against the door and closed his eyes. Several minutes later he let his head drop to the side, and he began to snore gently.

The boy picked up a pinecone and threw it in Billy's direction. It rolled to about two metres of his stretched-out legs, but Billy ignored it. And then another pinecone landed even closer. Billy continued to snore, and he could hear the boy giggle and come closer. Another pinecone hit one of Billy's boots, and he gave an exaggerated jump, opened his eyes, and blinked several times. With a blank look on his face, he and the grinning boy stared at each other for several seconds.

Suddenly Billy jumped up and ran for him, but the boy darted away. Billy followed close behind him, allowing the boy to be just out of reach until Billy purposely tripped over a young spruce tree, tumbled to the ground, and rolled over. The boy stopped and faced him and grinned again. Billy slowly stood up, and the boy scooted behind the stack of firewood, but when Billy moved towards him again, he headed for the back side of the cabin.

Billy slowly walked over to the small building, opened the door, and entered. He left the door slightly ajar and settled down on one of the bunks. About two silent minutes later, the boy cautiously nudged open the door a little farther. He poked his blonde head through the narrow opening causing his cap to shift. He quickly glanced around the interior but when he saw Billy, he slowly broke into a grin.

After Stanley led in another hymn, a visiting speaker approached the lectern. "It's good to hear the Word of God expounded," he remarked as he laid his Bible down. "Many messages today use the Word of God, but the preaching is watered down and doesn't have the power of the Holy Spirit, the Author of Scripture, to convict and convince not only the unbeliever, but the believer as well." He glanced over at Timothy and nodded. "So, thank you, Timothy Jack, for sharing with us the message the Lord gave you for us at this time."

The visiting teacher spoke on the Christian family. He reminded the people gathered in the barn that Satan brings many attractive things into our daily environment to draw our children away from the Lord in subtle ways. He told them, "Many of these influences cannot be avoided; they are all around us everyday. But we do have control of all that which comes into our homes. The mosquitoes and black flies are out there all around us, and we try to prevent them from entering our homes, so we do not allow worldly influences to come into our homes. It is our responsibility before the Lord to secure our homes to be safe havens for our children. When we can't avoid them, our children should be taught to resist harmful influences."

"Is this your cabin?" the boy asked as he pushed open the door and stepped in.

Billy frowned at him. "No, it isn't. It belongs to Camp Bethlehem." The boy straightened his cap and glanced around the interior once more. Billy demanded, "And what's your name, Boy?"

"Mitch."

"Mitch," Billy repeated and then added, "Mitch the Grinner."

The boy continued to examine the room. He noted, "This cabin has three bunk beds, a table to eat at, and a stove." He sat on the end of a bunk at a distance from Billy and then glanced up at the Bible text over the large window. The letters were formed with twigs fastened to a piece of painted plywood.

"Do you ever stay overnight here?" Mitch inquired.

"I come when I bring guys from camp. They like to stay overnight here."

"Can I come too?" he asked. "I'd like to stay overnight here."

Billy answered sharply, "No, you can't Mitch."

The boy was disappointed. "Why not?"

Billy did not answer. He tapped his boots together several times as he continued to frown at Mitch.

"Why not?" Mitch insisted.

"Because this cabin is for guys who obey their parents." Mitch quickly looked the other way. "Guys who run away and don't tell their parents where they're going, don't get to do exciting things," he said sternly.

Mitch hung his head and stared at the floor. After a long pause he said, "I was mad at Mom and Dad for making me come here when I wanted to go to the amusement park."

"Your mom and dad know what's best for you even if you don't agree with them. You need to obey them because they're responsible for you. They care about you; they give you nice clothes to wear, and they don't make you sleep outside under a bush, but they've given you a nice bedroom." Mitch looked up with a dumbfounded look on his face.

Billy glared at him. "Your parents don't throw stale, leftover food at you to eat, do they? They give you good food." Mitch was beginning to squirm, and Billy reminded him, "The Bible says children are to obey their parents, and if you want to be happy, you must obey your parents and then cheerfully cooperate with them. They love you."

Mitch looked glum. "Yeah, I know," he admitted.

Billy quizzed him harshly, "You know what, Mitch?"

The boy stared at the floor. "I'm supposed to do what they want me to do; because the Bible says so."

"And?" Billy prodded.

He fidgeted with his cap before answering. "Mom and Dad care about me, and they know what's best for me."

The cabin was silent for nearly a minute, and during that time Billy could see Mitch had looked up and had noticed the scratches on his arms. The boy was now even more uncomfortable.

Billy suddenly grinned at him. "Do you have a flashlight and a sleeping bag?"

Mitch quickly brightened up, and he moved opposite Billy on the bunk across from him. "Yeah, I have a flashlight and I can bring my sleeping bag and I have a brand new jackknife. Should I bring it, too?"

Billy stood up, stretched, and walked over to the door. "Mitch, after you apologize to your parents for your unaccept able behaviour, you can ask their permission to stay here overnight. We'll ask those other three guys, too, okay?"

Mitch jumped up. "Okay, that would be great! When can we come back to here?"

"And you're not going to wear your cap during mealtimes, Boy, or to any of the meetings inside. Do you hear?"

"Yes, I hear. I won't."

Billy then looked at him sternly. "And Mitch, I think you owe me an apology. It wasn't in my morning plans to go chasing through the woods for an irresponsible rooster." Mitch hung his head for several long seconds, but when he glanced up and saw a slight smile on Billy's face, he grinned back shyly.

"Come on, we better get back to the barn. Your parents will want to know where you are, and I have things I need to get at."

Billy and Mitch stepped out into the sunlight and moved along the path. "We don't go to the cabin until after the evening program, and you are to attend all the meetings with your parents and be involved in the other activities of family camp."

"What activities are you in charge of?" he asked as he looked up at him and beamed. "Can I join whatever you look after?"

"Yeah, you can join what I do if you like."

"Good! What activity do you do?" he asked once more.

"Oh," Billy answered casually, "I collect the garbage and do other important stuff like that."

After a mid-morning lunch for those who wanted a snack, one family left to see some of the local tourists' sights, and another family set off to visit with relatives in the area. Family camp at Camp Bethlehem was operated in an informal way, but it was not disorganized. Families came and left as they wished but there was always something to do on the grounds either for individuals or groups.

A few of the local Christians occupied private cabins on the grounds while others came only for the day. Several families learned about family camp through a notice which had been placed in a nation-wide Christian magazine. This resulted in some vacationing families coming from a distance who included family camp at Camp Bethlehem in their summer plans. One family brought their camping trailer and parked it near the housekeeping cabins.

Camp Bethlehem was a ministry which operated on faith and trust in the Lord. There was no charge for anything, but there was opportunity to contribute to this work through donations. Boxes were left in several locations, and the camp trustees experienced the provisions of the Lord and His blessings on this ministry. The experience of the trustees was that when a gift was given, even one that seemed small but was given for the glory of the Lord and the good of His people, that that gift was used effectively at camp. They also learned that when Camp Bethlehem was over-valued rather than the Lord being glorified that sometimes things would not go smoothly.

Jennifer enjoyed the warmth of the sun on her back as she sat on the grass near the flagpole with her arms resting on her raised knees. She watched a daddy long-legs stroll across the cover of her book on the identification of wildflowers. *If I can persuade this fellow to stay, I can explain to the others the difference between insects and creatures like this.*

Suddenly a shadow came over her, and she could sense someone behind her. Jennifer turned and squinted as she looked up towards the sun with her hand shading her eyes. She promptly sneezed. A volleyball was dropped next to her, and Stanley lowered himself and sat on it. He faced her and grinned, and Jennifer returned the grin.

Soon a little girl arrived pulling on her dad's hand. "Is this where we meet for the nature walk?"

"Yes, it is," Jennifer replied. She kept her eye on the daddy long-legs on her book as she tossed her braid behind her back.

Several others approached the little group, and Stanley stood up and left with his volleyball. "See you later, Stan." He waved and then trotted off towards the volleyball court.

Jennifer quickly glanced over the small group of men, women and children. "Does anyone know what this is here on my book?" she asked as she held it out. The people stepped closer.

"It's an insect," a boy informed her.

"It's a spider!" blurted out a young girl as she clasped her hands behind her back.

An older girl put in, "It's a daddy long-legs."

"Yes, that's right, it's a daddy long-legs. And how many legs does this fellow have?"

The boy stepped closer to have a better look. "Five, six, seven, eight. He has eight legs."

"Yeah, that's right. And spiders have eight legs, too. How many legs does an insect have?"

The older girl answered, "An insect has six legs."

"Six legs," Jennifer repeated. "But this guy has eight. So he's not an insect."

"It has eight legs," an older boy concluded as he scratched his bare arm. "It's only a spider."

"Spiders have fangs, and they can bite," Jennifer revealed to him. "This daddy long-legs does not have fangs, and he will not bite—he's not a spider." She lowered her book to the ground and tipped off the daddy long-legs into the grass. "The Lord has designed many interesting creatures, hasn't He!" she exclaimed as she stood up.

The group started to move across the field, and Jennifer summarized the discussion. "So we've learned that daddy long-legs are not spiders and that neither daddy long-legs nor spiders are insects."

The little girl stayed close to Jennifer and added, "And daddy long-legs don't bite." And then she asked, "Are there mommy long-legs?"

Several people laughed, and Jennifer replied, "Good question. No, both are called 'daddy long-legs'."

One of the men observed, "We learned all that before we even left the area!"

Timothy sat on the top step of the veranda of the barn. He leaned forward and placed his elbows on his knees and his chin in his hands. He glanced across the field to the little group examining something in the tall grasses, and then he looked beyond the campfire area to New Lake with the two little rowboats each with people wearing orange life jackets. He could see the House of Prayer situated prominently at the edge of the field. And he could hear the volleyball game on the other side of the pine trees nearby was getting more exciting by the minute. He marvelled, *The Lord has provided all this for the good of His people and for His glory!*

Timothy heard the screen door close behind him. Kathleen, who was wearing a long, flowered skirt, lowered herself onto one of the twig chairs. He sat up, rotated to face her, and smiled.

"Timothy," she began as she leaned back and crossed her ankles, "I could tell that the message you gave this morning was from the Lord. It had so much of His Word in it."

"Well, I'm glad you see it that way, Kathleen." Timothy grinned at her. "Thanks for the encouragement."

Kathleen smiled, stood up, and descended the steps. Timothy leaned back against the post, put his hands behind his head, and watched her as she went along the path. *Thank You, Lord, for not only providing these facilities but for providing the people to manage them for Thy glory. Your people have the opportunity to hear Thy Word here as well as have fellowship and family recreation.* Timothy stood up and stretched. As he headed for his cabin, he thought, *God is blessing the work here which He started through Mr. Charles. And Camp Bethlehem has gone far beyond all the dreams that godly man ever had.*

"You can grab that coil of rope there, Mitch," Billy told him as he reached for the ladder hanging on the hooks in the shed. "Let's go." The two fellows left the building and proceeded along the path. "Nice day if it don't rain," Billy remarked. When they reached the swings, he extended the ladder and rested it against the top horizontal piece. He then climbed to the top and began to cut the rope with his pocket-knife. "This rope is some worn," he said as he sawed away at it. "We wouldn't wish anyone to encounter sudden and intimate acquaintance with the terra firma, now would we?"

Mitch frowned at him. "Huh?"

When the rope fell, Billy said, "Slide the rope out of the seat." Then he cut through the other end of the rope and let it fall onto the boy. "Okay," Billy said as he descended the ladder, "we can thread the new rope through the seat now." Mitch grinned as he lifted the rope off his shoulder, and then he retrieved his cap. Billy told him, "Thanks for coming along and helping." He parted his lips slightly and quietly whistled a simple tune.

There were three cabins on both sides of the barn. These canvas covered buildings were used by campers during children's camp in July, and now Timothy shared one with Stanley and Billy. He liked this particular cabin. When inside during the sunny morning hours, he could see on the canvas wall on the east side the shadow of a large pine tree. In the evening, on the opposite wall could be seen the shadows of the spruce trees which were growing up close to the west side of the little building.

About ten minutes before noon, Timothy came out from his cabin carrying a small weather radio. He sat on the landing, and as he extended the antenna, his sister Jennifer came towards him through the tall grasses and daisies.

"Tim," she began as she fingered the edge of her straw hat trimmed with a pink ribbon, "I just had an interesting talk with Kathleen."

He switched on the radio. "Shh, I need to get the forecast for this evening. Oh, it's not for our area. Who?"

"Kathleen. She says she could play the piano since she was seven."

"Overcast for this afternoon," Timothy repeated when he pressed the radio to his ear. "Yeah, I know."

"She said she sometimes gives lessons."

"Chance of showers after midnight for our area. Yeah, I know."

Jennifer turned and started down the path. She stopped, faced Timothy, and revealed to him, "Kathleen says she'll be ninety-seven years old next month."

"Cloudy tomorrow with sunny breaks in the afternoon. Yeah, I know." He pushed the antenna back into his weather radio, stood up, and turned to enter the cabin as Jennifer left the area. *We could tentatively plan to have the evening program outside at the campfire circle,* he figured as he opened the door.

"Ninety-seven years old next month!" Timothy exclaimed aloud. He turned and frowned at Jennifer just as she walked out of sight around the back of the barn on her way to the kitchen.

When Timothy gave the announcements at noon, he could not help but notice the blonde-haired boy. Gone was the scowl, gone was the red cap, and when the boy glanced over at Billy sitting at the next table and had his attention, the boy would grin at him. Timothy wondered, *What did Billy do to change that irresponsible rooster?*

Timothy cleared his throat. "What can we thank and praise the Lord for?" he asked, and then he informed them, "Yesterday we received the funds for a new freezer. The old one is too small and is not reliable. A used bed and dresser and curtains were donated recently. We'll put them in the new cabin presently being built."

After the singing at noon and the clearing of the tables, Timothy returned the push broom to the closet. As he crossed the floor to the door to the veranda, he passed close to Jennifer and Kathleen who were wiping the tables.

"You sure work really well for an elderly lady, Kathleen," Timothy informed her warmly. "And you hide your age very well. Jennifer tells me you'll be ninety-seven next month."

Before Kathleen could swing around to face him, Timothy went out the door. She just stood there and stared at him, and her mouth dropped open. Before he crossed the veranda, he caught a glimpse of Jennifer out of the corner of his eye. She was frozen in place with her hand on the dishcloth, and her arm stretched across the table. After the door closed behind him, Timothy heard the two young ladies laughing.

Later that afternoon, nearly a dozen people attended the class for reading music. Mrs. Sonnet picked up a hymn book and stated that there is disunity when believers from one area sing tunes slightly differently than Christians do from another location. "When we are together and sing the music the way it is written," she declared, "we will all sing each tune the same way."

Mrs. Sonnet held the hymn book and informed them that the best tune to go with the words usually is the tune with the words there in the hymn book. "The music nicely supports the words," she expressed.

Mrs. Sonnet opened the hymn book and told the group that when we sing the four parts of the music, everyone can comfortably reach the notes. "And four-part harmony," she reminded them, "is pleasant to sing and nice to hear. All this brings glory to God and is beneficial to believers." Mrs. Sonnet leafed through the hymn book and told them, "Let's look at number three hundred and eighty-eight."

* * *

After the rowboats were hauled up onto the grass and the life jackets were put away, Stanley walked through several of the old apple trees and over to the picnic shelter. He sat at one of the tables under the large roof, and several minutes later Jennifer joined him.

"Hi, Jennifer," Stanley greeted. She moved under the roof and sat on one of the swings suspended from the rafters, but she said nothing. Stanley said, "I was thinking about Samuel. He was instructed to say, 'Speak, Lord, for Thy servant heareth,' but because Samuel didn't know the Lord yet, he didn't address Him as 'Lord'."

The wooden swing seat was too low for Jennifer to swing comfortably. She grasped the ropes and backed up to a standing position as she rested against the seat board.

"Yeah, that was interesting," she replied. "He was in the service of the Lord, but it says he didn't know the Lord." She leaned back and lifted her feet into the air causing her long hair to flow as she glided forward. After swinging back and forth several times, she planted her feet on the ground and stood up, and then she came over to the table where Stanley was seated.

Stanley said, "Samuel didn't know the Lord until the Lord had spoken to him, and we can't really know the Lord until we recognize Him speaking to us in His Word."

Jennifer sat down opposite him; she removed her hat and placed it on the picnic table. "Yeah, I agree with you, Stan," she informed him as she put her elbows on the table.

"I hope the others are getting as much out of the messages as I am," Stanley said.

"Yeah, I agree with you." Jennifer grinned at him and then told him, "I like the way you lead the singing, and the hymns you choose are suitable for each occasion."

Two girls and a boy approached them under the roof. "Stanley," one of the girls addressed him as the children stood next to the fireplace, "can we use the stilts?"

He pivoted around to face them. "Yeah, sure," he replied. "Help yourself. They should be just inside the door of the sports hut. Please put them back when you're through with them." The children ran off without replying. "And thanks for asking first," Stanley called after them.

More local people arrived for the ministry meeting during the late afternoon. Those who stayed to supper brought more than enough food for themselves and left it all in the kitchen to be shared with those who would be there. The parents of Timothy, Jennifer and Billy attended the afternoon meeting, and they stayed to supper and the evening program. The Jacks dropped off a dozen and a half large carrots freshly pulled from their garden, two raspberry pies baked that afternoon, and a four liter container of cherry-cheesecake ice-cream purchased on sale.

After supper, Mitch was anxious to get started with the garbage duties. He and Billy emptied all the trash bins on the grounds and placed what they had collected in the shed. "Can I help you again tomorrow, Billy?"

Billy suspended his monotonous whistling. "This is an important job—but you're a good helper," he said. "Guess I can use you again tomorrow."

The campfire was burning nicely that evening, and the heat from it caused the smoke to rise into the air away from those assembled there. The shadows were gradually lengthening as choruses were sung with the accompaniment of two guitars.

Ten minutes later the guitars were put aside, and Dr. Roop stood up. "If someone was to tell you that the waving of the trees makes the wind blow, would you believe them?" he asked, and he paused as he glanced over the people there. "This phenomenon of the trees making the wind blow is a fact easily observed," he stated in an authoritative voice. "The more the trees wave back and forth, the more windy it is. And when the trees move very little, there's not much wind."

Several children giggled, and Dr. Roop looked at them with exaggerated sternness. "It can be scientifically and mathematically proven that the amount of activity of the waving of the trees is in direct proportion to the velocity of the wind." And then he said very seriously, "Sometimes the trees wave so much in their effort to cause the wind to blow that they break some of their branches, and sometimes whole trees come down. This is clearly mother nature's way of culling out the older and diseased trees as well as getting rid of those trees which are overzealous in their activities." Several people chuckled, and then Dr. Roop gestured with one hand to emphasize his next point. "Many learned scientists who are greatly respected in their various fields of research have carefully documented thousands of such cases."

Billy leaned over and added more wood to the fire. "I don't need to tell you," Dr. Roop continued, "that theory is as foolish as the theory of evolution." He glanced at the children and grinned. "The biggest reason why anyone would choose to believe evolution is because they feel more comfortable with the lie. In order to believe the Biblical account they must also believe in God and what the Bible says about mankind and our sinfulness. And those people who believe evolution don't want to face up to their personal sin. It's easier to deny the problem and the consequences of sin by inventing something which would conveniently dismiss God from their lives. But believing incorrect information doesn't make that incorrect information true."

Dr. Roop explained to his listeners, "Evolution is a clever tactic of Satan. He invented the lie about evolution in order to cause disbelief in God's Word. No one can be saved from hell if they don't believe the Bible, for we need to believe and trust in God to be saved. We cannot believe only certain parts of the Bible. Which parts should we believe? Which parts are not true? Is there really a place called hell?"

The sky was nearly black as the evening program concluded. Some people stayed at the fire to sing, but most left to go back to their cabins. Billy and the four excited boys departed for the cabin back in the woods. As they traipsed along the path in the dark, the boys shone their flashlights into the nearby trees and in each others' faces.

"Don't use up the batteries of your flashlights when you don't need to," Billy advised them.

"Why not?" one of the boys challenged as he aimed his light into Billy's eyes. "I can recharge my flashlight at the cabin."

"Dummy!" Mitch promptly told the boy. "The cabin back in the woods doesn't have electricity."

"It doesn't?" he responded in disbelief as he turned his light on Mitch.

Kathleen was alone and playing the piano when Timothy arrived in the barn later that evening, but she did not acknowledge him as he approached her from behind. Her hair was done up in a bun at the back of her head, and she wore a shawl over her shoulders. Timothy stood a couple metres behind her and waited until she had finished the piece she was playing, and then he asked, "Kathleen, do you know the tune that goes with the words for 'The Happy Wanderer'?"

He stepped closer, and she began to play the tune. "Is this the one?" she asked when she had finished the first two lines. And then as she continued to play she turned to face him.

Timothy gasped and then laughed. Kathleen giggled and stopped playing. She had wrinkles painted all over her face. As she stood up, her shawl slipped off one shoulder. "If you'll excuse me, Young Man, I must leave now to get my beauty rest." She lifted the shawl back onto her shoulders and wrapped it around her, and then she hobbled across the floor towards the door.

Timothy politely called out, "Miss, I'll get the door for you." And he hurried over to where she was waiting for him.

"Why, thank you, Sonny," she replied with an elderly voice and a shy smile as she looked up at him.

He held open the door for her and said, "You're some pretty, even when you're a ninety-seven year old elderly lady."

"Oh, they all say that," she told him as the two of them stepped out into the cool night air and moved across the veranda.

The boys awoke in the cabin in the woods, and Billy lit the fire in the stove to fry wieners and eggs. "Nice day if it don't rain," he informed the boys, and he began to whistle softly through the narrow opening between his lips.

"I've never had wiener pieces mixed with eggs before," one of the boys remarked as he watched at Billy's elbow.

Billy stirred the mixture around before answering him. "It's my own special recipe, and the only thing that I can cook, besides bologna pieces mixed with eggs." The boy grinned at him.

One of the younger boys returned from the outhouse and joined the group in the cabin. "Knock, knock," he said.

When he was ignored by the other boys, Billy replied, "Who's there?"

"Ach," the boy told him.

Billy followed through and asked him, "Ach who?"

The young fellow giggled and answered, "Cover your mouth when you sneeze."

One of the other boys asked the group, "Did you hear about the guy who wanted to live a life of crime?" He snickered as he looked around at the other boys. "He had to give it up because he got caught and had to go to jail for a long time."

Several minutes later, Billy called, "Okay, Guys, come to the table."

When breakfast at the barn was nearly finished, Timothy made the announcements for the morning. "As you can see and can probably hear, we're putting up another building at the group of housekeeping cabins." He pointed with his chin.

"The floor is now ready to lay. If you'd like to help hammer down the floor boards, come on over. Jeff Bell, our carpenter says with four or five helpers, we can finish the floor in less than an hour."

Timothy glanced over the group. "Stanley will organize a soccer game for this morning. Be sure the boys who are away with Billy know about it when they get back from their night in the cabin in the woods."

After the morning ministry meeting, Billy loaded the garden cart with supplies needed at the construction site, and he pushed it along the path towards the area of the housekeeping cabins.

"Billy!" a voice called out to him. "What's up? Where are you going?" Mitch ran up to him and walked beside him through the waist-high, Queen Anne's lace. "Can I come too, Billy? Can I help?"

"Sure, but you tell your parents first," he replied without slackening his pace.

Mitch shifted his cap. "I did. I told them I was going to look for you. Mom said it was okay."

"Okay, Mitch, come on."

An older couple was sitting on one of the benches close to the sundial near the House of Prayer, and as Mrs. Charles walked towards them, they smiled at her. "Hello, Mr. and Mrs. Perry," she greeted them. "Are you comfortable in your housekeeping cabin?"

"Oh, yes, we certainly are," Mrs. Perry answered.

Mr. Perry said, "It's a lot more comfortable than some places we've lived in when we were in Bolivia." Mrs. Charles stopped and sat on the bench opposite them.

"Yes," Mrs. Perry grinned. "We haven't seen any rats running along the roof rafters while we've been here, and we haven't seen any poisonous snakes anywhere." Mrs. Charles chatted with the couple for several minutes and then headed for the kitchen.

As Kathleen left her cabin and walked along the path towards the barn, she hummed the tune for 'The Happy Wanderer'. She thought, *The words for 'Amazing Grace' go with that tune and so does 'The Lord's My Shepherd' and 'O For a Thousand Tongues To Sing'. And she sang a verse of each hymn as she went. What words can we use for the chorus? How about, 'Praise the Lord, praise the Lord! Praise the Lord all ye people, Praise the Lord, and bless His Holy Name.' Hey! That fits in well, and it's also suitable for each hymn.*

Suddenly there was a loud squawk coming from the tall vegetation at the side of the path. Kathleen jumped and gasped, and then she sputtered, "I'll never get used to that thing!" She turned to the side of the path, bent over, and spoke into the pipe next to a clump of goldenrod. "Hello. Hello? Who's there?" She heard giggles coming through the fifty metre pipe buried in the ground. The other end of the pipe was out of sight on the far side of the thick spruce trees next to the path to the housekeeping cabins.

"Is that you, Shelly?" Kathleen asked into the pipe. "No? Then it must be Susan. It can't be Jennifer." The giggles turned into a chuckle and quickly became an exaggerated deep laugh.

"Timothy! Is that you?"

"It sure is," he replied through the pipe. "Are you the happy wanderer?"

Passengers spilled from the two vehicles which had just returned from an afternoon at Rogers Cove. One of the girls ran towards her parents who were sitting on a bench near the raspberry bushes along the stone wall.

"Mom! Dad! You should've come with us!" she called out to them. "We went to the beach where Jennifer gets stuff to make those nice beach plaques you know that hang on the wall. We saw so many neat things at the sand flats and Jennifer told us about the starfish except they're called sea stars and we saw an orange one and we saw a hermit crab and he was in a big shell that he found and he was walking sideways and we saw lots of periwinkles and they make long tracks in the sand but you can't see them move because they go so slow and we saw thousands of barnacles and Jennifer says they don't move around any at all and we saw some big rocks called 'Fearful Rocks' out in the water where boats sometimes get smashed up." The girl was almost out of breath. "Did you know," she added, "that Jennifer can snap an apple in two with only her two bare hands?"

After breakfast on that overcast morning of the last day of Family Camp, most visitors said their good-byes to one another and left the property. Timothy packed his things and set them out on the landing of his cabin ready to be carried to the car. He could see Jeff Bell inspecting the hand railings next to the boathouse. As Timothy dropped his jacket over his suitcase, he also noticed Kathleen sitting by herself at the campfire circle.

Timothy stepped off the landing, strolled through the goldenrods towards Kathleen, and lowered himself onto the log opposite her. She was wearing a flowered blouse and a dark denim shirt. She briefly looked up at him and smiled. Neither one said anything, and each stared into the cold, gray ashes from the fire of last evening. As Timothy poked at a blackened piece of firewood with a long stick, he became deep in thought and Kathleen sensed his apprehension.

At the barn, Stanley and Jennifer sat on the top step of the veranda, visiting with Mrs. Charles. Several minutes later the lady stood up from the twig chair, excused herself, and entered the barn. Stanley's gaze dropped to the step beneath his shiny black boots.

"Jennifer," he said about half a minute later, "how long have we known each other?"

She smiled and glanced over at him. "Ever since you came to know the Lord nearly nine years ago."

He faced her, leaned on one elbow, and replied, "You know that I think highly of you."

She turned herself towards him and tossed back her long hair. "Yes. And I think very highly of you, Stan, especially because of your interest in spiritual things."

"Well, yeah," Stanley answered, and he shrugged his shoulders, "all believers should have an interest in spiritual things."

"Yes," she replied thoughtfully, "I agree with you."

He paused and then abruptly asked, "Jennifer, would you agree that you and I should be married?"

"Yeah," she answered without hesitation, "I would agree to that."

Stanley leaned forward towards her and questioned, "You would?"

"Well, of course! I always agree with you."

He looked at her in amazement and then informed her, "I've wanted to ask you to be my wife for several weeks now."

"I've been waiting several weeks for you to ask me," Jennifer admitted to him. "But you'll have to check with Dad first, because, as his daughter, I'm still under his authority and protection."

Stanley nodded in agreement, and then he became thoughtful. "Let's ask the Lord now to guide us in our lives together," he said, and he moved closer to her on the top step, and they bowed their heads.

With his long stick, Timothy continued to poke at the remains of the fire of the night before. Finally he took a deep breath and stated solemnly, "Kathleen, I need to ask you." She looked over at him against the cloudy sky. He dug the heels of his boots into the bare ground and then admitted, "Well, I don't know how to say it." He cleared his throat and then blurted out, "Will you marry me?"

"Marry you!" she gasped in surprise from her seated position across from him.

"Yes. Will you be my wife?" Without giving her the opportunity to reply farther, he continued, "I don't want to pressure you into answering right away. Would it be alright if I gave you until next week when you leave your grandma's?" He saw a frown come across her face.

"Next week!" she repeated.

"That's not long enough, Kathleen?" he asked as he flipped over a burnt piece of wood with his stick. "Do you need more time to think about it?" He tried to conceal his disappointment.

"No! I don't need more time," she answered him confidently. "I can tell you right now." Timothy's mouth dropped open as he stared at her. She then smiled and uttered, "My answer is yes."

He continued to search her face as he told her, "You realize the Lord has called me to serve Him full-time, and He is training me now as I get more experience?"

She nodded. "Yes, I can see that."

Timothy grinned. "I'll be—that is we'll be living by faith—trusting the Lord for everything," he said to her. "I won't have a salary nor will I be earning money on a regular basis."

Kathleen nodded again. "Yes, I know all that," she informed him. "I have felt since I first met you three months ago at the funeral of Grandpa Charles that the Lord wanted me to be your wife."

Timothy was astounded. "And I wondered at that time if you were the girl the Lord had for me," he blurted out, and they both laughed.

"Timothy, I would be pleased to be your wife, and I want to be with you and support you in all you do for the Lord."

Timothy grinned. "I'll speak to your dad since you are still under his care and leadership." He then concluded, "The Lord has brought us to each other. Let's give ourselves to Him as a couple, and we can serve Him together." After they prayed, they started up the path to the barn.

Jennifer could see Timothy and Kathleen slowly making their way up from the campfire area. "They look happy," she remarked to Stanley. He looked over and watched the couple coming towards them. Jennifer wondered aloud, "Do you suppose?"

In the other direction, both couples could hear a dull clomp, clomp sound coming along the path towards them at the barn.

Soon Timothy and Kathleen joined Stanley and Jennifer who were seated on the veranda. "Well, guys," Timothy said, "Kathleen and I have an announcement to make, and we want you two to be the first to hear it."

"You do?" Jennifer replied as she glanced from her brother to the young lady at his side. "So do we." And she looked over at Stanley.

The source of the clomp, clomp sound was now close at hand and could not be ignored. "Hey Guys!" Billy called out as he navigated himself on the stilts towards the group. "Guess what?"

"What is it, Billy?" Jennifer wanted to know, and she started to giggle.

Billy stepped off the stilts directly onto the veranda just when Mrs. Charles came out from the barn. "Hurray! Ladies and Gentlemen," he proclaimed with enthusiasm, "I have an announcement to make." Kathleen giggled along with Jennifer, and Mrs. Charles smiled at the group of young people.

"An announcement?" Timothy chuckled as he observed his brother. "What is it, Billy?"

"I made it on stilts from the far cabin to the barn," he stated proudly as he shook the stilts held high above his head. "This sets my bells a ringing. I've finally got the hang of it."

Stanley was laughing now, too. "Good for you, Billy, good for you," he told him. Billy was puzzled. He stared at Timothy and Kathleen, and then at Stanley and Jennifer who were all laughing.

Billy moved to the twig chair, sat down, and placed the stilts across its arms. "What's so funny, Guys?" he demanded with a frown.

chapter twenty-two

about two months later—autumn 1997

The Gentleman

Eighteen-year-old Billy crossed the veranda floor of the barn and lowered himself onto one of the twig chairs. He watched as his family's car driven by his brother left to return to their home about twenty minutes away. The vehicle soon disappeared from his view as it moved along the road through the thick spruce woods, but he could hear it as it continued towards the road.

The young man pushed back the left sleeve of his blue and red jack-shirt. "Fourteen minutes to five," he said aloud. He glanced down at his sleeping bag and pillow and the plastic shopping bag which contained a package of wieners and a large tin of apple juice.

The autumn air was cool, and Billy folded his arms across his chest and shoved his hands up into his armpits. He looked across the dull green field which was now void of colourful, summer wildflowers. He could see the House of Prayer, and then he viewed the picnic shelter this side of the old apple orchard. *I should put that swing away for the winter,* Billy reminded himself as he observed it hanging lifelessly from the rafters of the shelter.

His eyes wandered down to the lake. The few remaining bright fall colours of the trees on the other side of the narrow body of water were reflected in a distorted fashion on its slightly rippled surface. *It sure is different here today than it is in the busy summer months!* Billy noted. *I don't see anyone around, and I don't hear any activities either.* He leaned forward and turned to look over his right shoulder through the nearly bare trees to the deserted volleyball court.

Billy then leaned back and crossed his ankles. *My Heavenly Father,* he prayed as he had several times already today, *may I be the person You would have me to be, and may I be used by Thee.*

Several minutes later, Billy heard a vehicle coming along the dirt road, and he turned to face it as it came into his view. That's the Copton's van, he told himself as he shifted his brown corduroy cap. Doug and Davy are here. He stood up and crossed to the edge of the veranda where Mrs. Copton could see him.

The van came to a stop in the parking area near the old stone wall, the sliding door opened, and Davy jumped out and ran towards him. "Billy, we're here!" he shouted. He skidded to a stop and picked up his cap which had just tumbled to the ground. "Hunky-dory! Is anyone else here yet?"

"Hey Kid!" his older brother Doug hollered from the front seat of the van. "Like—come get your junk! And don't think I'm going to—like—carry it."

"Hello, Mrs. Copton," Billy greeted and then added casually, "Nice day if it don't rain." He came down the steps and crossed over to the van.

"Hi, Billy." She handed him Davy's sleeping bag. "The boys have been really looking forward to this—all week in fact." Billy grinned and nodded. "I hope they don't give you any trouble," she informed him. "They've been kind of hyper since they got home from school this afternoon."

Billy took on a tough appearance and looked sternly over at the two boys. "I can handle them," he told her firmly. "I know 'judo' and 'karate', and a few other Japanese words like 'tofu' and 'sushi'." Mrs. Copton giggled and climbed back into the van. She handed Billy a bag of food, closed the door, and started the engine. She rolled down the window, and Billy said, "Thanks, Mrs. Copton."

"Oh, you're welcome, and have a good time." She then called out to her boys, "Bye, Douglas, bye, David. You two behave yourselves, and don't give Billy any trouble, you hear?"

"Bye, Mom," Davy replied as he waved.

"Bye, Sweetie." Mrs. Copton pulled out from the parking area, and Billy placed Davy's sleeping bag on the veranda floor.

"Hunky-dory doodle! When are we leaving for the cabin, Billy?" Davy wanted to know.

Billy answered, "When the others get here, and when we're ready to go and not a minute sooner."

"Like—what do we have to eat?" Doug demanded. "I'm—like—starving." He began to poke into the bags of food.

"Hey, leave those bags alone, Doug," Billy told him, and then he said, "We're going to need your help to carry all this here stuff to the cabin." As Billy spoke, he noticed the front of Doug's t-shirt under his opened jacket, but he was unable to read the words there.

"I can help, too, Billy," Davy informed him, looking up at him. "Hunky-dory doodle all the day!"

Doug scowled at his younger brother. "Like—you can't help carry this stuff," he snapped. "You have enough problems carrying your own junk. And don't get the idea that I'm here to—like—help you."

Davy ignored him. He was looking off in the direction of the road. "Here comes Paul," the younger boy exclaimed.

The car pulled into the parking area, and when the vehicle had come to a stop, Davy ran over to it as both rear doors opened. Paul stepped out from one side, and another boy came around from the other side. Billy stepped up to the unfamiliar boy.

"You must be Brampton," he said. "My name's Billy. I'm glad Paul invited you to come along."

Paul's dad came around to the front passenger's side. "Come get your gear, Boys," Mr. Green told them as he opened the door. The boys hauled out their sleeping bags and their food contributions and carried them to the veranda of the barn.

Mr. Green turned to Billy. "Nice evening for a sleepover," he stated. "Wish I could come, too." Billy grinned at him. "You know," Mr. Green remarked, "I've been thinking. It might be a good idea if the elders got together and spent a day at the cabin to discuss things and have prayer and Bible study—mutual encouragement and fellowship time."

Billy looked over at him and then answered, "Good idea." As Mr. Green slid into the driver's seat, Billy mulled over aloud, "An elders' retreat, or maybe it would be an elders' advance."

Billy grinned at Mr. Green but quickly turned to the noisy group of boys on the veranda. "Hey, Guys, get out of those bags of food," he ordered as he promptly moved over to them. "We're not going to eat until we get to the cabin."

"I don't want apple juice," Doug objected. "What else is there to—like—drink?"

"Let's go, Billy," Davy interrupted. "We're ready to go to the cabin now. We need to get a move-along."

"No, we can't leave yet," Billy answered him. "There's one more guy to come."

"Who else is coming?" Paul wanted to know. Billy did not answer. He checked his watch again, and with his foot, he gently pushed the sleeping bags and food contributions back together to the centre of the floor.

"Like—who are we waiting for?" Doug demanded impatiently.

Billy looked him squarely in the eye. "Charlie."

Doug's eyes widened, and his chin dropped. "Charlie!" he repeated in astonishment. "Why would he—like—want to come?"

"Why would he not want to come?" Billy answered him. "He likes to have fun just like you do." Billy poked his finger into Doug's chest to emphasize his point, and Doug stepped back and dropped onto a twig chair.

"Yeah, but—like—Charlie's—" Doug protested from his seated position.

"Charlie's what?" Billy demanded, glaring at Doug. "Besides," Billy continued, "I invited him." He now gave the surprised young fellow a grin of satisfaction.

Doug tried to hide his feelings; he said nothing and stared up at the ceiling of the veranda. As he sprawled out on the twig chair, he stretched both arms out along the back of the chair, causing his jacket to open out wide.

Billy took this opportunity to read Doug's t-shirt. 'I'm not going to say what I'd like to, 'cause if I did, you'd smack me!' Billy snickered. When Doug saw he had read what was on his shirt, he raised one knee and brought his heel up onto the chair, and he leaned forward with his arm across his knee. Billy laughed at him and then he turned to look towards the parking area and the spruce woods beyond.

It was silent on the veranda for a few seconds until Doug spoke. "Hey, Paul—like—what do you want to do?"

"I don't know," he replied. "What do you want to do?"

"I don't know," he answered as he lowered his foot and sat up. "Like—what do you want to do?"

"When you two guys are through your discussion," Billy interrupted, "you might take advantage of the remaining time to go down to the lake. Have a look-see what we've done to the fishing boat there." Doug and Paul jumped over the steps of the veranda followed by Brampton and Davy, and the four fellows raced away.

"Guys," Billy called after them. "Come back when you hear the whistle." Paul waved, and the boys continued their run through the field towards the lake.

Billy removed the whistle from his pocket and placed the lanyard over his head. He started to check his watch when he heard a truck coming through the spruce woods, and he headed for the parking area to meet Charlie. The pickup stopped, and Charlie's mother rolled down the window. "Hi, Billy. Sorry we're late."

"No, it's alright. The other guys took off for a few minutes." He looked over at Charlie who was tightly holding his sleeping bag on his lap. "Come on, Charlie, let's go. Cool weather we've been having lately. You think there'll be frost on the pumpkins tonight?"

The boy looked over at him, grinned shyly, and opened the door. When he stepped to the ground, Billy could not help noticing the little fellow's worn sneakers, and his army surplus sleeping bag looked like it had survived several wars.

A little girl jumped from the cab of the truck and ran over to Billy. "Billy, can I come, too?" She pulled on his sleeve. "Mommy is giving these two loaves of bread. One from me and one from Charlie—see! Please, Billy, please, can I come, too?"

"I told you, Annie," Charlie replied to his twin sister, "this is for guys only."

"Come on, Annie," her mother told her as she grasped the steering wheel of the truck, "we've got to go home and fix supper for Dad and Grandma."

Annie returned to the truck, and her mother started the engine. "Bye, Charlie," his mom called to him.

"Bye, Charlie," Annie echoed through the open window. "Bye, Billy."

Billy turned and waved. "Thanks, Ladies, for the homemade bread. See you tomorrow about ten."

Charlie followed Billy to the barn as he carried his sleeping bag by the binder-twine wrapped around it. Billy brought his whistle to his lips, and when he faced the field with the lake beyond, he blew it sharply. Then he turned to Charlie who had his hands up inside the sleeves of his jack-shirt.

"I hope you like brown beans for supper," Billy said. Charlie looked up at him and grinned.

The four boys soon reappeared and bounded up onto the veranda. "That fishing boat's some neat," Paul said as he flopped down on a twig chair. "Now someone can sleep there overnight."

"Can we go to the cabin now?" Davy asked, and he glanced at Charlie who was standing close to Billy.

Doug pointed to Charlie's sleeping bag on the veranda floor. "Like—who belongs to that!" he blurted out.

Billy decided to ignore him. "Okay, Guys," he instructed them, "grab your stuff, and each guy carries a bag of food."

The boys scrambled for their sleeping bags, and they snatched up the shopping bags of food. "Hey," Billy cautioned, "watch those eggs, will you."

When all the food bags were picked up, Paul yelled, "Okay, let's go!"

"This bag's some heavy!" Davy grunted as he lifted it from the floor and started for the steps.

"Davy, trade with that tough guy over there," Billy told him as he nodded at Doug. After Doug and Davy exchanged their loads, the older brother ran ahead to catch up to Paul and Brampton who had already started along the trail into the woods. And then Davy and Charlie with Billy behind them, began their hike along the trail. Billy let the two boys walk at their own pace. Each boy carried his sleeping bag under one arm and a bag of food in the other hand.

The gap between them and the older fellows was gradually increasing. Davy snickered. "Wouldn't it be funny if those guys got lost!"

Billy chuckled. "Get lost? I hope not! Doug and Paul have been in this neck of the woods plenty of times."

"Hey, Billy," Davy exclaimed a short time later, "you're not carrying a food bag. How come?"

"Well, it's like this," answered Billy, "the leader of the group has privileges."

"Well, if you're the leader of the group," giggled Davy, "how come you're at the end of the line instead of the front?"

Charlie quickly answered him, "Billy's bringing up the rear." And then he giggled at his own joke.

"Hey, Billy," Davy asked, "what book has lots of people in it but doesn't tell a story?"

Billy looked puzzled. "How can that be? A book about people, but it has no story?"

"I know," Charlie answered. "A phone book."

Billy grinned. "Of course—the phone book." Both boys giggled again.

Billy could hear farther along the trail, the occasional loud talk and clamors of the three older boys. He could see them some of the time, but usually they were lost from view in the dips and rises of the woods and the thick clusters of spruce and pine trees. The sun was no longer penetrating deep into the woods, but the absence of the leafy canopy overhead still allowed the two groups of fellows some light as they moved along. It was noisy tramping through the dry leaves, and Billy could hear the chit-chat of the two young fellows with him. *It's nice that Davy and Charlie are getting along,* thought Billy.

"Turn to the left here, guys," Billy instructed them some time later. "That's the side path there to the cabin." Charlie stepped ahead and turned onto the narrow path, and Davy and Billy followed. They traveled along the path, and when they entered the small clearing, the cabin, which was painted a deep, dark green, could barely be seen in the twilight.

Davy said, "The other guys aren't here yet. I don't see them."

Charlie suggested, "Maybe they're hiding." And he giggled.

Billy could tell the three older fellows had not arrived. "No, they're not here," he revealed to them. "See the leaves on the path ahead of you? The fellows haven't walked through here yet."

Davy looked up at Billy and grinned. "We got here first," he said proudly and then added, "Those other guys got lost!"

Billy and the two boys approached the cabin, and Billy pushed open the door and entered. The boys followed him inside. "It's not very light in here," Davy commented.

Billy dropped his sleeping bag and pillow on a lower bunk and pushed back all the window curtains to allow in as much outside light as possible. "Put your bags of food on the table, Fellows, and grab a bunk." He removed his whistle and pushed it deep into his jack-shirt pocket.

"I want that upper bed there," Davy decided, and he tossed his sleeping bag up onto it.

Charlie said, "I'll take that one up over there."

Billy leaned out the door to listen for the three older boys. "Nothing," he said. When he came back in, he lifted the metal lid of the stove and held the brim of his cap as he peered into the black interior. He lit a match from the jar on the shelf and held it over the open stove. "Good," he decided. "It's ready to light." After he checked that the damper was open, he carefully dropped the burning match onto the birchbark and slid the cover back in place.

"Those guys are lost!" Davy mentioned once more and then added, "Dad says that Doug's horror moans are coming to life—whatever that means. But I think that Doug is practicing to be a pain—a real pain. Thing is, he's already quite good at it—he doesn't need to practice anymore."

"Don't worry about Doug and those other guys," Billy snickered. "You fellows hungry? Get that saucepan, Davy, and there should be a can opener in the drawer over there. Charlie, you unpack the bags of food. I hope we carried the brown beans. If those guys stay on the trail, they'll come to the barn where we started out." He grinned at the two boys, and Charlie giggled, and Davy joined in. Billy tipped back his head and gave an exaggerated laugh but then suddenly became serious. "If those irresponsible roosters don't show up in a few minutes," he informed the boys, "I'll go out looking for them." He felt for his whistle in his jack-shirt pocket.

Billy glanced out the window towards the path. It was getting dark in the woods, but it was even darker in the cabin. "Let's light some candles," he suggested. "See how many you can find, Guys, and bring them here to the counter." The boys found five candles in holders and lined them up on the counter. As Billy opened the can of beans, he said, "Charlie, would you like to light the candles? And Davy can carefully put them on the window sills so the other fellows can see us here."

Billy placed the saucepan of beans on the woodstove which was now throwing out some heat. "Now, where's the wieners?" he wondered aloud.

"We don't have the wieners," Charlie replied checking over their supply of food. "The other guys have them."

"No problem." Billy put the lid on the saucepan. "We'll add the wieners after they get here."

"We could get the frying pan ready for the wieners," Charlie suggested, "and when they come, we should cut them into small pieces to fry and then add them to the beans. They're good that way." He looked at Billy for his approval.

"That's a good idea, Charlie," he replied. "Do you mind if I add your idea to my personal collection of recipes?" And then he grinned at the boy who returned the grin.

The cabin was warming up, and Billy removed his jack-shirt. He rolled it into a ball and pitched it across the cabin to his bed. Davy took off his jacket, and Charlie unbuttoned his jack-shirt.

"Listen!" Billy suddenly commanded. The two boys followed his gaze out the large black window on the opposite side of the cabin from the path they came in on. Davy crossed to the window and pressed his nose against the glass causing his cap to tumble to the floor. He shielded his eyes from the candlelight as he stared out into the darkness. Three lights could be seen coming towards them through the trees.

"It's them alright," announced Davy. Soon one of the lights shone across the small clearing and through the window. It was followed by two more lights which momentarily lit up the interior of the cabin.

Charlie moved and stood next to Billy at the stove. The door abruptly swung open wide, and the three older boys bounded into the cabin with their flashlights on. They waved their lights all around the room and into the eyes of Billy and the two younger boys. "Yup, this is the right place alright," Paul determined. "I can tell."

"Well," Billy welcomed them, "if it isn't the late Paul, Doug, and Brampton! Good evening to you, Sirs. Nice day if it don't rain. Did you guys bring the wieners by any chance?"

"Wieners!" Doug piped up as he dropped onto a lower bunk and then sprawled out on it. "Like—if I had known we had the wieners, I would've—like—had one. I'm—like—some starved, Man!"

Paul sat on one of the kitchen chairs and muttered. "I would have eaten two wieners."

"I would have eaten three," Brampton bragged as he put his food bag on the table and glanced around the cabin.

Billy informed them, "Well, I'm glad you didn't know you had the wieners." He located the package of wieners and slit it open with a knife. "Here, Charlie—do your thing."

"Doug said he knew the way," Paul complained to Billy with a scowl. "It was the way alright! The long way!" He looked over at Doug in an accusing manner.

"You've been—like—here before," Doug snapped at Paul from his stretched out position. "Like—how come you didn't know the way?"

"Well," Billy said calmly, "at least you guys gave your flashlights a good workout. I hope they don't let you down when you go out to the outhouse in the dark in the middle of the night."

"Outhouse!" Brampton groaned as he looked over at Paul.

"Okay, Guys," Billy said, "clear off the table and then bring all the candles and put them there." Paul and Brampton moved the things to the counter, but Doug stayed relaxed on the bunk. "Doug," Billy ordered him, "you can set the table. We need six spoons and we better have knives for bread." Doug moaned but did not move, and Billy added, "And Doug, make sure we have six chairs around the table. And let's see, check if we need firewood from the woodpile outside. How about water from the barrel while you're out there?" Doug slowly sat up and swung his feet off the side of the bed.

"Brampton," Billy said to him, "you can put that carton of milk and the package of sausages in the fridge and the carton of eggs, too."

Brampton looked around the room and then at Billy with a puzzled expression. "Fridge?"

"Yeah," Billy replied as he put another stick of wood in the fire. "We use that window over there as a fridge. Open it a crack and put the food on the window sill and make sure the curtain is closed all around it. That's a heavy curtain. It'll keep the warmth of the room away from whatever we put behind it. And the window is on the north side. The sun never shines into there."

Brampton picked up the milk, sausages, and eggs. "Cool!"

"Hey, Charlie," Doug said to him in a sly way, "is your house—like—on the Old Trail Road?"

Charlie looked uncomfortable, and Billy wondered what was coming next. The younger boy answered hesitatingly, "Yes."

"Well—like—you better get your house off the road," Doug told him. "It's—like—blocking traffic." Charlie grinned in relief, and Billy snickered.

By the time the boys had completed their assigned jobs, and the three older fellows had squabbled over the unclaimed upper bunk left to them, the wiener snips were nicely fried and added to the beans. Billy served the beans and wieners in paper bowls, and Charlie set them on the table in front of each of the boys. Before Billy had placed the bread and a container of butter on the table, Brampton had started to eat, and Paul kicked him under the table.

"Hey!" He glared first at Paul and then Doug. "Somebody kicked me."

"Okay, Fellows," Billy said when he had sat down and pulled off his corduroy cap, "let's give thanks." Davy took off his cap and laid it down on the table beside his dinner. Billy thanked the Lord for the forgiveness of sin through the Lord Jesus Christ, and he thanked Him for the time they were spending here at the cabin. Finally he gave thanks for the food.

Doug reached over, snatched up his younger brother's cap, and spun it through the air across the cabin. It hit the floor and slid under a bunk. "Like—what's the matter with you, Kid," he snapped. "Don't you—like—have any manners?" He grinned at Paul and Brampton, but when he saw Billy glaring at him, he quickly sobered up.

"Douglas Leland Copton," Billy told him firmly, "would you please pick up Davy's cap for him and politely return it to him? We're roughing it here in the woods, but we still practice good manners and respect for others. Perhaps, Boy, you've forgotten the rule here about guys who misbehave. Do you remember what it is?"

"Yeah," Doug quietly answered.

Billy waited several seconds. "Well," he asked him, "what do you remember about guys who misbehave?"

Doug replied meekly, "They don't—like—get invited back."

"Who doesn't get invited back, Doug?" Billy insisted.

He finally admitted, "Guys who—like—misbehave don't get invited back."

"You're right," Billy answered him. "Thanks for reminding us, Doug." And Billy grinned at him. "Now get Davy's cap for him."

Charlie took a slice of bread and spread butter over it. Brampton did the same and said, "Maybe I should become a Christian like you guys. I don't mind going to church, and it would be fun to do other neat things."

Billy looked at him not knowing how to respond. *That's not what being a Christian means,* he contemplated. *But at one time I used to think that being a Christian meant doing Christian things like going to church, reading my Bible and praying and being good, too.* Billy stared at the flame of the candle near him and continued his thoughts. *But being a genuine, Bible-believing Christian first means we accept Christ and what He has done for us because of our sin, and then we live a life of doing Christian things like going to church, reading our Bibles, and praying in order to learn and grow, and be useful to the Lord.*

"Hey!" Paul exclaimed, "these little wiener pieces are alright fried like this."

"Yeah," agreed Doug as he loaded his spoon. "Like—some delicious good!"

"I agree with you, Doug," said Billy. "Charlie has good ideas. What do you fellows want for liquid refreshment? We have both milk and apple juice." He glanced around at them. "Doug, can you reach the paper cups behind you?"

"I'll have a swig of apple juice," Davy said.

Doug said, "I don't want apple juice. I'll—like—have milk."

After about ten minutes, most of the brown beans and wieners were gone. "Who wants more?" asked Billy.

"I do," Doug replied as he stuffed the remainder of his bread into his mouth.

"What's for dessert?" Paul asked when he looked over to the counter. "Let's have them donuts there," he suggested.

After everyone had eaten and the boys were getting restless at the table, Billy said, "We need someone to do the dishes." He looked at Brampton. "Brampton, would you gather up the bowls and drop them into the fire." The boy grinned as he stood up and collected the bowls and carried them to the woodstove. "I like doing dishes this way, Brampton, don't you?"

After the bowls were deposited in the stove, Billy turned to the boys and asked, "What would you fellows like to do now?"

"'Gut Feelings' is on television about now," Brampton replied after he checked his watch. "I love watching that program."

"I haven't seen it," Billy admitted.

Paul shrugged his shoulders and reported, "You haven't missed much."

"Like—boring!" Doug responded. "I'd rather—like—watch an old lady knit a pair of long wool socks or watch a dog upchuck his breakfast." And then he said, "Hey, Paul—like—what do you want to do?"

"I don't know," he replied. "What do you want to do?"

"I don't know," he answered. "Like—what do you want to do?"

"There's Chinese checkers over there," Billy quickly butt in as he pointed with his elbow. "We can all play."

"Chinese checkers? Like—what's Chinese checkers?"

About half an hour later, Billy pulled a tall plastic pail out from under the counter and took a half sheet of newspaper from the wood box. Paul studied him as he opened the sheet of newspaper and placed it over the top of the pail and pushed down the edges of the paper around the outside of the pail. As he worked, he whistled softly to himself.

"What are you doing?" questioned Paul, and he came over to him.

"We need a piece of string to hold the newspaper tight to the pail," Billy determined as he surveyed the cabin from his kneeling position on the floor.

Doug stated dryly, "Charlie has—like—a piece of binder-twine."

Paul asked, "What's the pail for, Billy?"

"No, Doug, I don't want to use Charlie's string. He needs it."

Charlie answered, "You can borrow my string."

"Okay, Charlie, thanks."

"What are you making, anyway?" Paul asked once more. He settled himself onto one of the wooden kitchen chairs nearby.

"A mouse trap," Billy revealed as he accepted the twine Charlie held out to him.

"A mouse trap!" Paul exclaimed. "How's that a mouse trap?"

"Here, Paul," Billy said to him, "hold the newspaper tight as I wrap this twine around and tie it."

Paul knelt down and held the newspaper. "How are you going to catch a mouse with this?" he asked doubtfully.

Billy tied the twine and then gently tapped on the paper covering the mouth of the pail. "Good," he decided as he stood up and reached over for a sharp knife on the counter. He sliced a five inch 'X' in the newspaper over the mouth of the pail. "Davy, hand me that jar of peanut butter over there," Billy asked as he ripped a small piece about the size of his hand from the corner of the newspaper against the outside of the pail. He opened the jar of peanut butter and smeared a small amount onto it.

Charlie came closer and remarked, "Mice like peanut butter better than cheese, don't they?"

"Oh, I get it," Davy said as Billy carefully laid the small piece of newspaper over the 'X'. "The mouse walks across the newspaper to get the peanut butter, and he falls through the 'X' and into the pail."

"You could—like—put water in the pail," Doug hinted, "and then it would be automatic curtains for the mouse."

"This is a live trap, Guys. We don't want to hurt the furry, little fellow."

"Yeah, but how does the mouse climb up the outside of the pail to get to the peanut butter?" questioned Paul, looking up at Billy.

"We place the top of the pail level with the top of the counter to make it easy for him," replied Billy, and then he wondered, "And how should we do that?"

"I know how," spoke up Charlie. "Let's hang the pail by its handle onto the back of that chair and move it to the counter."

"Good idea."

Brampton, who was watching from the lower bunk, observed, "The peanut butter is bait that isn't worth a decent meal for the mouse, and even when he gets it, he's caught by the trap."

"You're right, Brampton," Billy answered. "And if Doug had his way, the mouse would not only be caught, he'd be curtains."

"If we catch a mouse tonight," Charlie protested, "we should let him go in the woods tomorrow, shouldn't we, Billy?"

"I agree with you, Charlie. You know, Brampton says that the peanut butter is a temptation that isn't worth a meal for the mouse. He's right. And when the mouse falls for the temptation, he falls into the pail. That's the way it is with sin. We are tempted to do something which is wrong, and we think we really want to do it, and we fall for it. Later, we find out it wasn't really as good as we thought it was going to be." He paused to let that sink in.

Paul concluded, "What looked like a good meal for the mouse could end in curtains for him, and when we fall for temptations, we sin—we've broken God's laws, and we deserve to go to hell."

"That's right, Paul. You explained that very well," Billy replied. "But the Bible says the Lord Jesus provided the way of escape for us. Charlie wants to let the mouse go to start a new life in the woods. We have a choice—we can accept what Christ has done for us—He took our sin and died on the cross in our place, or we can reject Him."

The pail was positioned, and a half hour later Billy called out, "Who wants something to eat?"

Doug asked, "Like—what do we have?"

"There's a package of cookies, and we didn't finish the donuts." Doug grabbed for the lunch on the table.

"Doug's hogging the donuts," Paul called out. "Save one for me, will you!"

"Oink, oink," Doug responded.

"Charlie," Billy questioned him, "do you have a flashlight?" The boy shook his head.

"I'll share mine with you. We'll leave it on the table, okay?" Charlie grinned shyly and nodded.

The young fellows made trips to the outhouse with their flashlights, and as Doug went out the door, he muttered, "I'm glad I don't have to—like—brush my teeth this time before going to bed."

When they returned, Billy told the boys, "We're going to leave one candle burning all night, Guys, so blow out all the candles except the tallest one, and we'll leave that one here on the table."

The boys scrambled to the five candles spread around the cabin. The little flames quickly went out one by one, and the cabin became pitch black. "Hey," Billy called out, "where's the jar of matches?"

"Like—who blew out the last candle?" Doug asked accusingly.

"The last candle!" Paul reacted. "Who has the tallest candle?"

Billy asked, "Where were you when the lights went out?" When no one replied, he answered, "In the dark." He felt for the matches, lit the tallest candle, and placed it on the table, and the boys were soon ready for bed.

After they were settled in their sleeping bags, Billy asked, "What can we be thankful for?"

"Thankful?" Doug questioned from his lower bunk. "Like—why should we be thankful for anything?"

Davy responded, "I'm thankful we can come here to this cabin."

Charlie added, "We can be thankful for our friends."

"We can be thankful for the Lord Jesus Christ," Billy reminded the boys.

"I'm thankful," Paul spoke up, "that I'm saved."

"What does it mean to be saved?" Billy probed him.

Paul replied, "To be saved means to be saved from the anger and condemnation of God because of our sin."

"Yes, that's right," Billy agreed. "The Bible says, 'the wages of sin is death'. The Lord Jesus paid our penalty when He died for us on account of our sin, and we are saved when we believe and trust in Him. We become believers—we now trust in Christ."

Paul said, "I began to trust in Christ at camp last summer."

"Yes," Billy replied, "I remember that. And I was saved at camp, too, seven summers ago. Before that, I used to think getting saved was the way to be a part of the group where my family and all my friends were. Of course I wanted to belong in the group with them—that was only natural. But that's not the correct way to look at it, because being saved means we are saved from the penalty of our sin and from the power of sin in our lives, too."

After nearly a minute of silence, Billy decided, "Let's thank God for the Lord Jesus Christ and salvation through Him. Pray only if you want to, and I'll pray last." Paul prayed, and then Davy, followed by Charlie. Finally Billy closed in prayer.

"Good night, Doug," Billy told him. "Good night, Paul. Good night, Brampton. Good night, Charlie. Good night, Davy."

Davy spoke up, "Good night. Sleep tight. If the mosquitoes bite, squeeze them tight. And we'll have them for supper tomorrow night."

"Bzzz," could be heard from another upper bunk.

Doug reminded the others, "There aren't—like—no mosquitoes this time of year."

"Bzzz," was heard again. "I hear one. Bzzz. Listen! Bzzz."

And then from each of the bunks in this candle-lit place came, "Bzzz, bzzz, bzzz."

"Quick!" Billy called out to the boys. "Squeeze them tight. We'll have them for supper tomorrow night."

An hour or two after midnight, Billy awoke to the sound of someone stirring. By the light of the single candle on the table, he could see Charlie slowly climb down the bunk ladder with his jack-shirt slung over his shoulder. He then reached back to his bed for his sneakers. After he slipped into his jack-shirt and put his sneakers on, he quietly moved to the table where Billy had left his flashlight for him. He proceeded to the door, opened it, switched on the flashlight, and followed the beam of light out into the darkness.

I'll stay awake until he returns from the outhouse, Billy decided. Several minutes later, Charlie, who was now shivering, came back into the cabin. He was soon in his upper bunk again.

Billy had nearly fallen asleep when he once more heard a sound. It was Doug at his lower bunk. After Doug picked up his flashlight next to his pillow, he crossed the cabin floor to the door. In the light of the candle, Billy could see Doug cautiously open the door part way and shine his light through the darkness to the outhouse under the large pine tree. Doug switched off the light and closed the door without going out, and he stood there looking uncomfortable. Once more, several seconds later, the young fellow opened the door, leaned forward, and shone his light outside. Doug pointed his flashlight all around the small clearing and up into the trees nearby. Billy could feel a cold draft of air from the open door, and he could see the candle flame wavering slightly.

He figured, *Doug's afraid to go out to the outhouse in the dark even with his flashlight.* He could see the young fellow switch off his light and close the door again. Doug shifted his weight from one foot to the other several times as he tightly gripped his flashlight.

Billy now realized, *I should get up and offer to go out with him.* He was just about to crawl out of his warm sleeping bag when he saw Charlie sit up. The boy silently climbed down the ladder again carrying his jack-shirt. Billy could see Doug looking over at Charlie as the younger boy picked up his sneakers. Charlie crossed to the table in his pajamas as he pushed his arm into his jack-shirt.

Doug approached him and asked him in a whisper, "Like—you going to the outhouse? Can I—like—come with you? It's—like—kind of dark out there." Charlie nodded as he picked up Billy's flashlight, and the two boys went out and disappeared into the darkness of the night.

Well, what do you know! Billy thought as he stared at the closed door. *That Charlie's alright.*

Several minutes later the two boys returned, and as Doug quietly closed the door behind them, Billy could see both boys were shivering. Charlie had one hand up inside the sleeve of his jack-shirt, and with the other he placed the flashlight on the table.

"Like—thanks, Charlie," Billy could hear Doug whisper to him. Charlie looked at him, grinned, and nodded, and Doug returned the grin.

The two boys glanced over at the live mouse trap hanging from the back of the chair, but they could see the peanut butter was undisturbed. When they were back into their sleeping bags, Billy could hear a whispered, "Good night, Charlie."

Charlie didn't have to do that for Doug, Billy considered as he closed his eyes. He then rolled over and drifted off to sleep.

Several hours later when it was just as light outside the cabin as it was inside with the candle burning, Billy blew out the little flame and opened the curtains at the large window. He quietly built up the fire in the woodstove and placed on top of the stove the pan of water he had dipped from the rain barrel outside.

"Is it time to get up?" a groggy voice mumbled from the upper bunk.

He turned to see Davy sitting up and peering down at him. "You can get up if you want, Davy," he answered him.

"Did we catch a mouse?" the young fellow wanted to know as he picked up his shirt.

"Why don't you have a look," Billy answered, and he reached for the frying pan.

Davy dressed, climbed down the ladder, and came over to the pail hanging from the chair. "The paper with the peanut butter is gone," Davy noted. He carefully spread open the 'X' and peered in.

"There's a mouse in there!" Davy blurted out. "We caught a mouse. Look!"

Billy grinned, bent over to have a look, and then they were joined by Charlie. "Look, Charlie," Davy exclaimed as he stepped aside for the other boy, "there's a mouse in the pail."

Charlie pushed back the paper slit and stared into the pail. "There's two mice in there!" he laughed. "Look again, Davy."

Davy looked once more. "Yeah, you're right. Aren't they cute!"

"We caught a mouse?" someone asked from the bunk beds.

"Yeah," Davy informed Paul who was now sitting up. "We have two mouses. Come have a look-see." Paul came across the floor in his bare feet and peered into the pail.

Doug and Brampton were soon awake and had joined the group. "How come there's—like—two mouses in the pail?" Doug asked as he ran his fingers through his disheveled hair.

Brampton responded, "Maybe when one mouse decided to try the peanut butter, the other mouse followed him, and then they both fell in together."

"Yeah," Billy answered, "I think you're right. And that's like one guy falling for a temptation, and another guy is influenced by him and figures it's alright and he falls as well."

"Let's take them outside and let them go," Davy told the others.

"Get dressed first, Guys," Billy advised them. "It's cold out. Probably frost on the pumpkins." As the boys quickly dressed, Billy covered the bottom of the frying pan with sausages, and he lifted down another pan for the eggs.

Davy removed the pail from the back of the chair and gently lowered the mice to the floor. Charlie untied his twine, threw it to his bunk and dropped the newspaper into the wood box. Davy then carried the pail containing the two mice to the door of the cabin.

"Hurry up, let's go!" Paul urged the other boys as he opened the door and stepped outside onto the landing.

Doug saw them go out the door, and he quickly slipped into his shirt. "But I'm—like—not dressed yet," he protested. He hopped across the floor on one foot as he struggled into his jeans.

"Come on, we don't have all day," Brampton told him from the path outside.

Doug did not take the time to button his shirt nor tuck it in. "Like—wait for me."

"Okay, Fellows," Billy directed, "hold on for Doug. And don't be long out there. I'd like your help with breakfast."

Billy stepped onto the landing. It was now much lighter out, and he could tell it was going to be a fine, sunny day. "Don't let the mice loose close to the cabin," Billy called out. "We don't want them back here tonight. Dump them out away over there beyond those large balsam." He pointed with the fork he was using to roll the sausages.

Billy backed into the cabin and stood at the open door. He heard Doug who was barefoot, say, "Davy carried the pail, and now Charlie should—like—dump out the mice."

Billy grinned as he observed the boys. Before he closed the door, he contemplated, "Nice day if it don't rain." He then crossed to the sausages which were now sizzling on the stove. *Why do I keep saying that?*

After breakfast, but before the boys left the table, Billy told them, "We're going to read God's Word before we get anything else started." Brampton looked surprised but said nothing. He quickly glanced up over the large window at the text which Billy's sister Jennifer had made. It read, 'Trust in the Lord with all thine heart'. Billy pointed across the cabin with his chin. "There are Bibles on the shelf over there." As the boys each took a Bible, he told them, "If we didn't have the Bible we wouldn't know where we came from. We might think we evolved over millions of years from goo to the zoo to you. But God's Word tells us He created our first parents, Adam and Eve. It also tells us that sin entered into the world through the first man, Adam." Davy leaned on his rolled-up sleeping bag with one elbow.

Billy sat on the edge of his chair, leaned forward, and faced the boys on the lower bunks. He said to them, "If we didn't have the Bible we wouldn't know why we're here now. We might think we're here to eat and sleep and have fun, and grow up and then get a job and maybe get married and have kids, and that's it. But God's Word tells us we are under His judgment and condemnation because of our sin, but it also says, 'God so loved the world that He gave His only begotten Son that whosoever believeth in Him should not perish but have everlasting life.'" Billy grinned as he grasped his Bible in both hands. "We know we're here to accept God's gift of salvation, and that'll make us His children and He our Heavenly Father. And then we live the way He wants us to live. This book, the Bible, tells us how." Billy could see this information was new to Brampton, and he could tell Doug was uncomfortable as he sat staring at the floor.

"So if we didn't have the Bible," Billy continued, "we wouldn't know where we came from nor why we're here, neither would we know where we're going. We might think that death is the end of our lives. But God's Word tells us that those who trust in Christ have everlasting life, and when they die they go to Heaven to be with the Lord Jesus. Those who don't, are condemned already—right now—and will spend eternity in hell with the devil and his angels." Charlie listened politely, and Paul nodded in agreement.

After they read a passage of Scripture and briefly discussed it, Billy prayed. Then he stood up and stretched. "Before we go, Fellows," he said, "we need to bring in some firewood from the pile outside. Each of you bring in two pieces. That should be enough."

When the firewood was deposited into the wood box, Paul opened the guest book and read the names of the people who had been here at the cabin this past summer. "Girls stay overnight here, too?" he asked in surprise, looking over at Billy with a disbelieving look on his face. "I thought this place was just for guys."

"Well, no," Billy responded as he checked the water on the stove. "Jennifer has girls here once in a while, too." As he was tidying up, Doug and Brampton returned the clean forks to the drawer.

Paul went back to his reading. "Who's Mitch the Grinner?" he asked.

"Mitch the Grinner," Billy repeated thoughtfully. "Mitch the Grinner was a guy who came with his parents to family camp. He didn't want to be at camp so he took off into the woods. I chased after him, and we ended up here at this cabin. Mitch grinned a lot, and before we left to go back to family camp, Mitch the Grinner was a happy camper, and he joined in the camp activities. Well, anyway, that's the abbreviated but true version of the story."

Paul suddenly screwed up his face. "Some guy here wrote out, 'a e i o u.' Why would he do that?"

Billy snickered. “That was some kid at camp who liked to demonstrate his ability to burp the vowels.” Paul looked amused.

Davy asked, “Can we sign our names in the guest book?”

“Sure—go ahead.”

After the six sleeping bags were rolled up, Billy packed the leftover food to carry out, and the garbage was put in a separate bag. “Okay, Fellows,” he called when he glanced around the cabin one more time, “help with this stuff here, will you. It’s time to skedaddle. Hey! Who belongs to that there cap, the one with the funny looking head of a critter on the front?”

Billy and the five boys left the cabin, and Billy hooked the door. As they started along the path to the main trail, the three older fellows suddenly bolted ahead. Several minutes later, Billy, Davy, and Charlie turned to the right onto the main trail and Davy looked along the path through the woods in the direction the older fellows went.

“Those guys are ‘way ahead of us,” Davy commented. “I don’t see them.”

Billy snickered. “You think they’ll get lost again?”

“Let’s hurry and catch up to them,” Davy suggested with a grin.

Billy told them, “When they see us running towards them, they’ll go even faster. We’ll never catch up.”

“I know what we should do,” Charlie proposed as he shuffled through the dry leaves at his feet. “When we don’t see them, we should run towards them. But when we see them, we should walk real slow.” He and Davy laughed in agreement.

“That’s a good idea, guys,” Billy acknowledged. “They’re beyond those spruce trees. Let’s go.” They broke into a run, but because of their loads, they soon changed to a slow jog.

“There they are,” Charlie called out in a hushed voice. “Quick, walk real slow.”

Billy and the two boys walked at a leisurely pace until the three older boys dropped from view on the far side of a gentle hill. The two boys, followed by Billy, began to hustle up the slope towards them. When they reached the level area at the top, Davy suddenly eased off to a walk, and Billy almost ran into him.

"There they are!" Davy exclaimed, breathing heavily. "I think we're catching up to them."

Gradually, Billy and the two younger boys reduced the distance between them and the older boys. "When they look this way," Billy told Davy and Charlie, "we should look off somewhere else. We don't want them to think that we're interested in them or trying to catch up to them."

Several minutes later the three older boys were in view again, but out of earshot. "They see us," Charlie decided as he stopped and made out he was looking at something off to his right, "but they don't suspect anything."

Over the next few minutes, Billy and the two boys decreased the gap until they were within speaking distance of the three older fellows. Davy and Charlie giggled, and Doug suddenly turned around. He stared at Billy and the younger boys who were casually strolling along several metres away. "Like— where'd you guys come from?" he asked, and Paul and Brampton turned to face them as well. "You—like—know a shortcut?"

"Who, us?" Davy replied innocently. "Hunky-dory doodle. We're just heading out from a night at the cabin in the woods." The three older boys suddenly took off running along the trail leaving Billy and the two younger boys laughing at them.

Five minutes later, Billy could see the barn through the trees, and then three vehicles in the parking area came into his view. When he and the younger boys arrived, Paul and Brampton were in the car and ready to leave.

"Bye, Billy, and thanks," Paul called out to him. "See you tomorrow." His dad and Brampton waved as the car left.

Doug was sitting in the van with the sliding door open. He stepped out, handed the bags of leftover food to Billy and he took Davy's sleeping bag from him and placed it beside his on the seat.

Billy told him, "We had a good time, didn't we, Doug? We'll plan to go again sometime, okay?"

Doug nodded. "Like—sure thing."

"I like your t-shirt," Billy told him, and he gave the young fellow a quick nod. Doug returned a nod and then looked away.

As Mrs. Copton pulled out of the parking area, Doug leaned out the front window of the van. "Bye, Billy. Bye, Charlie," he shouted. "Like—see ya." Charlie grinned as he stood there with his hands up inside his jack-shirt.

As the Copton's van disappeared into the spruce thicket, Billy walked up to Charlie who was standing near the pickup truck. The beaming boy looked up at him. "Thanks, Billy, for inviting me to the cabin."

Billy replied, "Thank you for coming. And I saw what you did for Doug. You're a real gentleman, Charlie. I like that." Charlie opened the truck door and climbed in, and before he closed the door, Billy placed the plastic shopping bags of left-over food at his feet.

Charlie's mother said to Billy, "Thank you for thinking of Charlie." She started the engine, and they were off.

Billy hopped up the steps of the barn veranda and sat on one of the twig chairs. He folded his arms across his chest and pushed his hands into his armpits. *Thank You, Lord,* he prayed, *for using me to work in the lives of these young fellows. Some need to admit to their sin, and some need continued encouragement in their Christian lives.*

Billy heard a vehicle coming along the dirt road through the spruce trees. The family car driven by his brother was coming his way. He picked up his sleeping bag and pillow and headed for the parking area.

chapter twenty-three

the following spring—May 1998

"I Do." "I Do."

With one hand on the steering wheel, Timothy crept past the empty vehicles and drove to the far side of the parking area. "Lots of cars here," he remarked to Billy, and he turned and headed to the far side of the building.

Billy glanced at the clock on the dash. "Two, fifty-two."

Timothy parked his car near the rear door of the meeting place and shut off the engine. He and Billy emerged from the car, crossed the gravel, and joined Mr. Dodge and Stanley who were waiting on the grass.

"Gentlemen," Mr. Dodge greeted as he stepped towards them.

"Hi, Tom," Timothy replied as he nodded. Mr. Dodge shook his hand and then Billy's. Timothy then looked over at Stanley, and they grinned at one another. "Stanley," he said as he shook his hand. Stanley squeezed his hand firmly. When he relaxed his grip, Timothy gave him a quick embrace.

"Friend and soon brother," Stanley said to him.

"Twice brother," Timothy reminded him. Stanley grinned at him again, and then he turned and shook hands with Billy.

Timothy examined his watch, and Billy replied casually, "Nice day if it don't rain."

From the other side of the building, Mr. Two Rivers with his video camera approached the group of men. His little girl was a step or two behind him. "Can I get a quick shot of you fellows before the ceremony begins?"

"Sure, Levi," Mr. Dodge answered. Stanley ran his fingers through his blonde hair, Timothy pressed back his mustache, and Billy stood up straight.

"Hi, Jessica," Billy greeted the youngster at her dad's side. Her long, straight, black hair gently blew in the breeze as she smiled bashfully at him.

"Where do you want us?" asked Timothy.

"The way you're standing now would be fine." He shot about ten seconds of video tape of the four grinning men posing near the rear door.

"Thanks, Fellows," Mr. Two Rivers said. "Come on, Jesse Girl, let's go." She put her little hand up into her dad's hand.

A minute later the men heard a voice call out to them, "Hey, Guys, you're supposed to have these here flowers." A young fellow in his early teens hurried over and handed one each to Timothy, Billy, and Stanley.

"Thanks, Mark," Billy told him. "Looks like I forgot to pick them up."

Mark turned to leave. "See ya."

"Wait," Timothy let out. "Help me pin it on, Boy."

Mark stopped and faced Timothy. "No way! I don't pin no flowers on nobody. I'm mortified enough as it is—taking ladies to their seats. Can't they find their own way?" He made an exaggerated frown as he backed away.

"Well, Mark, what about me?" Timothy asked him as he returned the frown. "Don't you think I'll be embarrassed? I have to kiss a girl in front of all those people in there looking at me."

Mark's step-brother hurried into view. "They're ready, Timothy," he announced. "You guys have to go in now."

"Thanks, Mark," Timothy informed him, "we will."

"Come on, Mark," Mark Two told Mark One, "we're supposed to escort the mothers to their seats and then close the doors." The two young fellows turned and dashed off together.

"Here, Men," Mr. Dodge offered, "I'll help you with your corsages."

After the three corsages were in place, Mr. Dodge suggested, "Let's commit ourselves to the Lord again before we go inside."

The four men formed a huddle with their hands on each other's shoulders. "We come to Thee in the Name of the Lord Jesus Christ giving Thee thanks for Him," Mr. Dodge prayed. "May Thy presence be known to us at this time, and may all be done for Thy glory causing others to praise Thee." Mr. Dodge broke away from the huddle. "Okay, Men, let's go." Timothy stood tall, and once more he instinctively smoothed back his mustache. Mr. Dodge opened the rear door to the auditorium of the meeting place, and the four men entered.

The windows in the dormers overhead allowed in plenty of light on four sides, and a stream of sunlight filtered through the shears on the south side, making this room a pleasant place to have a wedding.

Timothy did not attempt to see who was there. He kept his eyes on the closed double doors at the opposite side of the large, square, white room. He could see through one of the long, narrow windows of the doors, the bridesmaid, the younger sister of the bride.

Mr. Knott signalled everyone to stand, and he started the hymn, 'Lord Jesus, Who Dids't Once Appear to Grace a Marriage Feast.' The singing people turned to face the closed double doors, and as they finished the first verse, the doors opened, revealing the wedding party. Anne slowly stepped forward. She wore spring colours of yellow and green. Several paces behind her could be seen a bride on the arm of her father.

Timothy watched as his dad and sister began their slow march across the room towards him but he promptly looked beyond them to Mr. Clayton and the waiting bride at his side. *There's Kathleen,* Timothy contemplated, and he could feel himself grinning. *She's beautiful!* As she came closer, Timothy could see through her veil that his bride was smiling back at him. Both brides with their fathers and the bridesmaid between, stood facing the four men. Timothy realized he was not nervous anymore, only pleased, and excited, too.

When the hymn came to an end, the people remained standing and Mr. Dodge prayed for the friends and families gathered to witness this double wedding. He prayed for the two grooms and their brides. The relatives and friends then sat down, and Mr. Dodge asked, "Who gives this woman, Jennifer Jean Jack, to this man, Stanley John Clark?"

Mr. Jack replied, "Her mother and I, with pleasure, give our daughter to this man, Stanley Clark."

Mr. Dodge then addressed Jennifer. "Your parents, Jennifer, are giving you away in marriage to this man. They now relinquish from this day forth all their responsibilities before the Lord for you their daughter. Your father no longer holds any authority over you, neither will he assume any responsibility for your care, well-being, nor your protection. Neither will you have your father's name from this time on." After pausing for several seconds, he asked, "Who gives this woman, Kathleen Rose Waters, to this man, Timothy Titus Jack?"

Mr. Clayton answered, "Kathleen's mother and I are happy to give her to this man, Timothy Jack."

Mr. Dodge turned to Kathleen and informed her, "Kathleen, your parents are giving you to this man in marriage. From this day forth they are giving up all their responsibilities before the Lord for you, their daughter. Mr. Clayton no longer has any authority over you, neither will he assume any responsibilities for your care, well-being, nor your protection. Neither will you have your natural father's name from now on." The two fathers then sat with their wives in the front rows of chairs.

Mr. Dodge then placed a small table with four handwritten agreements on it between the audience and the wedding party.

It was then that Timothy could see Mr. Fullerton, a friend of the Clayton family rise up in the audience and approach the wedding party with a white envelope in his hand. The man turned to face the people gathered there.

"Mrs. Clayton, mother of the bride Kathleen has requested that I open this envelope and read the contents aloud," Mr. Fullerton reported to the people. "On the front of this sealed envelope it says, 'To be read at the wedding of my daughter Kathleen Rose Waters.'" Mr. Fullerton reached into his pocket and withdrew his folding knife.

Kathleen looked startled. She first glanced over at Mr. Fullerton, then at Timothy who was showing surprise and then at her mom who had her eyes cast down. Finally Kathleen looked back to Timothy.

There was a great hush in the room filled with puzzled wedding guests. The only sound was the rustle of the envelope as Mr. Fullerton carefully sliced it open with his knife. Before he drew out the single sheet of paper, he returned his knife to his pocket, and after he unfolded the paper, he quickly and silently read what was written on it.

Timothy shifted his feet, and through Kathleen's veil, he could see a mystified expression on her face. And then he looked over at her mother who seemed distant yet somehow unconcerned.

Finally, Mr. Fullerton lowered the paper and turned to face Timothy who was watching him anxiously. When their eyes met, Timothy was somewhat relieved to see a smile slowly spreading over his face. Mr. Fullerton cleared his throat and addressed Timothy. "This letter is dated November nineteenth, nineteen eighty-nine," he revealed to him but loud enough for all to hear.

"'Dear Gentleman, bridegroom of my daughter Kathleen Rose Waters,'" Mr. Fullerton began to read. "'At the time of this writing, my daughter has just turned fourteen years old.'"

Kathleen looked up at Timothy as Mr. Fullerton continued to read. "'I do not know to whom I am writing. I do not know if you are one of the young fellows I see around here week after week or perhaps I have never met you—you are a total stranger to me.'" Kathleen grinned at Timothy. "'But I want you to know that Kathleen's mother and I have been praying for you since the day she was born. Therefore I am confident you are the Lord's choice for my daughter.'" Timothy glanced over at Mrs. Clayton who was now smiling at him.

"'I am sorry I cannot be there with you and Kathleen and her mother to share in that joyful time of your wedding as the Lord is soon to call me away to Himself.'" Mr. Fullerton faced

Timothy and continued to read. "'Take care of my daughter Kathleen, will you, Young Man. She now seems so young and vulnerable. Keep her in the things of the Lord, and may the two of you as a united couple be sensitive to the leading of the Holy Spirit in your lives. May you serve Him together for His glory.' And it's signed, 'Love, Isaac Waters.'"

Mr. Fullerton then turned to Kathleen and continued. "'P.S. Kathleen my daughter, you now belong to this man. I know he is a man of God, and I know you will love, honour and obey this man who is now your husband. From your daddy.'" Kathleen was pleased as she glanced from Timothy to Mr. Fullerton and to her mom, and then she looked at Timothy who grinned and took a deep sigh of relief. Mr. Fullerton refolded the letter, returned it to its envelope, and he handed it to Timothy who nodded and pushed it down into his inside jacket pocket.

As Mr. Fullerton returned to his seat with his wife, Mr. Dodge smiled and looked over the friends and families gathered in the meeting place.

"The first wedding was in a beautiful garden," he told them. "The Lord Himself gave the bride away. The Bible tells us He brought her unto the man. But first we need some background detail regarding this first wedding."

Mr. Dodge took a step forward towards the people and proceeded. "After the Lord God had made the man, He said, 'It is not good for the man to be alone.' And then He said that He would make for the man, a helper suitable for him. We see here that it's not good that men should be alone; they need suitable help." Mr. Dodge gave a quick glance back at Timothy and Stanley. "These two men are standing here this afternoon before you, admitting they need help. And each of these men are here to receive the bride the Lord has provided to help him. He has brought Kathleen and Jennifer into the lives of Timothy and Stanley, and just now these women have been brought before us and to these men to be united in marriage."

Timothy could see those in the room listening attentively. "Women are special," Mr. Dodge said to the people. "God's Word tells us He formed every beast of the field and every fowl of the air out of the ground, and also from the dust of the ground, He formed man. But the woman was special; her creation was different; she was made from one of the ribs taken from man. We have seen in the lives of Stanley and Timothy that they have recognized that women are special by the regard they have for them, and we are sure both of these men will always know that for them, these two women are the most special of all." Kathleen looked up at Timothy and smiled, and he winked at her.

"The first woman was fashioned not from the man's head to make her superior," Mr. Dodge informed the wedding guests, "nor of a bone from his foot for him to trample on or to disrespect, but she was formed from a rib of his side, close to his heart, and also from his side to be his companion." Timothy could see Mrs. Charles looking pleased.

Mr. Dodge turned around and spoke directly to the two couples. "Timothy and Kathleen, may you ever be close in the hearts of one another. And may you, Stanley and Jennifer, always be close in the hearts of each other. And remember: husbands and wives must be pleasant so each will be attracted to the other and will want to spend time together in companionship."

Mr. Dodge paused for several seconds before making his next point. "I must remind you, Stanley and Timothy," he said looking from one to the other, "that God's Word says husbands are to love their wives as their own bodies. Each of you men are to nourish and cherish your wife."

Mr. Dodge paused again and then spoke to the brides. "Likewise, Jennifer and Kathleen, Scripture says wives are to reverence or respect their husbands. Each of you is to submit yourself to your own husband because, before Christ, he is your head."

Timothy glanced out to the people gathered there. *I'm glad Uncle Drew and his family could come,* he reflected. *They live so far away.*

Mr. Dodge turned and faced the wedding party. "And Stanley and Jennifer, Timothy and Kathleen," he said to them, "we know that if the Lord blesses you by giving you children, you will bring them up in the nurture and admonition of the Lord. The will of the Lord is that not only you yourselves be saved but your houses—that is your children are to be saved as well. It will give you joy to have children, but your joy will be even greater as each of your children comes to the Lord. Make sure your homes are Christian homes, not merely homes where Christians live." Timothy looked through Kathleen's veil and into her eyes. She was smiling, and he knew he was too.

"And finally, let me say," Mr. Dodge faced the two couples and continued, "the man and woman who marry, begin a life of their own together, and this union is to be permanent. 'What therefore God hath joined together, let not man put asunder.' To each of you, the ring which you are going to give to your spouse is a promise of your commitment to your marriage, not only to yourselves, but it is a declaration of your promise before others."

Mr. Dodge rotated slightly and looked over his shoulder to the people assembled there and said, "May Timothy and Kathleen, Stanley and Jennifer, be shining examples of the permanency and the unity of marriage as God has intended, and may the harmony and fulfillment they exhibit in bringing Him glory be evident all their lives to those with whom they come in contact."

During the past several months both couples had taken counsel and had gleaned advice from their parents and a few older married couples who were known for their sound relationships. And now today after Mr. Dodge had handed the four agreements to Timothy and Kathleen, Stanley and Jennifer, the two couples read to each other the marriage vows they had composed. And then in the presence of all gathered there, the two couples approached the small table and signed their names to their handwritten agreements.

Mr. Dodge then informed them, "Timothy and Kathleen, Stanley and Jennifer, you have made these solemn promises to each other, and also you have made them before God." He then swept his hand back towards the people there and reminded the two couples that their families and friends were also witnesses to these agreements they had just signed. Mr. Dodge announced to all, "Timothy and Kathleen, you are now husband and wife. Stanley and Jennifer, you are now husband and wife."

After Timothy and Stanley each saluted their wives, Timothy could see Mark One off to one side. The young fellow appeared to be studying the dormers at the far side of the room.

Mr. Dodge faced the newlyweds and smiled. "The Lord bless you and keep you," he told them. "The Lord make His face shine upon you and be gracious unto you. The Lord lift up His countenance upon you and give you peace."

"Amen," several well-wishers could be heard agreeing.

Mr. Knott started the hymn, 'Saviour, like a Shepherd Lead Us.' Timothy and Kathleen linked arms together, and followed by Stanley and Jennifer, they wove their way through the crowd of their relatives and friends and to the open double doors and then outside into the sunlight.

After Mark One and Mark Two had set a small table outside just beyond the parking area, the people inside the building followed the two couples outside. Each person signed their names to the documents, thereby witnessing to the marriage agreements. The children and young people, as they added their names, realized the magnitude of this solemn but happy occasion.

The wedding party with their parents and grandparents, stood in the shade under the wide branches of several spruce trees which had had their lower branches removed up to about seven feet. A few people took pictures but found it was too dark to take photographs without flash. Jennifer told them. "Follow us to where Mrs. Bucket is going to take our wedding photographs. It's absolutely beautiful there."

"Barb, would you like to carry my train," Kathleen asked a little girl standing with her parents. The youngster grinned, slipped away from her mother, and came over to Kathleen. "Just hold it up so it doesn't drag on the ground."

"Can I help, too, Kathleen?" another young girl asked.

"Sure you can help. Ask your dad first."

Charlie called out, "Jennifer, can me and Annie carry your train?"

The wedding party with its increase of four young helpers crossed the gravel and entered the woods at the back of the meeting place property. They proceeded along the narrow, curved road through the maple, birch, and spruce trees. Most of the other families and friends followed them causing the group to quickly swell. Several nine and ten year old boys scurried ahead while a small troop of giggling girls skipped along just behind the wedding party. On the shoulders of two fathers were beaming children enjoying their rides while other youngsters accompanied their parents.

A young man guided his younger siblings down the road and occasionally prodded them on. "Come on, Kid," he coaxed one of them. "Don't pick up any of those spruce cones. You'll get your fingers all gucky, and you'll ruin your Sunday-go-to-meeting clothes."

The sun shone through the leafy canopy overhead creating a mottled pattern on the stream of people as they flowed along. The road curved to the right, and a large sunny field could be seen through the openings in the trees. Some married couples walked hand in hand enjoying this outing together. Gingerly making her way down the gentle slope with her husband and young child at their side was a pregnant young woman. Accompanying this growing family was another family, a girl in a wheel-chair who showed pleasure at being a part of the excitement, and her parents who carefully wheeled her along the rough road. Several seniors were having a good time sharing this celebration with their grandchildren.

The road soon emerged at a large field which tipped gently towards the lake. Timothy and Kathleen, Stanley and Jennifer led the crowd of people across the field, past the House of Prayer, and to the old apple orchard.

"The apple blossoms must be at their peak," Mrs. Bucket exclaimed. "They're gorgeous—we should get some great shots here." Mr. Two Rivers ran ahead and under the apple trees, and he taped the procession as it entered the orchard. The wedding party with the well-wishers tagging close behind passed between the rows of blossom-studded trees. Many of the thick branches were hanging low nearly touching the tall grasses.

"It's beautiful under here," Kathleen exclaimed to Timothy. "I can see why Jennifer wanted to have our pictures taken here."

"Here's our place here," Stanley said as they approached a pair of elegant wing chairs which had earlier been positioned under the wide branches of an apple tree. "There's room for about a dozen of us here, and people can take pictures from over there." He pointed to a large open area between the trees.

Kathleen pushed aside a branch laden with apple blossoms and looked beyond it to the roadway. "Here comes Dad now," she told the others. The van pulled into the tall grass and stopped. The doors opened, and four or five grandchildren spilled from the vehicle before Mrs. Clayton could help Mrs. Charles from the front seat.

"Hurry, Grandma," one of the grandchildren called to her. "Kathleen and Timothy are waiting for us in those pretty trees over there."

"I'm coming as fast as my old legs will carry me, Dearie. And as your Granddad would say, 'I have my gas pedal to the floorboards.'"

"Take your time, but hurry, Mom," Mrs. Clayton said to her. Mrs. Charles started for the apple trees with a grandchild on each side.

Before many photographs could be taken, some of the children and young people left for the swings under the roof of the picnic shelter or ran down to the shore of New Lake. Soon other people wandered through the campgrounds, but most of the wedding guests made their way over to the barn veranda where they could visit at the twig chairs and other chairs set out for this occasion.

When Billy and Stanley's brother Colin were not required for the wedding photos, they returned to the meeting place and drove the cars belonging to Timothy and to Stanley to the parking area near the barn.

Just before five o'clock, Mark One beat on the triangle which was several paces from the veranda. The loud clanging startled Grandpa Joshua Palmer who was snoozing on a plastic chair in the corner of the veranda. "I should've turned my hearing aid off," he snickered as he retrieved his cane which had just tumbled to the floor.

Groups of people began to move across the field towards the barn. Some wedding guests had been visiting with friends in the shade of the picnic shelter, and others had been wandering around near the edge of the lake. Several young people jumped from the retired fishing boat set up on cradles in the grass a few metres from the water, and a few seniors with their grandchildren made their way through the dandelions and up to the barn veranda.

Timothy sprang up from the log at the campfire circle close to the lake, and he assisted Kathleen to her feet. "I think we're expected to join all those people in the barn," he told her thoughtfully. "So let's go. Besides, I'm starving."

"So am I," Kathleen agreed and laughed with him. She adjusted her veil, and Barbara offered again to carry her train.

"Those other guys are coming along now," Mark Two pointed out to Timothy and Kathleen. He watched as Stanley and Jennifer and several others made their way along the path from the woods. Timothy and Kathleen reached the flagpole near the barn at the same time as Stanley and Jennifer.

"How was your hike?" Kathleen asked them. "A two kilometre hike in the woods is a long way to go in your wedding dress. Mr. Two Rivers probably took some interesting movies of you guys."

"It was great!" Jennifer answered. "I had two helpers to carry my train." She turned and grinned at Charlie and Annie. "Thanks, you two." And then she lifted her dress and put one foot forward. "And I didn't wear sneakers for nothing," she related with one foot out from under her long, flowing dress.

Jennifer grinned at Kathleen. "I always wanted to go for a hike in the woods in my wedding dress. Ever since I was a little—"

"So that's why you agreed to marry me!" Stanley exclaimed as he interrupted his humming. "Just so you could go for a hike through the trees in your wedding dress!" He ran his fingers through his hair and stared at his wife.

"Well, that, and a few other reasons," Jennifer assured him. "And the best part of the hike," she continued as she slipped her arm under his, "was that I was with you, Mr. Clark. You know, I've been on that trail many times, and so have you, Stanley, but this was the first time that we've been on it together."

"Yes, I know," he nodded and grinned at her.

Colin stood at the door of the barn and raised his hand. "Could I have your attention please." When it was quiet he announced, "We'll give thanks out here, and then the head table will go in first, followed by the rest of us."

After everyone had moved along the buffet table, they took their places at smaller tables throughout the large room. The tables were decorated with green and yellow streamers, and bunches of apple blossoms were placed at the centres of the tables. Several people served coffee, tea, and punch to the wedding guests.

Later, and just before the desserts were spread out on the buffet table, Colin stood to make an announcement. "Mark One and Mark Two tell me they have some greetings from away to read," he said. "Come this way, Guys."

The two young fellows tried to look serious as they approached the end of the head table, each having a sheet of paper in his hand. They turned to face the people and began to giggle. They stood extra tall and straight, holding their pieces of paper in an important manner. "We received two greetings we'd like to read at this time," Mark Two said as he glanced down at his handwritten note. He elbowed Mark One. "You start, Mark."

Mr. Two Rivers used his video camera as Mark One held out his paper and began to read. "'Dear Persons, Stanley and Jennifer, Timothy and Kathleen.'" He quickly glanced over at the couples and then continued to read with a poor attempt at a

French accent. "'Happy congratulations on your wedding day. We are so sorry we cannot attend to your wedding at this time. We have previous engagements to be sure.'"

People began to chuckle, and Timothy thought, *Well, at least I don't have to be concerned about these letters!*

Mark One giggled again, and he resumed his reading. "'Please give my sincere regrets to everyone on your happy occasion as we will not be in attendance. Your friend Jean C.'" All those in the room laughed along with the two Marks.

As the laughter subsided somewhat, Grandpa Palmer could be heard asking his daughter-in-law beside him, "Does the prime minister know our young people?" This caused the laughter in the room to increase even more.

When the laughter died down again, Mark Two held out his paper. "We also received this greeting." He cleared his throat and began to read. "'Dear Timothy and Kathleen, Stanley and Jennifer,'" he read with dignity and a poorly-done English accent.

"'Thank you for your most gracious invitation. We deeply regret to inform you that we are unable to attend your wedding. We trust it will be a jolly good affair.'"

The people began to laugh, and Mark Two grinned as he momentarily looked up from his paper. He started to read again. "'Please feel free to drop in on us sometime for a lovely spot of tea, Old Chaps, if you're ever in our area. We live in the smashing big house with the stone wall and iron gates. Don't let the guards give you cause to fret.'"

Mark Two joined the others in laughter but soon went back to his reading. "'You can't miss our charming place, but please knock quietly as Mom might be napping.'"

Mark Two glanced over at the two couples. "And it's signed, 'Your affectionate blokes, Elizabeth and Philip.'" More laughter broke out all over the large room of the barn, and as the two young fellows returned to their seats, they were applauded.

Stanley stood up, and as the noise died down he said, "Thanks, Fellows, for reading those two greetings to us. When you answer the messages will you tell each of them to visit us when they're in this area. In the meantime we'll set some wedding cake aside on the top shelf of the cupboard for them for when they get here."

Stanley paused and looked out over their friends and relatives there. "I have much to be thankful for," he expressed to the people sitting around the tables, and then he glanced down at Jennifer. "I now have a wonderful wife, and I'm sure I'll grow to love her more and more as the days go by."

Stanley then faced Mr. and Mrs. Jack and said, "I'm thankful for Jennifer's parents who have brought her up in the ways of the Lord. And I'm thankful for my friend Timothy who introduced me to the Lord."

Timothy stared at the apple blossoms on the table before him as Stanley continued. "Soon after I was saved, my sister became a Christian, and then my parents became believers, and then my brother Colin trusted in the Lord, and all within about three years of my conversion. So our whole family now knows the Lord." Stanley sat down as exclamations of gratitude were heard throughout the assembled people in the barn.

Stanley's dad then stood up and turned to his son and his wife. "Our prayers go with you, Stanley and Jennifer, as you serve the Lord in the north among our native people," he told them, and then he faced the other newly married couple. "And we'll continue to pray for you, Timothy and Kathleen, as you serve the Lord here at Camp Bethlehem." Timothy could see his family and friends nod their approval. "Ever remember, Stanley and Jennifer, Timothy and Kathleen," Mr. Clark reminded them, "the Lord whom you serve is a great God, and it's His will you are doing, not yours. Each day make yourselves available to Him as His tools for His use."

Timothy could hear several 'amens' coming from the well-wishers, and then Mr. Clark sat down next to his wife. Timothy quickly brushed back his mustache and stood up. "Thank you for your encouragement, Stanton," he said to him. Timothy then looked out over the people in the barn.

After quietly clearing his throat, Timothy began his talk. "I'd like to thank Mr. and Mrs. Clayton for instructing Kathleen in the things of the Lord and then today giving her to me for my wife." He smiled at them and then informed the people, "Kathleen has asked me to thank everyone for the gifts you've given us. We really appreciate it, you're all so generous and kind," he said to the wedding guests as he faced them in the barn.

"We've received so many practical things—nothing useless like umbrella stands for the front hallway. We don't have a front hallway—we don't even have any hallway. So, thanks for your thoughtfulness." He then told them, "Kathleen and I would like you all to come visit us when you can." And then he quickly added with a grin, "but of course not all at the same time."

Timothy paused and glanced over at Stanley and Jennifer. "Kathleen and I wanted to give Stanley and Jennifer a meaningful gift. A week ago we saw a platform rocker at the furniture store in town. Was it ever nice!" Timothy grinned as he looked out over his friends and family before him. "It was dark brown, imitation leather and it was the last one the store had for sale. Well, the other one there had a 'sold' sign on it. We decided the chair would make an ideal gift for them. So we paid for it and made arrangements to have it delivered to our place on Camp Beth property here. We planned to put a ribbon around it and present it to Stanley and Jennifer there. We knew that Mike knew where to deliver it so we didn't have to be there when it arrived." Timothy briefly looked down at Kathleen and continued. "When we got out to the car, I told Kathleen the chair was just what I always wanted, and I wished we had one."

When Timothy realized he was playing with his wedding ring, he abruptly dropped his hands down to his sides. "Yesterday afternoon, Kathleen and I went over to our place to see that the chair had arrived and to put a ribbon around it. When I opened the door, we were shocked to find that there were two chairs in the middle of our small living room." Timothy took on a look of alarm, and he continued. "I said to Kathleen, 'Oh no! They've made a mistake—they delivered two chairs to us.' I was about to call the store on the phone we had installed in the housekeeping cottage when Stanley and Jennifer drove up. Now what were we going to do!" Timothy looked shocked again, and he could hear Kathleen giggle. "We didn't have time to put the ribbon around the chair or even sign our names on the card. Stanley and Jennifer came right in—didn't say a word—they looked at the two chairs and then looked at us kind of strange."

Timothy could see Jennifer was giggling as he went on. "Finally Stanley said to us, 'Why are there two chairs?' And I said, 'That's what we'd like to know. Why are there two chairs? Kathleen and I ordered only one.' Jennifer said, 'So did we. We ordered only one chair, and Stanley and I are here now to put a ribbon around it and put your names on it.' Kathleen said, 'That's why we're here—to put a ribbon on the chair we ordered for you guys and to put your names on it.' So Stanley said, 'Well, thank you, Timothy and Kathleen, for the nice brown leather chair. And there's your chair over there,—or is it that one there? 'So I said, 'Well, thank you, Stanley and Jennifer, for the nice brown leather chair whichever one it is.' So Stanley said, 'You're welcome.' So I said, 'You're welcome, too. You two have good taste.' So Stanley said, 'I was just going to say the same thing about you two.'"

Timothy paused to allow everyone to laugh. He looked over at Stanley and Jennifer, and he smiled and continued. "So, Stanley and Jennifer," he informed them, "Kathleen and I know you'll enjoy the dark brown, imitation leather chair from us just like we'll enjoy the dark brown, imitation leather chair from you guys." Timothy grinned and nodded politely at Stanley and Jennifer. "And we can't hide the fact from you," he added, "that we didn't pay the full price of the chair for you. We got it on sale, and we know you're well aware of that fact." Laughter filled the room once more, and Timothy sat down and held Kathleen's hand under the table.

Billy removed his note from his inside pocket and stood up. "My brother is a man of many questions," he told the wedding guests in the barn. "He's been asking questions all his life. Mom says when Timothy was three years old, he'd ask questions like, 'How long is a cougar's tail?' And on another occasion he asked, 'Does our rocking chair have batteries?'" Kathleen giggled and Billy paused and the people laughed. "But lately Timothy's been asking questions of another nature," Billy continued, and he looked down at his notes. "He's asked Mom, 'Is my good shirt cleaned and ironed yet?' And then he often asks, 'Did she call when I was out?' Of course we didn't have to ask who 'she' was." Timothy could feel Kathleen squeeze his hand as she giggled again.

Billy turned and faced Kathleen. "Now, Kathleen," he said to her in a serious tone, "I must warn you, my brother is still going to ask questions, and you should be prepared." He looked down at his paper, and she grinned not knowing what was coming next. "You might hear him ask, 'Are you planning to sleep outdoors tonight?'" Billy paused a few seconds. "Don't let that one bother you, Kathleen. He's probably talking to the cat."

Everyone laughed, and when it was quiet again he glanced at his notes. "You might hear him ask, 'When does the next bus leave for Brazil?'" Kathleen giggled, and Billy advised her, "Just ignore him, Kathleen. He's been known to talk in his sleep."

When the laughter died down, Billy looked over at Stanley. "Stanley, there's a few things I think you should know about my sister," he said with a straight face. "More than once, Jennifer's got the whole family up in the middle of the night to see the—what did you call them, Jennifer?"

She grinned. "Aurora Borealis."

"Yeah, that's it," Billy agreed. "She got us up out of bed to see—that. Northern lights, to the rest of us. 'Aren't they beautiful!' Jennifer would say. We'd stand there a minute looking out the window and then go back to bed." Billy began to grin as the sound of laughter was heard.

"And Stanley, if you don't know or even want to know the names and the identification features of all the evergreen trees in our area—or coniferous as she calls them—she might look at you kind of strange." Jennifer laughed and glanced at Stanley who was grinning at her. Billy continued. "Oh, and another thing

Stanley, Jennifer can be very stubborn." He paused and looked over at his sister. "She's stubborn when she knows the truth. She knows what's right, and she will not allow false information or any wrong to prevail, and she's not afraid to stand up for the right even if it means she'll be personally disadvantaged."

Stanley nodded knowingly, and Billy turned towards the wedding guests. "I'm really going to miss my brother and sister," he told them. "Timothy and Jennifer have been a big influence on me, probably greater than they realize, and no doubt greater than I realize." He glanced at Timothy and then Jennifer and concluded, "Thanks, Timothy and Jennifer. I'm just your younger brother, but please keep in touch."

Several hours later, Timothy slowed down and signalled to turn off the road. He switched the headlights to low beam to travel along the gravel driveway. "Grandma Charles is still up," Kathleen noted as they crept past her house with a light in the window.

Timothy turned the wheel to head along another roadway through the dark spruce trees. "I'm glad our place is not in view of the other housekeeping cottages. No one will suspect we've come back."

"Yeah," Kathleen agreed in a near whisper. "In the morning, they'll be surprised we were so close, and they'll be even more surprised when we show up tomorrow at the meeting place." She gave a quick giggle.

Timothy and Kathleen glanced over into the silent blackness where they saw nothing, but where they knew the barn was, and where, several hours earlier today, celebrations in their honour had taken place.

The newly married couple traveled without speaking until a small building came into view in the headlight beams of their car. "Our first home," Kathleen said thoughtfully as she peered out the front window of their little vehicle.

"Yeah, that's right," Timothy agreed, and he could feel himself smiling. He backed into the empty spot near the door of their place and shut off the engine. He emerged from the car and circled around on the gravel to the passenger's side and opened the door. "We're home, Mrs. Jack," Timothy told her as he took his wife's hand.

Kathleen climbed from the car and stood beside her husband. "Yes, Mr. Jack, we're home," she replied.

chapter twenty-four

one year later—spring 1999

The Old Clock

"What about this here old clock, Mom?" Billy asked as he dragged his finger across its dusty top. "Don't work no more. Should I put it out for heavy garbage?"

Mrs. Jack looked up from the box of odds and ends she was sorting in the basement. "The hired man's clock? No, I don't feel right about getting rid of it yet, not while your Grandpa Palmer's still living, anyway. It's been in the family since just before he was born. That would be—well, Dad's eighty-second birthday was this past March."

"Maybe I should have a look at it," Billy decided as he put it aside. "But I don't know nothing about antique clocks." He reached for a box of junk and headed up the basement stairs.

After supper, Billy completed his job of hauling trash down to the end of their long, tree-lined driveway in preparation for heavy garbage pickup the following day. As he pushed the empty garden cart back up towards the barn where it was kept, he thought about the hired man's clock. *I don't like to keep stuff around that's no good—just clutters up the place. That old clock hasn't ticked since the summer we did all that extra work at Camp Beth after the fire; it just suddenly gave up ticking. That must have been four years ago.*

Billy pushed the garden cart into the darkened hayloft and returned it to its usual spot between the lawn-mower and his bicycle, and then he lowered himself onto its open end. *But the clock means something to Mom,* he concluded. *Her father gave it to her when she married Dad. Before that, the clock was given to Grandpa Palmer when he married Grandma. Before that when my great-grandparents were the lighthouse keepers on Bunchberry Island, their hired man gave them this clock. The story is that the old guy didn't like the ticking of the clock at night in the quiet of his room in the lighthouse—reminded him of his home on the mainland and his wife who had recently died. And then the hired man died several days before Grandpa Palmer was born. I don't know anything about the hired man's family.* He stood up, stretched, and tucked in his shirt, and then he left the barn and walked up to the house.

"Oh, Billy," his mom said to him as he sat down on the stuffed chair across from his parents who were on the couch, "did you read the letter from Jennifer and Stanley? It came in today's mail."

Mr. Jack held out the envelope towards his son Billy. "Nice letter," he remarked.

Billy stood up, took the letter, and returned to the chair. After he unfolded the sheets of paper, he leaned back and read, *'Dear Mom and Dad, Billy and Grandpa. Thank you for sending the information on fetal alcohol syndrome. So many of the kids here seem to be affected by this condition as well as some being neglected somewhat by their parents, and a few are physically abused. The people here in general have low self-esteem, and they feel they have little or nothing to live for. Our hearts go out to them. Pray for us as we seek the Lord's will for wisdom and skill in reaching the people here for Him.'*

Billy leaned forward and read the next paragraph. *'The school year will be finished in another two weeks, and we plan to explore the area around here a bit. Although both Stan and I have found that our first year of teaching has been hard, at the same time it has been rewarding and satisfying. Those students who at first showed little interest in school are now enthusiastic about learning. Behavioural problems are now greatly reduced, and those children who were once shy or withdrawn are now more outgoing and confident. We love each child, and they seem to sense our care for them. Here is a riddle which is going around here: What is black and white, black and white, black and white?'*

Billy flipped the sheet of paper over and continued to read. *'Several weeks ago we started a Bible study in our little house. That first evening, the parents of one of our students and the mother of another showed up. We began by looking at the Bible as a book. We showed them how many books it had and that it was divided into Old and New Testaments. We told them it was written by about forty different men over hundreds of years yet they were in complete agreement. Some of the books are history; some are poetry; and some are letters to churches and individuals. The next week, two more people joined the study. We were encouraged when one of the men noted that the Bible wasn't just for the white-man. You should have seen him grin when we told him that Jesus wasn't white-skinned, and that He probably was as dark as he is! One of the mothers who attends the Bible study walked home with me after school one afternoon. She had some good questions. The people here enjoy hearing Stan and me sing together. Please pray that the folks here would realize they are sinners, and pray for us that we would have the wisdom and skill to communicate Christ to them.'*

The large family cat jumped up onto the chair beside Billy and rubbed herself against him. When he ignored her, she stepped onto his lap and leaned on the letter he was reading. Billy gave her several quick strokes and then lowered her to the floor, and he went back to the letter. *'That's enough about us. How are you people doing? That's exciting news from Timothy and Kathleen. We wish them the best of course. Stanley says he can almost see Timothy do his fake grin and hear Kathleen giggle. I have to agree—I can too. And we can almost hear Bill's comment, "Babies make the cutest pets." What a rig! Now let's change the subject. It's good Grandpa Palmer can stay with you folks. I'm sure he appreciates being with you as much as you like to have him around. Be sure he sees this and knows we are thinking of him. We trust Billy is doing well at his work and is enjoying it. Good, reliable workers are hard to come by. Well, we better close for now. The weekly mail goes out tomorrow morning at daybreak. We are thinking about you folks, and we pray for you often. We plan to come home sometime later in the summer months before heading back for another term. Love, Stanley and Jennifer. PS, What is black and white, black and white, black and white? A skunk rolling downhill.'*

Billy returned the letter to its envelope. "Yeah, that's a good letter," he agreed, and he laid it on the wide arm of the chair. After he leaned back, the cat jumped up onto his lap again and laid down. "Mother Moose, sounds like you have your little motor running again."

Mrs. Jack suddenly looked up from her mending. "Where's Grandpa?" she asked as she faced the kitchen.

"Heard him heading upstairs when I came in through the kitchen," Billy informed his mom.

"He's been kind of quiet lately," Mr. Jack added as he stroked his short, well-kept beard.

"I think he's slowing down some, and I've noticed he has less energy," Mrs. Jack commented. "Do you know what Dad said this morning? He said that while he was still living, he didn't want his body to be used as a make-work project for the medical profession just to give them employment. And he said he didn't want to donate his living body in order to give someone some medical experience in order for them to look good on their resumé."

Billy grinned. "Nothing wrong with his mind," he concluded.

"He also said that if he took a turn for the worse, he didn't want us to pray for his recovery, but to pray that the Lord's will would be done for him."

Billy looked thoughtful. "We can still keep Grandpa here, can't we?" His mother smiled, and then Billy said, "I told Grandpa I got a letter from Henry. When he heard that Henry was with a Christian organization that worked with disabled kids, he said that Henry's experiences at Camp Beth must have influenced him in that direction. And then Grandpa said that Henry was real good at lip-reading. He could tell what you were saying even if you were chewing gum."

Mrs. Jack smiled knowingly and then decided, "Maybe I should go up and check on him when I'm through with this." After she had finished sewing the button on Billy's shirt, she went up to the room which had been Timothy's.

Mr. Jack asked Billy, "How's that job working out that you and Jeff are doing?"

"Fine," he answered as he stroked the cat's neck with his rough hands. "Jeff has several jobs lined up for this summer. We'll be busy alright. There's lots of renovations going on these days—older houses being fixed up or remodeled. It's a good business. Suits me fine—I like it." His dad nodded, and Billy added, "Jeff plans to take time off to attend a day or two of family camp as well as be there every evening." His dad nodded again. "Dad, you know that old house just above the wharf in Rogers Cove?"

"The one they call the McNeill place," Mr. Jack said.

"Been empty now a few years," Billy continued. "Some woman from the city's bought it. Hired us to fix it up for her. Plans to do pottery work on the site and sell it from there. Nice location for tourists, I'd say. And I see as we drove by, that the old place where Grandpa lived in Rogers Cove has been renovated real nice. Heard a retired couple from the states bought it up and spends the summer months there now."

Mrs. Jack came into the living room looking concerned. "Dad was asleep fully clothed on the bed with the light still on." She lowered herself to the stool of the pump organ and faced Mr. Jack.

"He's probably alright," her husband answered. "Did he mention anything about not feeling well?"

"No. But he did walk down to the end of the driveway and back before supper," Mrs. Jack remembered. "He likes to get the mail—he wants to be useful. Maybe I should take him to the doctor's tomorrow to be checked out." Mr. Jack nodded his approval.

Several minutes later Billy looked down at the cat relaxed and dozing on his lap. "Sorry to disturb you, Pussy," he informed her politely, "but I need to get up." Mother Moose ignored him. Billy gently worked his large hands under the limp cat, and without disturbing her curled form, he stood up, turned around, and carefully lowered her to the warm spot where he had been sitting. "I hope you find this turn of events to your satisfaction, Mother Moose. But have you ever considered engaging in a bit of mousing? I reckon the barn is good hunting ground." The cat continued to disregard him so he concluded, "Perpetual holidays for sure."

His mom looked across to her husband after their son had gone. "I hope he'll be just as courteous to his wife—whoever she is."

When Billy returned from the basement, he placed the hired man's clock on the kitchen table. "Mind if I work here, Mom?" he called into the living room.

"No. Go ahead, Billy." Mrs. Jack came to the kitchen and prepared a damp cloth to wipe down the dusty, old timepiece.

Billy moved the clock to the edge of the table with its back facing him, and he knelt on the floor. After he smoothed back his mustache, he opened the little door, reached in and removed the winding key from off its floor. When he realized he needed more light, he stood up and reached over for the flashlight on the top of the refrigerator. "That's better," he said aloud as he shone the light into the dark interior of the clock case.

Mrs. Jack sat at the end of the table as she watched him. "It may not be a valuable antique," she mused aloud, "but to me, it's a beautiful old timepiece."

"Thingy here is loose," Billy noted, and he poked at it with his finger. "And there's a small screw on the bottom on the other side of the chiming mechanism." He tipped the clock towards him, causing the pendulum to bounce against the chiming rods. "Does have a nice sound," he admitted. The loose screw rolled to where Billy could reach it. "Got it," he said with satisfaction.

He again shone the flashlight through the little door into the clock case. He frowned as he stared intently at its floor now lit up by the beam of the light. Mrs. Jack watched him with curiosity. Billy closed his eyes and gently blew onto the floor of the clock and looked in once more. "There's some writing in there. Can hardly make it out."

Billy's mom came around to where he was kneeling. He stood up and handed her the flashlight. Mrs. Jack shone the beam into the timepiece, and after about half a minute she said, "It looks like it says, 'Jedidiah and Myrtle Harriston, married—' and I think it says, 'September 10, 1868.' But I can't read the next line."

Billy looked over his mom's shoulder. "Jedidiah and Myrtle Harriston," he repeated. "Who were they? Jedidiah might have been your grandfather's hired man on Bunchberry Island for all we know. Would Grandpa know?" he wondered.

"Maybe he does. I'll ask him tomorrow," she said as she stood up. "Come to think of it—I don't remember ever hearing what the hired man's name was. We always referred to him as 'the hired man'."

Billy grinned. "Wouldn't it be something if Chord Harriston from the meeting place is a descendant of this couple here in the clock."

"Yes, it would," she agreed. "And Jedidiah and Myrtle are names that are easy to identify. I should ask Chord this coming Sunday."

"Well, I need a small, slotted screw driver," Billy decided. He crossed over to the tool drawer beneath the radio-tape-player on the kitchen counter.

The next afternoon, Mrs. Jack left with her dad for his doctor's appointment in William Station. After Mrs. Jack pulled onto the road at the end of their driveway, the elderly Mr. Palmer turned up his hearing-aid.

"That the hired man's clock I heard before we left the house?" he asked his daughter.

"Yes, Dad, it was."

He leaned his cane against the seat. "Thought that clock was gone."

"Well, the clock hasn't worked for several years, but Billy fixed it last night."

"Who?" he asked as he turned his head, and his snowy white beard brushed his left shoulder.

"Billy," she told him again. "Billy fixed it."

Her dad seemed thoughtful as well as pleased. About a minute later he spoke. "That clock has done a lot of ticking and chiming over the years. My mother gave it to me and your mother when we was wed, and then we gave it to you and

Richard when you married. Maybe you will pass it on to one of your children." He grinned with satisfaction.

"Dad," his daughter asked him, "tell me again, why was it called the hired man's clock?"

"What you say, Alice—I mean Martha?"

"I said, why was it called the hired man's clock?"

"Oh." And then he grinned. "Father's hired man on Bunchberry Island. Father—he manned the lighthouse there. The lighthouse and tower burned in the year nineteen hundred and thirty-five. August. Nobody could do nothing to help. I remember we were living on the mainland then, in Rogers Cove. I was eighteen years old—young man and strong back then—could work all day." He stopped talking and stroked his beard.

"Dad," his daughter interrupted his distant thoughts, "what was the hired man's name?"

"Hired man?" he repeated. "He worked for Father at the lighthouse. Died two or three days before I was born. I heard tell he died of a heart attack."

"What was his name?"

"Hired man's name?" he repeated, and then paused before he spoke again. "Hired man died before I was born. Never met the gentleman."

"Did you ever know his name?"

"What?"

"Did you ever know the hired man's name?"

"Oh, the hired man's name. His name was Jed - Jedidiah. Don't know his family name—never met the man. Died just before I was born - long time ago now. He gave the clock to Father." The elderly gentleman gazed out the window. A minute later he turned to his daughter. "Timothy and Billy went to Bunchberry Island a few years back, didn't they?" he questioned.

"Yes, Dad, they did."

"Lighthouse and tower are gone. There's a steel skeleton tower there now—unmanned. They say at night you can see it flash from Rogers Cove."

The following Sunday, Mrs. Jack spoke to Chord Harriston between the two morning meetings. "The clock has been in the family for years," she revealed to him. "Ever since before my father was born." And then she told him the clock had been given by the hired man to her grandparents when they had been the lighthouse keepers on Bunchberry Island.

Chord, who had been in the same cabin at Camp Bethlehem as Billy nine years before, grinned. He had heard this story several times. He had been told the hired man gave the timepiece away because its ticking and chiming at night reminded him of his home on the mainland and of his wife who had just passed away. He had also heard the hired man had died in the lighthouse several days before Billy's grandfather, Joshua Palmer, who was well known to everyone, had been born. Chord had been told the hired man had been an influence on Billy's great-grandparents who, as a result, became believers, and each generation since has had a strong Christian testimony.

At the same time as Mrs. Jack was relating this story, Chord was wondering why she was doing so. What Mrs. Jack was telling him was common knowledge in their circle of friends. He shifted his feet and tapped his Bible against his thigh.

"Now, Chord," Mrs. Jack said with a grin, "I've reminded you of all that to tell you this: the clock hasn't been working for several years until Billy looked at it the other night. When he had the door open—you know, the little door at the back of the clock, he found some writing on the floor of the clock case. It was in pencil, and it said, 'Jedidiah and Myrtle Harriston.' And of course we thought of you and your family. Could the person we know as the hired man be an ancestor of yours?"

Chord shrugged his shoulders. "I don't know the first names of my great-grandparents on the Harriston side of the family. Those names you have there could even be my great, great-grandparents for all I know, but I think I could find out. The Harriston family story is that my great-grandfather ran away from home when he was in his teens and never returned or kept in touch. I've heard that my great-grandfather sometime later tried to find his parents, but he wasn't successful. He got married and had children, and, well, here I am today, but what became of his parents, we'll never know."

Mrs. Jack listened with interest. "I didn't know that about the Harriston family back a few generations," she said to Chord. "That's sad, but you belong to the Lord, and you know Him, and that's good even if you are the only one in the Harriston family who's saved. Well, I've taken up a lot of your time, Chord, and it's just about time to sit down again."

"Yeah, well, it's been nice talking with you, Martha," he said as he backed away. "I'll try to find out those names for you."

Monday evening the phone rang, and after Mrs. Jack answered it, she heard an excited, "Hello, Martha!" The caller immediately launched into the reason for calling without identifying himself nor giving her a chance to respond. "Dad looked through the family records where he keeps stuff like that. My great-grandfather who ran away and then lost contact with his parents—well, his name was Dwight Harriston. His wife's name was Hannah. And I have here that Dwight's parents' names were Jedidiah and Myrtle. Aren't they the names you found in your hired man's clock? That means your clock used to belong to my great, great-grandfather, Jedidiah Harriston. And he was the hired man who introduced the Lord to your grandparents, that is Billy's great-grandparents who lived on Bunchberry Island."

"Well, isn't that something!" Mrs. Jack said as she spoke for the first time since answering the phone. "The person we have been calling 'the hired man' all these years was your great, great-grandfather. And do you realize, Chord, that your great, great -grandfather introduced the Lord to my grandparents, and then their great-grandson Timothy Jack introduced Christ to a great, great-grandson of the hired man, which is you, Chord. This is exciting! My family will be interested to hear about this."

"Yeah, they will," Chord agreed over the phone. "And now the story of the hired man's clock has more significance. Hey—isn't that the hired man's clock I hear now?"

"Yes, it is."

"Must be nine o'clock," Chord concluded. Several minutes later they hung up.

From that time on, whenever Mrs. Jack heard the hired man's clock, she thought she could hear the ticking say, "Myr-tle, Myr-tle, Myr-tle."

Billy and his mom attended the midweek meeting while Mr. Jack stayed home with Mr. Palmer. As the two men sat in the living room, Mr. Jack tried to make conversation.

"Did you get out for your walk today, Joshua?"

Mr. Palmer's thinning hair was disheveled. "What'd you say, Bobby—I mean Richard?" He turned up his hearing-aid.

"I said, did you get out for your walk today?"

"Yes," the older man answered. "I walked down to the road to pick up the mail. I may be past my best-before date, but I still have some usefulness yet." There was a long pause.

Mr. Jack was determined to have a meaningful conversation with the elderly gentleman. *Older people are physically weaker—they are somewhat feeble,* he reasoned as he glanced up at the painting of Rogers Cove his wife's father did many years ago. *They are slower in their actions and often appear to be absentminded, but older people have been around a lot longer than the rest of us have. They've had more time to learn more things. They are more mature than we are and have much to offer if we're willing to listen to them and to learn, and yes, even to be corrected by them.* Mr. Jack spoke up and said clearly, "Joshua, if you could live your life over again," he asked him, "what would you want to do differently?"

Mr. Palmer looked at him blankly for several seconds. And then a grin slowly broke across his weathered, old face. "Well, I've been wondering the same thing some, the past few days." Mr. Jack waited for the old fellow to collect his thoughts. "If I could live my life over again, I would spend more time in the Bible. I would take the Word of God in my hands everyday and read it. I would get the Word of God into my head so that I was very familiar with it. And I would have the Word of God in my heart so that living it out would be natural for me. Others around me would see that I take the Bible seriously, making it practical in all areas of my life." Mr. Jack listened with interest, and he nodded in response. He could see that although his wife's father was smiling, he seemed to be a bit sad; he also noticed he was thinking clearly, and he also had spiritual wisdom to offer.

The old gentleman sat quietly, staring at nothing for nearly a minute. Mr. Jack could see he was thinking. "If I could live my life over again," he began once more, "I would have a closer relationship with the Lord by talking to Him often throughout the day. I would keep in mind that prayer isn't telling the Lord what to do, neither is it asking for things to get what I want. But prayer is realizing my weaknesses, my shortcomings. Prayer is willingly submitting to His authority - His will for me. Prayer is me putting myself in the position of submitting to the Lord and lining up my will to His will and then asking that His will be done." A smile slowly spread across the face of the old man.

Mr. Jack nodded at the realization of this truth. He thought, *I haven't heard Martha's dad talk this much in a long time.*

Mr. Palmer then added, "If I could live my life over again, I would keep in mind that prayer is a privilege I have because I'm a believer, and that gives me the right to call Him my Heavenly Father." He paused as he and his son-in-law shared this thought. "You know, Richard, prayer not only is a privilege for us, His children, but prayer is a right which has been granted to us. We have the right to come boldly unto the throne of grace. That right given to us has been made possible at great cost—the death of God's Son the Lord Jesus Christ." He continued to smile, and Mr. Jack watched him slowly bow his head causing his snowy beard to settle on his chest.

Mr. Jack thought the old gentleman had fallen asleep. *After his wife passed away, and when he could no longer look after himself properly,* Mr. Jack recalled as he watched him, *he sold his house and land. He took great delight in dividing up the proceeds and giving it to his children and grandchildren at that time. He also enjoyed giving away the rest of his possessions including all the paintings he and his wife had on the walls in their home—they were surrounded with beauty. I remember he said that the family could make better use of his things than he could and that they should have his stuff now rather than after he passed away. He said he got enjoyment knowing others were putting his things to good use.*

About a minute later, the hired man's clock gave one strike. Mr. Palmer slowly raised his head and looked at Richard sitting across from him. "If I could live my life over again, I would live as a new creature. 'Old things are passed away, behold all things are become new.' I wouldn't spend a lot of needless time and effort on things which have no value in eternity. I wouldn't live to get ahead according to the thinking of unbelievers. But I would invest time and effort now in order to learn the ways of the Lord and to live by faith—that is, by believing what God has said, and living it. I would aim for myself and for my family to be the people the Lord would have us to be. And of course this would bring glory to His Name. Others would see that the Lord is great; He is good and they would be attracted to Him because of us." The old man sat looking thoughtful, and the eyes of the younger man moved to the Scripture text on the wall behind Mr. Palmer. It read: 'In all thy ways acknowledge Him and He shall direct thy paths'.

One evening the following week after the supper dishes were washed and put away, Billy drove his car down their long driveway and turned onto the highway. Mr. Palmer, who sat in the front seat, asked, "Where'd you say we were going?" He turned up his hearing-aid.

"To visit Timothy and Kathleen," Billy answered him.

The old man hesitated before speaking. "Oh, yeah, I remember now. That's what your mother said at supper time," he replied as he held his cane between his knees. "I have a good memory," he told Billy. "Problem is, it's kind of short." Billy grinned, and he geared down on account of a vehicle ahead indicating its turn off this road and onto a driveway.

"It's not very often we get to sit in the backseat," Mrs. Jack commented to her husband.

He smiled, reached over, and touched her hand. "Yeah, and I like to be chauffeured around once in a while especially with you beside me," he informed her.

Twenty minutes later, Billy signalled to turn off the road. He lifted his hand in acknowledgment of Mrs. Charles, who could be seen by the flower garden in the yard of her little house. He drove on and then pulled up to the winterized cottage where Timothy and Kathleen lived on the Camp Beth property, and there he shut off the engine. Timothy came out to the little landing. "Hey, Dad," he called out as he held open the screen door for Kathleen behind him, "I like your new hat."

"Yes," Kathleen agreed. "It gives you an air of dignity. Your hat commands respect."

"Well, I've noticed that when I wear this hat in public," he grinned, "that I get more respect than I usually get—well, that is from strangers. But I don't get any more respect from those who already know me."

Timothy held open the door, and his family entered their snug little dwelling. "Here, Grandpa," Timothy said, "you can sit in my favourite chair." He steered the old man over to the brown, imitation leather chair. He then pulled a kitchen chair over for Kathleen, and he sat on his bright red farmer's seat.

Timothy told his parents how things were progressing in regards to preparation for the Camp Bethlehem programs this summer. "The training sessions for counselors are going well," he informed them. "The young men and women take their responsibilities seriously; they're nice to work with. And the camper applications are still coming in. It looks like we're going to have to turn some away."

His mom looked concerned. "Oh, it would be too bad if we had to turn children and young people away. That can't be the Lord's will. The facilities here could be expanded, couldn't they? We could build more cabins, too." She glanced around at the others in the room.

Mr. Jack took a deep breath and let it out slowly before he spoke. "The Lord has blessed Camp Beth over the years," he said thoughtfully. "Children and young people as well as adults have been saved. Many have come to know the Lord better. They have been taught in His Word, not only the basic doctrines, but they have been taught the practical side of daily living with the Lord. They know that Christ has delivered them from this present evil world and that they are not to be conformed to this world but to be transformed by the renewing of their minds." He paused, and his listeners waited for him to continue.

"I've been thinking regarding the Lord's work here." Mr. Jack again took a deep breath. "Bigger is not always better. Sure, like we say, Camp Beth could expand—we have the room, and the Lord could make that happen. He brought camp into being thirteen years ago this summer, and He caused it to grow steadily since then—meeting every need. And people have come from miles around, but a larger camp would be less personal—we would lose that sense of belonging and the closely-knit fellowship would be less. A larger camp would be in danger of causing us to place too much pride and undue value on the facilities here, rather than on the purposes for the facilities—to encourage others in the Lord and to bring Him glory."

Billy spoke up. "A larger camp would be more difficult to run and to maintain, and like Dad says, that would be putting an emphasis on the camp property rather than on what the camp is supposed to do or be."

"But we can't just refuse to grow," Kathleen put in as she drew her fingers through her long hair. "What about these children and young people we're turning away?"

Timothy answered, "That's right; we can't refuse to grow. The camp committee prays for the Lord's guidance, and the rest of us support them in prayer as well."

The elderly Mr. Palmer who appeared to be not following this conversation and had remained silent up until now, raised his hand until he had everyone's attention. "Have two camps," he said simply, but with conviction. "Start another camp an hour or so away. Let's not think that the Lord can run only one camp at a time. Like you say, don't concentrate on the camp, but what the camp is for—it's the Lord's tool for His use. Two camps in separate areas would double everything including the Lord's glory." His listeners stared at him, and then the old gentleman spoke again. "Timothy here—he has the experience and the desire to serve the Lord, and he has a good wife to work with him. Timothy and Kathleen could be used by the Lord to start a sister camp up country or down country or even across country somewhere. And there's plenty of people being trained at Camp Beth right now who could take over here as well as at a new camp, too." He stopped speaking, and there was a long thoughtful silence.

After an hour of visiting, and just before Timothy and Kathleen's company left, Mrs. Jack drew Timothy aside. "Your dad and I," she informed him, "have decided to give you and Kathleen the hired man's clock. Grandpa's enjoying the clock now, so let's wait until he's gone."

On the way home, Billy could sense that the condition of the engine of his car was deteriorating quickly. "Levi says that it'll cost hundreds of dollars to fix it. It's just not worth it," he told his parents. "I've saved up enough to get another used car. Levi has several on his lot that might be suitable for me."

Timothy and Kathleen washed the plates and mugs from the evening lunch. As Kathleen put things away in the cupboard,

Timothy returned to the seating area of their little place. "Are you planning to sleep outside, tonight?" he asked. Kathleen giggled, and then Timothy decided, "Well, Mozart, maybe you shouldn't." He picked up the cat and moved it from his favourite chair. "You'll get eaten alive by the mosquitoes, Mozzy."

Kathleen sat down opposite him. "You know, Grandpa's right," she agreed. "The Lord has given us Camp Beth, and we value His work here, but we must not think that this camp—Camp Bethlehem is all there is. Perhaps His will is for this work to be duplicated in another location."

"Yes," Timothy responded. "And I must confess that having another camp-work in a different area is something that I've been thinking about. The two camps could have different programs so that children and young people could choose which camp to attend according to their personalities and interests."

Kathleen added, "And having specialty camps is also something that should be considered, like camps which specialize in music and art or survival, and also camps which cater to disabled young people and even adults."

Timothy nodded. "There's something else that's crossed my mind," he told his wife. "There are a few believers who need help—a little guidance and support in their lives. These people need a place, maybe a farm of some kind, where they can learn some life-skills, get experience at doing useful things, and have the satisfaction of contributing. Some might live right there on the property, and others would come there regularly for the day."

Kathleen listened with interest. "That's a great idea," she told him excitedly and then added seriously, "These needy believers are the responsibility of us, their brothers and sisters in the Lord."

Timothy agreed and then grinned. "There could be farm animals," he said, "a garden and orchard, a carpentry shop, and maybe a mechanics' garage. All for the benefit of needy believers."

Kathleen leaned forward and added, "And a kitchen for baking bread and pies. Maybe the farm could have a few cottage industries of some sort. And of course this property could be used as camp grounds, too."

"That's right," Timothy agreed. "This place—this farm would be a lot of work, but it would be so useful to the Lord's people by filling a need, and it would be to His glory, too."

"Well," Kathleen said, "we'll have to pray about this."

Timothy nodded again. "Let's pray about it right now," he suggested, and they did.

During supper a week later, the telephone rang, and Mr. Jack left the table to answer it. Billy heard his dad say, "I'll tell him, Levi." Billy looked over to his dad, and a grin spread across his face. "He'll be pleased to hear that." Mr. Jack grinned back at Billy. "Yeah," he added, "he'll be over this evening." Billy nodded to his dad. "Okay, Levi, thanks for calling." When Mr. Jack returned to the supper table, he said to Billy, "Levi says not to forget the ownership paper." Billy nodded once more.

Mrs. Jack asked, "When are you going to take us for a ride, Billy? And what colour is this car you're getting?"

"It's green—blowfly green, I'd say."

As they continued their supper, Billy and his dad discussed the advantages and disadvantages of diesel engines.

The elderly Mr. Palmer had not contributed to any conversation at the table. He slowly ate his supper, hunched over his plate, apparently oblivious to what was going on. The hired man's clock in the living room gave six strikes, and when it had completed its chiming, Mr. Palmer spoke for the first time during the meal that evening. "Saw Jennifer today," he said without looking up. Mr. Jack stopped in the middle of his story, his wife paused with her fork in the air, and Billy stopped chewing. All three stared at the old man.

"But Dad," Mrs. Jack reminded him gently, "Jennifer and Stanley won't be back home until later this summer." She looked with concern over at her husband.

Mr. Palmer informed them, "She was in the backseat of a car that went by."

"Must have been someone who reminded him of her," Mr. Jack said to his family.

Mr. Palmer raised his head. "I went for my walk this afternoon," he continued. "I stopped to rest in the shade of the fruit stand, and that's when I saw her. I saw Jennifer go by—and Stanley was with her," he insisted. "She was looking this way —she looked happy—you know, smiling, like she usually does." His three listeners glanced at each other with doubtful expressions.

When Billy had finished his supper, he dug out the ownership paper, and then he pulled on the work-boots he had left below his jacket in the porch, and he grabbed his cap from the hooks. "Bye," he called out and closed the door behind him before his parents could reply. He felt strange not inviting his dad when he knew he would enjoy this outing with him, but Billy had other plans this evening.

About two hours later, Mrs. Jack could see an unfamiliar car moving up their long driveway. *That must be Billy—and that's a nice looking car he has. Blowfly green is a nice colour, but I don't care for the name.* She held back the curtain at the kitchen window as the vehicle came closer. "Oh, Richard," she called to him in the living room where he was sitting with Mr. Palmer, "Billy's back, and it looks like Timothy and Kathleen are with him, too."

Mr. Jack left the old man, and he and his wife went outside as the car driven by Billy stopped several metres away. Billy got out of the car and let the door swing closed behind him. "Nice day if it don't rain," he greeted in a carefree manner. Timothy moved from the front passenger seat, and then he opened the back door for his wife.

"Well, hello!" Mrs. Jack welcomed. "We weren't expecting to see you folks until the weekend."

Kathleen fingered the end of her long braid and giggled. "It's hard to stay away, besides, Billy offered to give us a ride in his new car." She giggled again as she caressed her enlarging abdomen.

"I like your car, Billy," Mrs. Jack said to him as she quickly scanned the length of the automobile. "It's a lovely shade of green."

"Blowfly green," he reminded her. He lifted the hood and the three men examined the engine.

Kathleen looked towards her mother-in-law. "I don't know what men see under the hood," she remarked. "It's so jammed packed full of parts." She giggled as she and Mrs. Jack climbed into the front seat of the car. Several minutes later, Kathleen asked, "How's Grandpa Palmer? We missed him last Sunday, and at the midweek meeting, too."

"Well," Mrs. Jack answered, "he seems to be failing. He's in the living room now, resting. It seems he rests most of the time now. We should call him out; he'd enjoy this." She left the car and started for the house.

"Hey, wait," Billy called to her. "Don't you want to see the trunk?" He and Timothy tried not to grin, and Kathleen giggled yet again.

Mrs. Jack stopped. "The trunk?" his mom questioned. "Why would I want to see the trunk?" Kathleen took the arm of her mother-in-law and turned to face the car.

"Yeah, I'd like you and Dad to see the trunk," Billy told them and after he removed the keys from his front pocket, he stepped to the rear of the vehicle. Mrs. Jack said nothing, and Kathleen guided her closer to the trunk of the car. Kathleen tried to stifle her giggles, and Timothy signalled for his dad to come near.

Billy pushed the key into the lock and slowly lifted the lid. Mr. Jack gasped as he leaned forward and stared into the trunk. Mrs. Jack stood with her mouth dropped open, and her eyes grew wide. Billy, Timothy, and Kathleen began to laugh.

"Surprise!" could be heard from the trunk as Stanley and Jennifer sat up from their cramped position. Stanley vaulted out of the trunk, and then he turned and lifted his wife from the trunk and set her down on the ground. They stood several feet from Billy's car, and Jennifer straightened her skirt.

Mr. Jack exclaimed as he grinned, "But we weren't expecting you two for another month." He stepped up to Stanley and shook his hand, and then he hugged his daughter.

Mrs. Jack laughed. "Yes—this is a surprise!" She hugged Jennifer and then Stanley.

Stanley told his wife's parents, "Jennifer and I were offered a fly-out for this morning—we couldn't resist. We got into Billy's trunk down at your fruit stand. We plan to stay about six weeks before we go back."

"We drove by here this afternoon," Jennifer said to her parents. "It seems like we've been gone a long time—even when everything looks the same as when we left. But it's so good to be back!"

"Oh!" Mrs. Jack remembered. "Grandpa said at supper tonight that when he was resting in the fruit stand this afternoon, he saw Jennifer and Stanley go by. We didn't believe him—he's failing so much, you know."

"Where is he?" Timothy asked. "Grandpa should be out here with us."

"Timothy," his mom told him, "will you go in for Grandpa? He's in the living room. He'd love to see Jennifer and Stanley." Timothy left the group and entered the house.

"We want to hear all what's happened with you two," Mrs. Jack said to Stanley and Jennifer. "Your letters are so very interesting." Mr. Jack grinned and nodded in agreement.

"And Stanley and I want to hear about everyone here," Jennifer said. "It seems we've been gone so long."

Stanley laughed. "It's been nearly a year." He looked to the door where Timothy had gone for Grandpa Joshua Palmer, and he began to quietly hum.

Less than a minute later, Timothy reappeared alone at the porch door. He stood motionless with a somber look on his face. His family members stopped their talk and stared at him. "He's gone," he informed them. "Grandpa's dead." The little group stood silently, and then through the open door could be heard the steady strikes of the hired man's clock.